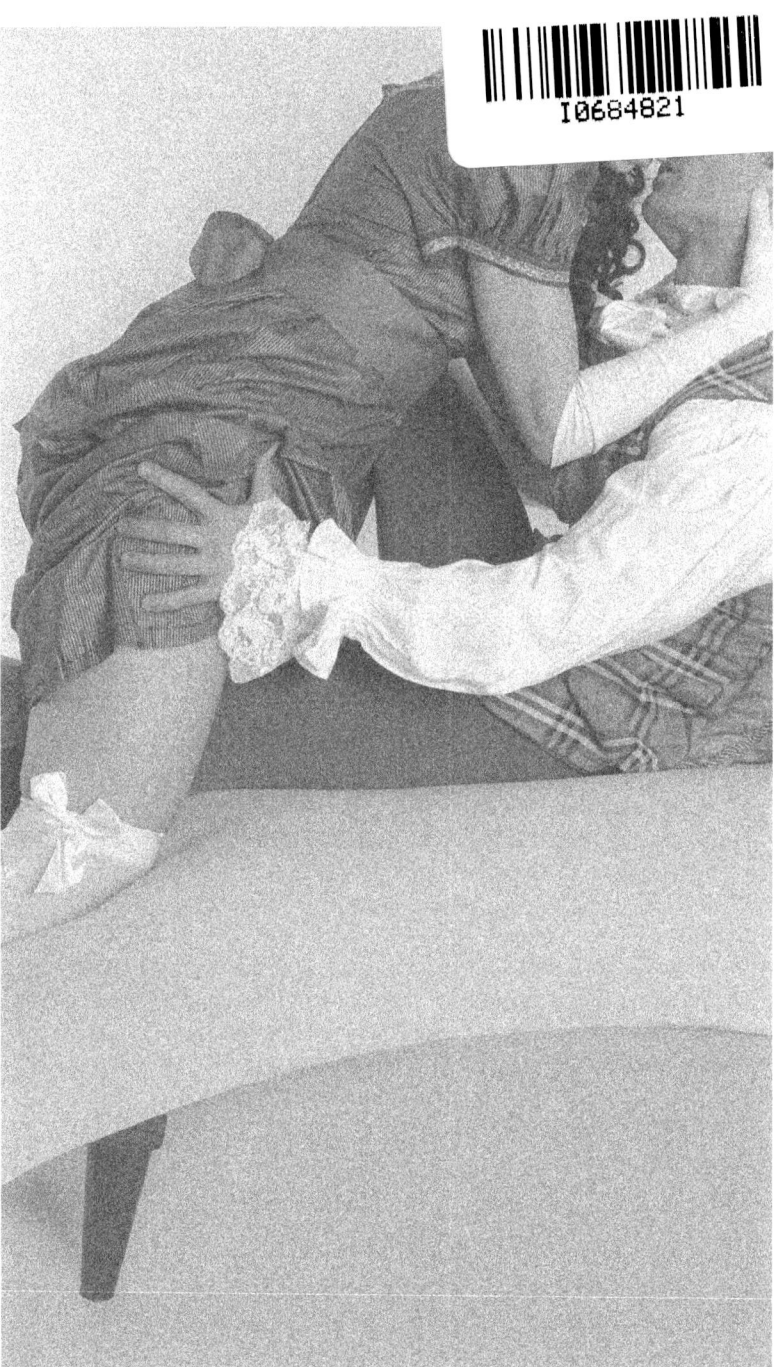

KING OF SWORDS
KINGS OF THE TAROT, BOOK 1
Published by HIGH PRIESTESS PUBLICATIONS
Copyright © 2017 by Anne Kenny

eBook 978-0-9989229-4-2
Paperback 978-0-9989229-0-4

Printed in the USA.

Cover Design and Interior Format

© THE KILLION GROUP INC.

KING of SWORDS

KINGS OF THE TAROT • BOOK 1

Love is in the cards.

ANNA DURBIN

For Mitzie, my once and future muse.

PROLOGUE

The Fool: The beginning of a journey, a choice of vital importance, wonderment, expanding horizons . . .

London
April 1804

THE DOWAGER LADY TREMAIN HANDED her well-worn deck of cards to her granddaughter. "Think on the question as you shuffle them, Cassandra."

Edges frayed, corners bent, the cards had seen better days. Cassandra handled them with care as she took them from her grandmother. Larger than playing cards, they proved difficult to hold, almost unwieldy, but she managed to shuffle them nonetheless as she thought and thought on the question.

"Are you concentrating?"

"Yes, ma'am."

"For the divination to work, you must concentrate on the question 'whom will I marry?' as you shuffle the cards," said the old lady, a twinkle in her cloudy blue eyes.

"Yes, Grandmamma, I know," said Cassandra, exasperated. "I am doing so." Or at least she had been doing so before her grandmother had interrupted her train of thought. She returned her mind to the question at hand and continued shuffling the awkward cards.

"When you are ready, set the deck down and cut it into three piles with your left hand."

Finally, after several more shuffles, Cassandra exhausted the question of whom she was to marry and put the cards down. She cut them into three piles and awaited further instruction.

"Now, draw one card from each pile from left to right and put it down in front of you, but do not turn the cards over yet."

She did as she was told. The three cards holding her future lay in front of her as the old lady took her hands and held them in her own gnarled fingers.

Closing her eyes, Grandmamma said a blessing in her native Welsh, words Cassandra understood only slightly. When finished with the blessing, she let go of her granddaughter's hands and said in English, "Turn the first card over."

The Fool stared up at Cassandra.

"Ah. Good. The Fool is the first card of the Tarot's Major Arcana. It means you've begun a journey. Tonight will take you further on your quest," said the old lady in reference to Cassandra's debut ball, which would begin soon—sooner than she felt prepared for. "Turn over the second card."

Again, she did as she was bid and saw the Nine of Cups upside down.

"Hmm. The 'wish' card, reversed." Grandmamma's brows drew together in apparent agitation as she regarded the card. "Listen very carefully, Cassandra." She tapped the card with a knobby finger. "You have the chance to receive the gift of your dreams, if you do not blunder and make the wrong choice this evening.

It is very important that you act with utmost decorum tonight if this dream is to come true. Do you understand?"

Cassandra nodded at the gravity of her grandmother's warning, confused as to what could possibly happen to make her behave badly.

"Now, turn over the final card," said Grandmamma.

The King of Swords lay in front of her, and she looked to her grandmother for explanation.

"Excellent, my child. A very good sort of man who is ruled by the season of Spring, the direction of East, and the element of Air. A gentleman of intellect, logic, and integrity—one with dark hair and light eyes who is fair and insightful—will come into your life. He will be the first one to ask you to dance tonight. This is the one you will marry."

Cassandra smiled. Perhaps, just perhaps, she would find true love after all.

Grandmamma gathered her cards together and placed them in a velvet drawstring bag. She stood and patted her granddaughter gently on her cheek. "Make haste, girl, for the guests will be arriving any minute now."

As the old woman hobbled from the room, Cassandra went to her dressing table and took one last look at herself in the mirror. She tucked a dark curl that had fallen from her coif back into place and smoothed a hand over the white silk dress that hugged her bosom and then fell from her waist in a straight line. She fingered a locket her grandmother had given her for this occasion, a sardonyx cameo depicting The Lovers, Grandmamma's favorite tarot card. The clock in the hallway struck the hour, and she knew a moment of trepidation. It was time to go downstairs.

Pausing by the window that faced the street below, she pulled back a panel of her curtains to sneak a glance at the first arriving guests. Her eyes landed on the profile of a breathtaking gentleman as he approached the front door. Almost as if he felt her looking down at him, he turned his head up to meet her gaze. Jolted by his intense eyes upon her, she dropped the curtain back into place, and a hot spark of anger coursed through her veins as her traitorous heart skipped a beat. *Oh no, not him. Not Lord William.* What was *he* doing here?

CHAPTER 1

Queen of Swords: A strong-willed, courageous, independent woman with dark hair and light eyes, who is perceptive, idealistic, humanitarian, and straightforward . . .

———◆———

Cumberland, almost twelve years later
March 1816

LADY CASSANDRA GARDNER OUTDID ALL expectations. Oh, most of the scandal sheets predicted she would somehow insult Lord William Poniard, as she was wont to do, at the Wellesley house party in the Lake District, but she surpassed all forecasts when she threw her drink in his face after overhearing the provoking comment he had made about her beloved sister Phoebe during the opening ball.

"Such a shame about Lady Abadon, is it not?" the oft befuddled Sir Lionel Farnsworth had remarked to Lord William.

Cassandra, who had been making her way across the ballroom, stopped in her tracks upon hearing her sister's name.

"Come again?" Lord William had asked. He stood on the periphery of the dance floor speaking with Sir

Lionel and appeared confused as to why the gentleman was suddenly talking about the Countess of Abadon, who had died a while ago.

Cassandra herself was also baffled as to why her sister's name had arisen out of nowhere in the conversation, so she stood riveted to the floor listening to the two men for clarification.

"I say, it's a shame about Lady Abadon, is it not?" Sir Lionel reiterated as if the question made perfect sense.

"A tragic shame. But why on earth do you ask all of a sudden?"

"Oh, I only bring it up because her brother, the duke, reminded me just a few minutes ago that it's been almost two years since she died. I was the duke's second when he called Abadon out over her death, you know." Sir Lionel's chest puffed out with such an obvious sense of pride that Cassandra thought he might pop a button on his waistcoat. He then leaned in toward Lord William to say in a quieter, almost conspiratorial tone, "It's unfortunate that Abadon survived the duel, don't you think? I mean, what do you make of the rumor that he killed Lady Abadon?"

"A horrendous crime, if it's true," Lord William had replied shaking his head. He then added in apparent afterthought, "Of course, if she was of the same temperament as her sister Cassandra, one could almost see how her husband might have wanted to hurt her, can't one?"

"Uh . . .," said Sir Lionel. It was all he could say before Cassandra stomped over to Lord William, tapped him on the shoulder to get his attention, and threw her punch in his face.

Most of the guests appeared to feign shock at such a display, when in fact it was common knowledge that most had accepted invitations to Lady Wellesley's week-long party so far away from London right before the beginning of the Season with hopes of being treated to just such a spectacle. Entertainment value alone had been the point of inviting the two to the same soiree. After all, their mutual animosity toward one another had been infamous amongst society since Lord William's return from the Continent last year after a ten-year stint in the dragoons, although Lady Cassandra's own hostility toward him predated his return as a war hero and began at her coming out party when she refused to dance with him, preferring instead to sit next to a potted frond. However, she eclipsed all past bad behavior with the beverage incident this evening.

Lady Wellesley herself appeared delighted at Cassandra's fit, even as she faked umbrage at the scene. "Lady Cassandra!" she exclaimed as a broad smile broke out on her face. She instructed a footman to assist Lord William with a towel.

Though outwardly Lady Wellesley remonstrated her, Cassandra guessed that inwardly, the woman congratulated herself at her own success. To deliver such amusement to her guests would be a definite feather in her cap. For his part, Lord William stared at Cassandra with incredulity, saying nothing, his utter astonishment evident as he blinked several times to clear the liquid that was probably stinging his eyes.

Cassandra, meanwhile, stood back and glowered at him. Well, it was his own fault that he now needed a new cravat from the punch dripping down his face onto its snowy folds. Had he not insulted her with his offhanded remark involving her sister, she might have passed by him without incident. Her response to his words, however, had come from her gut, not at all thought out.

After her own shock had worn off, she gathered her wits. "Oh, please do forgive me, Lord William. I must have slipped." Then she turned and walked away, leaving him perceptibly stunned and speechless.

Once alone and with a moment to think about the recent scene, she opened her fan and cooled her face. That had been very bad of her. Very bad indeed. Better to have come up with a verbal rejoinder to his comment than to physically assault the man. Yet, it had not been in her to think up a response to the affront he had just made at the expense of her dear sister. Furthermore, his insinuation that Cassandra herself had a defect in temperament that would drive someone to acts of violence also stung.

"Bad form, Cass," said her brother, the Duke of Benthower, as he came up alongside her in all his noble hauteur near the windows overlooking the moonlit garden.

She rolled her eyes. "Yes, I know it was, Your Grace." She called him that sardonically, mocking his arrogance at his own station. "However, I was provoked. Your erstwhile friend, Poniard, insulted the memory of Phoebe with something he said."

"Nevertheless, do try to rein in that temper of yours. Such a spectacle. You'll undo all the work I've done to get Sir Lionel to agree to marry you. I have him thinking he is quite in love with you, and I don't want you ruining it. I want to announce your engagement as soon as possible."

"If I've told you once, Michael," she said, using his given name this time because he didn't like anyone to address him by it, "I've told you a thousand times that I am not marrying anybody, least of all that half-wit

Sir Lionel."

"You're nearly thirty, old girl. At your ripe age, you're lucky to get anyone, even if it is Sir Lionel. Better to get at least a half-witted husband than none at all."

"Better for me? Or better for you? What unholy deal have you made with the man?"

"Now, now, Cass. The negotiations of men in these matters must remain between the men. You women wouldn't understand them."

She snorted in a most unladylike fashion at that statement. "Let me guess. You get half my dowry for his right to marry me? Aren't those the usual terms? That's what you did with Phoebe's and Julia's dowries, at any rate. Poor Bess died before you could get your hands on her money, and Violet is next after me, no doubt. Better get me married off, though, before I turn thirty and my dowry reverts to me for my own personal use, as it does on that happy day. Am I not right?"

"You make me sound so conniving. All I want is your happiness, Cassandra."

"All you want is *your* happiness. Having run through the dowries of two of your sisters, you're in need of a little blunt, I would bet. And now you're after mine." She turned to confront him head on. "Well, you can't have it, Michael. It will soon be mine to do with as I please. I have a purpose for my money, one you wouldn't understand."

"Oh, what ludicrous purpose could you possibly have for fifty-thousand pounds? Better to leave it to your husband to manage. You'll just fritter it away on frippery."

She eyed him warily and nearly told him what she intended to do with her money once it was hers to control. That she intended to build a refuge for unfortunate women whose husbands beat them, a place where they could find haven from the cruelty and abuse, a place where others understood and cared about their plights, a place where they could start afresh with new identities, if necessary, and funds to help them into new homes, as needed. All in honor of her sister Phoebe who'd been brutally beaten to death by her husband. But she remained silent and merely stared up at him as he looked down upon her in that condescending way he had of looking down upon those beneath him in rank and circumstance and making them feel like worms.

Finally, she said, "What I do with my money is my business. And you'll not get your hands on any of it."

"Tsk, tsk. Don't be so sure of yourself, my dear. Sir Lionel doesn't like a woman with so much self-confidence. He likes his women sweet and demure."

"Sir Lionel—and you—can go to blazes for all I care."

"Oh, you'll care, Cassandra. You'll care," he said cryptically—and with a hint of malice—before he turned and stalked away.

She gazed out the windows onto the terrace as she briefly considered what he had meant by his last comment, and then her mind returned to her earlier ruminations about the scene with Lord William. Throwing punch on him was not at all the thing to do, she silently chastised herself, especially if she hoped to drum up support for her shelter among the ladies of the *ton* present at this week's party. She must be on her best behavior to woo them to her cause. Another slip like the one she had just made could sink her ship before it set sail, and she blamed him for the blunder. Loathsome man.

Damnable woman. William silently cursed Lady
Cassandra as he tied a fresh cravat in his room. She had
the unique ability to irritate him as no other woman
could. She had been snide and surly to him ever since
his return to England following a distinguished ten-
year career in the 1st King's Dragoon Guards. Her
insult tonight with the punch had rankled him more
than anything she had yet done or said to him—but
then, he had to admit that his remark about her iras-
cible temperament had indeed been out of bounds.
He had certainly not intended for her to overhear it.
And though he had not truly meant to imply that a
man should ever hurt his wife, he had felt provoked
to meanness toward her by a comment she had made
to him two weeks ago at Lady Norris's dinner party
during a discussion of his service in the Battle of
Waterloo.

"Tell us again, Captain Poniard, about how you
rescued a dozen British soldiers from certain death,"
said Lady Norris's wide-eyed daughter Hermione in
breathless anticipation of the tale and, no doubt, the
gore.

"Well, it was nothing really," he began.

"No doubt it was—nothing really, that is," said Lady
Cassandra in her most withering voice, leaving him to
feel quite humiliated in front of the others. "In which
case, won't you spare us the dreary details of it, *Captain*?
We've all heard the story again and again." She placed
special emphasis on the word "Captain," as though she
didn't believe him worthy of the rank. She then rose
from the settee where she had been seated and left the

drawing room, giving him no chance to retort.

Having served his country faithfully, he might have thought a former army officer like himself, decorated for valor in both the Peninsular War and at Waterloo, deserved perhaps a little respect, but apparently not where she was concerned. No, she insulted him at every turn. He should have let it go, but he had been deeply embarrassed by her brusque dismissal of him in front of other people.

That she most truly hated him was obvious. Why, he couldn't imagine. What had he ever done to her to provoke such animus? Perhaps it had to do with his falling out with her brother. He and the duke had been the best of friends in their youth but had become estranged when they were both about twenty. Though, now that he thought about it some, Lady Cassandra's animosity toward him had begun a couple of years before that, sometime before he and her brother had ended their friendship. He recalled enduring many belligerent comments from her back then. He even recalled her turning him down for a dance at her debut ball. What had he done to set her so against him? Had he said something to her? Or done something to her? He would probably never know the answers to those questions, and frankly, he didn't care.

All he did care about was getting back to the ball. He had reserved a waltz with Benthower's wife, and he did not want to miss out on being able to hold his beloved for at least a few moments, even if it were only on a crowded dance floor. Though he avoided married women on principle and knew he shouldn't pine for one like he did the duchess, he couldn't help himself. Since his return from his service in the dragoons, he discovered that he was as much in love with her as he had ever been in his youth—before she had married the duke.

He made it back to the ballroom just in time for the coveted waltz with Her Grace, the Duchess of Benthower, Belinda Gardner. She sat on the periphery of the dance floor with some friends, and he greeted her with the customary gallantry before escorting her onto the floor.

"Belinda," he whispered to her in reverent awe, "you look breathtaking." And she did.

Gifted with the face of a goddess, she fairly glowed in the light of the beeswax candles illuminating the dance floor and lit up the entire room with her radiance. She was a fairytale princess: her eyes sapphires, her lips cherries, and her hair spun gold, and William—like most of the men of her acquaintance—had fallen in love with her the first time he had gazed upon her, which had been nearly fifteen years ago when he was eighteen and she was sixteen.

He had been heartbroken four years later when she married his erstwhile best friend Benthower after the duke had stolen her away from him. Then, after a few months of stumbling around in heartache, William purchased a commission in the dragoons just to get away from the situation with Belinda and the duke. Being away from her on the Continent had worked to dull his ardor for her to the point that he rarely thought of her while he was gone, but now that he was back home and near her once more, his old feelings had managed to surface all over again. In the months since he had been back from the war, he still yearned for her.

Despite the fact that he had come home from the war to look for a wife, he found himself dwelling more than was appropriate on Belinda and her charms. He cursed Benthower and his betrayal all those years ago. He might have been a happily married man now had Benthower not intruded and stolen Belinda away. Anger and resentment still gnawed at him over the entire situation. Would he ever see justice done for the duke's interference?

As he whirled the duchess about the dance floor, he looked into her eyes and tried to discern how she felt about him after all these years. She was as beguiling as a serpent, however; and like a serpent's eyes, hers gave nothing away.

Transfixed by her gaze, he said, "You look breathtaking, Belinda."

"So you have said." Her smile, calculated to entice, sent shivers down his spine.

"I don't suppose you know the effect you have on every man you meet?"

"Oh, don't I?" This time she gave him a seductive moue, as though she knew she could have any man she desired.

"I don't suppose you know the effect you have on me, do you?"

She laughed flirtatiously but said nothing in reply, seeming to enjoy his blandishments and to know that she need do nothing to earn them other than breathe.

"I must tell you something, Belinda."

"And what is that?"

"I must tell you that my feelings for you have never wavered—even after all these years away. I find myself thinking about you all the time."

"Is that so?"

"Yes."

She looked up at him bewitchingly, giving him a

provocative smile. "You flatter me, William, but how is it that your feelings have never changed after all these years?"

"You hold my heart, Belinda. In fact, I can still say that . . . that . . . I care deeply for you. I love you, in fact." The words were out of his mouth on a whisper before he even realized what he had said, and he blamed the wine he had drunk earlier in the evening for his candor. He decided, however, that he did not regret telling her how he felt and even went on to say, "I still love you as much as I ever did when we were together— before Benthower came between us." The sentiment just flowed out of him unchecked tonight much like the free-flowing spirits in the ballroom.

Her eyes grew wide, and she seemed truly astonished at his confession. "You do?"

"Yes, I do. I always have." He was stunned that she had not known it.

She appeared to think on what he said, and only after a few seconds of silence did she recover herself. She then replied with a sultry smile that belied her words, "I don't think it is a good idea to discuss such things, William. Benthower is eyeing us now. He will be very jealous that we have danced."

"Hang Benthower!"

She made no reply to that comment.

"I regret that there was never a time for us." He paused to gauge her sentiments on the matter, but her veiled countenance revealed nothing. "Don't you?"

She gazed at him a good long while and gave him another coquettish smile, which confused him. "Generally, I have no regrets."

Her response rankled him. "Don't you ever wonder what it would have been like had you married me instead of him?"

She seemed to consider the question a moment and then shrugged insouciantly. "I suppose I sometimes wonder about it, yes, but—"

Frustrated, he cut her off. "But I predict we would have been happy, you and I. It is you and I who should have married, not you and Benthower." She made no remark to that statement as they danced in silence for a few bars. Finally, he could no longer hold his tongue, and he asked her the question that had burned in his mind forever. "Did you . . . did you ever love me, Belinda?" The wine had affected him more than he realized, or he would never have been so bold as to ask her that question, but even so, he did not regret his audacity because he wanted—he needed—to hear the answer directly from her lips.

"Oh, William . . ." Her nervous laughter exposed her discomfort with the question. "I hardly know what to say. You are truly such diverting company. I esteem you greatly."

"Yes, but . . . but, did you love me?"

"I-I cannot say. I . . . I . . . just . . .," she said. Then she stammered around for more words, her composure overtly shaken, until he could no longer take her obvious rejection of his sentiments.

"No, don't. Please. Don't explain. I think explanations can only embarrass us both. I will always admire you, Belinda, and I bid you a good evening, madam." His voice was brusque and bitter even to his own ears. The set ended and he walked her to the sidelines of the floor where he left her without a bow. He did not look back her, not even a glance.

CASSANDRA WANTED to cast up her accounts. Watching Lord William fawn all over her sister-in-law was perfect torture and had been since the summer nearly fifteen years ago when he had visited her brother for a couple of weeks and met Belinda. He had been a favorite friend of Benthower's since their youth and had frequently stayed with the duke's family at their ancestral home in Northamptonshire.

That particular summer—the summer of 1801—Miss Belinda Hollowsley had been orphaned at age sixteen and had come to stay with her very wealthy aunt and uncle, Sir Geoffrey Hollowsley and his wife Maria, in the village of Raventon not far from Benthower Castle. Her uncle had bestowed upon her a generous dowry, making her the most sought after girl in the county, and she had received invitations to visit the castle because her Aunt Hollowsley had been particular friends with Cassandra's mother, the Duchess of Benthower. In the course of visiting the castle, Miss Hollowsley had become fast friends with Cassandra's sister Phoebe, who had also been sixteen at the time.

Cassandra, on the other hand, had not liked Miss Hollowsley from the start, having found her to be a shallow, vain, ill-tempered, uncharitable, and just plain mean creature, who concerned herself mainly with her appearance to the exclusion of nearly all other topics. She also belittled others who were not as fortunate as her, whether it was in looks or circumstance, and had nary a kind word for anyone. What truly irked Cassandra most about the girl, however, was how blinded people were by her beauty to her faults. She could do no wrong in the eyes of most, and in particular, Lord William. He had been so taken with her that he could not see her for the conceited girl that she was.

He seemed to think the sun rose and shone just to be nearer to her.

And oh, how Cassandra had wanted to be that girl to Lord William.

She had silently ached for years with feelings for him that she could only equate with love. She had developed a tendre for him early on, when he had first started coming to Benthower Castle because he had been so kind and attentive to her, not to mention fun and handsome, with his captivating emerald eyes and his dark brown hair. From the moment she had met him, she had dreamt of one day being his bride. At the tender age of fifteen, those feelings had been stronger than ever until Miss Hollowsley appeared—until the day Cassandra overheard Lord William tell her brother what he thought and how he felt, not only about Miss Hollowsley, but also about herself. The memory of it was like a fresh wound—still raw and sore.

That long-ago day had dawned brilliant and sunny, not a cloud to the sky. Her brother and Lord William awoke early with plans for riding that morning, and she sneaked along behind them to spy on them, as she frequently did whenever Lord William was visiting. She went undetected as she followed them to the stables and climbed up the ladder to the hayloft overlooking their horses. As they waited below for their steeds to be saddled, Benthower teased Lord William about being distracted by something.

"Lud, Will, what's got you in such a state?"

"I don't know what you mean, Benny."

Benthower laughed. "Don't you? One would almost think you're in love the way you pine about lately."

Cassandra's heart skipped a beat at her brother's pronouncement, while at the same time a strange wave of nausea overcame her. Lord William was in love? With whom? Though she feared she knew who it was, for a wild moment, she let her mind go to the possibility that it was she, until she heard him reply.

"You know me too well, old friend. I am in love. With an angel. The most glorious creature I have ever beheld."

"Who, pray tell, is that?"

"Miss Hollowsley, of course."

Cassandra's heart clenched, while Benthower went silent for a moment. She watched him through the floorboards of the hayloft as he eyed his friend warily with alarm and something akin to disapproval. Then he recovered himself and said, "Miss Hollowsley?"

"Yes. Don't you think she is divine, Benny? 'The all-seeing sun ne'er saw her match since first the world begun.'" Lord William even quoted Shakespeare over her.

Meanwhile, Cassandra's throat tightened up.

"Quite," the duke replied. He seemed to consider his friend's words before continuing. "What about my sister?"

"Which one?"

"The one who moons over you."

"Oh, you mean Cassandra?"

She gasped at her name, and both Benthower and Lord William looked overhead for the source of the sound. Apparently spying nothing out of the ordinary, Lord William asked offhandedly, "What about her?"

"I always thought perhaps one day you and she might make a match."

"Ha! Not bloody likely."

The force with which he said the words cut to her soul, and her heart met the floor in a crashing plummet.

"Why's that?" asked Benthower.

Lord William appeared to duck the question for a moment, and then he shrugged and threw a piece of straw he had been twirling into the air. "Look, I know she's your sister, old chum, but Lady Cassandra . . . just isn't for me."

Hot, stinging tears began to fill her eyes and fall from her lashes.

"Again, I ask you, why's that?"

"Because, and I hate to say this, but she is . . . well . . . she's rather homely. She wasn't always so, but now she's big and gawky and not at all attractive. She has spots all over her face and that nose." He shook his head as he spoke, as though there were no hope for her. "She's a very sweet girl, but I don't feel any attraction for her. I'd never tell her so, though."

"I really don't think she's as bad as all that," said Benthower, and despite the tears falling from her eyes, she felt a tenderness for her brother that she had never quite known before. "She has nice eyes, you must admit."

Lord William shrugged once more.

"And classic features, which she just needs to grow into. She's in her awkward years right now, but she *will* grow out of it, especially those spots."

Again, a shrug from his friend.

"She will be a real beauty once she is older, I predict," said Benthower.

Lord William practically snorted as he replied, "That I'd like to see."

A sob nearly escaped Cassandra, but she held it in until she climbed down from the loft and ran from the stables back to the castle where she broke down and cried for hours in her chamber. When at last her tears dried up, she vowed to purge Lord William from her breaking heart.

She was transported back to the present from her recollection of that painful day by the ending of the waltz. She watched him escort the duchess to her seat on the edge of the dance floor and noted with some satisfaction that they parted from one another with what appeared to be acrimony between them. What was that all about? As he went to claim his next dance with another woman, she also wondered—with something like regret—what it would be like to be the one in his arms.

Had she not snubbed him at her debut, had she danced the first dance with him like he had asked, she might have known what it felt like to have him escort her—if only for a dance—but she could never quite forgive him for his harsh words about her that summer long ago. Even though he had remained good to her and even kind to her in person while he was her brother's friend, she was from that moment on crushed at his opinion of her. That he considered her homely and could never feel for her as she felt for him was a devastating blow to her heart, and she could not be civil to him again. Her incivility had turned into open rudeness and even hostility toward him as the years wore on, and after his break with her brother, he seemed no longer able to hold his tongue to her barbs. When he returned from the Continent last year, he began to give as good as he got, and theirs became a relationship of intolerance and animosity.

Cassandra hated Lord William. And she would forever scorn him as he had done her.

CHAPTER 2

The Moon: Danger, deception, disgrace, peril, intrigue, and trickery . . .

———◆———

AS FINDLEY, HER ABIGAIL, DID her hair the next morning in her room at Wellesley Manor, Cassandra sat at the mirror and contemplated the reflection that stared back at her. She had gone to bed last night reliving the scene in the stables nearly fifteen years ago when Lord William had berated her appearance so thoughtlessly. Although she hadn't wept over the memory like she used to do, it had sent her into a melancholy from which she had been unable to shake herself even this morning. She wondered what his opinion of her would be now. What would he say about her nose, which perhaps had been overly large for the face of a young girl? Would he agree that she had grown into it since then? And her complexion? Would he even notice that her spots had completely cleared up? And what of her eyes? Would he merely shrug if he heard someone compliment them today?

Though many a man had called her handsome in the years since her coming out, and—unbeknownst to her family—a couple had even sought her hand in marriage, she had never quite believed that she had grown into a beauty as her brother had predicted she would. Instead, Lord William's assessment of her still haunted her, and she still saw herself as big and gawky and homely—words he had used to describe her. It was one reason she had never accepted an offer of marriage and why, at age nine and twenty, she remained unattached and on the shelf.

When Findley finished with her hair, Cassandra dressed and went downstairs for breakfast at eleven. She stood at the doorway just about to enter the breakfast room when she heard Lord William say something to someone inside the room. She knew his voice. It was at once grating to her and yet, somehow soothing also. Instinctively, she turned to walk back down the hallway and return to her room to avoid a possible meeting—and probable confrontation—with him. As she turned to retreat, however, she had the misfortune of making eye contact with Lady Wellesley, who was seated at the table.

"Lady Cassandra," the baroness crowed, "please do come in and join us."

All heads turned toward the doorway and toward her, and she was forced by the customs of decorum to enter the room at the invitation of her hostess. She walked through the doorway, and her gaze at once met Lord William's. What he was thinking, however, was not clearly written in his countenance. She hoped her thoughts were equally inscrutable, for she was immediately struck by his beautiful features, and though she hated to admit it—especially to herself—a reverent awe settled over her as it did every time she looked upon his emerald eyes. They stared at each other briefly, and she went to the sideboard to serve herself.

Lady Wellesley then arranged for Lord William to sit beside her at the table, and she invited Cassandra to sit across from him. What could she do but accept the invitation? To have turned it down would have been rude beyond measure. Meanwhile, several people who had been milling about the room noncommittally quickly got their plates and filled them with food and then sat down for the morning show. It did not take long for the entertainment to begin.

"So tell me, Lady Cassandra, what do you think about Mrs. Fry's work?" Lady Wellesley threw out the opening salvo, most likely knowing that Cassandra would have an opinion on the matter and that it would likely differ from Lord William's.

Cassandra cleared her throat. "I think she is a brave soul and one to be greatly admired. Her work on behalf of incarcerated women is unparalleled. My own hope, now that you mention that good lady, is to work with women who are abused by their husbands and help them in the manner that Mrs. Fry has helped female prisoners. In fact, I'd like to start a home, a shelter of sorts, for those unfortunate souls whose husbands beat them." She looked directly at Lord William, and he raised an eyebrow. "I was hoping to talk to you, Lady Wellesley, and several other ladies present here at the party about support for such a venture."

"Well, yes indeed, we must have that conversation, but first, what do you think of Mrs. Fry, Lord William?"

"While I might admire the work she does, I think the good lady would do better if she stayed at home and took care of her family rather than venturing into the bellies of such places as Newgate—but then, I am not her husband and cannot command her to desist."

Clink. Cassandra couldn't help herself. She set her

knife down a little too loudly upon her plate but remained quiet otherwise.

"You think her husband should rein her in, then?" asked Lady Wellesley.

A tempest was forming between Cassandra and Lord William and wanted only a little encouragement before it began to blow.

"Yes. Don't you?" Lord William took a bite of his kippered herring.

"Why, I don't know what to think on the matter. What say you, Lady Cassandra?" asked a positively glowing Lady Wellesley.

"As for myself, I think the lady should continue in her good works and not pay any attention to her husband."

"Not pay any attention to her husband?" asked Lord William, mild outrage resounding in his tone.

"Yes. Pay him no attention whatsoever."

"If I were your husband and I heard you say that, Lady Cassandra, I think I would put you over my knee," came his reply.

"If I were married to you, Lord William, I think I would poison your tea."

"And if I were married to you, I think I would drink it—providing, of course, that you didn't throw it in my face first."

Touché, she thought with regret, and suddenly she was no longer hungry. She forced herself to take a couple bites of her food for the sake of appearances, however, and then excused herself from the table and headed back up to her room. He had won that round. Odious man.

INFERNAL WOMAN. Why did she always bait him? And more importantly, why did he always take the bait? She was the most insufferable female he had ever met. Yet it had not always been that way. He recalled a time long ago when she had been sweet and good-natured toward him, a time when she had seemed to adore him. Girlish infatuation it had been, of course, but he could not account for her treatment of him in the present day. He wondered, yet again, what he had ever done to deserve the blatant antipathy that she showed him on nearly every occasion they met.

At least he had won that round with her, he thought, as he watched her rise from the table. He and the rest of the gentlemen rose as well, and she turned to throw him a final pointed look before she left the room. As her gaze fell upon him, however, his cock did a funny thing: without his permission, it grew hard, and not just sort of hard, but really hard, and he had to take his seat again immediately. He had not had an errant erection like this since his days at Eton, and he grew concerned about what it could mean. Surely, it did not mean he was attracted to Lady Cassandra, did it? Surely, all it meant was that it had been far too long since he'd been with a woman. Surely, abstinence—and not some latent attraction to Lady Cassandra—caused his current discomfort. Yet, she had looked remarkably good this morning, and this was not the first time he had noticed her looking so comely and captivating.

No, he had noticed her allure some years before on the evening of her debut. That night had been the first time he realized that she was not the homely, gawky girl of his youth, but rather, an elegant young woman. He had even asked her to dance with him despite the fact that she was Benthower's sister. Ironically, that incident had been the first time she had ever been rude to him in a public forum, preferring to sit out the dance than to be his partner. He had not known what to make of it back then, but he attributed her rudeness to the fact that he and her brother had no longer been on speaking terms.

Still, as enchanting as he had thought she had looked the night she debuted, she had looked perhaps even more so this morning, her alabaster skin offset by her sable hair. And this morning was the first time he had ever had a visceral reaction to her. With his member still stiff, he was uncomfortable for the rest of breakfast and had to remain seated for another few minutes to avoid embarrassment. When at last his phallus deflated, he got up from the table and went for a ride to clear his head.

Though the skies promised rain with their thick cover of clouds, William rode his steed hard until he was some distance away from the stables. He found himself near a thicket and turned his horse to ride slowly through the woods. As he rode along, he considered what he would do now. Though he wanted to find a wife this Season, he saw few prospects at the Wellesley party. No one compared to Belinda in his mind. Therefore, he saw no need to stay at this house party any longer, especially if Benthower and Belinda were going to be here. Why protract his misery at seeing them together and happy? Better he should go back to London and tend to business. With his brother, the Marquess of Kingspointe, out of the country in Italy, William had some affairs to see to for the marquisate anyway.

At length, he decided he would have Watts, his valet, pack his things when he got back to the house, and then he would leave for Town tomorrow at the latest. As he went over in his head all that he had to do in London, the clouds began to sprinkle on him. Droplets of water tinkled on the bare branches overhead and softly pelted his face and hands. Wonderful. He would be fairly soaked by the time he returned to the stables. He drew his coat around himself to stave off a chill and kicked his steed into a trot. As the rain began to fall in earnest, he turned the horse around to head back to the manor house and caught sight of a tall feminine form a few yards ahead of him. She was walking swiftly away from him, no doubt in an effort to make it back to the house and get out of the rain as soon as possible. Perhaps he could assist her.

He trotted the horse up beside her and said, "Good day, miss. May I offer you a ride back to Wellesley Manor?"

"No, thank you," came the hasty reply. She did not turn her head to look at him, which he thought strange. From where he sat, he could not make out her face for the bonnet obscuring it.

"You can have the horse, and I shall walk, if you are concerned about propriety."

"No. Thank you, but no." Her words were firm, and she kept her head down.

He pulled his mount to a halt and climbed down from the gelding. He rushed to her side, walking swiftly to catch up to her because she was moving so fast.

"Really, I insist. You ride the horse, and I'll walk beside you."

"Really, Lord William," said an overtly irritated Lady Cassandra as she stopped and turned to face him. "I don't think that is such a good idea, now is it?"

He remained speechless for several seconds, stunned

and captivated by her beauty. Even though she was damp and disheveled from the rain, she looked lovely. Finally, he recovered himself. "Nonsense. Surely we can be civil to one another for the short ride back to the house."

"I think it wise not to try. I appreciate your concern, but I shall walk."

"You'll be thoroughly soaked by the time you get back." As if to underscore his statement, thunder clapped overhead startling them both. "There. Now it will really start raining, and you'll catch your death of cold."

She shivered, probably despite herself. "I'll be fine. Thank you." And with that, she turned and began walking toward the house once again.

"Fine. I'll just walk beside you with the horse to make sure you get back to the house."

"Please do not. Please get on your horse and ride away, my lord." She did not look at him as she spoke, nor did she stop.

"I can't leave you stranded out here by yourself."

"And I really can't put you off your horse. You ride. I shall walk."

"Lady Cassandra, I insist you take the horse."

"You really needn't be so gallant for my sake. Besides, I'm not at all dressed for riding."

"Fine. As I said, I'll just walk beside you with the animal to make sure you get back to the house."

"Oh, for pity's sake, help me up onto the beast, but I insist you ride also. We'll make it back much sooner if we are both on the horse."

"That is very gallant of you, my lady." He flashed her an ironic smile as he climbed back onto his steed. He then held out his hands and pulled her up onto the saddle to sit as best as she could between his legs. He put his arms around her, while she settled her bum in front of him and sat with her legs to one side of the pommel.

He could tell how very tense she was as he took the reins and started the horse, but he made sure he had a tight hold on her so that she would not fall off. Her discomfort with the situation was palpable, which he found somehow endearing, as he pulled her even closer to him. She nestled her backside against him, and for the first time, he could smell her heavenly scent, a combination of roses and lavender, and just as had happened when she looked at him at breakfast, his cock took on a life of its own, jumping to attention at her proximity. He cursed himself but thanked the heavens for the skirts she wore. She most likely would not feel how hard he was for her through all the material surrounding her—or at least with her lack of carnal knowledge, she would not know what it was she was feeling.

———◆———

GOOD LORD! Was that . . . was that *him*? His male member pressed up against her backside? At the thought of it, her belly quivered, and her own arousal moved on down below. Though Cassandra had no firsthand carnal knowledge of a man, she knew enough of what was what, and what went where, to know what of Lord William's was poking her in the behind, for she had read a certain book that her sister Julia had brought back with her from her travels to India: the *Kama Sutra*. Julia had originally been introduced to the little known book when she lived in Calcutta. She'd received a copy of it from a friend and had it translated by a sage old man who traded in opium and who spoke English fairly well, and she had brought a copy home for each of her sisters when she returned from India several years ago, just before her husband, Niles Lacey, had died.

By the standards set for young women of her day, Cassandra knew she should have felt some shame in reading and enjoying the book and looking at its pictures, as well as getting aroused by its content, but she felt no contrition. Instead, she boldly pleasured herself whenever she opened the book. She might not ever have a man, but at least she knew an orgasm when she had one, thanks largely to the contents of the *Kama Sutra*.

As she rode along with Lord William, Cassandra was innervated by her contact with him and nearly swooned as he put his arms about her to keep her on the horse. His scent surrounded her as he pulled her close, and as she took it in, heat pooled between her thighs. He smelled so masculine and divine, like leather and sandalwood, and the warmth of a blush— several shades of red, surely—crept up her neck into her cheeks at the sensations he evoked throughout her body. She was only thankful that she faced forward, away from his view.

They rode several minutes without speaking, the silence between them awkward. At length, he cleared his throat and asked, "So, are you enjoying the Wellesleys' party thus far?"

"I would not say I'm particularly enjoying it, but then, I did not come here for the amusement of it. I came here with a purpose."

"And what, might I ask, is that?"

"I don't think you would comprehend, Lord William."

"You'd be surprised at my abilities, Lady Cassandra. Why don't you try me?"

"If you must know, I've come here with the intent of drumming up support with the ladies for the shelter I spoke of at breakfast."

"Ah, yes. A shelter for women whose husbands beat them. A very noble project indeed."

"And one that is very precious to me—as you may know."

He was silent for a heartbeat before continuing. "And how have you made out so far?"

"I have only just broached the topic this morning with Lady Wellesley. We need to discuss it further and then bring it up with the other ladies present."

"And what of the gentlemen? Are you not going to enlist us in your cause as well?"

"I don't know whether you all would be particularly sympathetic."

"Again, I think you'd be surprised at where our sympathies lie. I, for one, would be happy to throw in a couple hundred pounds for a good project such as yours."

"Really? That does surprise me, sir, as you would be one of many to discipline your wife should she stray from your strict authority."

"How's that?"

"You said yourself that you would spank your wife if she didn't heed your command."

"Don't you know a jest when you hear one?"

"I would not jest over something like that."

"And yet, you would jest about poisoning your husband. Or were you serious about that?"

"Only if you were my husband."

He chuckled at her remark. "Well, suppose you don't get very much support for your project at this party? Then what do you mean to do?"

"I mean to fund it myself. I turn thirty in two months, and my dowry will revert to me for my own personal use in the event that I don't marry before then."

"And you don't think you'll get a husband in the next two months?"

"I have managed to avoid getting one for twelve years. I don't see a problem with a couple more months."

Again he laughed, and she shivered with the tenor of his voice and with the rain, which by now had soaked through her pelisse and into her dress.

"Are you cold, my lady?" He leaned forward to ask her the question, and his breath caressed the back of her neck.

"Mmm. Perhaps a little," she admitted, but only with reluctance.

He halted his horse and then took off his coat and wrapped it around her shoulders. It was still warm from him, and she relished the smell of it and the feel of it on her body. She also noticed that he was still hard, pressed up against her bottom, and her belly quivered again with the thought of him aroused for her.

"There. Is that better?" he asked.

"Yes. Much. Thank you," she replied softly.

They rode the rest of the way in companionable silence, each lost in thought. What he was thinking remained a mystery to her, but she wondered for a moment what it would be like to be his wife, something she hadn't thought about since she was a girl. She imagined them riding together as lovers instead of bitter enemies, and again she shivered with the feelings those thoughts evoked in her body.

At last, they reached the stables, and he reined in the horse. He climbed down from the saddle and then helped her down as well. As she handed him his coat, she looked up into his face, and as her eyes met his, her heart skipped a beat. For one brief moment, they held each other's gaze until she could not stand the intensity of his scrutiny, and she looked away. In that moment, however, a bit of her old feelings for him crept into her heart, and she chastised herself for her silliness.

"Thank you again, Lord William. I am most obliged," she said sincerely.

"It was my pleasure."

"I'm sure it wasn't, but I thank you nonetheless."

"Lady Cassandra, what . . .?" His voice trailed off from his question.

"Yes?"

"Never mind. Go inside and get warm."

"You do the same." She smiled at him and turned to head back to the house. The smells of sandalwood and leather were all around her as she walked to her room. Dratted man.

———◆———

CONFOUNDED WOMAN. She had left her scent on his coat, and all he could smell as he put it on were roses and lavender. Then there had been the matter of her smile. It had nearly unraveled him as she turned away from him. And those eyes of hers. How had he never noticed those beautiful eyes? He was still as hard as granite from sitting so close to her on his horse. Why she was having this effect on him all of a sudden was beyond him, but he didn't much like it. He didn't like the feeling of not being in control around her or around any woman. Even around Belinda, he never got an erection unless he imagined them in the act of love-making. Why he was reacting to a woman—least of all *that* woman—as though he were some green lad was especially troubling to him. He was three and thirty, for the love of God, not three and ten.

The thing was that she had been fairly cordial to him during and after their horse ride together—so cordial, in fact, that it had nearly been like old times between them. He had almost asked her why she hated him so much, but as he looked into her eyes, he saw a spark of some emotion he couldn't quite name and thought better of the idea, letting her go without asking her to explain.

He walked the horse over to the stables and handed him off to a groomsman and then turned toward the house himself to get some dry clothes. He definitely needed to get away from this place as soon as possible. Whether he was running from the Duchess of Benthower or Lady Cassandra, he didn't know and he didn't care. All he did care about was getting as far away as possible from them both. He would have Watts pack his things as soon as he got back to his room, and he would head out after breakfast tomorrow. With good luck and good weather, he would be in London in three or four days' time.

Later that night after dinner, while the other guests played whist or faro in Lady Wellesley's drawing room, William wandered out onto the terrace that over-looked the vast gardens of the estate. It was chilly out, a March wind stiff to his face. April wasn't far away, for which he was thankful. He lit a cheroot, and as the smoke curled up from its tip, he watched the full moon climb high into the sky. His thoughts turned to Belinda then and how it would be to have her out here alone with him under the moonlight. Just what would it be like, after all these years, to finally feel her lips on his? He shook his head at the impossible fantasy as he wondered wistfully what she was doing at that moment.

He had seen her at dinner sitting to the right of Lord Wellesley, and she had outshone all the other women at the table. A pang of regret needled him at the way they had parted last night, and he considered approaching her to talk to her about it. He didn't see her after dinner, however, and as he listened to the wind whipping through the garden, he decided against talking to her or restating his feelings. He would feel too mortified having her spurn him again.

Yet, his yearning for her was as strong as ever. He recalled the moment he had fallen in love with her, a summer long ago when he had visited his friend Benthower and found Miss Belinda Hollowsley staying with Lady Phoebe at the castle. Miss Hollowsley had stopped his heart with her beauty, and even then, he knew that one day he would ask her for her hand in marriage. Unfortunately for him—and for his friendship with Benthower—Benthower had also fallen in love with her magnificence. And whether it was her beauty or her dowry that had so enamored his friend, William was never quite sure, but a rivalry had been born between them. Their friendship could not survive the competition between them over Miss Hollowsley, and the two eventually found themselves at odds over everything. It was not long after her debut, when she was officially on the market, that both men finally came to blows over the young woman, and their friendship was over. When the dust settled, Benthower had come out the winner, not because of his physical prowess, but because of his rank.

Much to William's chagrin, Miss Hollowsley had been conceived to wear a title, and with earls and marquesses and dukes in the offing, her hand had gone to the highest bidder of the Season, who happened to be the very dashing and eligible Duke of Benthower. Though William had proposed to Belinda before Benthower, she had chosen the duke over him, and William had always felt cheated, beaten at the game by his own best friend.

The memory faded like the smoke from his cheroot, and he stubbed out its last burning embers on the ground. The moon was so bright above the trees that the torches lighting up the garden were hardly necessary, and the folly at the far end of the yard caught his eye. He began strolling toward it along a narrow, lit walkway and was halfway down the path when he heard masculine voices coming from behind a tall evergreen shrub off the lane. He was struck mid-step when one of the voices said the name "Lady Cassandra." Though propriety told him he should keep moving and not listen in on the conversation, he was riveted to the spot where he stood when one of the men, whom he recognized as Benthower, said to the other man, "So, you've got it in your brain now, right, Farnsworth? You know what to do?"

"I think so, Your Grace."

"Well, why don't you repeat it to me?"

"Um . . . I am to ask Lady Cassandra to walk with me in the garden tomorrow night and . . . uh, then, I am to ask her to marry me?"

"Yes, yes, and then what?"

"Uh, then I am to try to kiss her?"

"Not just *kiss* her, man, but *compromise* her in some

way. So that when I come strolling down the path with several of the ladies and gentlemen in tow and we find you in this compromising situation, she'll have no choice but to accept your marriage proposal. Her reputation will be ruined, and she'll have to capitulate."

"But, sir, do you really want your sister's reputation ruined?"

"I regret to say that it's the only way, my man. It's the only way. She'll never accept you unless she is compromised."

"I'm not sure I can go along with this plan. She is the woman I love, after all."

"And don't forget that you do love her. Don't you want to be with her?"

"Of course, of course."

"Then you want to do whatever it takes to be with her, don't you?"

"I do?"

"Yes, yes, you do, you do. Now, I have the special license that we obtained for you before we left London all ready in case we can get the wedding performed while we are here, all right?"

"Yes, fine, but what if she slaps me?"

"Oh, I guarantee she'll try to slap you, but compliment her eyes. She's a fool for a compliment about her looks."

"Her eyes . . .," Sir Lionel absently mumbled the words, and even through the darkness, William could see the look of utter bewilderment on the man's face. He was probably having a difficult time committing all this information to memory.

"Yes, her eyes. Tell her they are the color of celadon, and she'll be most impressed. But remember, above all else, you must persevere in your course. After all, don't forget that you also want to make sure you have enough money to keep your mother and sister in the circumstances to which they have grown accustomed, don't you?"

"Er, yes, yes. My mother and my sister."

"You're doing this as much for them as you are yourself. You will need your half of my sister's dowry to keep them in comfort."

"I will?"

"Yes, you will. Don't look so horrified, my man. It will all work out for the best this way. My sister will get a good husband and a stable marriage, and you will get the love of your life and a sizeable sum of money. Now, head on back up to the house before someone sees us out here."

"Yes, Your Grace." Sir Lionel sounded doubtful but acquiescent, and then he moved from behind the bush and headed up the path to the house.

"And I shall get the other half of my sister's dowry to pay off my creditors. And none too soon," said Benthower to himself after Sir Lionel had left him. He then turned toward the house and left William hiding behind another evergreen shrub nearby.

Well, well, well.

So, Benthower was broke, was he? And evidently, he needed half of Lady Cassandra's dowry to sustain him, so he was conspiring with Sir Lionel to bilk her out of the money she was going to use to start her shelter. William considered what he should do with this intelligence as he lit another cheroot. He walked slowly back up the path toward the house and contemplated his options. If he wanted to be cruel to Lady Cassandra, he could do nothing and watch to see how this ill-begotten scheme of her brother's played out. Or, if he wanted to perturb Benthower, he could warn his sister of his perfidy. Of the two choices, he liked the idea of socking it to Benthower the best.

CHAPTER 3

Eight of Swords: Crisis, obstacles, powerlessness, being trapped by circumstances, inability to remove oneself from a difficult situation . . .

————◆————

CASSANDRA BREAKFASTED IN HER ROOM the following morning to avoid seeing Lord William. She had heard that he meant to leave the party for London soon after breakfast, which was perfect. The less she saw of him before he left, the better. She was still too shaken from her horse ride with him yesterday to trust herself not to blush profusely around him—or worse. She was afraid she would start being congenial toward him because he had been so kind to her during the rainstorm. What could he have meant by his solicitousness? It had been like the olden days when they were youngsters and he had treated her with genuine concern and respect.

He had always been such a nice boy to her, which was one of the reasons she had developed her *tendre* for him in the first place. He had been more amiable to her than her own brother had ever been. She had never had a kind word or gallant act from Benthower, except for the time she had overheard him tell Lord

William that she had nice eyes when she was eaves-dropping on them in the stables so long ago. And she was fairly certain the only reason Benthower had been so complimentary of her at the time was because he was trying to steer his friend away from Belinda. But Lord William had always been very concerned for her feelings when they were younger—other than the time he had called her homely. Of course, he had not known she was listening to him then, and though she could never forgive him the comment and would always hate him for it, she still had fond memories of him from her childhood.

She recalled the incident in which he retrieved a doll for her after her dog had dragged it into a pond near the castle. She had been just seven at the time and had come down from the nursery on her way out-side to play with her sisters, and she was carrying her favorite doll, which her dog Tramp promptly tore from her arms. He scampered outside with it, and she ran from the castle screaming that the dog had stolen her dolly. She raced after Tramp down to a pond where Benthower and Lord William were fishing. The dog splashed into the water with the doll still in its mouth and swam out to the middle of the pond.

While Benthower doubled over in hysterics at Cassandra and her plight, Lord William jumped into the pond and swam out to get the doll from Tramp's jaws and then swam all the way back with the doll tucked into his shirt. He came ashore dripping out of the pond with the toy, knelt down on the ground beside a sobbing Cassandra, and handed her the doll. When that failed to calm her and she continued crying, he patted her head to soothe her and then took her in a tender embrace. When she was pacified, he broke from the

embrace and kissed her on her cheek. She looked up at
him, into his big green eyes and loved him from then
until the moment he had said she was homely.

A knock at her door startled her from her reverie.
She opened it to find a chambermaid standing outside
with a letter for her. The maid curtsied and gave her
the note, and Cassandra stepped back into her room to
open it. The seal had the letters "WP" on it, which she
thought odd. Whom did she know at the party with
those initials but William Poniard, Lord William? She
broke the seal and anxiously read the contents of the
letter, which was dated today at noon. What was he still
doing here at such a late hour when he meant to go
back to London?

> *Dear Lady Cassandra,*
> *Please meet me straight away in the conservatory.*
> *I must speak to you in private about an urgent*
> *matter.*
> *Sincerely yours,*
> *William Poniard*

Her heart skipped a beat when she read the signature. What could he want to speak to her about? Did
he want to talk to her about yesterday? And if so, what
would he say? Her heart pounded, while her mind
raced with the possibilities as she checked herself in
the mirror to assess her appearance. Fortunately, she
had worn a light green dress, for the color of it brought
out her eyes. They veritably glowed—whether from
the dress or the prospect of seeing Lord William in private, she could not tell. She laughed at her own folly as
she pinched her cheeks and bit her lips to add color to
them. She then raced from her room to the south wing

of the house where the conservatory sat.

She slowed her pace as she entered the greenhouse so that Lord William would not think she had rushed to meet him. When she did not immediately see him, however, she suspected for a moment he had sent the letter to her in jest. She was just about to leave when she heard footsteps behind her, and as she turned, he emerged from behind a lemon tree.

"Lady Cassandra," he said as he bowed to her. How handsome he looked standing there beside the tree. Heat rushed to her cheeks with memories of the horse ride yesterday, and her belly fluttered. "How good of you to meet me here. I had wished to speak to you at breakfast, but I was told you ate in your room."

She curtsied. "It is probably better we speak in private anyway, my lord. If we are overly cordial to one another in public, we run the risk of confusing our hostess and the other guests." His laughter warmed her inside. "What is your urgent matter?"

He appeared to be giving some thought as to what he was about to say, as though he chose his words judiciously. Finally, he said, "It regards your brother."

"My brother?" Disappointment snaked through her veins, and she hoped her face did not reveal it. "What about him?"

"Something he said has me quite concerned for you."

She was astounded that not only had he talked to her brother after so many years but also that he was concerned about her. "I'm surprised, Lord William. I did not know you were on speaking terms with my brother."

"I am not. My concern is over something I overheard him saying to Sir Lionel about you."

"Pray tell. What is it?"

"There is no easy or delicate way to say this, my lady, so I will just state the facts as I heard them. Your brother and Sir Lionel mean to compromise your virtue in a plot to get you to marry Sir Lionel."

Her face fell as a thousand questions filled her mind. "I don't understand. Where did you hear this?"

"I was in the garden last night when I overheard the two of them talking about their scheme."

"What exactly did they say?"

Lord William repeated for her all he had heard the two men discussing last night, giving her the details of their plan and telling her that they had spoken about splitting her dowry as their motive.

"Forgive me, sir, but that is absurd." And yet, deep in her heart, she knew it wasn't. It was consummate Benthower to devise such a nefarious intrigue to get her money. Yet, she couldn't admit this to Lord William. It was simply too mortifying, and precisely because it was so mortifying, she was suddenly irritated at his apprehension over her. What gave him the right to care so much about her affairs? His interference on her behalf was intrusive and condescending, and she was suddenly suspicious as to his motives. What could he mean by his interest?

"Nevertheless, Lady Cassandra, do be on your guard with respect to Sir Lionel. He may not be the brightest candle in the sconce, but he's no dummy either. He sees the obvious advantages of a match with you. Just be careful that you do not walk alone with him in the garden."

"Why are you so concerned for me all of a sudden? After all, we are not on the best of terms, you and I."

"Be that as it may, I could not stand by and just watch this happen. My conscience would not allow me."

"How very noble, but I'm sure I shall be fine. There is no need to distress yourself. Good day, sir," she snapped. She then turned and left the conservatory with as much hauteur as she could command.

His voice chased her out the door as it trailed off. "Just take care, madam . . ."

His consideration for her irked her on several levels, and she couldn't quite explain her perturbation with him even to herself. What bothered her most, she supposed, was that he was merely acting only out of some higher honorable intention and not out of any genuine heartfelt concern or care for herself. There. That was it. He quite simply would not like to see a woman—any woman—treated so contemptibly. He had no particular regard for her above and beyond his conscientious duty. Rescuing her was a matter of course and probably always had been—even back to the days of their youth. All those occasions when he had saved her from some particular tragedy or other, he had been acting out of his overblown sense of conscience or duty rather than any real regard for her. Irritating man.

BLASTED WOMAN. She did not seem to believe him about Benthower. That, or she did not take the threat to her virtue seriously. Well, he had done his part and cleared his conscience by telling her what he knew. Moreover, he had wasted all morning doing it. Now it was nearly one-thirty, and he considered whether or not to leave for London at this late hour or to wait until tomorrow to go. Given that it was raining much as it had yesterday, he decided he would wait until tomorrow and get a fresh start early in the morning. Besides, he had some correspondence to tend to that he could take care of this afternoon in his room, away from the nonsense of the party and away from Lady Cassandra.

He certainly needed something to take his mind off her. She had smelled like roses and lavender once more and had looked so pretty standing there beside a potted fern that his member had stiffened again as she had passed by him on her way out of the conservatory. He had once again noticed her eyes, which Benthower had once said were nice. Nice? They were thoroughly lovely, exactly the color of celadon, as Benthower had said, and they seemed to glow in the dress she wore. She really was a very striking woman, with her sable hair and alabaster skin, much more attractive than the girl he had known as Benthower's younger sister, though why he suddenly was having these thoughts of her was beyond him. He was, after all, supposedly still in love with Benthower's wife, much good though it did him to yearn for her after all these years. Yet, Belinda still held his heart just as she had done since the day he had met her.

To distract himself from thoughts of both Lady Cassandra and the duchess, he set to work on his correspondence. He had to communicate with his beloved but errant brother David, the marquess, about the state of disrepair of many of the tenants' cottages on the family's ancestral lands in Essex. David, who was currently in Italy as he gallivanted across Europe on one of his many sojourns abroad, was in many ways ill-suited for the title he held. A libertine, a drinker, and a gambler, he tended to his vices more than to the marquisate and left the responsibility of the title to his younger brother in his absence. As for William, he wanted nothing more than for his brother to return home and take care of his own business. He was just thankful that he was not the marquess, for the title seemed more trouble than it was worth.

Besides his letter to his brother, he also had to tend to other correspondence, which he had brought with him to the house party. His mail took him all afternoon and into the evening to read and answer, and when at last, he had finished with it, he dressed for dinner and went downstairs to dine with the rest of the guests.

As he sat at the table, he caught sight of Belinda who sat next to Lord Wellesley again, and a feeling of sorrow washed over him that he would never have her. At least he was leaving in the morning and wouldn't be subjected to much more of the torture of watching her at this house party. He wondered how Benthower felt about her after all these years, whether he were still in love with her—or her dowry—the way he had been when he married her. He glanced at the duke down at the other end of the table seated beside Lady Wellesley. He seemed preoccupied with other matters at the moment, however, and didn't appear to notice his wife. William could only guess at what engaged Benthower's attention and figured it had to do with Sir Lionel and Lady Cassandra.

Lady Cassandra, meanwhile, sat across from him two seats down looking especially bewitching this evening with her low-cut gown that revealed perhaps too much of her captivating décolletage, and he experienced the usual visceral reaction as he watched her. What the deuce was the matter with him? Yet, he couldn't help himself. He wondered what it would be like to touch her breasts, the tops of which peeked out of her dress. He was transfixed as he watched her taste her first dish. She ate her soup so artfully that he imagined her lovely full lips doing all sorts of decadent things to his body, and he grew more uncomfortable still. He also fantasized about all the indecorous acts he would perform on her luscious form were he given the chance, and before long, he was hard as stone.

Though he tried to turn his attention away from her to the repartee around him, his eyes kept wandering to where she sat, and he found himself trying to catch what he could of her conversation. The occasional sound of her throaty laughter only served to increase the discomfort in his groin. Inevitably, as he stared at her, his eyes met hers, and rather than look away, he held her gaze for what seemed an eternity. Neither of them blinked, as the air between them veritably crackled with some unspoken emotion. Dare he call it desire? He raised his glass to her in a subtle salute, and she looked down at her plate, as if she were embarrassed.

He was brought out of the moment when the Lady Drayton, who sat beside him, said, "Won't you, Captain Poniard?"

"Won't I what?"

"Won't you regale us with your exploits on the Continent with the dragoons? I would dearly love to hear about your bravery at Waterloo."

He glanced up at Lady Cassandra once again then, expecting her to deliver one of her set downs, just as she had done the last time someone had asked him to recount his tale of Waterloo, but she merely cocked her brow at him and smiled.

"Perhaps another time," he said. "I'm sure you have all heard the story before."

Lady Cassandra cleared her throat. "Nonsense, Lord William. Please do tell us all about Waterloo."

He stared at her in genuine surprise and then returned her smile as he obliged those seated near him, recounting for them what it had been like at the infamous battle. When he finished his harrowing story of how he had rescued a dozen men and wounded his leg doing it, Lady Drayton said, "How very brave of you, Lord William."

"Yes! Let's toast to Captain Poniard," said Lord Drayton who sat next to Lady Cassandra.

Those few seated around him, Lady Cassandra included, raised their glasses in salute to him. Her gaze fixated on his for another long moment, and he smiled at her once more as she drank from her glass. Eventually, they both became distracted from one another, each engaging in conversations closer to them as the meal wore on. Finally, dinner ended after several courses, and while the ladies adjourned to the drawing room, the men remained in the dining room to smoke cheroots and drink their port.

He lit a cheroot, while Benthower made his way over to Sir Lionel at the hearth, and the two of them fell into a quiet tete-a-tete. William wanted to eavesdrop on them but couldn't approach them without drawing attention to himself, so he watched them intently from where he sat. Though he couldn't hear what they spoke about, he would've sworn he saw both of them mouth the word "Cassandra" a couple of times. Apparently, they were reviewing the plot to compromise her in the garden, and he only hoped for her sake that she would heed his warning of this afternoon.

At last, the men joined the ladies in the drawing room for cards. Sir Lionel made a beeline straight for Lady Cassandra who sat near the French doors leading out onto the terrace and the garden. William watched as the other man engaged her in a brief conversation and then sat down with her in some card game or other, just the two of them. Alarmed, he couldn't believe that she had the poor judgment to associate with Sir Lionel after what he had told her about him, and he tried to catch her eye to warn her with a look. After several unsuccessful attempts at trying to capture her attention from where he stood, he was shocked when she finally looked straight at him and simply smiled and raised a brow as if in open defiance of his admonition and her own good sense.

———◆———

THERE. THAT should do it. That smile should stop him from incessantly trying to gain her attention. He had been looking at her—staring at her, really—throughout the evening, especially during and after dinner. It was unnerving, and for a moment, as they shared a gaze across the dining table, she had the oddest sense that he was somehow *attracted* to her. It was nonsense, of course, but it had unnerved her so that she actually found herself being cordial to him, inviting him to go ahead and recount his Waterloo story, as Lady Drayton had asked him to do.

Nitwit. Of course, he was not attracted to her. He was just trying to get her attention to warn her about Sir Lionel, but that didn't leave her any more at ease under his intense scrutiny. What he didn't know was that she was no fool. She knew exactly what Sir Lionel was about and was just having a little fun with him by pretending to be interested in his advances.

"Lady Wellesley's party is going remarkable well, wouldn't you say, Lady Cassandra?" Sir Lionel asked her as she dealt the cards.

"It's going along fairly well, but you must admit that it did not start out so favorably when I threw my punch in Lord William's face at the opening ball."

"Er . . . well, I'm certain it was just an accident on your part. Did you not say so yourself when you apologized to him afterward?"

"Oh, did I apologize to him? I have no recollection of that. I had not intended to apologize to Lord William. If anything, *that* was the accident."

"Uh . . . yes, well, um . . .," he said, faltering for words, apparently not knowing quite how to reply to her acerbic comment.

She turned the conversation to more mundane topics. "How is your port, Sir Lionel? The Wellesleys serve only the best, no doubt."

"Yes, yes, only the best. And your sherry?" he asked, catching on to the trend.

"It is the finest."

He was not the most gifted conversationalist, and their talk soon lagged after that for want of a topic. Finally, she introduced a subject she knew would stir him to speak. "How is your estate in Gloucestershire, sir? Do you not have some of the finest *gardens* in the county?"

"Uh, yes . . . yes, I do." Apparently animated by the topic, he then continued as if he had hit upon an idea. "The *gardens* here are particularly nice during the spring. Do you like gardens, my lady?"

"Who doesn't? They are candy for the eyes."

"Um, then, might I interest you in a stroll through Lady Wellesley's gardens after we are finished with cards? She has some delicate jonquils that have just come up that I would like to show you."

"Perhaps another time. I should think it would be

difficult to see anything in the dark, after all, even with the torches lit." She laughed to herself in merry delight at the fact that she had just foiled his and Benthower's plan.

"Oh, uh . . . yes." A look of utter confusion crossed his face. "We hadn't . . . er, rather, *I* hadn't thought of that."

They played their game of piquet in relative silence after that. It was evident that his mind was not on the game whatsoever. His furrowed brow seemed to reflect how profoundly perplexed he was by something. Thanks to his lack of attention to what he was doing, he lost to Cassandra. He asked her to play another round with him, but she politely declined, telling him she would be retiring soon for the evening.

After they parted, he headed straight for Benthower, and Cassandra laughed to herself as her brother's face fell into a scowl when Sir Lionel spoke to him, probably informing him that she would not walk with him in the garden. Benthower had to be fuming. It did her good, however, to know she had thwarted him and his plans—for once.

The duke was notorious for his manipulations of his sisters and their dowries. Cassandra was sickened at how he had coerced their sister Phoebe into marrying the depraved Richard Slayer, Earl of Abadon, so that the two men could split her dowry. While Abadon mercilessly beat Phoebe, Benthower proceeded to gamble his portion of her money away and was soon in need of more funds to support his and the duchess's lavish lifestyle.

He then coaxed their younger sister, Julia, into marrying Mr. Niles Lacey, a man fifteen years her senior who was a merchant with the East India Company and who saw Julia's dowry as the perfect means to increase his holdings in the Company. Benthower and Lacey conspired with one another, both convincing Julia that Lacey was madly in love with her so that she would marry him. For his part in the deal, Benthower again received half his sister's dowry, which he mostly gambled away.

Their even younger sister Elizabeth was next in line for Benthower's machinations, but she disappeared the night before she was to marry the very old, very decrepit, and very impoverished Rudolf Atwell, Earl of Breningreal. Benthower had browbeaten her into an engagement with the ancient earl, who needed her dowry to make whole his earldom in Wales.

What happened to Elizabeth—or Bess, as she was known to her family—remained a mystery. The presumption was that she drowned in the Serpentine because her bonnet and pelisse were found floating on its surface the day of the wedding. Her body, however, was never recovered, and the earl died shortly thereafter—whether from grief or old age, it could not be determined. Cassandra was certain that Benthower was grieved, not for the loss of Bess or Breningreal, but for the loss of half her dowry, which was what he would have received for his complicity in getting Bess to marry the old coot. Even now, he had petitioned the courts to have her declared legally dead so that he could get his hands on her estate.

With Phoebe, Julia, and Bess out of the picture now, and no guarantee that he would have success in getting Bess declared dead, Benthower was left with only their youngest sister Violet—and Cassandra, of course—to cheat. He still had not found a cad with whom he could conspire to bilk Violet out of her fortune, but

Cassandra was certain he was working on it. He had plenty of time, though, for Violet was only nineteen and had been out for only a year.

Cassandra, on the other hand, was set to turn thirty in two months, at which time her dowry would revert to her for her own personal use. That arrangement had been part of their parents' marriage settlement and had been meant to provide for their daughters in the event that they did not marry. Though she was certain that Benthower had tried over the years to find a complicit suitor for her to marry, he had obviously been unsuccessful—probably thanks to Cassandra herself. For one thing, she rebuffed the few suitors who approached her on their own, and for another, she had such a bad reputation as a harridan that evidently no man whom Benthower himself had approached about a possible engagement arrangement had found even half her dowry enticing enough to take her along with it. No man until Sir Lionel, that is. He had just the perfect combination of stupidity and submissiveness to make him the ideal subject for Benthower to manipulate.

An immense sense of relief that she had not fallen prey to their plans consumed her, and she even felt some gratitude toward Lord William for the first time for interfering as he had done and warning her of the plot. She would not tell *him* she was thankful, at least not tonight. Perhaps twenty years from now, after she had her dowry and her women's shelter and her life to herself, she might mention to him that she was grateful that he had told her about her brother and Sir Lionel's scheme, once upon a time.

As she attempted to escape the drawing room for the evening, Lady Wellesley invited her to watch a game of faro in action, and she acquiesced, thinking it would be a good time to reopen the subject of donations for her shelter project. Before she spoke to Lady Wellesley, though, she searched the crowd for Lord William and saw him playing whist across the room. He seemed to be intently studying Benthower and Sir Lionel as they conversed, and then he glanced over to her and gave her a very subtle nod of approval, solemn though it was. When she saw him looking her way, she smiled so prettily at him that he raised both brows in apparent surprise. Irksome man.

ANNOYING WOMAN. She was mocking him with her smile. He thought they had shared a moment between them at dinner, a sort of silent truce, as it were. He had been especially touched when she had encouraged him to recount his tale of Waterloo. But later on, she had seemed wholly committed to ignoring his warning of earlier this afternoon and putting herself in harm's way by playing cards with Sir Lionel. Of course, she *had* managed to ditch the man after their card game, but William was not entirely convinced things were over. Now, she sat across the room next to Lady Wellesley, obviously pleased with herself. By all appearances, she had thwarted Benthower and Sir Lionel. William knew better, however, because he knew Benthower. Though she may have won this small skirmish, the war was far from over. Benthower would not stop at one little set-back, and William fully expected another onslaught—if not tonight, then another night. Well, the problem was not his. Why he even cared so much was a mystery to him, except that he hated to see anyone used in such a villainous manner and especially by Benthower, whom he could not stand.

As the evening waned after a couple of hours of cards, he stared at his hand. He couldn't concentrate on the game he was playing, and consequently, he and his partner lost, and he left the table shortly after that to smoke a cheroot. On his way across the drawing room for the outer doors, he looked for Lady Cassandra. She was nowhere to be seen, so he searched for Sir Lionel and Benthower. He saw neither of them in the room, and alarm skittered across his nerves. As he stepped out of the room into the garden, a commotion at the folly caught his attention. Several people, including Benthower and Lady Wellesley, were gathered at the structure. What on earth was going on? He walked down the torch-lit path to the folly, and as he got closer to it, he saw Sir Lionel. The man appeared edgy and nervous, his arm around Lady Cassandra. As for her, she appeared mortified, and when William caught her eye as he approached, she put her hands up to her red cheeks and looked about to cry.

Good lord, she'd been compromised.

CHAPTER 4

Six of Cups: A gift from a childhood friend, a new friend-
ship, new opportunities . . .

———◆———

O*H, NO. NOT HIM, OF all people. Not Lord William,*
too, to witness my downfall.

She sighed deeply and put her hands to her face as he
approached the folly where she stood with Sir Lionel
next to her, his arm around her shoulders caressing her
in an effort to comfort her, the bounder. Benthower,
meanwhile, gloated, and Lady Wellesley appeared truly
horrified. Cassandra was mortified that she had been
caught with Sir Lionel kissing and groping her, never
mind that she had not been a willing partner to his
depravity.

A few minutes earlier, having had perhaps too much
sherry, she had grown warm as she watched the faro
game with Lady Wellesley. She then excused herself
and stepped outside onto the terrace for some fresh
air. The moon above looked so beautiful shining down
upon the folly in the middle of the garden that she had
wanted to see the scene up close, so she walked down
the lit pathway to the small pavilion. She stepped up
into the structure and stood for a moment reveling in

the sights and sounds of the garden under the moon-light when, from out of nowhere, Sir Lionel accosted her.

"Lady C-Cassandra," he stuttered her name. "How n-nice to see you. May I say you look very enchant-ing?"

"Sir Lionel! You startled me. Where did you come from?" Alarmed at his sudden appearance, she glanced around her for an easy escape and spied the stairs just a few feet away.

He gulped loud enough for her to hear him. "I saw you step out into the garden, and I must admit that I followed you out here. There is something I have been meaning to ask you."

"Yes, well, perhaps another time. I've grown a bit chilly, and I think I would like to go inside now." She turned away from him toward the steps.

He grabbed her hand and genuflected before her. "L-Lady Cassandra, will you do me the honor of becoming my wife?"

"Oh, sir, do get up," she entreated him. "I implore you. Do not stay down there on bended knee."

"But I must. Until you ease the aching in my heart, I must remain a supplicant before you. Please say you will marry me." He peered up at her as he slathered kisses all over her hand.

"I cannot, sir!"

"Oh, please, do not make me beg, my lady. I love you so very much that I'm in misery whenever we are apart."

She almost laughed at the absurdity of his statement, given that they barely knew one another and were, therefore, perpetually apart. She maintained her poise, however. "I do not mean to cause you any pain, Sir

Lionel, but I do not feel for you as you say you feel for me." She attempted to take her hand out of his and go, but he only gripped it tighter as he stood up.

"Perhaps you could come to love me once we are married, my lady. Such is often the case when two people are together long enough."

"But sir, I do not wish to marry you. I don't know how I could be any plainer. Now, really, I must go." Once again, she turned to step down from the folly.

"Oh, but you cannot!" He immediately took her into a frenzied embrace and crushed his lips to hers. She tried to pull away from him to slap him, but he grasped her more tightly in his arms, and she was unable to move.

It was then that she heard rather than saw people approaching, and as the footsteps got ever closer, Sir Lionel did something completely outrageous. He shoved his hand down the top of her dress and groped her breast most indecently, all the while still kissing her like a wild man.

"Lady Cassandra! Sir Lionel, I must say!" Lady Wellesley said with palpable indignation as she approached the scene. Her reaction to the scandal seemed genuine this time, unlike the other night when she only feigned indignation after Cassandra had thrown her drink in Lord William's face.

Benthower, who had approached the folly dragging Lord and Lady Wellesley along with him, said, "Choose your seconds, sir."

Several other people from the party then caught up to everyone at the pavilion to witness what was going on.

Sir Lionel at last broke the kiss, and Cassandra pulled away from him just as he took his hand from her breast. "Your Grace!" The man's voice squeaked and he appeared to tremble in real fear, for Benthower had sounded so serious. "I have asked Lady Cassandra to m-marry me."

"And what is her answer?" Benthower demanded as he climbed onto the folly and stood within inches of Sir Lionel, menace in his countenance. "Are you to be married?"

"I do believe so now, sir."

"Cassandra? What have you to say for yourself?" the duke asked her accusingly.

"I . . . I . . . he . . . he . . ." Tears threatened as words escaped her. Her attempt to defend herself and tell her side of the story was thwarted by her inability to form coherent words or even thoughts.

"Well?" Benthower shouted.

She recovered herself after a moment and said with as much indignation as she could muster, "This is hardly my fault, and *you* know it."

Benthower took her by the elbow and drew her away from the crowd. "After such a display as that, Cassandra, why, you must marry Sir Lionel. There is no other alternative."

"Oh, Benthower, how could you?" she said through her teeth. Anger laced her words. She swallowed more threatening tears and said adamantly, "I cannot—will not—marry that man."

"It must be so, Cassandra. You are to marry Sir Lionel." He was unyielding in his command.

"I daresay you certainly must, my dear," said Lady Wellesley, who had climbed the stairs of the folly and now stood beside Cassandra caressing her arm in what she supposed was meant to be a comforting gesture. "Why, only think of your reputation."

"But . . . but I . . . do not love Sir Lionel." Her voice sounded almost forlorn, even to her own ears. Sir Lionel, meanwhile, stepped over to her and put his arm around her shoulders once again. The gesture was surely meant to placate and comfort her, but it only embarrassed and angered her. She might have reached up and slapped him had she not seen Lord William approach the scene. Distraught by his appearance, she put her hands to her face to cool her flaming cheeks.

"Well, never mind that now," Lady Wellesley said. "We'll announce your engagement to Sir Lionel here at the party. Tomorrow night. We'll have a special celebration in honor of it."

Cassandra could only nod as a single tear escaped her eye.

"There. It's decided then. Tomorrow, you and I will discuss the settlements, Sir Lionel," said Benthower.

"Come, my dear, let us go inside. I can tell that you are cold. We'll sneak in through the library doors so that we don't have a scene in the drawing room." Lady Wellesley took her by the hand and led her up one of the paths to the house. As she passed by Lord William, Cassandra noted that he looked truly sympathetic, not at all triumphant, which was what she would have expected from him. Confusing man.

———◆———

POOR WOMAN. William never thought he would again have compassion for Lady Cassandra as he had done when they were younger, but her situation now was truly pitiable. And her brother, who was standing there obviously relishing his triumph, was the worst kind of blackheart for orchestrating the entire scenario. William glowered at the duke as he watched him shake hands with Sir Lionel.

Benthower, who evidently noticed William staring at him, said, "What is it, Will? You look as if someone has stolen your prize."

"I don't know how you can be such a rotter to your own sister, Benny."

"What care you?" Benthower said dismissively as he laughed. "At least, it's none of your concern. You don't even like the woman."

"That may be, but nonetheless, I know what you did in order to orchestrate this calamity, and I can't abide it."

"And I can't abide a paragon. Night, night, Will. Sleep tight." And with that, Benthower took his leave with Sir Lionel trotting faithfully behind him up the path toward the house, like a well-trained puppy.

William walked back to the house himself, and as he walked, he contemplated Lady Cassandra's predicament. Somewhere deep inside himself he was consumed by that old need to come to her defense and protect her, just as he had done when they were much younger, and he couldn't explain the urge—even to himself. She had looked so tragic standing up there on the folly next to Sir Lionel that his mind immediately calculated what he could do to help her, to make things right again. What was she doing at this moment? For the life of him, he could not say why he even cared. In truth, what did it concern him anyway? As Benthower had said, it was not as if he liked the woman. Yet, what Benthower and Sir Lionel had done to her had been truly abominable. He would not treat a dog with such indignity.

The guests had fairly well dissipated by the time he got back to the house, and Lady Cassandra was nowhere to be seen. He supposed Lady Wellesley had somehow managed to assist her to her chamber discreetly. He wanted nothing more than to be in his own bedroom at the moment, so he left the drawing room and headed down the hallway toward the staircase.

On his way past the library, a woman's gentle weeping stopped him, and when he peeked inside the room, he saw Lady Wellesley trying to comfort a downcast Lady Cassandra. The baroness poured a glass of spirits and said, "There, there, Lady Cassandra. It's not the end of the world, this. Why, Sir Lionel is a very good sort of man, all in all."

Lady Cassandra dried her eyes and opened them wide as she regarded her ladyship in apparent astonishment. Even William had to wonder how anyone could conceive of Sir Lionel as a good sort of fellow after what he had done.

"You know, love is not everything in a marriage. Wellesley and I were not a love match, and yet, we have got on pretty well over the years. I can even say I love him now."

Again, Lady Cassandra did not answer. Instead, she held her handkerchief to her eyes in a clear effort to hold back tears.

"Your brother seems to think it a good match."

Those words seemed to send Lady Cassandra over the edge, and the tears fell despite her obvious attempts to staunch them.

"You know, I don't think I am helping much. Why don't I just leave you alone with your sherry?"

Lady Cassandra nodded and appeared thankful that Lady Wellesley was going. As Lady Wellesley walked toward the door, William slipped into an alcove in the hallway so that she would not see him, and when she had left the room and was out of sight, he entered the library. Lady Cassandra jumped when she noticed him.

"I'm sorry. I didn't mean to startle you," he said.

She recovered herself somewhat when he approached her and sniffled. "Come to gloat, have you?"

Compassion washed over him. Her defenses down, Lady Cassandra did not appear as formidable as she usually did. "Forgive me, madam. I only came to say how sorry I am that things have turned out as they have." She stared at him for a moment, not responding to him. Then she shrugged and wiped her eyes with her sodden handkerchief. He handed her his own handkerchief, which she accepted somewhat warily. "You have my profound sympathy," he continued.

She attempted a feeble smile, but her bottom lip trembled as though she might start crying in earnest. She regained her composure, however, and said barely above a whisper, "You were right, Lord William. I should have heeded your warning more carefully. I should never have given Sir Lionel the opportunity to be alone with me. I shouldn't have gone out into the garden by myself where he could follow me."

"He is a scoundrel."

She looked down at the handkerchief she wrung in her hands. "Careful now. That is my future husband of whom you speak." Her attempt at humor failed miserably, and with lip quivering, she inhaled sharply as if she might start sobbing. She remained strong, however, and finally recovered herself. "Of course, this means my plans for the women's shelter are crushed. He will get my dowry—or at least half of it. The other half will go to Benthower for his complicity in the plan."

"Do you really mean to marry Sir Lionel then?"

"My reputation is ruined. What alternative do I

have?"

William remained silent for a moment, and then, hitting upon an idea, he said, "Marry me instead."

She regarded him as if he had spoken a foreign language, and then she laughed out loud at the very notion.

"Or pretend to marry me, at least."

When he did not also laugh, she gave him another odd look. "What on earth can you mean by 'pretend to marry you'?"

He did not answer her immediately as his mind sorted through the scheme he was concocting. Finally, he said, "We'll 'elope,' but we won't really elope."

"You have lost me."

"What I mean is that we'll arrange it so that everyone will think we have run off to be married, but we won't actually marry. However, when we return, everyone will think we are husband and wife. As your 'husband,' I'll get your dowry and hold onto it for you until you turn thirty. Then, I will give it to you, and we shall part. Your money will be yours to do with as you please."

She stared at him in stunned silence. When it was obvious to her that he wasn't joking and when at last she seemed able to formulate words, she asked him, "How will we arrange it so that everyone will think we have run off to be married?"

"We'll actually run away together."

"To where?" Utter disbelief resonated in her voice.

"Gretna Green, of course. We are only forty-some miles away from the border. If we leave tonight, we shall be there sometime tomorrow morning."

"You're mad."

"On the contrary. I'm perfectly sane. And perfectly serious."

"How will we convince everyone we are married if we don't actually marry? Won't my brother seek proof of it before he allows my dowry to go to you?"

William pondered that excellent question and took a moment to answer her. "We'll procure a phony marriage certificate when we are in Gretna Green. It will look like the real thing, but it will be utterly fraudulent."

Lady Cassandra narrowed her eyes in apparent doubt, dubious as to the plausibility of his plan. "But what about when we return? Won't we have to live together to make everyone believe we are married?"

"For a time, perhaps. But there are couples who live apart much of the year. We'll return to London and put on a show. Then you can live where you please, and I'll live where I please. It's only for two months, after all."

"Yes, but what about afterwards? My reputation will be in ruins if I live with you for any period of time when we are not actually married. I'll never be able to go into society again."

"I hate to say this, my lady, but your reputation is in tatters already unless you marry that nitwit Sir Lionel. Only with him, the marriage would be real. At least with my proposition, you will one day have your freedom and your money."

Her shoulders slumped at the truths he had just uttered, but she nevertheless appeared to give his suggestion some serious thought. At length, she said, "I don't understand, Lord William. Why do this for me? What do you get out of it?"

He contemplated that very good question for a moment. "The pleasure of seeing Benthower foiled for once." He didn't say it aloud, but he relished the idea of being able to thwart Benthower's pursuit of Lady Cassandra's money in a way that was comparable to how Benthower had thwarted William's pursuit of Belinda Hollowsley's heart years ago. It would very much do him good to finally have his retribution against Benthower—and in a way that would hit the duke where he would feel it most: his pocketbook.

Lady Cassandra stood from her chair and raised her arms in question. "How will we ever pull it off? We do not get on, you and I."

"Neither do half the married couples in England."

"But won't people get suspicious of our artifice?"

"They might, but by then, it will almost be over."

"And you will give me my money free and clear after I am thirty?"

"Yes. All of it. Free and clear."

She walked over to a window and peered out into the darkness. "Suppose I wanted a formal agreement signed between us that you will give me all my money?"

"I'll have my solicitor draw something up immediately upon our return to London."

After several moments of silence, she turned to him, and the gratitude and vulnerability in her expression undid him. "And you would really do this? For me?"

He nodded and thought to himself, *not just for you, but for myself, also. It is my justice for Benthower's betrayal after all these years.*

Aloud, he said to her, "What say you, Lady Cassandra? Will you 'marry' me?"

She hesitated for a couple of heartbeats and then squared her shoulders. All tears subsided, and she was once again the formidable force he knew her to be. "Yes, I will."

———◆———

BACK IN her room, Cassandra let her abigail assist her with readying herself for bed so that the woman would not get suspicious, and when the maid was gone, Cassandra quickly doffed her night rail for a traveling dress. After she changed, she packed a small valise with some clothes and a few necessities and thought about the plan she had just made with Lord William. It dripped with irony. That she was now running off to "marry" the man she had dreamt of marrying as a girl was truly unbelievable. It staggered the imagination that it would even come to pass as it had, especially given the fact that she disliked him with such vehemence. The thought of marrying Sir Lionel, however, was even more ludicrous—and worse, it was revolting. His kiss and his touch, especially upon her breast, had repulsed her to the point where she didn't believe it was possible to have enjoyable relations with him, the kind of relations detailed in the *Kama Sutra*. She'd rather remain a virgin her entire life than to go into such an objectionable marriage with such an objectionable man as Sir Lionel.

When she had completed the task of packing, she wrote her brother a brief note explaining what she was doing and with whom.

> *My Dear Duke,*
> *By the time you read this in the morning, I will be in Gretna Green with Lord William Poniard. He and I are going to marry, and there is not a thing you can do to stop us. Do not bother coming after us as you will be too late. You have lost, Michael.*
> *Yours sincerely,*
> *Cassandra*

She addressed it to Benthower and placed it on top of her pillow where her maid would easily spot it in the morning. She then paced her room, waiting for the prearranged knock on her door from Lord William. They had agreed to leave around two in the morning, when the house was quiet and after most people had likely gone to bed. As she paced, a moment of doubt about the scheme flickered across her mind. Should she—or could she—really go forth with this? Doing so would mean the ruin of her name in society. Yet not doing so would be worse. Not only would she be united to Sir Lionel for life but she would also lose the opportunity to start her cherished shelter for battered women, a dream she had held dear in her heart since the tragedy with her sister Phoebe. Helping unfortunate women was more important to her than her own reputation, however, so she resolved to go through with Lord William's mad proposition.

The hour approached when they were to leave, and she waited in agitation for a sound at her door. Finally, there came a light tapping, and she went to answer it, opening the door just a crack.

"Are you ready to go?" Lord William whispered.

Heavens, but he was breathtaking. She could only nod as he took her valise.

"Good. The carriage is waiting for us by the stables. I've scouted the house, and I think we should sneak out through the garden. We won't run across any servants that way."

Again, she only nodded and followed him down the deserted hallway toward the staircase. When they reached the bottom of the stairs, he led her to the library, where they had formulated this outrageous plan, and then through a set of double doors that led out onto the terrace across from the drawing room entrance. Fortunately, the moon was still high in the sky and lit the garden like a torch. She could make out the folly where she had been caught earlier with Sir Lionel and the pathway leading toward it. She carefully followed Lord William as he maneuvered his way down the path and around the folly to the far side of the garden, away from the house. They wended their way around beds of flowers not yet in bloom and past evergreen shrubbery of all shapes and sizes until they reached a stone wall at the very back of the garden.

In the darkness, she could not see how they were to get over the wall, but Lord William led them down a path to a wooden door that opened out onto a broad lawn. As they stepped out of the garden onto the lawn, she could just make out the stables in the distance, and she followed Lord William as he walked swiftly toward the darkened building some fifty yards away. Horses whinnied and stomped their hooves as she and Lord William approached the stables, and as they walked around the building to the other side, she caught sight of a large carriage, which even in the dark appeared to be a well-appointed town coach. A groomsman opened the door for her and assisted her up the steps into the carriage where she took the seat facing forward. Lord William spoke to the coachman, talking in hushed tones, and then he climbed up the steps and seated himself across from her. He rapped on the ceiling of the carriage, and they began rolling away from Wellesley Manor.

A sudden rush of nerves seized her, whether from their escape from the manor house or from being alone with Lord William in the shadows of the carriage, she could not tell. Her heart pounded and her stomach roiled with a distinct queasiness as they began gaining speed on the road leading away from Wellesley Manor. They had done it. They had gotten away without being detected, and she was free of her brother's tentacles—for now. How would she ever show Lord William her gratitude for what he had done? She supposed there was just no way she could ever express it. She wanted to know more than anything what he was feeling and thinking at that moment, but she couldn't make out his features in the darkness that enveloped them, and she couldn't calm herself enough to get up the nerve to speak to him. His silence as they rode in the carriage only served to make her more apprehensive. Perplexing man.

———————◆———————

BAFFLING WOMAN. She had not spoken one word since they had absconded with one another. He could not tell what she was thinking or feeling as they rode for a few moments in utter silence, and he wanted more than anything to ask her. He was, however, still too wound up from their escape to speak calmly, even though eluding detection had been fairly easy. He supposed that had been due to the hour at which they had departed. Then he thought of the duke. Was he even now sleeping soundly, believing that all was right with his world because he would get half his sister's dowry? What would he do in the morning when he found out that his sister had left and with whom? He smiled to himself, and suddenly he was curious as to whether or not Lady Cassandra had left a note for her brother.

"Did you leave a note?" he asked.

"I did." Her voice wavered a bit, but at last she cleared

her throat. "I told Benthower that I had eloped with you. Was that not the thing to do?"

"That is perfect. I only wish I could see his reaction to it."

"Me, too."

He paused a moment and then asked her, "Any regrets?"

She hesitated but only briefly. "None. You?"

"No. None."

Then, for the first time, he thought about what he had actually done by pretending to elope with a woman he did not really like. Well, it was not so much that he didn't like *her* as that she didn't like *him*. He supposed he had no real quarrel with her, other than the fact that she loathed him, and not for the first time, he wondered what he had ever done to deserve her acrimony. She had always seemed to like him when she was a girl. Was it his dispute with Benthower over Belinda that had soured her on him? Benthower and William's rivalry for the attentions of Belinda and their subsequent contention over her had always been common knowledge, but somehow he couldn't imagine Lady Cassandra having that much loyalty to her brother or his cause. No, surely it wasn't his relationship with her brother that had alienated her. It had to have been something he himself had said or done to make her dislike him so much over the years. But what it was, he hadn't a clue.

Perhaps someday he would ask her what it had been, but for now he sat back against the squabs of his brother's coach and contemplated how having her in his life for the next two months would affect him. He really didn't see how it would change his life that much. Once they got back to London, he would put up the pretense that they were married, but he could essentially go about his affairs as he had always done. One thing he definitely had to tend to, however, was this business of his apparent lust for her. Once again, he grew hard as he thought about her. He didn't even have to see her to have this reaction to her. Just her scent in the coach's cabin was enough to make him erect, and he decided he would have to do something about this bothersome effect she had on him. Perhaps he would have to visit—with discretion, of course—a woman of the demimonde once he was back in London.

Even Belinda had never had this effect on him physically, and thinking of her left him wondering how she would react to his "elopement" with Lady Cassandra. Would she in any way be jealous that he had left the party with her sister-in-law? Would she perhaps be forced to admit that she had some feelings for him after all these years? He waited for his heartrate to increase at the possibility, but then the strangest sentiment washed over him: he found himself on the verge of ennui over the question. He furrowed his brows. How strange. A couple of days ago, he would have wanted only blistering jealousy from her, but as he sat there in the carriage staring out the window, he was astonished at the realization that he simply had no desire for her to burn with envy. What on earth did that mean?

As he contemplated this perplexing question, the time of day finally caught up with him, and he drifted off to sleep. He dozed dreamlessly for what must have been a couple of hours and awoke to find that the sun's first rays illuminated the peaks to the east. He checked his pocket watch for the time and then noticed that Lady Cassandra, who had curled up onto her seat and gone to sleep, was not yet awake.

He watched her slumber in the early morning light and could not help himself from noticing how lovely she looked as she lay with her head resting on her arm. She was not Belinda, yet there was something indeed beautiful about her. Whereas Belinda was fair and angelic, Lady Cassandra was dark and as alluring as a siren. As he watched her, his groin tightened once again. What would it be like to kiss her lush full lips? She had a mouth made for sin, and he considered what it would be like to taste her. Would one kiss satisfy this strange desire he had for her? As he thought these thoughts, he slapped himself lightly on the cheek to remind him exactly whom he was thinking of kissing. This was Lady Cassandra, after all—not some biddable miss who would relish the thought of kissing him. What was the matter with him? He silently contemplated his sanity for another few minutes until they reached the Cross and Dragon Inn in Penrith where they were scheduled to change horses.

As they pulled to a halt and ostlers from the inn came to take charge of the animals, Lady Cassandra awoke and stretched seductively along her seat, and William had to cross his arms over his lap to prevent her from seeing his arousal. She glanced at him with her beautiful celadon eyes and then sat up hastily. "Where are we?"

"In Penrith."

"Already?"

"Yes. I thought we could get out and stretch a bit here, but if it's all right with you, we'll wait until we reach Carlisle before we eat, unless you are terribly hungry, my lady."

She shook her head no.

"Good. I would like us to keep moving, though I don't think Benthower will see your note for another few hours, will he?"

"What time is it?"

"Almost six."

"No, he won't. I instructed my abigail not to come for me until around ten this morning, so we have a few more hours before Benthower knows anything."

"Well done." Then he couldn't help himself. He smiled.

CHAPTER 5

Two of Cups: The beginning of a new friendship, cooperation, partnership, first love, a kiss . . .

———————◆———————

LORD WILLIAM'S SMILE NEARLY TOOK her breath away with its beauty, and Cassandra had to turn her heart away from it. Oh, what would it be like to have him smile that smile for her every day, as though they were lovers? And then she mentally had to slap herself back into reality. This was Lord William, after all, not some erstwhile beau of hers. He would never smile at her as though he loved her and only her, and when that thought broke her heart anew, she chided herself for her foolishness. She thought she was past this pointless yearning for him, but evidently, she could fall into silly girlhood habits with just an errant smile from him.

After the horses were changed and Lord William and she had both had a brief respite from the carriage, they resumed their journey toward Gretna Green. The closeness of the cabin felt more cloying now in the daylight than it had last night in the darkness, and not comfortable with attempting conversation with him, she watched out the window at the passing scenery to avoid looking at him more than was necessary. At length, drowsiness overtook her as they continued down the road, and she fell into a light sleep. She dozed for what seemed like minutes but what must have been a couple of hours, and before she realized it, they were preparing for yet another stop along their route.

She opened her eyes to find him silently watching her as he sat across from her in the carriage. What had he been thinking as he stared at her? His face was inscrutable, and though she thought she detected a trace of amusement in his emerald eyes, she couldn't be certain. Warmth rushed to her cheeks, and she looked away from him out the window where she saw the carriage pulling up to the coaching inn in Carlisle.

After the vehicle came to a complete halt, a footman from the inn assisted her down the steps and into the inn's lobby. She watched through a window as Lord William talked with the ostlers who handled their horses. He then came into the establishment and procured a small private room for them in which to eat their breakfast. The inn was nearly deserted, but even so, she was thankful for the privacy of the little room. Others dining at the inn would likely presume they were married since they were traveling alone together, and she was grateful that they would not be ogled by anyone as they ate—or worse, asked what their situation was.

Their breakfast was served quickly and efficiently, and she managed to eat her eggs and toast and drink her tea with a modicum of grace that belied her state of agitation from the trip so far and from her proximity to him in the small room. As they ate in silence, she looked over at him. He seemed to be contemplating something, and she longed to ask him what he was thinking. She dared not speak, however, for fear she would trip over her tongue.

As if reading her thoughts, he said to her, "I talked with the ostlers outside about Gretna Green. In truth, I know nothing about eloping and what we should do, so I asked them what the usual steps were. They suggested starting with the blacksmith in town. They say he performs the marriage rite. Does that sound right to you?"

She took a deep breath, trying to keep her voice slow and even. "I know next to nothing about it myself, but I believe that is correct based on what I've heard."

"And what is that?"

"Well," she said, pausing to calm her nerves so that she could speak in coherent words, "I heard from my sister Julia, who heard it from her maid, whose cousin told the story of a dear friend that ran off to Gretna Green to be married before she was one and twenty because her parents wouldn't approve a match to her beau. The couple ran off from London and were chased all the way north across the border to the blacksmith's shop by the girl's father. It was quite melodramatic."

"Quite. Were they married?"

"Yes, by the blacksmith, I understand."

"So, I suppose we ought to see the smithy then about obtaining a phony marriage certificate. I only hope the man can be bribed to give us one."

"Oh, I believe everyone has his price, don't you, my lord?"

"I certainly hope so. Or this has all been for naught." She must have appeared alarmed by his pronouncement, for he smiled and patted her hand in an apparent effort to sooth her. "Don't worry. I'm sure we'll find a way to procure a fake certificate."

She looked down at his hand on hers. His touch produced a fluttering in her belly, and she had to remind herself that this was Lord William touching her, not some intimate beau. When she returned her gaze to his face, he withdrew his hand as though the contact with her skin had stung him.

She returned her attention to her food. Breakfast took them a few minutes longer, and by the time they were finished, it was nearly nine-thirty. Though they were making good time, she grew worried that the duke would soon be reading her note, so she asked Lord William as they walked back to the carriage, "Do you think Benthower will try to follow us once he reads my letter to him?"

"It would be foolish of him to do so. He is much too far away to be able to make up the distance between him and us, even on the fastest horse. No, he will stay where he is and curse me for a blackheart."

She paused when they reached the carriage steps and glimpsed up at his face. "Lord William, I don't know how I'll ever be able to repay you the kindness you've shown me. I will, however, repay you all the expenses you will have incurred on this trip. I'm deeply indebted to you."

Flustered when he put out his hand to help her up the steps, she accepted it nonetheless, and her belly fluttered once again when they touched. Worse, his gaze met hers, and in that instant, she nearly lost her footing as she attempted to step up into the carriage. He was just so devastatingly handsome that she could hardly stand next to him. She could only stare at him in silent reverence. He grasped her arm when she faltered in her step and, in helping to right her, clasped her to his side, which only served to addle her all the more. Eventually, he assisted her up into her seat and then let go of her altogether.

"Think nothing of it," he replied as he joined her in the carriage. "After all, I get the pleasure of seeing Benthower thwarted in his devious plans."

Why did he find so much gratification in such a small thing? Strange man.

———◆———

PECULIAR WOMAN. She was the oddest mixture of sweetness and acerbity he had ever met. She could be calling him an arse one moment, and the next, she could be staring up into his face with the most sincere look of appreciation—almost adoration. Although she had not been unkind or mean-spirited toward him since they had started their trip, he knew that just beneath the surface of that charming celadon gaze of hers, there lurked a real shrew. Yet, the expression in her eyes as she had thanked him a minute ago had nearly undone him, and he had felt that now-familiar tightening in his groin as he had peered down at her.

Earlier, before they had stopped in Carlisle, the tightening had been severely uncomfortable as he had watched her sleeping, and he had only to laugh at himself for his own folly at finding so attractive a woman he could never have. And he knew without a doubt that he could never have her. She would not stand for it. Still, he contemplated once again what it would be like to kiss her as they made their way up the road to Gretna Green. And though he longed to know what she would feel like in his arms, he quelled the notion with the thought that she would probably be a cold fish, not at all the passionate creature he wished her to be and not at all as he imagined Belinda would have been had they married.

They made good time to Gretna Green and rolled into the village shortly before eleven. In all likelihood, Benthower knew their scheme by now. Curiosity plagued William as to how the duke was taking the whole thing. Undoubtedly, he was livid at this moment. William truly believed that it served him right for stealing Belinda away all those years ago that he had now stolen the duke's golden goose. He smiled with secret satisfaction just as the coach stopped in front of the blacksmith's shop at the junction of Headless Cross.

He descended from the carriage and then turned to help Lady Cassandra step down from it as well. They proceeded together into the workshop where a tall, burly man stood sweating over an anvil as he forged a red-hot piece of metal into the shape of a horseshoe. Clang, clang, clang. The clattering of his sledgehammer as it hit the shoe resounded throughout the shop.

William approached the smithy and said loudly enough to get the man's attention, "Pardon me, sir . . ."

The man, who stopped hammering mid-stroke, looked up from his work and smiled. "Ah, what have we here? A couple of lovebirds come to see about getting married, I would wager." He spoke with such a heavy Scottish brogue that William had difficulty understanding him.

Despite that, he said, "Well, now, we're more interested in procuring a marriage certificate than in actually getting married."

The smithy leaned on his sledgehammer, which he had rested on the anvil, and gave a look of utter confusion. "Excuse me?"

"Let me introduce myself. I'm William Poniard, and this is Cassandra Gardner." He figured that if he left the "lord" and "lady" out of their names, he might not have to pay as much for his request in the end.

"How do you do?" The blacksmith took William's hand in a firm handshake. "I'm David Lang, at your service."

"Pleased to meet you, Mr. Lang."

"Likewise, good sir. Now, what was it you said before? I'm not sure I quite understood you."

"Well, my fair lady here is in an awful predicament because of her brother," said William. "She has run away from him to avoid an unfortunate marriage, which he would force her into."

"I see. And like a good knight, you've come to her rescue, then?"

"You might say that."

"So, you would like to marry the lady instead?"

"Well, not quite. Er, rather, you see, the lady would prefer not to marry at all, but she must make it look like she's married—at least for a short time until she can get her dowry."

"I'm not sure I follow you."

William then explained how Lady Cassandra stood to receive her own dowry as an inheritance on her thirtieth birthday in a couple of months if she remained unmarried. And how her brother, who had designs on the money himself, had concocted a scheme to force her to marry a man of his own choosing, a man who was a nitwit and a knave who would split her dowry with her brother. He further explained his and Lady Cassandra's plan to pretend to be married to one another just until she turned thirty, at which time she would get her dowry and they would part.

"We don't want a real marriage because we're not in love with one another."

David Lang raised a brow and scratched his forehead. "So, you've come all the way to Gretna Green to make it appear that you have married?"

"Indeed."

"Ah, I see. That's a fair piece to come just for appearances. Is the brother on his way here, too?"

"No, sir. Not that we're aware of. But we need to make it seem somewhat authentic, or her brother will never believe us."

"So, now you're here, what need have you of a priest if you don't mean to be married?"

"We don't so much need a priest as just a marriage certificate to show to her brother as 'proof' of our marriage," said William.

"And you'd like me to provide the certificate?"

"That we would. We'd be willing to pay handsomely for the certificate."

"Well, now," said Mr. Lang as he appeared to contemplate the offer William had just made. "I might be willing to help you with a blank certificate, but I don't think I could in good conscience sign the thing under false pretenses. However, makes no difference who signs it as priest. For your purposes, you could even make up the names of your witnesses and your priest. But for added authenticity, you might want to get a couple of the locals to 'witness' and 'sign' your certificate."

"But would they do it under pretense?"

"For a dram o' whiskey, they'll do just about anything, I'm certain. Just head over to the Hind's Head down the lane and offer up a round of spirits. You'll find your priest and witnesses there, I'm sure."

CASSANDRA HAD stopped listening to the conversation between Lord William and the blacksmith after Lord William had said, "We don't want a real marriage because we're not in love with one another."

Her mind had stuttered to a halt because the words had pierced her heart. Well, it was the truth, wasn't it? What had she expected him to say, anyway? Obviously, they weren't in love with one another and never would be. Otherwise, this would be a very different trip.

As a consequence of not paying any attention to the conversation, she missed how much he had paid for the blank marriage certificate. She only knew that he had obtained one, and without further ado, they were walking down the road to the Hind's Head Pub. Why they were headed to the Hind's Head she wasn't entirely certain and asked him as they stood in front of the establishment.

"Forgive me, my lord, but why are we here?"

"To get a couple of people to witness the certificate and one to sign as the 'priest,'" he replied. "Mr. Lang said it would add to the authenticity of the document if we had some of the locals sign it, remember?"

"Oh, yes," she lied. She must have missed that portion of their conversation caught up in her own thoughts as she was.

"You had better follow me into the pub rather than wait alone out here in the street, Lady Cassandra." He opened the heavy oaken door to the Hind's Head and led the way into the dark, smoky interior.

Her eyes had to adjust to the low light in the room. The pub was well populated with most of the patrons probably there for luncheon. All eyes turned toward her when she and Lord William entered. Several men gawked, no doubt surprised to see a lady dressed so finely in their grimy establishment, while she put her handkerchief to her nose to prevent herself from gagging on the smell of stale ale, pungent smoke, and sweaty bodies.

"Oy!" said Lord William by way of greeting. It got everyone's attention. "I could use two fine men to witness this marriage certificate and a third to sign it as the priest. There's a bottle of whiskey in it for each of the takers."

Several hands went up, including the bartender's, and Lord William chose the two men closest to him, along with the bartender.

"My good man, I appreciate your willingness to oblige us," he said to the bartender.

"Aye," the man replied as if it were a matter of course. "So, you be wanting to marry the lassie, eh?" He spoke in a strong Scottish brogue, which Cassandra had difficulty understanding.

"Aye, that's correct," said Lord William.

She leaned in to him to whisper, "Shouldn't we tell them it's a pretense only?"

"Nah," he replied also in a whisper. "It won't matter at all to these gents. The less said, the better. They're just in it for their whiskey, after all."

"It won't be legal, will it?"

"I don't think so, no. Not as long as the blacksmith doesn't perform the rite. Don't you agree?"

She shrugged and nodded her assent.

"And you, lassie, you wish to marry this fine young buck?" the bartender continued.

Again, she nodded.

"Is that an 'aye,' lassie? You must speak up."

Cassandra cleared her throat. "Aye. That's correct."

"It be done, then," said the bartender, and a general

cheer went up from the crowd.

"Kiss her!" one of the men shouted to the whoops and whistles of the other men gathered round.

"Oh, yes, you must kiss her!" The bartender's booming voice resonated in the pub.

The floor seemed to crumble underneath her. Her eyes were probably as big as a pair of full moons, while Lord William appeared for all the world as if he didn't understand the command.

"Kiss her!" someone shouted again as the other men crowed.

Then a general chant went through the crowd. "Kiss her! Kiss her! Kiss her!"

"You want . . .," Lord William began and then cleared his throat before continuing, "you want me to kiss her?"

"Aye!" After shouting in unison, the men started banging their tankards on the tables in a steady rhythm indicating they would not be satisfied with anything but a kiss.

He turned to Cassandra who was fairly certain she had gone white. He took her hand in his and whispered softly into her ear, "I don't think we can get out of this without a kiss, my lady." His warm breath on her neck nearly undid her, while he seemed to search her eyes for a sign of acquiescence. "I do apologize."

She could only nod as he leaned in close to her, the smell of sandalwood and leather filling her senses. She closed her eyes as he lightly brushed his lips against hers and held them there for what seemed like an eternity. In actuality, he lingered but a few seconds, and then he pulled away. She opened her eyes, and a soft sigh escaped her lips. As he looked deep into her eyes once more, her belly bottomed out from the intensity of his gaze, and the men in the room roared for more.

He obliged them by drawing her into his arms and kissing her more firmly on her mouth. She let out a small whimper as his lips caressed hers, and then instinctively, she parted her lips for him. He slid his tongue into her mouth and teased her own with light, delicate strokes until she was on fire. She caught on quickly and returned his kiss with equal ardor, their tongues sparring in an endless erotic match. The world spun away as their kiss turned ravenous, each devouring the other. Oh, to be kissed in such a way by this man was everything she had ever dreamt of. She could die after a kiss such as this and not care. Finally—almost reluctantly, it seemed—he broke their union of mouths and pulled away from her. Bewildering man.

———◆———

ASTONISHING WOMAN. That kiss . . . that kiss had been unearthly, certainly not the kiss of a cold fish as he had presumed she would be, but rather the kiss of a warm-blooded sybarite, and he had reveled in it, his cock jumping to attention as he had gazed into her big celadon eyes before his lips had even touched hers. Briefly, as he had closed his eyes and their lips met, he had thought of Belinda and wondered for a moment whether kissing her would be so otherworldly. Then his thoughts had returned to Lady Cassandra. Where, oh where, had she learned to kiss like that? He had looked into her eyes once again as the crowd around them cheered their approval of the kiss and thought he saw that same adoration he had seen earlier in the day when she had thanked him for his help. But no, it couldn't be adoration. This was Lady Cassandra Gardner he was talking about, not someone in love with

him. She hated him, and not just him, but the very
ground he stood upon. Yet, from that kiss he could get
the idea that perhaps she did not hate him quite as
much as she liked the world to believe.

Still reeling from the kiss, he turned to the bartender
and said, "You'll sign the certificate now, my good
man?"

"Aye. Of course."

"And see that the other two gentlemen sign it as
well, won't you?"

"Aye."

He thanked the men and handed over the coins for
three Scotch pints of whiskey. After obtaining the sig-
natures, he folded up the certificate and placed it in
his inner coat pocket, and he and Lady Cassandra then
left the Hind's Head to return to the full sun of the
early afternoon. He shielded his eyes so that they could
adjust to the bright light as he searched the street for
their coach. The coachman had followed them down
the road from the blacksmith's shop and had waited
for them across from the pub, so they didn't have far
to walk to reach the carriage. As he turned to help her
up the steps of the coach, he noticed that her lips were
still red and swollen where he had kissed her, and he
wanted more than anything at that moment to sweep
her into his arms and ravage her mouth once again.
He refrained, however, and instead assisted her into the
carriage. He then climbed into it himself and sat across
from her.

As the coach turned around to head south back to
Carlisle, the atmosphere in the carriage was thick with
awkwardness. She sat primly in her seat with her hands
folded in her lap as she stared out the window in an
effort to avoid eye contact with him, no doubt, so he

followed suit and stared out the opposite window. What was she thinking at this very moment?

They had covered quite some distance and were practically to Carlisle when he determined that he should ask her about the kiss and what it had meant for her. When he turned from the window to speak to her, however, she was asleep. This would not do, he thought. Well, he supposed she could sleep, if that was what she was really doing, but he would either ask her about the kiss after they rested briefly in Carlisle or when they stopped for dinner in Penrith.

───◆───

OH GOD, oh God, oh God, *oh God*. Please do not let him ask about that kiss, she prayed. She had closed her eyes pretending to be asleep, hoping that he would forget about what had happened between them in the Hind's Head. Surely, he would have the decency and discretion not to mention it.

And yet, what *had* happened between them back in the pub? Had they actually kissed like lovers? It had certainly felt that way as he had pulled her body close to his and she had felt his arousal. And he had been aroused, as aroused as when they had ridden the horse together. Did that mean he had enjoyed the kiss as much as she had? He had certainly kissed her with as much or more ardor than any of her suitors ever had. And none had ever kissed her with such intensity. Oh, what did it all mean? She wanted to know, yet she didn't want to discuss it with him for fear that he would tell her that it meant nothing to him, that he had just gotten carried away with the situation. She wanted to remember the kiss into her old age as something special, even if it had been nothing special for him, and so, as the coach pulled into the inn at Carlisle for a brief respite, she determined that she would avoid all mention of the kiss now and when they ate dinner in Penrith.

The stop in Carlisle took them but a short time, and they were back on the road within fifteen minutes. In three hours, they would be in Penrith. *Surely, he'll have forgotten about the kiss by then.* She closed her eyes once again, pretending to sleep so that he would not speak to her as they journeyed along the road. Still, she could not forget about the kiss, and as she sat in her seat, ostensibly asleep, she relived it, every glorious second of it.

His mouth on her mouth. Hot and sensual. His lips on her lips. Soft and sweet. The gentle rasp of his whiskers against her sensitive skin. His teeth nipping her lower lip and his tongue wrangling with hers. His arms holding her in a tender embrace as his hands caressed her back. All these memories of the kiss flooded back to her and made her ache for more. Sensations surged throughout her body and made her ready for him . . . weak for him . . . melt for him. She wanted nothing more than to go to him, slide across the carriage to him, and resume that kiss with him. She thought about what it would be like to have him take the kiss to another level, to have him feel her, fondle her, stroke her, her breasts, her thighs, and yes, that special place that only she had ever touched. She grew heated as she continued in her reverie and had to squeeze her legs together to relieve some of the arousal she was feeling. Oh, she should never have thought about that kiss.

At last, they arrived in Penrith, and she was roused from her fantasy when Lord William nudged her gently to wake her. He said nothing to her, however, and they both descended from the carriage without a word to one another. Though he remained silent, his demeanor told her that something still hung in the air between them. She, however, dutifully followed him into the Cross and Dragon where he obtained a private room for them in which to eat. She had rather hoped they would take their meal in the general dining room this time, as he would be less likely to talk about what had happened at the Hind's Head amidst a crowded room, but she went along with him into the small room nevertheless.

After their meal was served, he said matter-of-factly, "There's something we need to discuss, Lady Cassandra."

Oh, lord. He was going to bring up the kiss. Heat rushed to her cheeks, but she remained silent and looked down at her plate.

"I've been giving the matter some consideration since we left Gretna Green and want to know what your thoughts are. Do we want to return to Wellesley Manor where everyone will be curious as to our situation or head straight for London without informing anyone of our plans?"

Oh. Was that all? "I don't know. What are your thoughts?"

"Well, I've left my valet back at Wellesley, but I can always send for him and my belongings via post-chaise once we arrive back in London, as you could do with your lady's maid and your things. I think in the end it would be more dramatic if we were to be gone from view for several days and then show up together in Town."

"That's what I was thinking as well," she said. "People would expect us to be gone together for a time if we were really married, anyway, so the few days it takes us to reach London would be a perfect little 'honeymoon.'"

"Fine. It's settled then. We'll stay here the night—in separate quarters, of course—and then be off to London in the morning. And what about that kiss?"

What?! She nearly choked on her roast beef. Had he just asked her about the kiss? "I'm sorry, what did you say?"

"That kiss? That very passionate kiss we shared at the Hind's Head. What are your thoughts about it?" His eyes twinkled with mischief.

"Well, I-I don't . . . Really, Lord William, I hardly think this is an appropriate topic for the dinner table."

"Perhaps you are right, but I think we need to discuss it. Otherwise, it will always be out there between us."

She chewed her food with severe deliberation and then said, "I have nothing to say on the matter."

"Really? I, for one, have more questions than I can formulate about that kiss. For instance, did you—"

"Ple-e-ease, Lord William, you torture me. Let us drop the subject."

"After you tell me—"

"Good lord, sir! It was just a kiss! It meant nothing."

He pondered her statement a bit, doubt crossing his features. "Really? Nothing?"

"Really. Not a thing."

"Very well, then. If you say so." Amusement sparkled in his eyes and resonated in his voice. "However, if you ever wish to talk about it—"

"No! I'm certain I never shall."

"You have only to ask," he said, and then he winked at her. Horrible man!

CHAPTER 6

Three of Wands: Beneficial collaboration, a quest or adventure . . .

———◆———

FUNNY WOMAN. SHE REALLY WAS quite attractive when she was riled, as she was now. And she would have him believe that that kiss had meant nothing to her. Likely story. He had ceased tormenting her with questions, however, because she was getting so flustered, but her countenance had told him all he needed to know regarding how she really felt about the kiss. It had meant something to her, which was interesting. It begged the question: was Lady Cassandra perhaps hiding her true feelings about him behind a show of dislike for him? Perhaps things hadn't changed so much from when they were children after all. Perhaps the look of adoration he thought he had seen in her eyes earlier today had been just that—adoration. Perhaps she still had a slight tendre for him, as she had when they were younger.

The thought intrigued him, and he was very much tempted to ask her how she felt about him—not because he cared necessarily, but because he found the possibility that she actually liked him . . . interesting.

Not wanting to embarrass or harass her any further, however, he let the subject drop. Although he was curious as to how she really felt, he figured he would not likely get a truthful answer to such an inquiry from her now. Perhaps in time she might tell him, but it was just as likely he would never know. And what did it matter anyway? Their association would be over in two short months, at which time they would both resume the lives they had led before the Wellesley party. Well, perhaps her life would change in that she would not go into society as much, what with the debacle with Sir Lionel and the fake elopement with himself, but his life would pretty much return to what it had been.

He sighed at that thought, for his life had not been much of anything at all, in truth, after returning from the Continent, other than the endless parade of engagements he found himself invited to in the mindless pursuit of leisure. This was not to imply that he was a hedonist. Far from it. In fact, the thing that bothered him most about his life was that it now seemed so devoid of direction that he felt as though he were drifting through it—not really living it, just existing in it. He craved a purpose, a reason to get up in the morning, something at least to aim for, something that was missing from his life right now.

It was time he found himself a wife and got married for real. Perhaps having a family to care for would give his life the meaning he sought. He wasn't entirely sure, however. The only thing about which he was certain was that he should be doing more than just wandering through his life as he had been doing for the last several months, like a feather on the wind. Perhaps this sense of pointlessness had been one of the reasons why he had offered to help Lady Cassandra out of the quandary she had been in with her brother. Perhaps he had just needed something noble to do.

They finished dinner, and afterward, he procured separate rooms for each of them in which to spend the night at the Cross and Dragon. He made certain she was safely secured in her room before going to his own next door. Though their rooms adjoined one another's, he used the hallway to get to his chamber rather than going through her room because she seemed uncomfortable with him there, as though she expected him to revisit the subject of the kiss as he said goodnight to her at her doorway in the hall. He said nothing about it, however, as she closed the door after him, and instead went silently down the hall to his room.

He unlocked his door and leaned against it for a moment after he shut it. For the first time that evening, he realized how tired—exhausted really—he was from the day's journey and events. He shucked his coat and waistcoat and then untied his cravat and tossed it onto the floor. Yawning loudly, he put the small satchel that he had brought with him on his bed and sat down on a nearby chair to remove his boots. He yawned yet again as he pulled his boots off one by one and sat there without ambition for a several moments, his elbows resting on his knees, as he ruminated about what he had done that day. For all intents and purposes, he'd gotten "married" today, and his "wife" was a woman who claimed to dislike him but whose kiss told him a different story.

Interesting, that kiss. It had been simply a kiss, guileless, artless, given by an ingénue. Yet for all its simplicity and innocence, it was one of the most perfect kisses he could ever remember partaking of. And one of the most erotic. He had, of course, grown rock hard as

Lady Cassandra's sensual mouth had met his own, as he had tasted her honeyed lips and as the swordplay of their tongues had heated up between them. She had wrapped her arms around his neck and caressed the hair at his nape, which had nearly undone him. In an effort to relieve some of the agony in his groin, he had pulled her even tighter to him. Embracing her, however, had only served to increase his torment, for her sweet scent had driven him mad, and he had wanted nothing more than to throw her down upon the floor and ravish her. Had they been alone, that was likely what he would have done, lord help him. He definitely needed to visit a willing woman and soon, or he would feel nothing but torture from his proximity to Lady Cassandra over the next couple of months.

He was silently contemplating whom he could visit on his return to London for the purposes of relieving his lust for Lady Cassandra when a loud scream interrupted his thoughts. It came from the compartment next to his—her room. He stood up abruptly and rushed to the door that adjoined the two rooms. On finding it locked, he pounded on it to get her attention. Within seconds, he heard the turn of the key in the lock, and a frightened Lady Cassandra flew into his arms.

Without thinking, he embraced her and held her tightly to him while she clutched at his shirt. After a moment, however, he became self-conscious holding her so close to him in nothing but his trousers and shirtsleeves, and he let go of her. He took a step back from her, and for the first time since he had entered her room, he noticed her. Really noticed her.

Her hair was not pinned to her head as she usually wore it. Instead, it cascaded like a waterfall of dark lustrous curls down her shoulders to the middle of her back, and she wore nothing but her night rail—and moreover, nothing under that. Her breasts peaked beneath the white muslin, their dark tips standing at attention, and the dark triangle of curls at the apex of her thighs was just visible through the gown. She looked thoroughly alluring standing there discomposed, and he tried to distract himself from her far too lovely figure with a question.

"Lady Cassandra, are you quite all right?"

She shook her head no.

"Are you hurt?"

She closed her eyes and, again, shook her head no. Well, she was not injured at least.

"What's the matter then?" He tried to maintain some control over the sensations her state of undress was causing in him but wasn't having much luck at it.

"A m-m-mouse," she stuttered the words, and then her whole body visibly shuddered.

"A mouse?" He suppressed a laugh. A mouse had caused all this fuss?

She nodded frantically.

"You saw a mouse? Where?"

She pointed to the window.

"Outside?"

"N-n-n-o-o-o! It c-climbed up the curtains inside the room, and then it ran across the rod and onto the dresser and then into a hole in the wall." Her horrified whisper amused him.

He went to examine a small crack in the wall near the top of the dresser. As he turned away from her, she clutched onto his back and followed closely behind him to the wall. On seeing nothing in the crevice, he turned back toward her. She clenched his shirt again and stood provocatively close to him, and he said to her as gently as he could, "Well, it's gone now, my lady. There is nothing more to be frightened of."

"Are you s-s-sure?"

"Yes, I'm certain." Growing uncomfortable with her clinging to him, he plucked her hands from his shirt and tried to disentangle himself from her so that he could once again take a step back from her.

"Lord William," she began fearfully and then stepped forward and grasped his sleeves, "do you think it will come back?"

She had no idea what she was doing to him as she gripped his arms. Her touch warmed him to the core of his being, and for one very unreal moment, he had the urge to take her in his arms and kiss her. He was in very real danger of succumbing to her charms—and she was in very real danger of being pounced upon. He gathered himself together, however, and kept his voice slow and even. "No, I don't think it will be back here tonight. It's gone on its way now."

"I'm just so terribly afraid of rodents, my lord. I cannot stand them."

"I don't understand. Why are you so frightened of them?" he asked, trying not to sound as though he were ridiculing her.

"Because of Benthower."

"Benthower? What does he have to do with it?"

She closed her eyes tightly and shivered as though she were recalling a truly horrific event. "He used to tease me with them," she whispered. "He would scare me out of my wits by putting them in my bed at night. And then, this one time, he . . . he put a mouse down the back of my dress. I could feel it crawling all over me, and I nearly fainted from fright. It was horrible."

"I remember that, and it was horrible. I was visiting the castle, and I remember you ran screaming out of the drawing room after Benthower's twisted little trick."

"Yes, and you helped calm me down so that we could get the creature out of my dress. You were always so very gallant." She touched his cheek with what felt like affection, increasing the discomfort he already felt from her proximity.

"Well," he said brusquely, dismayed by her touch, "it's gone now. You've nothing more to worry about." He reached up to remove her hand from his face, but she grabbed onto his arm and wouldn't let go. Instead, she followed him to the door as he made an attempt to leave.

"Must you leave?" Her voice rang with desperation, and her eyes pleaded with him not to go.

"I think it best." On seeing her frightened reaction to his words, however, he added, "But we can leave the door open between our two rooms if you would like—in case the mouse returns."

"Oh, yes. Please, please leave the door open."

"As you wish, my lady. Good night." He took her hand off his arm, and with monumental control, turned, and strode into his room.

———◆———

CASSANDRA WAS too scared to move as Lord William left her room for his own. She stood immobile for several moments after he had gone, trying to decide what to do next. Although she would credit herself as a levelheaded woman when it came to most topics, she was irrationally afraid of mice and rats, thanks largely to her brother. In fact, she was so frightened at the very thought of a rodent running around inside her wall at that moment that she didn't know if she could stay in her room alone for the night. Lord William had said the creature would likely not return, but she knew better. The wretched beast could pop its furry little head out of that hole at any time, and what could she do about it? She could only scream. This would not do.

She gathered every bit of courage she could muster, however, and climbed into her bed where she said a hasty prayer that the mouse would not come back. She blew out the candle at her bedside and sat there in the darkness staring towards the hole into which the mouse had crawled and reliving the horrible moments she had spent watching the thing scamper about her room. She shuddered at the thought. Then she felt entirely cork-brained at her behavior in front of Lord William. How could she have acted so foolishly? He must have thought she had a head full of feathers as he made his escape. He certainly acted as if he couldn't get out of her room fast enough. Well, at least he had not laughed at her outright. At length, she decided to forgive herself her folly and closed her eyes. Not long after that, she drifted into a fitful sleep sitting upright.

She must have dozed for a couple of hours because a clock in the hall struck midnight, which woke her. Then she heard it—a scratching inside the wall beside her bed. She jolted fully awake and heard it again—the distinctive sound of tiny paws.

Scritch-scratch.

Scritch-scratch.

Silence.

Scritch-scratch, scritch-scratch. Faster. More furious.

Scritch-scritch-scritch.

Scratch-scratch-scratch.

Oh lord, the mouse was back.

She shivered with revulsion. Though she didn't scream, she quickly shimmied off the bed at the thought of the little beast so near her. She grabbed her wrapper and stood stock still in the middle of her room wondering what to do next. Lord William! He would know what she should do. A gentle light subdued by cloud cover spilled in from the window and illuminated the open door to his room. She tiptoed to the doorway and peered inside his chamber. All was dark and nearly silent except for the rhythmic strains of his breathing in the stillness of the night. He was asleep.

"Lord William," she whispered.

Nothing.

"Lord William," she said a little more audibly.

Still nothing.

She stepped inside his room toward him and stood right next to the bed as he slept. He lay on his right side facing away from her, and she considered shaking his shoulder to awaken him. Thinking he would probably be cross with her if she did that, she let him sleep as she pondered what to do. She didn't really want to wake him if it weren't absolutely necessary. All she really wanted was to feel safe from the mouse. Standing next to him as he lay in his bed made her feel more peaceful and protected than she felt alone in her own room. Yet, she couldn't just stand there all night. Perhaps if she sat on the bed next to him she would feel better. Gingerly, she climbed atop the bed creating as little disturbance as she could. Fortunately, he was either such a sound sleeper or so very tired that he didn't even stir as she nestled her bottom onto the mattress close to him.

Only after she had settled in a bit and began to feel safe and secure did the thought occur to her that she really should not be on his bed with him. The impropriety of it was enormous, given the fact that they were not truly married. Of course, just traveling alone with him as she was doing was completely inappropriate and something for which she would surely be censured once they parted company, once she was on her own, and once it was evident that they had lived together without the benefit of marriage. So, why should she fret about sitting on his bed alone with him now? Worrying about it was of little consequence in the long run and would serve no purpose tonight.

He turned to lie on his back at that particular moment, and she fretted that he would wake up with her sitting next to him. He remained asleep, however, and she breathed a sigh of relief, for she was afraid that he would make her go back to her own room if he were to awaken and find her in bed with him. So she sat there utterly still, making no sound at all but just watching him and listening to his steady breathing. It was hypnotic, his breathing, and as she watched him, it began to lull her to sleep.

She was just about to doze off when thunder rumbled overhead startling her awake. She looked down at him to see whether or not he would awaken with the sound, but he continued sleeping. Again, she sighed with relief that he continued to slumber. Then lightning lit the sky, while thunder crackled outside the window nearly causing her to jump off the bed.

Once again, she worried that he would awaken. She watched him intently for several seconds, but he did not move. Instead, he looked so handsome and peaceful lying there next to her that she wanted to stroke his perfect brow. Absently, she put her hand out to do just that as thunder boomed even louder outside, shaking the building and rattling the window. She yanked her hand back and closed her eyes in fright waiting for him to awaken from the sound, but he remained asleep.

Rain began falling outside with drops of water pelting the roof and windows in a rhythmic tattoo. When he still did not wake up with the fierce sound of the rain pounding the inn, she was a little more confident that he was out for the night, and she shimmied underneath the bed covers to lie next to him. And even though being so close to him when they weren't married seemed somehow wrong, she took comfort in lying safe beside him in his bed. Perhaps she might actually get some sleep herself tonight.

Before she closed her eyes, however, she turned on her side and watched Lord William again as he slept. She reveled in the scent of sandalwood and leather that was his and imagined what it would be like to be his wife in reality, to have the privilege of lying next to him every night. Just as when she was younger, her heart ached with the thought of him as her husband, and the old yearning for him sneaked up on her again. Could it be that her resolve to hate him was melting just a little because of what he had done for her? Essentially, he had saved her from a fate worse than death, which was marriage to a half-witted knave like Sir Lionel Farnsworth. And in saving her from that marriage, he was also making it possible for her to get control of her own dowry and build a new shelter for battered women. He was really behaving too nobly for her to remain as bitter toward him as she had been for nearly fifteen years. For that, she leaned over and kissed him on his bristly cheek—softly, though, so that he didn't awaken.

Oh, dear. If she weren't careful, if she didn't guard her heart from him every moment, she would find herself very much in love with him once again. Dear man.

———◆———

UNBELIEVABLE WOMAN! What on earth was she doing in his bed? And snuggled up against him like she belonged there, for pity's sake? He blinked his eyes several times to make sure he wasn't seeing things— that he wasn't just imagining her there. That he wasn't perhaps in some bizarre dreamscape with her.

No. She truly was lying on her side right next to him, her head on his shoulder, her hand on his arm almost affectionately. He scrubbed his free hand through his hair in frustration. What should he do next?

"Lady Cassandra," he whispered, thinking that if he woke her, then perhaps she would jump out of bed and the situation would right itself.

She did not respond.

"Lady Cassandra," he whispered a little more loudly.

Still nothing.

He smelled sweet lavender and roses, which predictably aroused him. Though he was hard from just having awoken, his groin tightened even further because of her presence. He was fortunate, however, that he had fallen asleep wearing his trousers and shirtsleeves and that he wasn't lying in bed naked as he otherwise would have been. That would have been truly awkward with her next to him.

He peered over at her sleeping peacefully beside him. She looked like a wanton woman as she lay there with her hair strewn all about her. It aroused him even more than her scent to see her in such dishevelment.

Didn't she braid her hair before bed like most other women? Or had she been too upset by the mouse to worry about her hair last night?

The mouse. Of course, the mouse. That was why she was in his bed this morning. The little rodent must've shown itself again, and she must've come into his room to get away from the damned thing. Then he heard a scratching noise coming from inside the wall just now. Definitely the mouse.

But why hadn't she just awoken him about it? Why had she gotten into bed with him? Perhaps she had not wanted to disturb him, but she was certainly disturbing him now—just by being so near him. Her hair, her scent, her hand on his arm—all unnerved him. Her very presence made him go insane with lust. His pulse quickened with every breath, leaving him confused and apprehensive, and if he didn't escape that bed soon, he couldn't be held responsible for his actions. He gently pushed her hand off his arm, disengaged her sleeping head from his shoulder, and rolled off the bed.

He stood there in the middle of the room and watched her for a moment still sleeping where he had just been. How beautiful she looked lying there. What would it be like to wake up to her like this every morning? What a bizarre thought. They would never suit in a real marriage arrangement after all, not an affable arrangement anyway, not with her ardent dislike of him. Well, perhaps it was a little less ardent now that he was helping her save her dowry. But still, she hated him, didn't she? And why did that thought leave him so glum? Why did he suddenly care one way or another how she felt about him?

Needing to clear his head, he walked over to the window and opened it to let in some fresh air. A cool breeze washed over his face as he looked out on the courtyard two stories below, and he gathered from the amount of mud present that it had rained last night. He wondered that he hadn't heard it. Of course, he'd been very weary when he lay down after the long day, and he hadn't heard much of anything after he'd fallen asleep—including Lady Cassandra coming into his room or getting into his bed with him.

"Lord William?" A soft voice came from the bed.

He turned to find that she had just awoken and looked completely disoriented, as if she herself could not remember how she ended up in his bed. "Yes?"

"How . . . I mean, have you been awake long?"

"Only a few minutes."

She sat up in bed, and the covers fell from around her in complete disarray. She wore her wrapper over her night rail and looked utterly stunning, and he fought the urge to go to her and kiss her, knowing he couldn't stop at just a kiss. "When did you come into my room?" He asked her the question more to distract himself from her than because he wanted to know the answer.

"Sometime after midnight. I am sorry . . . the mouse . . ."

"No need to apologize, my lady, though I was a little confused when I first woke up and found you there. I figured the mouse had something to do with it, however."

She nodded. "I heard it—or something like it— scratching around inside the wall beside my bed. I couldn't bring myself to stay in my room after that, so I came to find you. Only, you were asleep, and I didn't want to wake you, so I just sat down next to you. And then I felt very tired so I lay down next to you. I'm terribly sorry."

"No need to be." He waved his hand in dismissal. "Are you hungry?"

Again, she nodded. "A little."

"Perhaps you should go get dressed while I shave. Then we'll eat our breakfast and be on our way."

"Very well." She got out of his bed and shuffled into her own room, closing the door behind her.

He was alone. At last. He had his room to himself, as it should be. And yet, strangely, he missed her. What on earth did that sentiment mean? Not wishing to contemplate it, he distracted himself with the business of his toilette. When he had completed his customary shaving and ablutions, he dressed and headed downstairs where he rented a private room in which Lady Cassandra and he could take their breakfast. Fifteen minutes later, she came down to join him. They ate in relative silence, so the meal did not take them long to finish, and when they were through with it, he gathered their few bags and ordered up his carriage.

They set out by eight o'clock on that gloomy morning with rain looking imminent. They had not gone very far from Penrith when the clouds began sprinkling on them. A few miles more, and the rain fell hard on their carriage. The muddied course proved difficult to manage when deep ruts formed in the roadbed, but their coachman nevertheless trudged forward despite the slow pace and the bad conditions.

William observed Lady Cassandra as she looked out the window upon the dreary day. She appeared to be lost in thought rather than watching the scenery as they passed it, and he asked her what she was thinking.

"I was just considering where my sister Julia and I ought to locate our new shelter," she replied.

"And what have you decided on the matter?"

"I believe Durham would be the best place for it."

"Why there, may I ask? Why so far north?"

"Mainly because I will come into some land there with my dowry, so we would only have to build a new structure on the land rather than acquiring land also."

"Very wise."

"Julia is already secretly housing women in her home in Hampshire, but it is becoming overcrowded with women from London, and we desperately need a new place to take in the overflow of unfortunate souls. Our new shelter will have to operate clandestinely also." She stared out the window as she spoke.

"I don't understand. Why the secrecy?"

She turned and looked at him in surprise. "Well, you must know, Lord William, that our mission is hardly condoned. The biggest obstacles to creating a shelter to house battered women are the law, the church, and society itself."

"How so?" he asked, truly astounded.

"You are well aware, no doubt, that all three institutions sanction a husband's right to chastise his wife. The wife has little or no recourse from such abuse. She could, in fact, be imprisoned or sent to an insane asylum if she were to run away from her husband."

"I hadn't thought of the situation like that. You and your sister must have quite a task in helping these women escape their tormentors in secret then."

"Herculean, it is, but we've created an underground network of helpers and aids in our essentially illegal activity. We have to operate in utter concealment, however, because the law is not on our side. It was dangerous of me even to mention our work to Lady Wellesley in hopes of raising funds for our cause, but funds are so desperately needed that I didn't know what else to do until I gain control of my dowry."

"You are very impassioned by this topic."

She then peered down at her hands, which lay motionless in her lap. "Who that had a sister as good as Phoebe would not be impassioned by the senseless cruelty and danger some women suffer at the hands of their husbands?"

A gnawing guilt ate at him with her statement, and he paused a few seconds before saying, "Lady Cassandra, I am terribly sorry for the comment I made about your sister at Lady Wellesley's ball. It was unconscionable. I do hope you can forgive me."

She returned her gaze to his, tears shining in her eyes, and he was touched that his words had moved her so much. She replied evenly, however, saying, "Yes, my lord. I can forgive you now that you have helped me win my dowry back."

He smiled at her, and she looked away.

CHAPTER 7

The Chariot, reversed: Forward momentum stalled, ill luck with travel . . .

———◆———

ONCE AGAIN, CASSANDRA HAD TO look away from him because his smile was so beautiful that it nearly knocked the wind out of her. She wanted nothing more than to fly across the carriage and embrace him for his words, but she restrained herself. Instead, she pretended to watch out the window at the passing scenery, such as it was in the rain.

The rain itself wearied her. They had been traveling for nearly four hours now, and fatigue had crept up on her. She was ready for a break from the road. Though only a few miles from the nearest town, she grew restless as the carriage plodded along. The road worsened with each drop of water, it seemed, and she feared that soon it would be impassable. As it was, the going was slow, and the carriage, though well-sprung, rocked and lurched with each rut it hit.

As they teetered through one particularly bad spot, Lord William said, "We may have to stop in the next town until tomorrow if the road becomes any more perilous."

"It is quite bad, isn't it?"

"I don't know that I've traveled worse."

At length, however, the rain let up as the sun came out, and she was heartened by the change in the weather. The road, however, remained bad, and as the carriage splashed its way through puddles and grooves, she prayed that they wouldn't get stuck in any of the muddy ruts.

Eventually, they pulled into a quaint little burg that bustled with activity despite the morning's earlier weather. They rolled past shop fronts that veritably teemed with life, people running to and fro in the street, shouting out greetings to others as they passed. Small crowds gathered here and there, and children raced around their parents or jumped in puddles created by the rain. Meanwhile, vendors with their carts peddled everything from fruit and flowers to bread and cheese. The town was abuzz with excitement. What was all the clamor about? She looked at Lord William in question, but he merely shrugged in answer.

The carriage came to a standstill at a small coaching inn on the far edge of the town. He opened the door, stepped out of the carriage, and held out his hand to assist her down. He then turned to an ostler handling the horses to ask him a question.

"My good man, what is all the fuss here about town?"

"Why, it's the annual spring festival, sir. People from miles around have come to Nether Wrigsby to partake of the fair and feasting here. We thought the weather would ruin it for us, but now the sun's out, people are coming out for the festivities."

"I see. Thank you." He turned to Cassandra and said, "Well, let's go in and eat. I'm going to inquire about accommodations in case we wish to stay the night here and head out tomorrow when the roads are better."

She followed him into the inn, and they stood at the front desk waiting for the innkeeper to acknowledge them. Finally, the man looked up from his work and smiled.

"Have you two rooms, sir, for my wife and me for tonight?" asked Lord William.

Her heart skipped a beat when he referred to her as his wife.

"I'm sorry," said the man. "We are full up. We haven't even one room to rent to you for tonight. It'll be that way all over town, too, with the festival and all. You'll have to go on to the next town for a room."

"How far is that?"

"Oh, about fifteen miles."

"Hmm. That's pretty far on these roads. Haven't you *anything* that we might rent?" asked Lord William.

The innkeeper tapped his temple with his finger as he thought a moment. "Well, we haven't any regular rooms. If you wanted, though, I could let you have an old empty room above the stables, but I wouldn't recommend it unless you was really desperate. It's pretty rough."

"Thank you, but I suppose we're not really that desperate. We'll brave the road for a while more, but we would like a meal here, if we may?"

"That I can accommodate you with."

They ate a light luncheon and were back on the road in a little over an hour. Their carriage trudged forward down the muddied and rutted thoroughfare. They had traveled two arduous miles from Nether Wrigsby when their coach got stuck in the muck and mire. The coachman valiantly tried to coax the carriage out of the rut it was stuck in, but they were well and truly affixed to the roadbed. Then, without fanfare or warning, the problem wheel fell off the vehicle. The coach crashed down on its body toward the right rear end, and Cassandra slid down the seat and hit her whole right side against the interior of the carriage.

Lord William leapt from his seat and rushed to her side. "My lady, are you quite all right?" He seemed truly distressed at seeing her thrown about the coach as she had been.

More embarrassed than anything, she merely laughed at her predicament. "I assure you that I am quite fine." Though battered and bruised by the experience, she did not want to create more anxiety for him.

He opened the carriage door and assisted her to the ground. The coachman had already descended from the driver's box and was surveying the offending wheel when she and Lord William approached the back of the vehicle.

"It's lost a linchpin from what I can tell, my lord," said the driver. "And the wheel's badly damaged, besides. Might even need a new one. In any case, I'll likely need the assistance of a couple of men from that town we just came from to help me repair it."

Lord William frowned as his brows creased together. He said nothing for a moment, but she sensed his agitation. She had no clue as to the workings of wheels—other than that they turned—so she could not tell how imperiled they were as a result of losing a linchpin with this one. And could the damage to the wheel be fixed in a matter of hours, or would it take days? No matter what, they would all have to return to Nether Wrigsby for assistance.

"Well, drat," Lord William said at last. "We'll have to walk back to town, I suppose. Unless—is there any possibility we could ride the horses back to town, Mr. Sullivan?"

"I don't think so, sir," replied the coachman. "None of them is broke to riding, so it would be difficult at best to get them to stand still long enough for you to mount them. Then, of course, we have no saddles, so it would be a precarious ride, especially for the lady in her dress."

"True. I hadn't thought about that," said Lord William. "Well, then, we walk. I do apologize for the inconvenience, Lady Cassandra. Will you be able to manage the distance back to town?"

"I believe so." Although she had her doubts about trudging two miles through the muck and mire in her dress, she downplayed her consternation. Perhaps she'd be able to rinse the dress once they returned to Nether Wrigsby. If not, she had fortunately packed another garment in her satchel, for just such emergencies.

They started out in silence toward town, with him walking beside her and Mr. Sullivan well behind them carrying her valise and Lord William's small bag. She tried to think of something to say to pass the time but couldn't come up with a topic.

Finally, he broke the silence. "You're awfully quiet. Are you terribly upset that we have to walk to town?"

"No, not at all." The statement was a bit of a fib because of her dress, which had already begun to accumulate mud along the hem, but she didn't want to worry him.

"I don't believe you, but you are a very good sport for not complaining. I tell you what. I will make it up to you when we get to town."

She laughed. "You really needn't, Lord William. A little exercise never hurt anyone."

"Ah, but I insist."

He stopped then and bent down to pick a flower growing alongside the road. She stopped as well and watched him as he twirled the flower in his fingertips.

"Do you know what this is, Lady Cassandra?"

"A buttercup?"

"Yes, indeed. Very good." Reaching out toward her, he rubbed the flower under her chin. He chuckled at the results. "Aha! You turned yellow. You know what that means, don't you?"

"That I like butter?"

"No, silly. That you're in love."

"It means no such thing."

"Oh, but it does."

"Where did you ever hear such drivel?"

"From my mother. And she would never lie to me."

"I don't know what part of the kingdom you mother hails from, but I have never heard that rubbing a buttercup under your chin and it turning yellow means you are in love."

"My mother hails from Essex, and she believes in all things magical and romantic," said Lord William. "Now, tell me, whom do you love?" His eyes twinkled with mischief as they had done on more than one occasion during their trip.

"Ha! No one."

"Well, buttercups never lie."

She plucked the flower from his hand and rubbed it under his chin then. It turned his skin yellow. "Then you, too, are in love, sir," she said while he laughed heartily. "But I won't be so indelicate as to ask with whom." And besides, she feared she knew whom he loved.

He took the buttercup back from her and placed it

in her hair, which sent a shiver down her spine and, she was certain, a blush to her face. He smiled at her sweetly then, as though they were friends. Silly man.

———◆———

CHARMING WOMAN. She had reacted so prettily to his teasing with the flower that he began to see in her a little of the girl he had once known when he was younger. She really was behaving quite well under the circumstances, given the disabled coach and them having to walk two miles back to civilization. She had not complained once about their situation as most others of her sex would have done by now, and he had to commend her for her fortitude and her temperament. Moreover, he was actually enjoying her company as they trudged toward the village. They laughed and talked of sundry topics, and as they walked, he wondered exactly what she was thinking. More to the point, what was he thinking? Could it be that he was having a change of heart toward Lady Cassandra? Could it be that she was not the harpy he had taken her to be merely five days ago when she had thrown punch in his face? Could she actually be sweet and affable, like Belinda? Perhaps there was another side to Lady Cassandra, one he did not know or credit.

At last they arrived in Nether Wrigsby. The coachman left them with their things to make his way to the wainwright's shop in town, while Lady Cassandra and he stopped at the coaching inn where they had lunched. They entered the establishment to ask the innkeeper about the room he had mentioned earlier. If it were still available, William would let her have it, while he himself would bed down somewhere else in the stables.

"Ah, you're back, I see," said the innkeeper by way of greeting.

"That we are. Our carriage lost a wheel a bit up the road from here. I doubt it can be fixed today, so my wife and I have come to see about that room you mentioned earlier. It seems we are desperate now. Would the room still be available?"

"Aye, it would, but I must warn you. It is not fit to be slept in currently. Oh, there is a bed in there, but it's certainly old and will be mighty uncomfortable. But I'll have the room swept and aired for you and the bunk made up for you. Why don't the two of you take a turn about town and partake of the festivities meanwhile?"

"We will do just that, and I thank you for all your accommodations with the room."

"Don't be too hasty in thanking me, sir. Let's see how you feel about it in the morning."

William chuckled and said goodbye to the innkeeper, and then he and Lady Cassandra left to tour the town. His belly growled as they passed a vendor selling tarts. Dinner was a few hours away yet, so he purchased a couple of the treats for them. They nibbled them as they strolled around the town, stopping at other carts and stores until they came to a jeweler's shop.

"Let's go in here for a moment," he said. "There's a certain purchase I should make before we return to London, and I need your assistance with it."

Lady Cassandra looked at him quizzically but followed him into the store nonetheless where he regarded a case of trinkets at the front of the shop. To the jeweler who approached them, he said, "My good man, I am interested in purchasing a wedding ring for my new wife here. You see, we've just come from Gretna Green, but I haven't yet got a ring for my lady to wear."

"Felicitations!" said the portly gentleman. "And may I say you make a fine couple? I have some rings over here, which you might like."

William followed the jeweler to the ring cabinet. "Cassandra, come here, my dear. Let's have you try on a couple of these."

The jeweler laid out several samples and styles of gold rings for the both of them to consider. William picked up a simple gold band and took her hand and placed the ring on her finger. Her hand trembled as he did so, which he found endearing. After they looked it over, he removed it and tried several other rings on her finger, her hand still trembling with the last one.

"Which one do you like best?" he asked. She hesitated as if she were uncomfortable making a choice. "Go on, my love, don't be shy." He used the endearment for the jeweler's benefit, but there was an unmistakable hitch in her breath when he uttered it.

She cleared her throat, but her voice still came out soft and low. "I think I like the first one you chose the best, my lord. It's the prettiest, and it fits the best."

"Are you sure?"

She nodded.

"That one it is, then." He smiled broadly at her.

He paid the jeweler on credit, and then he put the ring on her finger once again. He kissed her hand afterward, and they left the shop together.

"Thank you, Lord William, for thinking of the ring," she said. "It is hardly necessary, however."

"Nonsense. We have to make our ruse appear as authentic as possible, or your brother will never believe it. A ring makes it 'official.' He can't deny that."

"But such an expense, my lord. I will pay you back out of my dowry."

"Think nothing of it." He waved away her offer of repayment. "Besides, I told you I'd make it up to you for the carriage breakdown."

They returned to the street where a crowd had gathered around a juggler, and they stopped to watch the entertainment. Both he and she became engrossed in the juggler's act until he saw a movement out of the corner of his eye. He turned to see what had caused the motion and noticed a delicate piece of material floating to the ground—a woman's handkerchief. He picked it up and handed it to the young lady who had dropped it and was astounded to see a beautiful woman of about one and twenty who resembled Belinda when she was that age. She looked so much like her with her blond hair and blue eyes that he thought they could have been sisters. He would've thought her a long lost relative of Belinda's, except that she had no near relations other than her aunt and uncle in Raventon.

"Thank you, sir," said the young woman.

"You are most welcome." He watched her walk away with something like wistfulness. He then turned to Lady Cassandra to see whether or not she had caught a glimpse of the woman, but she was too captivated by the juggler to have noticed anything else. He returned to watching the woman with the handkerchief as she wended her way through the crowd to another amusement, and then he lost sight of her.

Seeing her, however, brought memories flooding back of the first time he had seen Belinda and how he had fallen in love with her on sight. An ache, an ache which hadn't affected him since he had left the Wellesley party with Lady Cassandra, settled in his chest at the very thought of Belinda. That he was not over her was obvious. Some feelings still lingered. He had loved her as none other, and he sighed at the notion that he would probably never know love like that for anyone else. She had been everything to him at one time, and now he had nothing. How he hated Benthower anew for stealing her from him so long ago. He then looked at Benthower's sister, whom he had essentially stolen away from the duke. She laughed at the juggler, and William laughed along with her—only, not at the entertainment. Rather, he laughed with some satisfaction at the thought that he had at last seen justice rule over Benthower.

CASSANDRA OBSERVED Lord William. She liked his laugh. When he laughed, his beautiful emerald eyes crinkled at the edges, and his smile radiated the warmth of the sun. She basked in it, just as she had done when they were in the jeweler's shop together. He had called her "his love," and she had nearly come undone at the words. They had only been spoken for the jeweler's benefit, of course, and not because he truly felt that way, but somehow she had taken just a little piece of them to heart and then chastised herself for her folly. When he kissed her hand, she was lost to all reason. She couldn't keep thinking this way, or her heart would end up in peril where he was concerned.

Lost in thought, she did not hear him ask her a question. "I'm sorry. I was distracted. What did you say?"

"I just asked you if you were ready to head back to the inn. We've been gone for some time now, and I'm sure they have that room ready by now."

"Oh, yes, I am definitely ready to return to the inn."

She sighed and continued, "I know it is too much to hope for, but I would dearly love a bath when we get back."

"Well, we will see if that can't be arranged."

They returned to the inn where they ate a leisurely dinner before the innkeeper led them through a rear courtyard to the stables and then up a back staircase to a tiny unoccupied room that must have housed a groom at one time. He unlocked the door and let them into the chamber, which now stood stark and nearly empty. The smells of leather and straw and horse rose from the stables below and met them as they entered the room. A rickety bed freshly made up—but uninviting, nonetheless—stood along one wall, while a hearth with a small fire burning low in it occupied the wall opposite. At the foot of the bed were a chair and small table.

Before the innkeeper left them for the evening, Lord William asked, "Would it be possible, my good man, for you to have a tub and water brought up so that my wife could bathe?"

"I believe we can accommodate that request. I'll see to it straight away."

"Very good," said Lord William.

After the innkeeper had gone, Lord William put Cassandra's things on the bunk and then stood back and surveyed the room. The warmth of a blush crept up her neck to her face at the realization that they were alone together, and she turned away from him in embarrassment.

"It's not much, is it?"

"No, but it will do. Thank you, Lord William, for asking for the bath. I really do appreciate it."

"Do not mention it. Once it arrives, of course, I'll

leave you alone for the evening and sleep elsewhere in the stables."

The hackles on the back of her neck rose in alarm at that statement, and she turned back to him. "Oh, must you stay elsewhere?"

He raised his eyebrows at her question. "I think it only proper, don't you?"

Fear gripped her by the throat at the thought of staying in that room by herself. "What about . . . ?"

"What?"

"Mice?" she whispered the word as if it saying it loudly might make one appear. "Or worse—rats? They are everywhere in stables like this. Oh, Lord William, please don't leave me alone."

He seemed to consider her request for a moment. "How about if I sleep just outside the door? All you'll have to do is call me if something should happen."

Doubt must surely have clouded her face, but she nodded.

Sometime later, footsteps up the back staircase heralded the arrival of the tub, and Lord William answered the knock at the door. Two men entered with the tub and set it on the floor by the hearth, while several others carried in the hot water and towels. They left after they finished filling the tub, and once again, the heat of embarrassment crawled up her neck and face at finding herself alone with him.

"I think you have everything you need. I'll just be outside this door." He exited through the back door of the room to the loft over the stables.

Once alone, she went to her satchel and took from it a pouch containing dried rose petals and lavender buds. She threw the cheesecloth pouch into the bath and let the flowers steep a bit while she removed her clothing. Fragrance rose from the steaming water, leaving her a little more at ease as she climbed into the tub with her rose and lavender soap and a washcloth.

Water sloshed around her, and the floral scent tickled her nose. She lay back against the tub and closed her eyes, the worries of the day melting away in the warmth surrounding her. She sat suspended in the water, various thoughts sprinting through her mind, but always returning to Lord William. Good sense evaporated like steam where he was concerned, and the old feelings of adoration for him filled her with an aching for him that she hadn't known since she was a girl. Why, oh why, did he have to be so kind to her today? She lifted her left hand from the water and admired the ring that glistened there. Oh, if only it were a real token of his love.

She distracted her mind from such thoughts by sinking down into the water to wet her hair. She lathered it up with the soap and then sank down again to rinse it. She soaped up the cloth and washed her body with it, rinsed, and then stood up in the tub. Stepping out of the basin, she reached for the towel on the bed and froze. There on the floor by the bunk was a rat—a small rat, but a rat nonetheless.

She shrieked, dropped the towel, and climbed dripping wet and shivering atop the chair by the table as the rat scampered across the room and under the door leading out to the stables. Lord William rushed into the room and saw her standing nude upon the chair. He gaped for a moment and then averted his eyes and turned away. Decent man.

—————◆—————

IMMODEST WOMAN! Where was her towel, for the love

of God?

"Are you hurt?" He stood with his back to her, but the thought of her naked on the chair behind him undid him. The smell of roses and lavender overwhelmed him as well, and he nearly lost his wits.

"No." Her voice shook when she uttered the word. "But there was a rat on the floor by the bed."

"Is it still there?"

"No, it's gone. It ran out of the room under the door."

"Then I'll just leave you to get dressed."

"No! Don't go! Please don't leave me alone."

"But you're naked."

"Ahhhh!"

"What is it now?"

"Another rat—or perhaps the same one—just darted into the room and under the bed. Oh, please, please don't leave me!"

He scrubbed his hands over his face in exasperation. "Where is your towel?"

"On the floor in front of me."

"Can you get down to get it?"

"Impossible. Not with the rat still under the bed."

"Likely it isn't there anymore, my lady. It probably crawled into a crevice and is gone by now."

"It could come back."

"Botheration. Very well. I will get your towel." He backed up toward her without turning around and spied the towel on the floor at the foot of the chair. He bent down to retrieve it, and standing up, he put one hand over his eyes and handed her the towel. His other hand brushed hers as she took it from him, and his groin tightened.

"Thank you." She did not get down from the chair, and he heard her rub the towel over her body drying herself. "Can you hand me my night rail?"

Oh, for the love of . . . "Where is it?"

"In my bag right there on the bed."

Without looking at her, he turned toward the bed and rummaged through her satchel until he found the garment she'd requested. He closed his eyes and handed it over to her.

"You can look now. I am dressed."

He opened his eyes one at a time and gazed up at her on the chair. She looked lovely standing there in her dishabille, and he couldn't help himself. He imagined her naked underneath the night rail, just as he had seen her when he burst into the room. Her perfect breasts, full and ripe, the dusky nipples standing pert at attention. Her long slender waist flaring out to her hips and the triangle of dark maidenhair at the apex of her milky thighs. In her fright from the rat, she had not even tried to cover herself. It had all been too much for him—and still was, for that matter. He needed a drink.

"Now that you are settled, my lady, I think I am going to go out for a bit, just for a short drink."

A look of horror crossed her face, and she stepped down off the chair and raced over to him. She clutched the lapels of his coat in apparent desperation. "You cannot leave me alone. What if the rat should come out from under the bed?"

"Lady Cassandra, the little thing is probably not even there anymore. And even if it is, I assure you, it will not bother you. It's more afraid of you than you are of it. Now, I'll only be gone a short while. It's beginning to get dark. Why don't you try to go to sleep?"

"Sleep?" She shuddered. "You can't be serious. I couldn't possibly sleep with that rat under the bed."

He went to the bed and moved it out from the wall to prove to her the rat was gone. She, meanwhile, shrieked once again and returned to her perch on top the chair. The rat, however, had vanished. It was not to be found underneath the bed, at least.

"See? It's gone. You can come down now."

"Are you sure?"

"I am certain." He held out his hand to her to help her down. She took the proffered hand and reluctantly stepped down from the chair. She did not let go of him, however, and instead, clutched it to her chest, driving him mad.

"You won't be gone too long, will you?"

Just long enough to forget about seeing you naked. "No, not long at all. You just try to relax."

He left her and walked to a pub across the street from the inn where he drank a couple glasses of whiskey in an effort to wipe the vision of her naked form from his mind. She had looked so beautiful standing on that chair that he had had the devil's own time refraining from plucking her off it, laying her down on the bed, and climbing on top of her then and there. And the worst thing—or the most endearing thing, depending on how he looked at it—was that she'd had no idea of the effect she'd had on him at the time. Whereas Belinda would have been all too aware of her effect on him—or any other man, for that matter—Lady Cassandra was not. She was oblivious to her charms.

Two hours later, he walked back across the street to the inn and around behind the main building to the stables. He climbed up the staircase to the outside entrance to the room and knocked on the door when he reached the top landing. He heard the chair scrape across the floorboards, and soft footsteps padded near the door. She was still awake.

"Who is it?"

"It is I, Lord William."

The key in the lock turned from inside the room, and the door opened to reveal Lady Cassandra. Oh lord, he should've drunk more whiskey. She looked entirely too enchanting backlit by the soft candlelight coming from the table. She had donned her wrapper and brushed her hair, which had dried to a satiny, sable sheen.

"Thank goodness you're back."

"Why? Did the rat return?"

"No. I was just growing concerned is all."

She stepped back from the entrance and let him pass into the room. It was then that he noticed that she had been playing cards on the table.

"What game are you playing?"

"Not a game really." She hesitated and then continued, "I was doing a reading for myself while you were gone."

"A reading?"

"Yes. With tarot cards."

He stepped over to the table to look more closely and saw several stunning, ornately illustrated cards depicting different scenes laid out in the shape of a cross.

"Where did you learn to read the tarot?"

"From my grandmother—my mother's mother. She was from Wales, and she learned to read the cards from her own grandmother who was part French. The cards were popular in Europe, especially in Italy and France, beginning around the fifteenth century. My grandmother's grandmother was also part Gypsy, which is where my grandmother got the gift of second sight.

Between the cards and her gift, she could tell the future with surprising accuracy."

"Do you have the gift, too?"

"A little, but I just dally with the cards, mostly."

He fingered the edges of one as it lay on the table. "What do they say?"

"They indicate I will soon come into great wealth—and happiness."

"Oh really? Which card means that?"

She picked up a card that showed a hand coming out of some clouds and holding a single round gold disc with a pentacle on it. She handed it to him and said, "This card. The Ace of Pentacles—or Coins."

Intrigued, he regarded the card for a while. "Do a reading for me. Please."

CHAPTER 8

The Lovers: Attraction, a choice, a union, passion, making love . . .

———◆———

HER HEART POUNDED, BUT SHE managed to project confidence as she motioned for him to sit in the chair while she took a seat at the end of the bed and gathered the cards together into one pile. "Here," she said, handing him the deck. "Shuffle the cards until you feel comfortable with them, and I will do a simple 'past, present, and future' reading for you."

He took the oversized cards into his large hands and shuffled them several times with little effort. When he finished, he placed them on the table.

"Very good. Now, cut them into three piles with your left hand," she said.

"Why my left hand?"

"Because, according to my grandmother, your left side is more attuned to the mystic forces of the universe, and you are, therefore, more likely to receive arcane messages from the higher realms through your left side."

He shrugged but did as he was told, cutting the cards with his left hand.

"Pick a card from each of the three piles. Then place the cards in front of you, but do not turn them over yet."

Once again, he did as instructed and picked the top card from each pile and placed each one before him.

"Now go ahead and turn them over, one by one."

Again, he did as she instructed.

"The first card represents the past, the middle card—the present, and the third card—the future."

The candle flame flickered on the table, casting his handsome features in a warm glow. "How does it look?"

She wavered before answering. "Well, the first card, your past, is the Queen of Wands. Reversed as she is, she denotes a cruel and petty woman, one who is vain and conceited." She paused a moment, giving him time to let that sink in. In her mind, the card represented Belinda, but she hesitated in suggesting that connection to him, wondering whether he would make the association himself. She doubted it.

She then read the next card. "The second card, the Lovers, represents the present." Her cheeks warmed as she glanced at his face for any signs of discomfiture, but he merely stared stoically at the cards. "It could mean the obvious—lovers in love, or it could mean an important choice is at hand for the querent." Her heart squeezed a little in grief at the thought of him in love with the Queen of Wands, but she tried to remain cheerful and not let her feelings show. Besides, it was entirely possible that it portended nothing more than an important choice coming up for him to make.

She hesitated once more before reading the last card because she didn't like the meaning of it. She hated when certain cards came up in readings, and this was one of them. "The third card, or the future, is the Ten of Swords. It can represent ruin . . . or death, but not violent death." She paused as his eyes widened. "Generally, however, it is better to think of it as the end of a cycle. Which always means the beginning of something new."

After several moments of silence, he said, "Well, hopefully, it's the lesser of those evils. Are the cards usually very accurate for you?"

They were usually always right for her, but she did not say that aloud. Instead, she said, "It is difficult to gauge how accurate they are for others. I do not do that many readings for other people." Which was the truth.

"I thank you for doing a reading for me. We'll see what happens, won't we?" He stood from the chair and then yawned and stretched. "Well, perhaps it is time we turn in. You take the bed in here, and I will go bed down in the hayloft outside the room."

She stood in alarm. "Oh please, Lord William, must you leave me alone? Can't you just stay in here with me? I would feel ever so much better with you here, especially with that rat around." She vacillated a moment before continuing with her next suggestion. "We could . . . we could even share the bed, I'm sure. Then I would feel truly safe." Heat crawled up her neck at the very idea of them sleeping in the same bed together as they had done last night in Penrith, but she was too agitated to worry about the impropriety of it.

He chuckled a little at what she said. "I do not think that is a good idea, my lady." Disappointment must have shown on her face, for he continued, "I'm afraid I would crowd you out of the bed."

"No. No, you wouldn't. I can sleep on my side very

easily. Please. Please just lie down next to me. Just until I fall asleep. I would feel so much less vulnerable with you there."

"Oh, very well." He seemed resigned to granting her request. "Just until you fall asleep."

She smiled at him, removed her wrapper, and hung it over the back of the chair. She climbed onto the sagging mattress and scooted against the wall. She lay on her side to give him enough room to lie down beside her.

Her heart raced as he shucked his coat and waistcoat, laying them both over her wrapper on the chair. Her breathing quickened as he untied his cravat and laid it over his clothes and then sat on the edge of the bed to remove his boots and stockings. Her belly quivered as he stood and blew out the candle sitting on the table and then padded over to the bed where he hesitated. His expression was lost in the darkness, so she had no clue what he was thinking or feeling. She could only feel the weight of his presence as he sat—and then lay down—on the bed. He faced away from her on his right side, and she could just trace the outline of his broad shoulders in front of her in the darkness.

He was so close to her that heat radiated off his body and warmed her own. His earthy scent intoxicated her. Sandalwood. Leather. And something altogether different. Him. The scent of him. She stared at his back, and as her eyes adjusted to the darkness, she could make out his form quite clearly. His hair was rumpled on the pillow, his shoulders bunched in what she could only assume was agitation. The temptation to reach out and touch his hair and run her fingers down his back was so mighty that she nearly succumbed to it and had to put her both her hands under her pillow to refrain herself.

She closed her eyes but couldn't sleep. He was too close, and images of him turning and kissing her flooded her mind. She grew aroused thinking of him embracing her, and her heart missed a beat at the thought of him on top of her. Poised to enter her. And then taking her by degrees until he was all the way inside her. She throbbed down there, ready for him. Wanting him. Aching for him, until suddenly he sat up.

"Lady Cassandra? Are you asleep?" he whispered in the darkness.

"No. What's the matter?"

"This is not a good idea, this arrangement. I should go."

She sat up behind him, alarmed that he might leave her. "But why? I don't understand."

He hesitated as if trying to find words. "Because I . . . I am a man. An ordinary man. And if I stay here with you—like this—I am likely to succumb to my baser instincts. And you are in very grave danger of being compromised."

Her belly quivered and bottomed out at his pronouncement, and of their own volition, her hands reached out and stroked down his back.

He sat rigid as she continued to massage him. "That isn't helping the situation, my lady."

She was awed by how solid he felt beneath his shirt, like stone under her fingers, and his hard muscles twitched and then relaxed under her touch. She ran her hands up his shoulders to his neck and then through his hair, which was damp with perspiration.

"Please stop." Though he whispered the words, he remained where he was, as if he were anchored to the bed.

"I cannot," she whispered back.

He shook his head. "Do you *wish* to be compromised?"

She sat on her knees and leaned in to him, and then she said softly in his ear, "What if I do?"

In a heartbeat, he turned around toward her and grabbed her hands. His gaze found hers in the darkness, and his eyes sparked with desire. "Be certain that you do because I am not sure I can stop myself."

"Then, do not try."

She was delirious as he pulled her head to his own and kissed her, roughly at first, raggedly, savagely, as if she were sustenance and he were a starving man. His tongue parried with her own as he consumed her. His hands moved from her face to her arms to her waist, and encircling her there, he pulled her close to him, so close she could feel his heart beating in his chest. He held her tightly, caressing her back, squeezing her bottom. Then he gathered her night rail up from the hem as he broke the kiss to pull the garment over her head and toss it onto the floor behind him. She, in turn, pulled his shirt up until it was over his head, and when it was off, she threw it behind him as well.

Even in the darkness, the heat of his gaze on her naked form scorched her to her soul. He touched her breasts, making her shiver, and squeezed her nipples until they peaked. Then slowly he bent down to take a nipple between his lips.

She shuddered.

He suckled that breast while his hand pinched her other nipple until it, too, peaked and she groaned with pleasure. She swept her hands up through the fine hairs on his chest to find his own nipples and squeezed them, while his lips moved to her other breast and suckled it.

So good it felt. She arched her back to give him fuller access, and he laid her down on the bed following her until he lay next to her.

His mouth moved up from her breast in a hot path across her décolletage. He kissed her neck, sucked on it, and then licked a wet course along her jaw until he reached her mouth once again. He took her in a deep kiss, and she fell into heady delirium. His hand, meanwhile, moved south from her breast down her belly to the top of her maidenhair. Instinctively, she parted her legs for him, and he stroked through the soft hairs until he found her swollen flesh, wet, throbbing. Ready. Waiting.

She whimpered her pleasure into his mouth, and he groaned his own into hers as he parted the tender lips between her legs. Gently, he traced the flesh around her entrance putting sweet pressure on her bud and causing her hips to lift off the bed in anticipation of his next move. Softly, slowly, he penetrated her with his finger, and she gripped him in a pre-orgasmic spasm so tight that it clenched him between her walls.

She broke from the kiss panting, moaning, as he continued his digital ministrations to her delicate flesh. Wanting more, she moved her hands down his chest and belly to his crotch, where she felt his hardness still ensnared by his breeches. She stroked his manhood through the cloth and whimpered her frustration at not having access to it. He took his hand away from her to unbutton his placket and then pulled his breeches and small clothes off and threw them in a pile on the floor. He kissed her once again and returned his attention to her tender, wet flesh as she caressed his rod with her hand. Even in the darkness, she could feel how big he was, and that made her contract in yet another pre-orgasmic quiver.

She moaned with pleasure and squeezed up his shaft, familiarizing herself with its shape and texture. She marveled at how thick and long it was and how soft the skin was over the turgid flesh beneath. Finally, she clasped the head and found a sticky substance leaking out of a slit there, which she spread down the shaft.

"Careful." He tore himself away from her mouth. "Or it will all be over before we have begun."

With first one knee and then the other, he spread her legs apart and climbed between them to mount her. He rubbed the head of his penis between the silkiness of her wet lips and positioned it to enter her.

"I'm sorry, my lady, but this could hurt," he whispered a tender warning to her.

"I'll be fine," she assured him. She wanted nothing more than for him to continue.

As he nudged himself slowly into her, she felt a slight pinching and a stinging discomfort, but mostly, there was little pain. He then tunneled inch by inch until he was fully sheathed within her walls, as he seated himself inside her.

"Are you quite all right?" His breath caressed her shoulder.

"Yes . . ." Her answer trailed off as he began to move inside her, slowly, almost imperceptibly. Yet, she could feel him rocking his pelvis against hers, and the sensations it evoked inside her drove her mad.

He pulled out of her and pushed back into her with gentle force. And then he did so again. And again. She marveled at how good it felt to have him inside her, and she moaned. Then he began to drive himself into her more forcefully in a wondrous rhythm that astonished her with pleasure. Each thrust brought her closer to the edge of that sweet threshold she longed to cross until she was teetering on the brink of oblivion.

And all the while, it never left her that she was making love to Lord William.

William.

The man of her dreams.

Oh God, he was inside her. Deep inside her. Thrusting into her. They were one. She was his. And he was hers. At least for now . . .

He moaned his own pleasure in her ear, and his voice pushed her up, up, and over the precipice of bliss until . . . "William . . . " she was there, and she uttered his name on a prayer as she convulsed around his manhood in an orgasm so powerful it seemed to shake the room.

He felt it. She could tell he felt it. "Yes, my love," he said on ragged breaths. "Come for me, my love. Come for me." And she did so—again. And then, as he pounded into her, he whispered those three words. Words she could not believe. Words she thought she would never hear him say to her. But she heard them. He said them, and she heard them.

"I love you . . . ah—ah . . . I . . . love you," he whispered as he continued inside her.

She . . . she couldn't believe what he said, could she? And yet, he *had* said it. . . . He had said it! Joy spread throughout her like warmth from the sun. And then they were out of her mouth, those same words. She couldn't take them back. She could only feel them.

Live them.

Be them.

"I love you, too." And she did. She did. She loved Lord William. She loved him. She had always loved him.

He moaned in acknowledgement of her words. And then she could feel it start in him. His release. His orgasm. His breathing hitched, and he thrust into her hard twice, once, no more. She could feel him explode inside her, releasing his seed into her. And he said on one final ragged breath, "Belinda . . ."

Then nothing.

Silence.

No movement. No breath. Only screeching silence. In her mind and in the room, the roar of silence.

Had he said, "Belinda?"

Or had she imagined it?

No.

She had not imagined it. He had said it.

He had said another woman's name. That woman, of all women.

Sweat—his, hers, theirs—trickled between them bringing her back to the moment.

"Get off me," she said.

She wanted to be free of him. Free of the cloying scent of sex and of him. Free from the sticky, sweaty closeness she felt to him.

He didn't move at first, and she was sickened by the intimacy of their bodies. "Get off me. Get away from me!"

"Cassandra, I . . . I'm sorry."

"No. Don't. Do not apologize. Just get away from me. Leave. Leave me."

"But what about the rat?"

"The rat be damned. Get out. Now!"

He got up off her and off the bed. He scuffled around the room gathering his clothes, the ones that were in a heap on the floor and those that were draped over the chair. She could hear him feeling around on the floor for his boots and stockings, finding them at the foot of the bunk. Then he padded over to the door and left the room. Despicable man.

———◆———

IMPOSSIBLE WOMAN. She was upset. And now, she was crying. He could hear her through the door. If she'd just let him explain . . .

But no.

There was no explanation, was there? Other than the obvious: he'd been thinking of Belinda toward the end. Belinda. He shook his head with disgust. As he had pounded into Cassandra, Belinda had slinked into his mind, as she so often did on a daily basis, an hourly basis. And soon, it had been Belinda he was making love to. And it had felt so damn good to be inside her. She was tight. So tight. And it had been so easy to lose himself in her, to lose the sense of time and place—and person. Especially in the dark, where he couldn't see whom he was with. And suddenly, before he realized it, he was calling her his love. Telling her he loved her.

Bloody hell.

Had he really told her he loved her? And what had she said in response? She had said something in response, hadn't she? Oh, yes: she had said she loved him, too. He had heard it. He had thought it was Belinda talking to him, but it had been Cassandra. Cassandra had told him she loved him.

Good lord. What did *that* mean? Had she meant it? Had she meant to say she loved him? Or had she been thinking of someone else, too?

No. She had clearly been thinking of him. She had said his name as she came. She had said, "William," and she had said it reverently. Worshipfully, almost like a prayer.

Good God. What an arse he had been. Here she had said she loved him, and he had just done the most egregious thing possible. He had taken her maidenhead while thinking of another woman. The woman with the handkerchief he'd seen at the festival this afternoon had stirred some memory of Belinda in him. And so entrenched in the habit of fantasizing about his former love, he had thought about her as Cassandra had climaxed, imagining it was Belinda who was reacting to his lovemaking with such passion. And carried away in the fantasy, he had told her he loved her.

Arse. Bloody arse.

Cassandra was still crying. He could hear her sobbing, really. His heart ached for her, and he wanted to go to her, to hug her, to hold her, to tell her he was sorry, and to make it better. But how could he make it better? The only way to make it better would be to tell her he loved her, too—and to mean it, which he couldn't do. He couldn't say he loved her like he meant it because he was still in love with Belinda, wasn't he?

His heart stuttered as he considered the question.

Well, wasn't he?

As he stood on the other side of the door, he shook his head in confusion. He did love Belinda, right? Or were his affections changing somehow? He searched his heart for a ready answer and found only that it wasn't as full of the sentiment he had felt for her just a few days ago. Panicked and conflicted, he asked himself why. Why didn't he feel for Belinda what he'd felt for her before the Wellesley party? Did it have something to do with Cassandra?

And what about Cassandra? Where did she fit into the puzzle of his emotions? And moreover, why hadn't he known she loved him? Why hadn't he seen the signs all along? She didn't hate him. She had never hated him. She loved him. It was now so obvious to him that he thought himself a simpleton. He certainly had been one where she was concerned. All her animus toward him, all the hostility she had directed at him all these years had not been out of hatred for him, but rather, out of love. Unrequited love.

Oh, he should never have suggested this ill-begotten scheme of retribution of his. He had just broken a woman's heart as a result of his need for revenge on Benthower. He would not be in this situation right now had he not suggested they run off to Gretna Green and pretend to marry. But, on the other hand, where would she be without him? Better off, probably. Better off mildly unhappy with Sir Lionel than miserable and broken-hearted with him.

Still standing naked outside the door to her room, he dressed himself quickly and headed through a narrow passage to the hayloft. He lay down in the hay and tried to sleep, but sleep eluded him. Her scent was still with him, so he couldn't calm his mind even as he took refuge from his actions. All he could smell were roses and lavender. It was all around him. Her. Cassandra. Not Belinda. Did he even know what Belinda smelled like? No. Had he ever noticed her scent like he had Cassandra's? No.

His thoughts returned to Cassandra and the fact that she loved him. What was he going to do now that he knew how she truly felt toward him? Nothing, probably. What could he do? He didn't return the sentiment, but the fact that she loved him certainly changed everything between them. In fact, all of tonight changed everything between them. They should probably marry for real now that they had made love. She could become pregnant, after all. He would broach the topic of marriage tomorrow. As he grew tired, he smiled to himself. Perhaps she would feel elated to marry him for real, given how she felt about him, and perhaps in time he could come to feel something for her, too. He drifted to sleep determined to ask her to marry him in the morning.

SUNLIGHT FILTERED through the stables waking him. He sat up, scrubbed his hands over his face, and looked around. For a brief moment, he couldn't remember where he was or how he had gotten there, but then the woes of the previous night began to return to him, one memory at a time. Cassandra. He had made love to Cassandra. And called her Belinda. He hung his head in shame as that recollection hit him, but in a way, he was going to make it up to her by asking her to marry him.

He stood and righted his clothes, tying his cravat as best as he could without a mirror and putting on his waistcoat, coat, and boots. He needed to see the coachman about the carriage, to find out whether they could travel today, and if so, to get them on the road. He also needed to see Cassandra, to talk to her about last night, to ask her to marry him.

He walked down the narrow passageway from the hayloft to her chamber, and when he got to her room, he knocked lightly on her door. There was no answer. He pressed his ear to the door and heard the gentle rhythmic sound of her breathing. Evidently, she was still sleeping, so he went by himself in search of the coachman.

Hours later, after the coach was repaired with a new wheel and it stood waiting for them in the courtyard of the inn, he went to retrieve her. He had been to her door twice before to update her on the progress of the coach and to invite her to breakfast, but each time, she had merely told him to go away without letting him in. This time, however, she would have to come with him because it was time to leave.

He climbed the stairs to her room and knocked on her door once again.

"It is nearly one o'clock, my lady, and the coach is ready," he said through the closed door.

Finally, after several seconds, it creaked slowly open, and he was greeted by a dressed and groomed Cassandra. She looked beautiful—despite the fact that her eyes were red and puffy.

"Good morning." He attempted amicability with her.

"Morning."

"How are you?" He was afraid to ask, but he truly wanted to know out of concern.

"Fine."

"Did you sleep well?"

"Oh, really, Lord William. You know I did not. Can't we please dispense with the pleasantries? In fact, let us, from now on, only speak to one another when it is absolutely required. Like we used to do."

"I'm sorry, but I cannot accommodate you there. We need to speak. We need to talk about last night."

"No, we do not. We never have to mention last night again. Now, my things are on the bed, if you please. I will be down by the carriage." She marched down the stairs, leaving him behind to carry her belongings.

The coach ride was tense with her not speaking to

him. He had attempted several times during the first hour to introduce a conversation only to be rebuffed by her ignoring him. Exasperated, he finally said, "Cassandra, we need to talk about last night."

"No, we don't. As I said to you back at the inn, we need never mention that topic again. I think we are better off forgetting that anything happened."

"I don't think we can just forget about it and pretend nothing happened between us."

"I have. You can, too. It's simple. Just do not think of it. Put it out of your mind."

"You know I cannot just put it out of my mind. Nor should I. We made love."

"Ah-ah." She waggled her finger at him. "We had coition. There is a difference."

"We did not simply have coition, and you know it."

"Oh, you poor, dear man. Are you suffering under some delusion that what happened between us had any meaning? We had coition, and that is all. Nothing more. There. We have discussed it. Nothing more remains to be said. The topic is closed."

"The topic is not closed. We must discuss marriage—real marriage."

"Goodness, I can't think why." She flicked an imaginary fleck of something off her dress.

"Because we made love, and you might become *enceinte.*"

"No, I shall not. And even if I do, that is none of your concern."

"None of my concern?" He almost came out of his seat. "It is deeply my concern. I have a duty to marry you now that you might be carrying my child."

"You are too noble with your offer, I am sure, but I decline to marry you. You are off the hook. Now . . .

please . . . may we stop this discussion?" She looked out the window to indicate she had finished talking about the matter.

"No, we may not." He jumped to her seat and sat close beside her, intentionally close so that their bodies touched. "We made love, Cassandra," he whispered into her ear.

"That's 'Lady' Cassandra to you," she whispered back.

"I've been inside you, my dear. I think I can call you just 'Cassandra.' Besides, do not forget. If we are to fool others, I should call you by your given name, without the honorific."

"Well, be that as it may, we did not make love. We only had coition."

"Call it coition if you want, but we made love, and you know it." He rendered his voice low, hot, full of carnal subtext, and she shifted in her seat. Good. He was getting to her. "You came in my arms. Around my cock. Twice, if I recall . . . and . . . you said you love me. Do you remember?"

"I remember I was delirious. That's all. I didn't mean it."

He lightly brushed his fingertips across her breast and the nipple pebbled in response. "You love me, don't you, Cassandra?"

Her breath quickened in response to his question, and she replied, "No . . . I was . . . I was thinking of someone else when I said that."

"No, my dear, you were thinking of me. You said it way too earnestly to have been thinking of someone else."

"And you are way too certain of yourself, my lord. Though I did not call out another's name as you did, perhaps, I was thinking of someone else nonetheless."

"That's what your affectation is all about, isn't it? That I called out someone else's name. You're angry, aren't you?"

She paused for a moment as if she were trying to control her words. Calmly and evenly, she spoke. "Why no, I am not angry. I understand how it is. I know what happened between us and what did not. We engaged only in coition, my lord. We did not make love. You lost yourself in the act and called out another woman's name. That is all. Now, if you please, this discussion is finished."

"It would be a very different discussion if I hadn't called out another's name, wouldn't it?"

She seemed to think about that. "Perhaps. But then I would be laboring under the misapprehension that you had some feelings for me, and you would be laboring under the same misapprehension about me."

"But you would consider marrying me nonetheless, wouldn't you?"

"As I said, do not be so sure of yourself."

"Will you marry me?"

"Absolutely not. I do not love you."

"I think you do."

"I think you are an arse."

He agreed with her.

CHAPTER 9

Nine of Cups, reversed: A wish granted in an unusual way . . .

———◆———

THREE DAYS LATER—AFTER MANY MORE attempts on Lord William's part to have a conversation with Cassandra about the necessity of marrying—they arrived at his residence in London. It was past ten-thirty at night when they pulled in front of his townhouse, and she was exhausted. She wanted only to sleep in her own bed. That not being possible, she wanted to sleep in *any* bed. She dragged her tired body up the stairs to the entrance where the two of them were greeted by those servants who had not yet retired for the night. Lord William ordered them to ready the room next to his for Cassandra, whom he introduced as his new wife. After much bowing and curtseying, the staff did as requested and prepared her room.

About an hour later, she lay in bed marveling at the fact that just eight days ago she had thrown punch in Lord William's face, and now, here she was pretending to be his wife. She also ruminated on the fact that they had made love—or had coition, as she preferred to think of it—just three nights ago. She had mixed feelings about having had coition with him. Part of her deeply regretted it for the way it had turned out. That he had called out Belinda's name at the end had wounded her to her soul. Yet part of her would do it all again just so she could say she had held him in her arms and taken him in her body.

She refused to think about the fact that she had told him she loved him, however. That topic was off limits, both as a subject for thought and for conversation. Though he had tried to get her to talk about it on the way home to London, she would not discuss it. He had also continued to badger her into marrying him, in the event that she ended up pregnant, but she had remained adamant that marriage was out of the question. The reason she gave him was that she preferred to remain single and in control of her own destiny and her own fortune. In truth, however, she would not marry him because he did not love her, and worse, he loved Belinda. She simply could not marry him when he was in love with another woman. If she ended up with child . . . well, perhaps she would go abroad for a while, but she would not marry him.

She finally drifted off around midnight and slept until nine the next morning. She wouldn't have awoken at such an early hour except for a great clamoring downstairs in the entrance hall. Someone was yelling for Lord William. She jumped out of bed, threw on her wrapper, and ran into the hallway to see what was going on.

"Poniard!" bellowed a familiar voice. "Poniard, come down here at once. Your man here insists you are not in, but I know better."

Benthower.

"Cassandra! I know you are here as well."

A door opened near where she stood, and Lord William came out of his room yawning and wearing nothing but his open banyan. Heavens, but he looked handsome standing there all disheveled from sleep. She caught a glimpse of his naked body as well, and he was glorious. He pulled his robe closed when he saw her standing in the hallway also. He yelled down to her brother, "We'll be down in a minute, Benny! Give us a chance to dress." He winked at Cassandra and went back into his room, presumably to put on some clothes.

Benthower grumbled from the vestibule as Cassandra returned to her room also to dress. From the way he sounded, he was in a foul mood, so she dressed and did her hair as quickly as she could without her abigail to assist her. She would try to be downstairs as soon as possible in an effort to appease her brother. She figured the less irritated he was, the less likely he would be to doubt their story.

"Good morning, Benthower." She attempted cheeriness as she entered the drawing room.

He was not alone but had brought his solicitor with him, and the two of them were huddled together talking. Benthower stopped the conversation when she entered and said quite simply, "No, it is not, Cassandra. It has not been a good morning for several days now." He paused for effect and then continued, "How could you, Cass? How could you do it? Sir Lionel is heartbroken, and I have been worried to death about you."

She snorted at his false concern and lack of sincerity. "I am sorry to have caused anyone any heartache or worry." Her reply was laced with as much earnestness as he'd shown.

"What have you to say about the fact that you have

brought shame and scandal down upon our family by eloping, my dear sister?"

"Only that, again, I am sorry." Wishing to change the subject, she asked, "How did you know we were back?"

"I have my spies. So, where is he? Your new husband. I'm anxious to congratulate him."

"I'm sure you are. He'll be down shortly."

"Here I am, Benny," said Lord William as he entered the room. He strode over to Cassandra, took hold of her left hand, and kissed it. Her heart skipped a couple of beats until she realized what he was really trying to do. He flashed the wedding ring she wore toward her brother so that he would notice it. Benthower appeared to seethe, which was evidently the reaction Lord William was going for, judging from the smile to cross his handsome mouth. To Benthower, he held out his hand, which the duke reluctantly took in a hand-shake, as Lord William said, "So, now we are brothers!"

The proclamation had the predicted effect of making Benthower's expression even more dour than it had been before. "So it would seem. That is, *if* you and my sister are truly married."

"What do you mean 'if' we are truly married? We're married."

"You'll forgive me if I am skeptical. It's just that I find it hard to believe you two are in love."

"Your sister is the love of my life." Cassandra's heart leapt at that statement as he put his arms around her shoulders and pulled her close. In her mind, though, she knew he was lying.

Benthower snorted. "I trust you've the documentation to *prove* that you're married?"

"Yes, of course."

"I'd like to see it, if you don't mind." It was more a command than a request by his tone, and he continued, "I've brought my solicitor, Hopkins, here to look it over, too."

"Don't mind at all. I'll just go and get it. Care for tea while you are waiting?"

Hopkins looked hopeful at the offer, but Benthower said, "Tea? No, no tea."

Cassandra's brow and hands began to perspire as she waited for Lord William to return with the signed marriage certificate. Oh, why had Benthower brought his solicitor with him to look at the document? What if it did not pass muster with Hopkins? She wrung her hands, worrying that he would see that it was fraudulent.

"What's the matter, Cass? You look nervous. You're not afraid that the certificate will prove to be fake and your marriage a sham, are you?"

"What? No, of course not. I am not nervous whatsoever."

"Nervous about what?" asked Lord William as he returned to the room.

"Benthower thinks that I am nervous that the certificate will prove to be a fraud."

"Nonsense. Hopkins will aver that it is a bona fide marriage certificate, real and valid," said Lord William, as he kissed Cassandra's cheek making her heart flutter once again. He then handed the certificate over to Benthower, who looked it over briefly and gave it to Hopkins, who perused it more carefully and read it aloud:

Kingdom of Scotland
County of Dumfries
Parish of Gretna.

These are to Certify to all whom they concern:
That Lord William Joseph Poniard from the Parish
of East Welkin in the County of Essex and Lady
Cassandra Marguerite Gardner from the Parish
of Raventon in the County of Northamptonshire
being now both here present, and having declared
to me that they are Single Persons, have now been
Married after the manner of the Laws of Scotland:
As witness our hands at Gretna, this 30th day of
March, 1816.

Parties Lord William Joseph Poniard and Lady
Cassandra Marguerite Gardner
   Witnesses Edmund Stewart and Robert Mac-
Donald
   Priest Thomas Campbell

The solicitor then looked up at Benthower.

"Well, Hopkins? What say you? I don't trust them not to have devised some clever scheme to fool us all. Does it look authentic to you?"

Cassandra wrung her hands again as Hopkins paused a moment before speaking. "Yes, Your Grace. Most authentic, in fact. It is a legal and binding document."

Cassandra blinked twice, and then her eyes went wide at this statement, but no one paid her any attention. All eyes were on Hopkins.

"How so?"

"Well, Your Grace, as you can see, they declared themselves in front of two witnesses. That is all that's required to marry in Scotland." Hopkins paused, and Cassandra scanned Lord William's face for his reaction, but his countenance displayed no emotion. Hopkins continued, "As a matter of fact, sir, it used to be much the same way here in England up until the Marriage Act of 1753 when Parliament put a stop to such marriages. Fleet marriages, they were known as. Now the law requires that banns be read three times in the parish before a wedding can take place."

"Thank you, Hopkins. You're a fount of knowledge. But what about this priest here? This Thomas Campbell?"

"His signature looks authentic."

"Yes, but is he a real man of God? How can we know that for sure?"

"He doesn't need to be a man of God in Scotland. Anyone can perform the rite."

"*Anyone*?" bellowed an outraged Benthower.

Cassandra looked to Lord William again for his reaction to this statement, and this time he looked back at her, one of his eyebrows raised.

"Yes, anyone. I've heard people traditionally go to the blacksmith in Gretna Green for the marriage ceremony, but anyone in Scotland can perform it."

She turned to Lord William again, but he merely motioned with his hand for her to calm down. His stoic expression told her not to worry, that everything would be fine. What if they were really married, however? Perspiration leaked down her brow as she clenched and then opened her hands over and over.

"So, there is nothing we can do about it? They are well and truly married?" asked her brother.

"It would seem so, sir," replied Hopkins.

"And he gets her dowry? Is that what I am to

believe?" Benthower's tone became increasingly hostile.

Hopkins loosened his cravat at his employer's voice but answered nonetheless, "I would have to look at the terms of her trust, but it would seem that Lord William would be entitled to the money. He is, after all, her husband."

Benthower stomped in a circle for a moment, fuming and cursing. Then he stopped in front of Lord William. "I want you to know this is far from over, Poniard. I know something rotten is afoot, and I will discover it. Mark my word." His blustering deeply disconcerted Cassandra, but he and the solicitor left without further ado.

She made sure they were well out of the townhouse before she turned to Lord William and said a little desperately, "I did not know that just *anyone* could marry two people in Scotland with just two witnesses, did you? We essentially declared ourselves in front of many witnesses and a bartender, who signed as the priest." She paused as an unthinkable realization popped into her head. "Please tell me we were not legally wed in a crowded pub."

"Now, now. Don't get upset based on what one solicitor says. I will ask my solicitor as soon as I can whether Hopkins is correct."

"You would think, however, that if anyone would have seen through our fake marriage certificate, it would have been my brother's solicitor. And yet, he thought it was valid."

"That's to our advantage, though. Your money will soon be yours to do with as you please. Don't you see?"

"Oh, but what shall we do about Benthower's threats?"

"He is all bluster. He will not find anything amiss if we continue to act as though we are truly married." He caressed her cheek as he spoke.

Warmth rushed to her face, and she turned away from him.

Their discussion, however, was interrupted by the announcement that her sisters, Julia and Violet, had arrived for a visit. Moreland, the butler, showed them into the parlor where Lord William and she were, and as soon as they entered the room, they both rushed to hug Cassandra.

"We know it's early in the day, but we had to come when we heard you were back. Is it true, Cass?" Julia asked incredulously. "Are you really married to Lord William? Are you really his wife?"

Cassandra hugged her sisters back. "Well, yes and no, but how did you know we were back?"

"I have my ways," said Julia. "What do you mean 'yes and no'?"

"Well, I will tell you."

"First, would you ladies like some tea?" asked her "husband."

"Yes, thank you, Lord William. We would love some tea," Julia answered for both herself and Violet, who nodded.

"Please. Just call me 'William.' We are family now."

"Thank you, and please won't you call me just 'Julia'?"

"Very good. I will have some tea sent in and leave you three alone to visit. Good day." He bowed to them and then he left the drawing room.

Julia turned to Cassandra. "I have so many questions. When I heard that you were run away to Gretna Green with Lord ... er ... with William, I nearly had an apoplexy. As did most of the *ton*. Right, Violet?"

Shy, unassuming Violet merely nodded once again.

Julia continued, "No one could believe it. No one. But tell me, how did it all come to pass?"

Cassandra recounted for her sisters the events leading up to Lord William's unusual proposal of marriage and his scheme that they pretend to marry to help her keep her money.

"I cannot believe that Benthower was such a cad," said Julia.

"Let me assure you, he was," Cassandra replied.

"But what I really cannot believe is that you agreed to let Lo . . . that is, William—of all people—assist you, given your history with one another."

"I know," said Cassandra. "I can hardly believe it myself."

"How have you managed to be civil to one another?"

"I am not certain, but I think I have been able to tolerate him because of all that he has done for me in the past few days. And he has been able to tolerate me because I haven't been so catty to him as usual. He really has been, for the most part, most kind."

Tea arrived at that point, and Cassandra served the three of them.

"What do you suppose his motive to be? I mean, what does he get out of it? Have you promised him any money?" asked Julia.

"He says the pleasure of seeing Benthower thwarted is his only reward. I have promised him no money, though I do plan to reimburse him for the expenses of our trip and perhaps even give him some extra money for his pains. I worry about Benthower, however. He has threatened to expose our marriage as a fraud."

"Never mind Benthower. What is it like to be married to William, of all people?" Julia's eyed glowed with mischief. "I mean, you had such a tendre for him when we were all younger. Do you remember?"

Cassandra rolled her own eyes, while heat rushed to her cheeks. "How could I forget? It is so very strange to think of myself as his 'wife,' even in pretense, that I don't quite know how to fathom it yet."

"So, tell me, is it just a pretense, Cassandra?" Julia leaned in to ask her. "Or have you two—you know—been intimate?"

Cassandra nearly choked on her tea, and her cheeks flamed even warmer than before. "Julia, really! In front of Violet?"

"You have. I can tell by the way you blush that you have. And don't worry about our dear Violet. She knows all about the subject. She has read the *Kama Sutra*, too, you know. Haven't you, dear?"

Violet's cheeks reddened to the color of cherries, but she said nothing.

"Shush! *Please* be quiet," Cassandra said.

"Oh, Cassandra, but that is wonderful. Perhaps you two will stay married."

"We are not really married, though, I told you. At least, I don't think we are. He said he wants to marry me for real—now, but he does not love me, so I will not consent to marriage."

"What if you are *enceinte*, though? Have you thought about that?"

"Yes, I have thought about that. I think I would go abroad for a while. I want to maintain the freedom I would not have as his wife."

"Having been married to Niles as I was, I can certainly understand your position. He did not care for me, and I was nothing more than chattel to him. However, I do think that it might be different with you and William."

"I don't see how it could possibly be different. There is no affection between us, and it would be only a matter of time until he took a mistress, which I could not stand to watch."

"Still, perhaps he could come to love you in time."

"The way Niles came to love you?" Cassandra asked.

Julia's eyes widened in apparent disbelief at the question, and when tears glimmered in them, Cassandra chastised herself for having gone too far. "Forgive me, Jules. Please forgive me. I did not mean to be cruel. It's just that Lord William will never feel for me the depth of affection that I could wish from him."

Julia set her teacup down. "Then I can understand your reluctance to marry him. Better to guard your heart than to have it crushed."

"Indeed," said Cassandra.

"Even if you two aren't really married, however, you simply must come to my ball tonight. I will make you my guests of honor."

"No, really, do not. We couldn't come. We shouldn't come. We are too scandalous right now. No one will want to be around us."

"That's what they will all say. And many may perhaps scorn you because of your elopement, but I can tell you that *everyone* is dying to see you two together— you know, to see if the marriage is real."

Violet nodded her agreement.

"You must come. You must," Julia continued. "There will be such a crush there if you two attend. With so many ladies there, perhaps we could even raise some funds for the new shelter at the ball."

Cassandra evaded answering for a moment and then

said, "I don't know. I have neither my clothes nor my Abigail here."

"Oh, please say yes. Your maid is at Benthower's along with your clothes. We will go get them both this morning. Besides, you and William will want to put on some sort of a show so that you appear as authentic as possible to throw Benthower off."

Resigned to the fact that she must make her "marriage" appear as authentic as possible, she finally capitulated. "Oh, very well. I will see if he is willing to go, but I cannot guarantee that he wants to be such a spectacle." She was tired, however, of discussing herself and her "husband," so she changed the subject. "So, tell me, how are things with everyone who has sought haven in Hampshire?"

"Not good. We are overcrowded as it is at the moment, and there are so many more women who need our help. We desperately need a new place for them."

"I have decided to build the new place on my land in Durham."

"What a wonderful idea!" said Julia. "It never occurred to me to build on land you would inherit."

"Lord William thought it a good plan."

"I agree. You know, Cass, I like him. I always did."

Cassandra, however, couldn't determine how she felt about him. Love him, perhaps she did, deep down inside. Though she didn't like to admit that even to herself. But like him? That was an entirely different matter, given the fact that he was in love with another. Heartbreaking man.

———◆———

ENCHANTING WOMAN. William was bewitched as he

watched Cassandra descend the stairs that night for Julia's ball. She looked so elegant in her gold silk gown with pearls around her neck and woven through her sable hair that he considered taking her in his arms and kissing her. He had been tempted to kiss her earlier today as well at her delightful reaction to Hopkins's proclamation that the marriage certificate was real. She had appeared so upset—appalled, really—that William had had difficulty refraining from laughing. He had wanted to kiss away her frown at that moment and pull her down to the floor and make sweet love to her to quell his raging arousal. Lord help him, making love to her hadn't squelched his lust for her in any way. If anything, it had only increased his desire for her.

The carriage ride home to London had been damned uncomfortable because he had thought about nothing but making love to her during the whole of it. And ever since they had arrived in London, he had wanted to seize her and kiss her, especially when he had seen her in the hallway this morning. She had looked so lovely standing there in her wrapper with her hair all down around her shoulders that he'd had a hell of a time controlling himself.

He had been about to kiss her when her sisters had arrived. Damned poor timing, that. How far would he have gotten with her had he tried to kiss her? Would she have even allowed it, or would she have balked because of the way he had called out Belinda's name during their interlude together? Probably the latter, damn it. He was in a real quandary. How would he survive the next two months until she turned thirty without kissing her or making love to her again? Most likely, she would never allow them to be together ever again because of his stupidity in calling out Belinda's name. What a mess he had created for himself there.

At least he had found some comfort in Benthower's reaction to the pronouncement from Hopkins that he and Cassandra were married. He really couldn't have asked for a better show of indignation from Benthower. His outrage had been palpable and priceless. At some point, William had to find out if what Hopkins said were true, however. A small, strange part of him hoped that it was. Then he wouldn't have to worry about convincing Cassandra to marry him for real in the event that she were pregnant.

At the moment, however, he was tasked with the business of getting to the ball without giving into the increasing urge to reach across the carriage for his "wife" and pull her into his arms. She sat across from him and veritably glowed in the darkened interior in the dress she wore. The scent of roses and lavender filled the air between them, doing nothing to abate his arousal for her as they rode to Julia's townhouse.

She broke the silence between them. "Thank you for agreeing to accompany me to this ball."

"Not at all. It is my pleasure. We shall make our first appearance as husband and wife for Benthower's sake."

"Did you not like his reaction to our elopement? Was it not classic Benthower?" She laughed as she spoke, and he found her amusement enchanting.

"It was everything I could have hoped for—and more." Strangely, though, the triumph he felt over having bested Benthower was not because he had finally had his revenge on the man for stealing Belinda away all those years ago. No, the pleasure he felt in having foiled Benthower derived from a new, surprising sentiment in William, one he couldn't quite put a name to, one that had nothing to do with Belinda and everything to do with Cassandra.

"Indeed," she continued. "He was so incensed when Hopkins said that *anyone* can perform the marriage rite in Scotland that I thought he would have an apoplexy right there."

"I thought so, too, for a moment."

"You do not think we are truly married, though, do you, Lord William?" Distress crept into her voice.

"No, I do not, but I will ask my solicitor on the morrow." Then something made him ask, "Would it be so very bad if we were married in reality?"

Even in the dark, he could see the look of horror that crossed her features. "It would be disastrous, don't you think? We do not get along, nor do we love one another."

He smiled to himself and considered pointing out to her once again that she had told him she loved him during their lovemaking. He thought better of it, however. "Well, in the meantime, why don't you call me just 'William,' and I will continue to call you 'Cassandra'? Using our more intimate names with one another will give people the impression that we are truly married, which is what we want."

"Very well, then . . ., William," she said hesitantly. She repeated it a couple of times as if testing it on her tongue.

He smiled again in the darkness. He liked the way his name sounded on her lips, and he was beginning to like her more and more.

They arrived at the ball not long after that, and an unequivocal hush fell upon the crowd when they were announced as "Lord William and Lady Cassandra Poniard." All eyes turned toward them, and William leaned in to her and whispered in her ear, "May I have the first and the last dances with you, Cassandra?"

"Yes, William." She flushed with her reply.

Julia rushed forward to greet the two of them, and Violet followed quietly in her wake. "I am so happy you could make it," said Julia.

"Thank you for having us," William said as he bowed to her.

The first dance of the evening was a quadrille, and he and Cassandra were forming a set with three other couples when Benthower bullied his way into their group with his wife, displacing one of the other couples. William noticed Belinda then, and although she looked pretty enough tonight, she did not overshadow all the other ladies present as she was wont to do on other occasions. Instead, she looked tired and worn, whereas to his surprise, Cassandra outshone the lot of them, looking positively radiant in the dress she wore, with several men eyeing her rapaciously, which, to his even greater surprise, made him prickle with irritation.

"Poniard," Benthower said by way of a greeting, "don't mind if we join you, do you?"

"As a matter of fact, we were just—"

"Didn't think so."

Benthower's reason for joining them could only be to assess the state of William and Cassandra's so-called marriage, so he squeezed her hand affectionately for the duke's benefit. Benthower fumed at the gesture, and Belinda looked none too pleased with it herself, which should have given him pleasure, indicative as it probably was of her jealousy toward Cassandra. Belinda's reaction had little effect on him, however, which he found ironic given that not long ago he would groveled at her feet for just such an indication of her fondness for him. He then noticed that she greeted

Cassandra with something akin to disdain, which also should have given him pleasure, indicating once again her jealousy. Her reaction did nothing for him, however, except perhaps to make him chafe for Cassandra's sake. More astonishing was the fact that he didn't feel the devotion toward Belinda that she'd elicited from him for so long. His attitude toward her was definitely changing. His regard for her was certainly waning by degrees.

The first two sets ended, and he reluctantly let Cassandra go to dance the cotillion with the foppish Lord Wakefield, one of the men who had been ogling her during the first dance. She blushed when William kissed her on the cheek as they parted, which endeared her to him. Benthower, meanwhile, rudely left his wife standing alone on the dance floor as he went to claim the hand of another lady, which left William with no honorable choice but to ask Belinda for her hand in the next dance or to escort her off the dance floor since she'd been abandoned by her husband.

"May I have the honor of the next dance?" he asked her more out of politeness than a real desire to dance with her.

"I'm sorry, William, but I am already promised to Lord Ryder and then to Mr. Allen."

"Perhaps a later dance then, Your Grace?" he replied, again to be polite.

"Yes, indeed. A waltz." Her flirtatious smile gave him the impression she was doing him a kindness. A week ago, he would have thought she *was* doing him a kindness to make room in her dance schedule for him—and with a waltz, no less. Now, however, he was slightly annoyed by her condescension toward him.

"Very well, then. I will see you in a while," he said as

Lord Ryder approached her.

William made his escape from the ballroom to the card room and joined a game of faro to while away the time. He won prodigiously and then returned after a while to the ballroom to find out how the dancers fared. He made it back in time to see the most recent dance ending and both Cassandra's and Belinda's partners escorting them off to the sidelines where Belinda sat with a group of her friends. It was not yet time for the waltz, and evidently, Belinda did not have a partner for the next dance, so she sat out. Cassandra, however, was immediately accosted once again to dance with Wakefield, one of the worst rakehells in London. William's gut tightened as some strange emotion washed over him. What was this he was feeling?

Jealousy.

CHAPTER 10

Nine of Swords: Despair, worry, death of a loved one . . .

HE REMAINED CALM BUT SNEAKED behind a pillar not far from where Belinda and her friends sat, not so he could eavesdrop on their conversation, but rather so that he could watch Cassandra dance with Wakefield and make sure nothing untoward happened with him. The earl could play the gentleman well enough at any given function, but beneath his cultured exterior, the man was a reptile. Not knowing what he was saying to Cassandra as they danced nearly drove William insane. Who knew what proposition he was making to her? It was obvious when she blushed and turned her head away that Wakefield had said or suggested something inappropriate, and William's first instinct was to rush to the dance floor and clobber the lout. He stopped himself short when he overheard Belinda talking in a low voice on the other side of the column.

"Can you believe her?"

"Who?" asked one of her companions.

"My sister-in-law Cassandra. Can you believe that dress she is wearing? The décolletage is utterly immodest given her endowments."

"I wholeheartedly agree with you. It is scandalous."

"No wonder Wakefield has swooped in on her. She belongs in a brothel, dressed like that. Half the men present are salivating over her, which makes me wonder what's in the punch. She is no great beauty, as you know. Oh, she looks tolerable enough this evening, I suppose. But for the most part, she has never been a truly handsome woman, not at all like her sisters Phoebe and Julia—or Violet, for that matter. She is so very tall as to put one in mind of an Amazon. How Lord William could ever have been duped by her, I cannot fathom. It must have been the money she brings to the marriage that hooked him."

It was Belinda's voice saying these things, but she spoke with such venom that he had to peek around the pillar to make she it was she who was talking. Sure enough, it was the duchess. Her obvious jealousy over Cassandra should have pleased him, but somehow her unkind remarks left him cold instead. This was a side of her he had never seen.

"Indeed," said one of her companions. "I heard that he rescued her from a marriage to Sir Lionel Farnsworth who only wanted her for her money."

"What else has she to offer a man? She is certainly more of a harridan than any decent man would want to involve himself with," said Belinda, her tone bitter. "I tell you this, also, that she will be shunned by society for eloping. The only reason she is here at all is because her sister invited her. I didn't want to come tonight because she was going to be here, but Benthower insisted. Her behavior is most scandalous. Speaking of scandalous, I have also heard that she and her sister hope to raise money at tonight's ball for their haven for women whose husbands are cruel to them. What a travesty that enterprise shall turn out to be. I don't know any of my acquaintance willing to get involved in such a plot."

"What husband here would allow it?" asked Belinda's companion.

"None that I know. It is a cork-brained scheme of such notoriety that no one will back it."

William fumed as he stood behind the pillar in a state of astonishment that Belinda was not at all who she seemed to be. Rather than the sweet, alluring woman he'd always thought her to be, she was instead a shallow, acrimonious creature. How could he have been duped all these years? Of course, all they had ever discussed together had been topics to do with her— her interests, her pastimes, her views on fashion or the weather. He had never had an in-depth conversation with her about any other subject, and he was surprised and disappointed at her spitefulness, especially where Cassandra was concerned. For her to say that Cassandra was a harridan of no great beauty cut him deeply, and to his own astonishment, he was seconds away from coming out from behind the pillar and defending her to the lot of them when the cotillion ended and the next dance was to be the waltz he had promised to Belinda.

Though he didn't care to do it, he had no choice but to claim her hand for the dance. The irony of the situation was not lost on him. Nine days ago, he had danced a waltz with her grace and told her how he felt about her. He had even fantasized about asking her for an assignation at the Wellesley party. Whereas a little over a week ago the thought of making love to Belinda would have undone him, now it left him cold and empty. Why was he having this change of heart with respect to her? Perhaps it had to do with his change in perception of her.

He reluctantly approached her and led her to the dance floor, bowing politely to her as she curtsied to him. The waltz began, and as he took her hands in his, he wanted nothing more than to have the set over with. An awkward silence followed the first bars of the music. He had nothing to say to her.

Finally, Belinda broke the peace. "How are you this evening, William?

Still incensed by her unkind remarks about Cassandra, he shrugged. "I'm fine, I suppose. And you?"

"I am good, but you don't seem to be doing as well." Faux concern laced her voice.

"I don't understand. What do you mean?"

"Why, only that you look tired and worn. I don't think marriage agrees with you. At least, not marriage to Cassandra."

Needles of annoyance pricked his skin as she spoke. "I'm probably just fatigued from our travels. We've only been back in Town a day, you know." She was treading on thin ice with respect to the topic of his wife.

"Still, I worry about you, especially with someone as . . . shall we say, spirited and opinionated as Cassandra can be?"

"She has been perfectly amicable and well-behaved, I have to say." His declaration was adamant, which he hoped would end the topic.

"She has not yet thrown a beverage in your face then?"

"No," William said. "Don't you think she looks bewitching this evening?" He posed the question to rankle her.

"Oh, I don't know. I suppose *some* men would think so."

They danced in silence for several bars until she sighed heavily in an obvious attempt to get his attention. "What is it?" he asked.

"Only that you have not once mentioned us tonight, William." She pouted as she said the words.

"Us?" he asked in utter confusion.

"Yes. You and me. You have not once mentioned the two of us. You have not once told me how I look or that you love me this evening."

He was momentarily dumbfounded and simply stared at her for a moment. "I thought we had settled this at our last meeting, Your Grace. You indicated that you were uncomfortable with such talk. I had rather doubted that much has changed since then."

"Oh, but everything has. I have found out that Benthower has taken a new mistress. I am sure of it. They're dancing together now."

He couldn't help himself. He turned to see who Benthower danced with. Ah, the widow, Mrs. Taylor. The duke did indeed look to be engaged by her charms. William turned back to Belinda and shrugged. "I don't see how that affects you and me."

She put on her sultriest smile and spoke in her most seductive voice. "Why, must I spell it out? You must know that I am thinking about a liaison between us. You even said last time we danced that you wished there could have been a time for you and me." She leaned in and whispered, "I am telling you now that there could be."

He was at once suspicious. Why all of a sudden would the duchess suggest a liaison between the two of them just because her husband was involved in one of his own? Had Benthower set her to this task? Was she was in league with him to prove that William's marriage to Cassandra was all a pretense by seducing him? He kept his mistrust to himself for now, however. "I'm a married man, Belinda. A liaison would jeopardize my marriage." The statement was rubbish, of course, because he had no marriage. Still, he wouldn't give her any indication of that fact.

"Really?" She pouted again as though she were wounded.

"Yes, really."

"Perhaps in time you could come to change your mind about the matter."

"Perhaps, but I don't—"

"Let us just leave it at 'perhaps' for now." She smiled coyly as the set ended and he led her over to the sidelines.

He was flummoxed by her proposition—and more so, by his reaction to it. He should have been overjoyed that she'd asked him for a liaison, but he was not. In fact, he was strangely put off by the suggestion. What did that mean in terms of his feelings for her? Could it have something to do with Cassandra? As he thought of his wife, he scanned the ballroom for her to see whom she was with. To his great annoyance, she was dancing yet another dance with Wakefield. How outrageous. Dancing twice with Wakefield had been cause enough for William to be jealous, but three times was positively unheard of. The worst of it was that she now appeared to be flirting with Wakefield. If they did not watch themselves, the two of them would create a scandal of huge proportions amongst the *ton*.

CASSANDRA FUMED. How dare William dance the waltz with Belinda, the love of his life, when he was supposed to be creating the illusion that he and she were really married? She was of a mind to ask for a glass of punch just so she could throw it in his face. Well, there was no reason not to give Lord Wakefield a third dance then. What did appearances matter anyway when William was so unconcerned with them?

He was watching her now, so she played up the flirtation that Wakefield had begun with her. He had earlier insinuated that they ought to meet privately in Julia's library for an assignation, a suggestion that had left her blushing wildly and not just a little nauseated. She had told him no, that she had not wanted to cheat on her new husband. Had Wakefield asked her now, however, she might very well have taken him up on the scheme just to spite William. Oh, but what would he have cared anyway? He had no regard for her or her feelings. He was, after all these years, still madly in love with the duchess, and Cassandra had to deal with that reality. She, however, couldn't wait to rid herself of William and the heartache he caused her. She looked forward with relish to the day she turned thirty and could be free from him and have her money to build a new refuge for battered women.

Her dance with Wakefield ended, and he escorted her to the sidelines.

"My, but I am parched," she said.

"Would you like some punch, my lady?" asked Wakefield.

"Oh, yes, please. If you wouldn't mind."

He went in pursuit of punch, and she was mildly surprised to see William accosting him at the refreshments table in the room adjoining the ballroom. What could he be saying to Wakefield? Julia approached her at that moment, however, distracting her from the two men.

"Are you enjoying the ball?" asked her sister.

"I am." Though she had detested seeing William dance with Belinda, she was nevertheless having a good time.

"You look stunning, Cass. Every gentleman here has his eyes on you tonight, and I daresay that William is jealous. I would bet he is scolding Wakefield as we speak for dancing with you three times this evening."

"Oh, I highly doubt that."

Julia's brows shot up in apparent shock at the sarcasm in her tone, but Cassandra made no apologies. She no longer wished to discuss her husband, so to change the subject, she asked her sister how the efforts to raise funds for their new shelter were going.

"Alas, not at all as well as I had hoped. The ladies present here at the ball are reluctant to throw in much of their pin money to help us. We have raised only a couple hundred pounds tonight."

"I don't understand. Who could not see the need to help women whose husbands beat them?"

"It is not that they do not see the need. It is that they fear the repercussions such support would have with their husbands who do not see the need."

"How infuriating. Well, it won't be long now before I have my money and my land, and then we can build a new home in Durham."

William approached them at that moment and handed Cassandra a glass of punch, which she took from him in surprise. "Thank you, but Wakefield was going to bring me a glass of punch as well."

"So he said," William remarked. "I told him I would

save him the trouble because I wanted to have a word with my *wife*."

"I'll just leave the two of you to talk," Julia said. She then whispered in Cassandra's ear, "Dance the last dance with your husband, and I will make sure it is another waltz because it will be so much more romantic than any other dance."

Cassandra raised a brow, giving her sister a look calculated to wither but said nothing in reply. She then turned to William. "What is it that you wished to discuss?"

"I am concerned that you danced three dances with Wakefield and what that will look like to everyone here tonight."

"I should think it wouldn't matter at all."

"Dancing more than two dances with one man is nothing short of scandalous, and we *are* trying to give the impression that we are married for real, Cassandra."

"That's odd coming from you, especially since you danced with the Duchess of Benthower," she said peevishly.

"Yes, but only one set and not a very pleasant one at that, I might add."

"I find that difficult to believe, my lord, given how you feel about her."

"You know nothing of how I feel about her."

"Oh, don't I? I seem to recall you saying you loved her during a recent loathsome interlude between you and me, one which I would dearly love to forget."

"But which you can't forget about because you're in love with me." He stepped closer to her and caressed her cheek.

"You insufferable, odious man. I told you I was thinking of someone else at the time. The only one in love with you is yourself."

"Careful, or we'll create a scene. Now, come. The last dance is about to start, and we should make a good show. Your brother is watching us."

Cassandra forced a smile and reluctantly took the arm he offered, following him onto the dance floor. As he settled his hands on her, she was transported to the other night and what it had been like to be in his arms, what it had been like to have him kissing her and touching her and making love to her, and she flushed with the memory. When she looked up, he was watching her with his sensual green eyes, and her belly bottomed out. What had he been thinking? Unnerved by his gaze, she focused hers on his shoulder where she didn't have to look directly into those eyes.

After a few turns in uncomfortable silence, he finally said, "I'm going to visit my solicitor tomorrow to find out if what Hopkins said is true and whether or not we are truly married."

"And don't forget to have him draw up an agreement stating that you will give me my money when we are through with this sham of a marriage."

"About that . . ."

Alarm skittered along her nerves. "Yes?"

"If we're not married now, I think we should marry posthaste in case you are *enceinte*."

"You have said that over and over, and I thoroughly disagree. As we agreed to before, you and I are through after I get my dowry. If I am with child, I shall take part of my money and go abroad for a while. Tomorrow, I am going to visit my solicitor to find out the particulars of my trust and exactly when it will become available to use. I assume it will be soon, which is good because we need that money to start the new shelter in Durham as soon as possible. We aren't having much luck convincing the women here tonight to contribute to our cause, and we're desperate for funds."

"You would leave the country with my child?"

That's all he'd heard of what she had said? "For a time, yes. Until the scandal dies down, for there would certainly be a scandal if I had a child while I was unmarried. Or perhaps I would marry someone else. Perhaps even Lord Wakefield would do me the honor."

"That I will not stand for. It's absurd. Why don't you just marry me?"

"Because you and I are not in love."

"You would not be in love with whomever else you think you might marry, like Wakefield. Nor he with you, most likely."

The comment stung, and the pain in her chest rivaled her indignation. "Are you saying that no man could find himself in love with me? Am I so disagreeable that no one would want me? Is that what you are implying?"

"Of course not. I was only saying that most likely you would not find a love match before you would have to marry someone if you are *enceinte*. Also, be reminded that anyone you do marry will want control of your dowry."

"And you would not?"

"I have no need of it. My investments are serving me well, and I neither need—nor want—your money. I would let you use it as you see fit."

Cassandra considered this for half a second, but in the end, she said, "It is of little consequence, as I still would not marry you. Besides, the point is probably moot because I doubt I am with child."

"This discussion is far from over, my dear. We shall

see in time what the cards hold for us, won't we?" The dance ended, and he led her off the dance floor with a wink. Infuriating man.

———•———

EXASPERATING WOMAN. To think that she would not consider marrying him but would consider marrying someone else—especially that fop Wakefield—if she were carrying his child was thoroughly aggravating. He spent the rest of the evening stewing over the issue. Having slept poorly, he was up early the next morning and rode out to visit his solicitor before Cassandra had come down for breakfast.

The traffic was awful for the early morning, putting him in a foul mood, worse than the mood he was already in from thinking of her marrying someone else. In due course, however, he pulled up in front of his solicitor's office and tied his horse outside. Once inside, he waited patiently for Sedgwick to see him. Eventually, a clerk showed him back to Sedgwick's desk.

"Ah, Lord William, how good to see you," the solicitor said as he stood to greet him.

"Sedgwick, my good man, likewise, I am sure."

"How can I assist you?"

"Well," he began, "this may come as a surprise, but I need to find out if I am legally wed."

The solicitor raised his bushy brows, and William explained the events leading up to his and Cassandra's decision to pretend to elope to Gretna Green. He also explained how he and Cassandra had obtained the blank marriage certificate from the blacksmith who would not, in good conscience, sign it under false pretenses, and how they had gone to the Hind's Head in search of people willing to sign the certificate, think-ing that having local witnesses sign it would add to its "authenticity" for Benthower's sake. He recounted for Sedgwick how they had both told the bartender in front of a crowd of witnesses at the Hind's Head that they wished to marry one another. He then showed him the certificate itself, signed by themselves, the bar-tender, and two of the witnesses.

The solicitor eyed the document carefully, and after several minutes, he exhaled, clearing his throat. "So, let me understand this correctly: you and Lady Cassandra had no real intention of marrying, yet you declared that you wished to marry to the bartender and several witnesses?"

William nodded.

"Did the bartender or any of the witnesses know at the time that the two of you were not serious in your declarations?"

"No," said William cautiously. "I saw no need to explain our situation to them, thinking it would only confuse them."

"I see. So, at no time did they know that you and she were seeking only to have the certificate signed with-out the actual rite of marriage."

"That's correct."

Sedgwick tapped his finger on his temple as if deep in thought. After pondering the situation for several moments, he said, "You realize that all that's required for two people to marry in Scotland is for them to state their intentions in front of two witnesses?"

"I do now, sir."

"Based on the fact that you did just that and now have a signed certificate to prove it, I would say that you two are truly married."

William let that statement sink in. "But we didn't mean to be."

"Be that as it may, I believe you and Lady Cassandra have legally wed under Scottish law."

"Do we have grounds for an annulment?"

"Only if you have some illegal consanguinity between the two of you or you could prove one of you was insane or feeble-minded at the time of the vows or one of you is . . . oh, how should I put this? Impotent."

"I see." William began to pace the small space in front of the solicitor's desk. "What if the marriage was never consummated?"

"'Tis not grounds for annulment, unless you can prove that the non-consummation was a result of impotence. Plus, you must realize that it could take years to prove impotence to the satisfaction of the consistory courts. Then, too, there would be all the prurient details that the court would have to know in order to render an annulment for impotence. It wouldn't be worth it in my opinion, for the story could reach the press and become nightmarish in its salaciousness."

William stopped mid-step and sighed. "And suppose my lady does not wish to be married to me?"

"She, perhaps, should have thought about that before she married you in the first place."

"Bloody hell. I wish we had fully understood the laws of Scotland before setting off for Gretna Green."

"Indeed."

He thanked Sedgwick for his time and left for home. He did not know how he would break this piece of news to Cassandra. He only knew she would be truly vexed to find out they were married for real. For his part, he was glad of it, for the fact that she could be *enceinte*, but he did not relish telling her that they were legally wed.

Even though it was still early, he stopped off at Brooks's for a drink and a diversion, and when he arrived home several hours later, he saw a coach and four waiting outside his townhouse. He recognized the vehicle and the livery of the footmen and coachman. His mother had come for a visit. Wonderful. She would certainly not be pleased about his elopement—or having had to wait for him to return home. He steeled himself for a possible confrontation and walked up the steps to his front door.

He found his mother sobbing on the settee in the drawing room. He had no idea that she would be this upset over the elopement.

"Good afternoon, Mother," he said as cheerfully as he could manage.

She looked up and dabbed her red and swollen eyes with her tear-soaked handkerchief. "Oh, William, there you are." She stood and rushed to his arms.

"Goodness, Mother, why so glum?"

She sniffled, managing to control a sob. "You have not heard, then, have you?"

"Heard what?"

"Oh, William, William, whatever shall we do?"

"Come, sit down and tell me, what is the matter?" He led her over to the settee.

"It's David . . ."

"Davey? What about him?" Every last nerve jolted in alarm at the mention of his older brother.

His mother stifled another sob and said as best she could, "I have just had a letter from his friend Lord Howell in Italy. Oh, William, David has died."

His mother's words were a punch to the gut. He was silent for several seconds and then whispered, "Died?

But how?"

"He caught a fever—malaria, the doctors think it was—and he died very suddenly. Howell didn't even have time to write us that David was ill. That is how quickly the fever took him."

"Good God. When?"

"I just received the letter by special courier today. You will probably be getting one as well. He died a little over a week ago. Oh, William, they have buried him already—and in Italy, no less. He could not even be laid to rest on his ancestral soil." She began crying once again.

"Oh, Mother, don't cry so. At least he went quickly and did not suffer long."

"But he was so young. Only six and thirty. And he died without an heir." She scrutinized his face for a moment and then took his hand in hers. "You are now the marquess, William. You are Kingspointe."

That realization hit him like a thousand bricks. Just as it was seeping into his brain that he was now the Marquess of Kingspointe, Cassandra walked in.

She stopped short in the doorway and appeared alarmed when she saw him consoling his crying mother. He stood and motioned for her to come into the room.

"Cassandra," he said wearily, "come and meet my mother."

Cassandra stepped forward and curtsied as he made the introductions between his mother and his wife.

The now dowager marchioness said to him through her tears, "In all my grief, I had forgotten you had run off to get married, you naughty boy." She sniffed once again. "I don't know why you couldn't have waited until you got home to do it properly."

"Well, that's just it, Mother. We fell quite madly in love while we were at the Wellesley house party, and since we were so near Gretna Green, you know, we decided to elope."

"Still," said the dowager marchioness as she sniffled, "I would have liked to have seen you wed, William."

"I'm terribly sorry, my lady," said Cassandra. "I'm afraid it is all my fault. William eloped for my sake. Please do not be so upset about it."

"She is upset by news about my brother." William sighed heavily. "He has died suddenly of a fever while in Italy."

An expression of apprehension crossed her features. "Oh, William, I am so terribly sorry. I had no idea."

"Nor did I. No one did until just today."

"Is there anything I can do for you?" Her kind and gentle offer nearly undid him.

"Thank you, but no. There's nothing anyone can do at this point." He sighed once again. "Have you been out, my dear?"

"I have been to see my solicitor."

"And I have seen mine this morning, as well. We have a great deal to talk about."

"I know." The gravity in her tone was not lost on him.

"Perhaps I should leave," said Dowager Lady Kingspointe.

"No, no, Mother. You must stay for tea at least. You are welcome to dinner as well."

"Yes, Lady Kingspointe. Don't go. I'll order us some tea and cakes," said Cassandra.

"Please, no. I hate to be so rude as to run off before we have become acquainted, my dear, but I am really far too fatigued for tea. I believe I shall go ahead and take my leave, William. We will talk more soon."

"Of course, Mother. Let me help you out to the carriage."

He returned after assisting his mother to her coach to find Cassandra pacing the drawing room. She stopped abruptly when she saw him standing in the doorway. They both stared at one another for several seconds and then both said in unison, "We are married."

"I know," they both replied, again in unison.

After a moment of silence, he said, "So, your solicitor confirmed it as well."

"Yes. Oh, William, this is disastrous. Whatever shall we do? We cannot stay married. We simply can't. We have to come up with a way out of this. Perhaps I could say that I was not in my right mind when we were in Scotland. My solicitor said that if one of the parties were insane, the marriage could be annulled. Well, I could certainly say I was quite insane to have married you."

Perhaps she did not mean it to be rude, but with the mood he was in, he couldn't help but take her words the wrong way. They stung prodigiously, and after a moment, he said in a sullen voice, "Is it really so horrible, Cassandra?"

Her face softened, and she crossed the room to him to touch his cheek tenderly. Again she spoke with kindness. "How cruel of me, William. How utterly heartless. We will discuss the marriage business another time. Please, let me get you something to drink."

"Whiskey, if you don't mind." Tears formed in his eyes, but he blinked them back, refusing to let them fall.

"Oh, William." She hugged him where he stood. "I am so sorry about your brother. So very sorry. I know how hard it is to lose a sibling."

He took consolation in her words as she led him over to the settee where she continued to hold him and rock him for a while. He lay his head on her shoulder and let her comfort him. She ran her fingers through his hair to soothe him, and he felt better having her there. Finally, she kissed his brow, and when she rose to get him his drink, he was lost without her.

She poured him three fingers of whiskey, and he gulped it down and asked for another glassful, which she gave him. He sipped it more slowly this time as he leaned back on the settee, and she sat next to him again. She took his hand, kissed it, and then clasped it in both of hers, and he was touched by the gesture.

When at last he could speak, he said, "We were pretty close when we were younger, he and I. We did everything together. . . . We grew apart, however, the older we got—once he became Kingspointe—but I still loved him. I didn't love how he lived his life, though. I think what killed him ultimately was his lifestyle. Despite what Lord Howell told my mother about how he died of malaria, I think he died of something far more insidious, something he caught from a . . . well, never mind that." He let out a long sigh. "He's gone now. It's best not to sully his memory. Bloody hell, maybe it was malaria and nothing more."

"I am so sorry." She touched his face with tenderness once again as she peered into his eyes. "Please, William, if there is anything that I can do . . ."

"Just . . . thank you for listening. Did you . . . did you wish to discuss more about the marriage?"

"Not now. We'll talk about it another time. For now, just know that I am here if you need to talk." She kissed him on his cheek.

Despite how bereft he felt, he took solace in her presence. Whether from the whiskey or from her company, warmth seeped into his chest as she stroked his hair.

CHAPTER 11

Five of Coins: Loss of possessions, material impoverishment, destitution . . .

———◆———

HE DIDN'T SEE MUCH OF Cassandra for the next several days, and to his surprise, the hours seemed somehow empty without her. She left little notes of consolation and encouragement for him here and there, and they soothed his grief and touched his heart. He didn't have time to seek her out, however, because he was busy attending to affairs of the marquisate. To his dismay, his brother had left *everything* in rough shape. Deplorable shape, really. David had not yet begun to molder in his grave, and yet, his creditors had come out of the woodwork in droves demanding payment for this item or that service. Then there was the matter of the tenants' cottages in Essex, which he had written to David about at the Wellesley party. His brother, no doubt, had never received the letter, so he had little idea how much the cottages had deteriorated in just the last year. William was appalled at the squalor in which the tenants were living. It was inexcusable really, and he blamed David for not taking better care of his lands and the people farming them. Though he loved his brother, William was angered and ashamed at how poorly the man had run his affairs.

William sat in his study late one morning going over the land steward's latest reports when a footman announced a visitor. He was shocked when Belinda glided into the room with practiced grace. He was even more astonished that all he felt was annoyance at seeing her. He stood, however, to greet her, and she ran to him and engulfed him in a stifling hug.

"Oh, William, I came as soon as I found out. How devastated you must be." She stepped back and regarded him with a sultry stare, which was meant to entice him, no doubt, but which did nothing but irk him.

Nevertheless, he remained calm and adeptly disengaged himself from her embrace. "Belinda, what a surprise. May I offer you something? Tea, perhaps?"

"I'll have some whiskey, if you don't mind."

He raised both brows at her, and she vacillated. "Perhaps it is a bit early for whiskey. Do you have sherry?"

He thought it a bit early for sherry, too, but he poured her a glass and offered her a seat on the settee by the fireplace, while he stood by the mantle.

How strange it was to be alone with her here in his study. Only weeks ago, he would have relished this time alone together with her. He would have drooled at her feet for a morsel of attention, but today, he wanted nothing more than for her to be gone.

"Come and sit by me, William." She patted the space next to her.

The settee was just big enough for two people, so it would have been a very close fit had he chosen to accept her invitation. Instead, he said, "Thank you, but I have been sitting all morning. I prefer to stand."

"Nonsense." She rose and moved to him. She took

his hand and pulled him over to the settee and made him sit. Then she sat next to him—right next to him with their knees touching. "There. That's better." She patted his leg. "Well, so, tell me, how have you been managing?"

He loosened his cravat. Sitting so close to her was not at all comfortable, and strangely, it was not at all arousing. In fact, it was slightly revolting. Even more than that, it felt like a betrayal of Cassandra. Nevertheless, he remained seated. "It's been difficult, I must say. I never wanted the title, you know."

"Really? But it's so prestigious that you are the marquess now."

Irritation sliced through his gut at her comment. "You always were impressed by a title, weren't you Belinda?"

She laughed and rubbed her hand up and down his thigh in an obvious ploy to tempt him. He took hold of her hand and set it between them on the settee. "Now, now, Belinda. I'm a married man."

She creased her brow and pouted at him. "That may be, but you still have feelings for me."

"I'm married, Belinda." He stood to emphasize his words and crossed to the mantle, his back to her.

She stood also and followed him, putting her hand on his shoulder. "Have you given any thought at all to what I suggested about the two of us at Julia's ball?"

Vexed with her again, he turned to face her. "Only that I will not be taking you up on your offer. I'm committed to Cassandra."

She huffed and retreated back to the settee. "Cassandra, Cassandra. I am sick of Cassandra. Only two weeks ago you'd have jumped at the chance to be with me."

"And that would have been wrong of me. You're a

married woman, Belinda."

She scoffed. "There's not a couple among the *ton* who haven't had a dalliance or two outside the marriage bed. Why not me? Why not us?"

"I've told you. I'm with Cassandra now."

"Yes, but do you love her?" Her tone was petulant, almost adolescent.

He closed his eyes and tried to say that he did, but for the life of him, the words would not come. They wouldn't come because although he felt something for his wife, something like affection, he could not say that he loved her, truly loved her.

"Just as I thought." She smile and then smirked. "You do not love her. It is a marriage of convenience, is it not?"

Again, he tried to say that it wasn't, but the words would not come.

"I don't understand your false loyalty to that woman, but I tell you this, William: one day, you and I will be together." She stood from the settee and approached him once again. Laying her hand on his cheek, she said, "One day, you will tire of her, and you'll come to me. And do you know what? I'll be waiting for you. Only think of it—you and I together, as you've always wanted."

He was mildly surprised that her hand was cold where she touched him and that he felt little for her but a desire to be rid of her. "I think it's time that you go, Belinda."

"Perhaps. But think on what I've said. You love me, William, and you've always wanted me. And that will never change."

But something inside him *had* changed. Although he could not say he loved his wife, he also could not say that he was in love with Belinda anymore. He narrowed his eyes at her and nearly told her so, but she patted him on the cheek and turned to go. She left him in his study to contemplate his feelings—or lack of them for her.

———◆———

CLOUDS CAST the London sky in a leaden gloom twelve days later as Cassandra peered out the window of her room at the mews behind William's townhouse. She had come to think of this chamber as her own. It was warm and comfortable—too comfortable, perhaps. She would regret leaving it in a couple of months and not just because it was so commodious. She would regret it for the fact that she would never be this close to William again. His room was just beyond the dressing room behind her, and their closeness to one another was constantly on her mind. Whether or not he ever thought about how near they were to each other when he was alone in his room was a different story.

She doubted it.

For her, however, their proximity to one another sent a little thrill through her whenever she imagined them acting as if they really were man and wife, in which event he would probably come to her in the night to make love to her. But they were not really man and wife, nor lovers, nor partners, nor even friends, so it was with some wistfulness that she looked to the door that led to the dressing room connecting their two bedrooms. Was he in his room right now? Probably not, as he rarely slept in. He was an early riser, she had learned, and since taking over the marquisate, he had much business to tend to.

She'd rarely seen him in the past week-and-a-half—only in passing really, but she had left little notes for him now and again consoling him over the loss of his brother. Whether or not he appreciated the notes she had yet to learn. He spent his mornings in his study, but where he spent the rest of his days and where he ate his dinners she hadn't a clue. He was preoccupied with condolences from friends and acquaintances and his pressing business to do with the marquisate, and so she hadn't had the opportunity to speak to him about their matrimonial situation. Although she had yet to talk to him about it, the question of their marriage loomed uppermost in her mind. She could not quite absorb the fact that she was actually married to him and how horrible that was for her.

Horrible because she loved him so. She did. She had to admit it. Making love to him had been the worst thing she could have done because it had opened up all her old feelings for him. They had all come crashing back to her, as surf to the shore. She loved him as much or more than she ever had. But he did not love her.

No, he loved Belinda, and was probably having an affair with her. After all, he had called out her name and told her he loved her while he made love to Cassandra and had lost no time in seeking her out to dance at Julia's ball. Then there had been the peculiar way that he had allowed her into his study alone with him when she stopped by to express her condolences after finding out about his brother. She had spent an hour alone with him "consoling" him, and although Cassandra did not know what they *actually* did together during that time, she had a pretty good idea of what they *probably* did together.

Belinda aside, Cassandra could not imagine spending

the rest of her life with William—or Kingspointe, as he was now known—feeling as she did for him when he felt nothing for her in return—and worse, with him having an affair with Belinda, of all people. Oh, she supposed they could live as some couples did, apart from each other with a laissez-faire attitude about their peccadilloes as long as they were discreet about them, but she really did not want a marriage of so little convenience to herself. In truth, she didn't want a marriage at all. Marriage would end her rights to her property and money. In fact, her entire legal identity would be given over to her husband and she would have no legal say on anything whatsoever.

No, it would be better if she could return to being a single woman in possession of her own fortune with the ability to dispose of her property and her money as she saw fit. The problem was that she and William had no real grounds for annulment, although she still considered insanity—her own, at least—as a distinct possibility. Whatever else, it was still too soon to ask him to discuss their marriage, given all that he had been burdened with in losing his brother and inheriting the title. She would wait until sometime next week to broach the subject with him.

She resigned herself to the fact that, once again, she would be eating dinner alone in her room until a chambermaid delivered a note mid-afternoon from William requesting her company later on.

> *Dear Cassandra,*
> *We must discuss our situation. Please have dinner with me this evening. I will be home by six.*
> *W.*

His note sounded almost ominous. Whatever did he mean by it?

Though she was leery of the conversation they must have, she dressed for dinner in her most flattering gown, a green muslin with pink silk flowers along the hem and a décolletage that revealed her bosom nicely. Findley did her hair and wove green gems throughout the updo, and Cassandra even put a little lampblack on her lashes and rouge on her lips and cheeks. She might as well look her best since this was the first time she had really seen him in nearly two weeks. Upon entering the dining room, she found him pacing behind his chair as if he were deep in thought or deeply troubled by something or both. He started when he saw her but quickly regained his composure. Did her appearance please him? It was difficult to tell because he looked wearied and worn, as if he hadn't slept in days, making his thoughts hard to read.

"Good evening." He came around the table to help her be seated. "Thank you for having dinner with me. I fear I have been neglectful of you these past several days, but business has kept me quite occupied. I really must thank you for the notes you've left me regarding David. Your kindness has meant a lot to me." He squeezed her shoulder and kissed her cheek affectionately, and warmth rushed to her face. What could he mean by showing her such sentiment? He seated himself and indicated to the footman to begin serving them. "How have you been?"

"Oh, I've been fine. And yourself?"

"I've been doing as well as can be expected under the circumstances."

"You mean with respect to your brother?"

He released a long sigh and nodded. "Yes, that. And,

oh so much else."

She raised a brow at that statement. "Please. Tell me what has been going on."

"Oh, Cassandra . . .," he trailed off as though he were at a loss for words. "It's hard to know where to begin. It's all so overwhelming."

"What is?"

"The title. The marquisate. I never wanted it, you know. Never wanted the hassle or the responsibility that goes with it. It's all too much. . . . And now to find out about all the trouble it's in . . ."

"Trouble? What trouble?"

He hesitated before he spoke, his shoulders slumping somewhat. "It turns out that my brother, God rest his soul, ran the estate into enormous debt. It is virtually in financial ruins. What wasn't subject to entail he sold for cash—and he used everything he gained from property sales and incomes from his tenants to support his lifestyle of gambling, drinking, and traveling—oh, and other unhealthy habits, which I won't go into. At any rate, I've found out that he was virtually living off his creditors these last few months. I think part of the reason he went to the Continent was to escape the invoices that were piling up. I've received so many dunning notices in the last week-and-a-half as would cause your head to spin. Bloody hell, I've even begun to receive notices from his creditors abroad. My savings and income from investments have barely made a dent in the mountain of debt. As it is, I will have to sell this townhouse to pay off creditors, and we will have to move to Kingspointe House in Mayfair—which I suppose we'd have done eventually anyway, but I just didn't realize how dire the circumstances were that would force me to sell most of what I own to pay his debts."

"Oh, William, I am so sorry. Is there anything I can do?"

He paused and stared down at the untouched food on his plate. "As a matter of fact, I hate to ask you for your help, Cassandra, but . . .," he paused again and then said plaintively, "but I really could use some of the money from your dowry to assist me. That is what I wanted to talk to you about regarding our marriage situation."

"Oh." She got a sinking feeling in her gut. This was not good.

"We are married. I know you don't like it, but we are married. I've talked with your solicitor, and—"

She cut him off as her temperature rose. "You talked with my solicitor? When?"

"Just the other day, and he says—"

"Without informing me?"

"I didn't want to burden you at the time until I knew exactly what I was up against."

"What did you discuss with him?"

"Your trust fund—your dowry. I wanted to know what the terms were."

She gasped at his audacity. "And what did he tell you?"

"That—that it is mine to claim whenever I want it."

The heat of anger flared in her blood, but she tried to force some calm. "And are you trying to tell me that you do want it? Is that what this is all about?"

"I'm asking if I may use some of it—with your permission, of course. To help pay the debts and the servants and to repair the properties of his . . . er, my tenants in Essex."

"How much are we talking about?"

He grimaced. "At least thirty-five thousand pounds."

"Thirty-five thousand pounds!" She practically yelled the words as she stood and threw her napkin on her chair. "But—but that would barely leave me with enough to build a new house for the women I hope to shelter and all the expenses that would go along with it, not to mention having anything left to live on myself for the rest of my life."

"You will be living with me for the rest of your life, and I will take care of you."

"You must be joking. I don't want to live with you. I want an annulment." She turned and stormed out of the dining room. He followed her into the hallway.

"An annulment would be virtually impossible to obtain. We have no grounds."

"I'll have a doctor declare me insane or fee-ble-minded. Lord knows, it's true enough."

"And wind up in an asylum? You'd be worse off than you are now."

"I'd do anything—anything at all—to get out of this sham marriage that we have." She threw her arms up in exasperation.

"Is it so bad—really?" He moved closer to her. "You'll be taken care of, and it doesn't have to be a sham."

"What on earth do you mean?" She narrowed her eyes at him in suspicion.

"We could make it a real marriage, Cassandra. We could live as husband and wife."

"Just what are you suggesting? That . . . that we have . . . conjugal relations?"

He chuckled. "That would be part of living as man and wife, but we would also have each other."

"Absolutely not. I'll not consent to conjugal rela-tions, not with you having an affair with Belinda.

There is no way."

"Who told you I was having an affair with Belinda?"

"No one had to tell me. I can read the signs. You called her name out in the throes of passion; you couldn't wait to dance with her at Julia's ball; and then there was the way she spent an hour alone with you in your study after she learned about your brother. What else am I supposed to think with evidence like that?"

"She and I are certainly not having an affair. I danced with her at Julia's ball only to be polite, and she just dropped by to offer her condolences. Nothing more, I assure you."

"For a full hour?"

"Yes, for a full hour. I wanted her to leave, and in fact, I finally did ask her to leave."

"I don't believe you, nor do I care," she said dismissively. "I'm still not going to act the part of your wife."

"Really? Haven't you at least thought about it since you've been living here?" He moved closer to her and clutched her hand. He brought it to his lips for a kiss. "Think of it, Cassandra. We could be man and wife . . . in every sense of the words. I could come to you at night and make love to you." He stepped even closer to her, and the smell of sandalwood and leather overwhelmed her senses as he looked into her eyes with his hot, green gaze. She shook her head no, but it was an empty gesture because her eyes most certainly said yes, and he kissed her. He brought his lips to hers, and her mouth betrayed her desire for him when her lips parted for his tongue to enter. He embraced her then, and her arms went around him in another act of betrayal. And as his kisses intensified and his caresses grew bolder, her barriers fell completely to his advances. He touched her breast, taunting the nipple, and she moaned with pleasure when it peaked.

She wanted him. She shouldn't want him, but oh, how easily she slipped into his sensual trap. He guided her backward until she came up against the wall, and his mouth left hers to trail kisses from her jaw to her earlobe, which he nibbled irresistibly. He kissed her neck then and continued his attention to her breast, which he revealed by pulling down her sleeve and then the bodice of her dress and, finally, her corset and shift. He dipped his head and took the nipple in his mouth, and she was in ecstasy—or agony, depending upon how she viewed it. To have her body betray her will under his seduction was too much, but part of her wanted this so very badly that she couldn't stop it just yet.

"William . . .," she managed to say in her delirium. "I-I don't know. How shall we make this work?" She regained some of her composure and said more coherently, "I mean, I want to build a shelter, after all. How shall we build it and run it with such meager funds?"

By this time, he had already gone to work on her other breast, and he tore himself away from that nipple, lifting his head to gasp some air before responding. "Well, that's another thing altogether. I was thinking we wouldn't build anew, but use an existing building on one of my lands in Essex."

She stiffened in response to that. "But what about my land in Durham? What's to become of that?"

He hesitated for a heartbeat. "I'm having it inspected for mineral deposits, and if all checks out, I think it will work to mine coal there. I hope so, anyway. Then at least the land is producing some income for us." He returned his attention to her nipple.

"But what if I don't want to have it mined? What if

I want to build a new refuge there?"

He kissed her petulant lips in an obvious effort to divert her attention. "It makes no sense to build a new building to house the women when I have a perfectly good structure sitting empty and unused in Essex. I will have to visit Essex sometime next week. You can come with me and view the house for yourself. You'll see. It's perfectly appointed for your purposes. Plus, you won't have the added expense of transporting the women from London so far north. And you should come with me anyway as the new marchioness to meet my tenants. Now, let's go upstairs where I can make love to you properly."

She stiffened once again and pushed him away from her as she righted her undergarments and her dress and concealed her breasts once more. "No. You're deliberately trying to distract me from talking about these issues. You know I will object, so you're trying to get me in a state of passion where I'll say yes to anything you want."

"That is not so. I'm trying to get you upstairs to make love to you—like a husband should do with his wife. Now, let's go." He took her hand and began to lead her to the staircase.

"Oh, no. No, you don't. I still have not agreed to be your wife for real. Or to any of your requests—for my money or my land in Durham."

"You are my wife, damn it—for real. You will eventually have to act the part."

"Act the part?" She laughed at that statement. "I shall not. It is a part that I am ill qualified to act. I am not some weak-willed, biddable girl here. I am a grown woman, and I know what I want and do not want."

"Well, what you want seems to be at odds with

what you've got, my dear. You have yourself a husband whether you like it or not. One who is entitled to your dowry without asking your permission to use it. And one, I might add, who is entitled to conjugal rights whether you like it or not. I *will* eventually need an heir, Cassandra."

"Bloody hell! We were married by mistake." Her use of the expletive and her tone of voice shocked even her. "Are you telling me you would use my money as you see fit and take my body as you like it? Both without my permission?"

"No, I am not saying that. I *am* saying that I am entitled to both your money and your body without your permission, but I would never behave so egregiously. I value you too much, Cassandra. I want us to have a good marriage, one of mutual respect."

"And what of love?" she asked quietly.

He did not respond to her, and his silence spoke volumes. After several moments, he said, "Please think on my requests—all of them. For the money, the land, and an heir." And he left her to go to his study. Aggravating man.

———◆———

ILLOGICAL WOMAN. Why couldn't she see the benefits a real marriage with him had to offer her? He brooded at his desk and poured himself some whiskey. She would have all her basic necessities met during her lifetime—food, shelter, and clothing—and all the rights and privileges of being his marchioness. Plus, they could make love any time they chose. He was still hard as granite from their encounter in the hallway. She was so passionate with him, and God, he wanted to tap the unplumbed depths of that passion. Perhaps he didn't exactly love her, but his physical reaction to her was unparalleled. He had never reacted to any of his lovers like he had reacted to Cassandra. Not even Belinda, though the two of them had never been lovers per se, but one thing was certain: he had never had the kind of physical reaction to Belinda that he had had with Cassandra.

The trouble was that Cassandra put too much emphasis on being in love. Why couldn't she just accept their relationship for what it was? He felt something for her. He truly did. Something warm and tender was forming in his heart for her. It was just not love yet. Love was overrated. He had loved Belinda for so long—to no avail—that he didn't know whether or not he could even invest himself enough to love another woman. He didn't know whether or not he could leave himself vulnerable again to the kind of rejection Belinda had so firmly given him until recently. She had hurt him, and he was happy that he no longer thought about the duchess as obsessively as he had done before.

He was also happy to admit that his love for her had diminished so much over the course of the last few weeks that he rarely thought about her. For one thing, he had lost respect for her at Julia's ball when he had overheard her being so petty and critical of Cassandra. And then there had been her visit here to console him, during which he had been thoroughly unmoved by her charms. She had, in fact, mildly repulsed him with her advances. He did not want her, not as he had at one time.

He wanted Cassandra, and the revelation stunned him—boggled his mind really—and left him with an ache he'd never quite known before—not even for Belinda.

He opened a desk drawer for a cheroot, lit it, drew on it deeply, and considered his problem. The crux of the matter was he needed some way to convince Cassandra that a real marriage between them was the best thing for both of them—and not just because he needed her money now that he had inherited all this debt from his brother. A real marriage, one in which they made love to one another, was the best thing for both of them because of the underlying passion between them. He would need to convince her of that. He would need to woo his own wife.

He would start tomorrow with flowers—three dozen fresh red roses, a dozen for every week they been together so far. He would have them interspersed with sprigs of lavender because the two scents combined reminded him of her. Though he could ill afford the expense of such extravagance, he had to do something to show her that he cared about her and wanted a real relationship with her. Then he would visit his jeweler, Rundell and Bridge in Ludgate Hill, sometime tomorrow to commission a special piece of jewelry just for her, perhaps a diamond necklace. It would cost him a small fortune, but he could buy it on credit. And if it would help him to captivate her, it would be worth it.

He would also have to see his mother about the house he had told Cassandra she could use as a haven for battered women. The house was actually the dowager residence not too far from Springwinds Hall, his ancestral home near East Welkin in Essex. His mother rarely used the dowager residence in the country, preferring to stay at her townhouse in London most of the year. He sincerely hoped she would not object to his using the country house for Cassandra's purposes. It would be a waste of resources to build a new home on her land in Durham when they had a ready-made building in Essex.

He crushed out his cheroot and decided to turn in for the evening, so he went upstairs to his room. As he passed Cassandra's chamber, he put his ear to the door but heard nothing. Was she asleep or still awake? He contemplated knocking on her door to see if she were up and amenable to talking some more about their current situation and their future together, but he thought better of the notion. Talking could wait for another day.

He went to sleep thinking of her and dreamed of making love to her. He awoke early, frustrated and hard for her. Would she allow him into her room this morning to partake of his conjugal rights? He sincerely doubted it, so he ordered up a tepid bath, thinking that the cooler water might douse his ardor. The bath worked to some extent but he still couldn't help remembering how responsive she had been to him in the hallway yesterday evening, and the memories of her full, supple breasts in his hands and in his mouth made him ache for her more than was comfortable.

Eventually, he banished her from his mind enough that he could get out of the tub and towel off. His valet helped him shave, and then he dressed with care for the visit to his mother. Before he left for her house, however, he sent a couple of his footmen out to buy the flowers with which he hoped to impress Cassandra.

The ride over to his mother's townhouse in Mayfair was tedious because of the traffic and the fetid smells rising from the streets even at this early time of day. He was dropping in on her before a fashionable hour, but he doubted she would mind, as she was an early riser like himself. She was indeed up and, like him, dressed in mourning garb. The black bombazine made her look so much older than her fifty-five years that he had difficulty hiding his surprise as he joined her in the breakfast room for tea.

"William! How good it is to see you. Won't you join me for breakfast?" said the dowager marchioness as he bussed her on her cheek.

"Thank you, Mother, no. I hope to eat breakfast with Cassandra later this morning, but I will have some tea."

"Very good." She directed a footman to bring an extra cup, after which she served William from the teapot on the table. "Well, what you have been up to? Have you petitioned the House of Lords for your writ of summons yet?"

He took a drink of the tepid beverage. "No, not yet. I've been too busy with other matters to worry about my seat among the Lords just yet."

"You must see to it sometime soon, though, my love. Well, tell me, what brings you by so early?"

"I have a rather large favor to ask of you, Mother," he replied.

CHAPTER 12

Ace of Cups: Intimacy, emotion, joy, falling in love . . .

———◆———

"OH? AND WHAT IS THAT?" She took a sip of tea.

William began by explaining to her how poorly the marquisate was doing for cash, and she gasped when she heard the story, telling him she'd had no idea how badly his brother had been doing with his creditors and his money situation. She explained that she had been so nicely taken care of by her dower since being widowed that she had never had a need to go to David for anything. She had not known that he had sold all of his unentailed property and that he was basically bankrupt.

"What did he do with all his funds?" she asked.

"Poor investments mostly. And then there was his lavish lifestyle." William didn't mention the grittier details of David's existence—his drinking, gambling, and whoring—and let her believe that he had just been foolish with his money. How much more she read into the story was another matter, but she didn't pry too deeply into the issue.

"So, how is it that I can help you?"

"Well, I'm sure you heard the awful stories around two years ago of Cassandra's sister, Lady Abadon. You remember her, don't you? She died as a result of falling down a flight of stairs after her husband beat her."

"Oh, my good lord, yes. That was hideous. Just hideous."

"Well, Cassandra would like to start a refuge for women whose husbands beat them, a place where they may go to seek haven from their tormenters, in honor of her sister."

"Commoners as well as noblewomen?"

"All women."

"What a grand and noble idea," said the dowager marchioness.

"Another part to the story is the fact that Cassandra had stood to gain her entire dowry for her own use when she turned thirty in May, and she had wanted to use some of that money to build a new shelter for the women on her land in Durham." He then went on to explain about how her brother and Sir Lionel Farnsworth had conspired to compromise her and force her to marry Sir Lionel, who was then going to split her dowry with Benthower.

"How devious!"

"Yes, well, I suggested that she pretend to marry me instead in a fake elopement to Scotland, and after a couple of months she would be free to go her own way with her dowry intact. The only thing is that we were actually married for real in Scotland due to their bizarre marriage laws, and she and I are now truly husband and wife."

"That was very gallant of you, dear, but I thought you said you two were in love and that's why you eloped."

He fiddled with the handle of his teacup, unsure how

to explain his earlier deception. Finally, he chose to be simple and direct. "I fibbed, Mother."

"I wondered if there weren't more to that tale than you were telling me. I mean, I wondered why you would marry the one woman in the kingdom who could not stand you." Her eyes twinkled at the irony.

Flabbergasted that she was aware of his and Cassandra's animosity toward one another, he asked, "How did you know?"

She shrugged. "A mother hears things. Plus, I must confess. I do read the scandal sheets now and again. So, are you and she on better terms now?"

"We were—until last night, that is, when I asked her if I could use part of her dowry to pay off David's debt and fix the homes of the tenants."

"How much did you ask to use?"

"Thirty-five thousand pounds. That is how much it would take to make the marquisate whole again."

She gasped. "Oh, for Heaven's sake, William. That is a vast fortune. Can her dowry support it?"

"It could, but it would leave her with very little money to build her shelter *and* fund it properly."

She set her napkin on the table and sat back in her chair. "I see, but I still don't understand how I can help."

"Well, I told Cassandra that rather than build a new building in Durham to house the women who need it, we should use a building that already exists in Essex. That is how you can help, Mother. Could we use the dowager house near East Welkin? At least for a little while, until her land in Durham turns a profit from coal mining and we can afford to build a new house for the women?"

His mother sat silently while she appeared to contemplate his request. It was indeed a huge favor he was asking of her. That, he knew. Though she had not of late gone to the country much, it was important for her to know she had a place to go when she chose to do so, so he said, "You are free to use Springwinds Hall as your home in the country, Mother. We'll have the west wing converted to apartments entirely for your use, if you like."

"That won't be necessary just so long as I have visiting rights. You may use the dowager house for as long as you need it."

William rose and kissed her on her cheek. "Thank you, Mother. I don't know how I can ever repay you."

"No need to do so, son. No need."

He left his mother's house and headed for the jeweler's shop in Ludgate Hill with the goal of having something appropriate designed for Cassandra on his credit there. He walked into the shop and gaped in surprise when he saw Benthower being helped at the counter.

He walked over to the duke and regarded the necklace he was admiring. "Benny! Fancy meeting you here. What brings you to this fine establishment?"

"Ah. Will. Or should I say, 'Kingspointe' now? I imagine I'm here on the same business you are."

"You're buying something for Cassandra?"

"Ha. You always were such a wit." Benthower did not appear amused, however. "No, I am purchasing something for a special lady." He proudly pointed to a necklace with an ostentatious array of large emeralds. "It will complement her eyes."

"I see. I'm sure the duchess will love it, given that her eyes are blue."

The duke scowled. "I'm surprised to see you here buying anything at all, given the woes of your brother's estate." Then he whispered loudly enough for every-one in the shop to hear, "Do they know you are broke here?"

In an equally loud whisper, William responded, "How soon you forget, Benny. Unlike you, I have your sister's dowry to right everything. Do they know *you* are broke here?"

The jeweler raised his eyebrows at that question.

"Not that it is your business, Will, but my credit here is impeccable." The words were said through his teeth, after which he turned back to the jeweler. "Box it up, if you would, my good man. I will take it today."

"Yes, Your Grace," said the jeweler.

"See you later, Will." Benthower parted with a wink and a smirk.

Odd. What had Benny meant with the wink and smirk? Did he have something up his sleeve? Oh, never mind. He banished the duke from his thoughts as he stepped up to the counter to speak to the jeweler. "I would like to commission something special for my wife. Something simple, yet elegant, in diamonds."

The jeweler retrieved his sketchpad and a pencil. "May I suggest a rivière necklace, my lord, to look something like this?" He drew a picture of the design he'd just suggested and showed it to William.

"That, my good sir, would be perfect. About how long will it take? I'd like it as soon as possible."

"A week?"

"That will work fine. I'll see you in a week."

Very happy with the design, he left the shop and headed home, hoping that Cassandra had not yet come down for breakfast because he wanted to see the look on her face when she beheld the roses and lavender that he had sent for. Luckily, he arrived home before she had come downstairs. He instructed his house-keeper to make up a large bouquet of the roses with the lavender sprigs interspersed among them in a vase. When it was completed, the arrangement smelled so much like Cassandra that he had difficulty preventing himself from getting aroused just by sniffing it. He managed, however, to avoid embarrassing himself as he climbed the stairs to her room so that he could deliver the flowers to her personally.

He knocked on her door, and a muted voice came from within. "Who is it?"

"It is I—William."

"I am taking a bath."

"That's fine," he said as he opened her door and walked into the room.

Cassandra squealed in alarm and covered her breasts with her arms. "William, what on earth?"

"You are excused," he said to her abigail, who stood next to the tub holding a towel waiting for Cassandra. The maid left posthaste.

William, meanwhile, ogled his wife, who had crouched down in the tub so that only her head was above the rose and lavender scented water. He set the bouquet of flowers on her dresser. "I wanted to give these to you personally. I got you some roses and lavender because they remind me of you. There are three dozen roses, one dozen for each week we've been together now."

Rather than yell at him like he thought she might do because he had invaded her privacy, she appeared dumbfounded for a moment. "You have kept track of how long we have been together?"

"Practically to the minute. It has been a rather memorable three weeks, wouldn't you say? Plus, you were so kind with the consoling notes after my brother died that I wanted to repay you in some small way."

"That really wasn't necessary, William, though they are beautiful."

"Are you done with your bath?"

"Yes, but—"

"Why don't you let me help you out of the tub?"

"But—but I am naked."

"Well, obviously that. I have seen you naked before, or don't you remember? After you saw the rat in the stables in Nether Wrigsby? Then there is the fact that we have made love, you know."

"Had coition. Yes, but—"

"Come, now. I won't look at you, if you are feeling bashful. I'll just hold the towel up so that you can step into it." He unfolded the bath sheet for her to wrap herself in, and then he closed his eyes.

The water sloshed around as she stood in the tub, and he heard rather than saw her step out of the water and onto the oilcloth beneath it. She took the large towel from him, and he opened his eyes as she wrapped herself in the cloth. It took all his might to not to grab her and take her over to the bed and ravish her, right then and there.

Cassandra, meanwhile, padded over to the dresser to smell the flowers. "They smell divine."

"As do you."

"Thank you for them, William. Although I see what you are doing, you know."

"Oh? And what is that?" He tried to sound innocent.

"You are trying to win me over with these flowers to your notion of us as a true married couple."

"Am I so transparent?"

"Yes, you are. And you know you are." She paused

while he smiled. "I have thought about all you said yesterday evening. I was up most of the night thinking about it, in fact. I have decided that I will perhaps let you use my land in Durham for mining. However, I would first like to see the house in Essex you have in mind to use for the women's refuge."

"Excellent. We'll leave for Essex next week. We have to move our things from here to Kingspointe House first, but that should take only a few days, and then we'll be on our way." He stepped closer to her as though he meant to take her in his arms, but she moved away from him.

"I still have not decided about the other things yet. The money and the heir, that is. I will need some more time to consider those issues."

He paused a moment pondering whether or not he would argue the points with her now but decided against it. "As you wish, my dear. I am glad about the land in Durham, however. You won't regret it, and I think you'll like the house in Essex."

"Yes, well, I hope so. . . . Will you excuse me while I get dressed now?"

"Must you so soon? We could . . . make love . . ."

"*No.*"

"Oh, very well, then," he said as if she had spoiled his fun. "I will send your maid back in to assist you. Come down for breakfast when you are ready."

———◆———

CASSANDRA WATCHED him as he left her room, with an aching in her heart at his departure. She wanted him so very badly but knew he was only interested in her money—which, for all intents and purposes, was his to use as he pleased anyway. She supposed she should feel some gratitude that he wasn't looting her funds indiscriminately and was at least seeking her permission for using them, but in the end, she knew how it would all turn out. She would capitulate and let him use her money to pay his brother's debts and to fix his tenants' homes, and she would bear him his heir. There seemed no sense in fighting the inevitable, so she would eventually give in to his requests. She would not, however, tell him her decision right away. For one thing, she did want to see the house in Essex that he said she could use to shelter the women to make certain it was fit for that purpose. For another thing, she wasn't ready to act his wife just yet—not when he didn't love her. Maybe given some time, the pain of her unrequited love would not be so intense, but for today, it was too much to bear.

She joined him for breakfast and was half-way through her eggs when the butler announced that Benthower had stopped by to see her. Never one to stand on ceremony and wait politely in the entry hall, her brother burst into the breakfast room and stood by the table waiting for her to acknowledge him.

"Benny. To what do we owe this . . . uh, pleasure?" said William in complete surprise.

"Well, Kingspointe, I have come to see my sister."

"Pull up a chair and join us for breakfast, why don't you?"

"Alone. I prefer to see Cassandra alone. If you don't mind."

"I believe that's up to Cassandra."

She narrowed her eyes at her brother, until he finally spoke. "It's important, Cass."

After some contemplation of the request, she acquiesced. "I will see you, Benthower, but only for a few minutes." She looked back at William whose face registered irritation at her decision. Nonetheless, she led Benthower out of the breakfast room and into the hallway.

"Can we talk some place a little more private?" he asked.

Warily, she led him into the drawing room. "What is it, Michael?"

"Cass," he began, "I know your marriage is a sham. Don't try to deny it. I've had someone investigating your 'wedding' for me in Scotland, and he has it on good authority that you never meant to be married."

Her gut sank. "Oh, really? Whose authority?"

"He talked to the blacksmith in Gretna Green who said that a couple resembling you and Will came to him for a blank marriage certificate on the thirtieth of March. The blacksmith told my man that the lady in question had run away from a nasty situation involving her brother who was forcing her to marry another gent. My man said the blacksmith told him that the man she was with was willing to pretend to marry the woman in order to fool her brother. They didn't want a real wedding, just a certificate from the blacksmith, which he gave them but which he wouldn't sign in good conscience."

He paused. She guessed he wanted to see whether she would admit to anything he had told her so far, but she remained silent. "The blacksmith said this couple then took the certificate with them up the street to a pub, where they were going to try to find some locals to sign it for authenticity's sake. Then my man talked with the barkeep at this pub who said that on March the thirtieth, a couple resembling you and Will came into the establishment and basically pledged their troths to one another in front of a crowd of men who were there for lunch. The barkeep said he and two of the witnesses signed the blank certificate and that he made a notation of the event in a register he keeps of weddings he performs. He showed my man the entry with your names in it. The bartender said that at no time did the couple say that they were marrying only under pretense, or he'd not have performed the wedding."

Cassandra moved to the window and looked out upon the street below. "So, what is your point?"

"Only that I know you did not really intend to marry that jackass in the other room, and I know that, by Scottish law—and thereby English law—you are legally wed to him, unfortunately. I thought that if you wanted to be legally unwed to him, perhaps I could help you."

"I don't see how. We have no grounds for annulment."

"Ordinarily, I'd say you are right and that your petition for annulment would be doomed in the ecclesiastical courts. But I've approached the bishop in Raventon who said he would be willing to rush this through his chancellor at the consistory court for that diocese, and my own personal physician in London is willing to help us out as well."

"Us?"

"Yes. You and me. I feel we are in this together. To some extent, you would not be in the situation you are in if it were not for me."

"To *some* extent?" Her eyes widened, and she laughed, despite the fact that her temper escalated. "I'd say you are wholly responsible for my situation."

"Let's not fight about it, Cass. Let me tell you how I

can help you."

"Or is it how I can help *you*? I know you, Michael. You do not do something for nothing. What is the catch?"

He pursed his lips at her assessment of his motives. "Well, the thing is that it will cost you. The bishop requires a certain fee for his assistance granting an annulment and rushing it through the consistory court with as little hassle as possible. And the doctor also requires a certain fee for his services in diagnosing you with a mental defect at the time of the marriage."

"And I bet you require a 'certain fee,' as well. Am I right? How much are we actually talking?"

"Five thousand apiece for the doctor and the bishop. The doctor will declare you insane and give testimony to that fact. You will need a proctor to represent you in the consistory court, and we can pay enough witnesses to aver that you were not in your right mind when you married Kingspointe. That should be another five thousand pounds at most. Meanwhile, the bishop will rush an annulment through the court based on the witnesses' depositions. Then you give me fifteen thousand for helping you out and keep the other twenty thousand plus your land in Durham."

"I would not have to go to Bedlam or some such similar asylum?"

"No. I would see to it that you are remanded into my personal care."

She shuddered. "I can think of nothing worse than to be remanded into your personal care."

"Fine. You can retire quietly to Durham where no one will bother you."

"I don't know, Benthower. Thirty thousand pounds is a huge sum."

"It is. But annulments do not come cheap, especially if one wants to influence the court in one's favor."

"What about William? He will fight this now that he needs my money. He will appeal the decision of the consistory court. Besides, he has legal rights to and control of my dowry right now. I do not have access to my money or the ability to use it as I see fit."

"He will have to return your dowry once the annulment goes through, and the bishop and the doctor are both willing to do this on my promise that you will pay them when you have access to your money. Has he spent any of it yet on the debt he inherited?"

She shook her head. "No. He wants to use the funds to pay the creditors, and he wants the land in Durham for coal mining, but he's waiting for my permission before he proceeds."

"How very noble, but that works to our advantage."

"I don't know about this . . ."

"Surely you want to be free of him, don't you?"

"Well, yes, but I . . ." Her voice trailed off as she thought better of what she was going to say.

"Don't tell me you've fallen in love with him."

She turned away from him to look out the window once more so that he would not see her expression. Benthower, however, approached her at the window and turned her so that she had to look into his eyes. "Because he does not love you, Cassandra. Believe me when I say that, and make no mistake about the fact. He will fight you on the annulment because he needs your money, but that is the only reason. I say again: he does not love you."

She swiped at a tear that threatened to spill over her lashes. "I know he doesn't. I know."

"Then, why are you hesitating?"

"Because . . . oh, I don't know! For one thing, I do not get to keep all my money with your plan."

"You don't get any of it if you stay with him."

"Oh, just give me time to think about it, will you?"

"Yes. But don't take too long. I don't know how long the bishop and the doctor are willing to wait. And for God's sake, Cassandra, I hate to be indelicate, but do not have conjugal relations with him."

"Michael! Really!"

"Do not let yourself get with child is all I am warning you about, or the bishop will not agree to do the annulment—even for the money."

"I understand."

Benthower left her dazed. Only minutes before his visit, she had been doomed to marriage with a man for whom she suffered an unrequited love. Now, she had the opportunity to get that marriage annulled, but shockingly even to her, she was hesitant to do so, precisely because of how much she loved the man she was married to. Perhaps she really was insane. Here she should be shouting with joy that her brother had found a way out for her—a way which left her with five thousand more pounds than what William offered her after he paid off his brother's debts and made the necessary repairs to his tenants' homes. Yet, here she was balking at Benthower's plan because of her silly emotions.

Perhaps if she just went back to bed, she could forget the entire problem, but she rejoined William in the breakfast room. He looked up from perusing the newspaper as she entered. "So, what did the duke want?"

She bit her lip in hesitation. "He just wanted to see how I was doing is all."

"*Really*?" he drawled. "The great Benthower deigned

to check in on his little sister, did he?"

"Yes. He was concerned for me after hearing about your brother's financial woes."

"You mean he was concerned for your dowry, don't you?"

"Yes, that's pretty much it." She didn't exactly lie, but she didn't tell him the whole truth about the annulment offer, fearing that if she told him anything, he would set in motion steps to stop it. And since she wasn't certain she didn't want the annulment, she left her options open.

She picked at her eggs and nibbled on her toast, but in the end, she excused herself to go lie down, telling William she had a headache. Though he was quite concerned for her, he saw her to her room and kissed her on her cheek as she left him. Considerate man.

———◆———

ARTFUL WOMAN. She had concocted a headache to avoid discussion of Benthower's call, but the visit had obviously depressed her spirits. Benthower was up to something devious. What nefarious plot did he have in mind this time? If Cassandra wasn't going to tell him what was going on, he would have to use other means to find out. Perhaps he would write to his friend Alfred Baker, a Bow Street Runner who sidelined as an investigator into private affairs for the *ton*. Baker could find out what underhanded tricks the duke was up to, if anybody could.

He went to his study and penned a quick letter to Baker asking him to snoop into Benthower's business and see what scheme he was cooking up with respect to Cassandra.

In the meantime, he set his household staff to packing items to be moved to Kingspointe House and had his and Cassandra's personal items moved to the house the following Monday. They settled into their new residence quite comfortably, but Cassandra, meanwhile, continued to remain silent about the real purpose of Benthower's visit. On Wednesday, William's friend Baker stopped by Kingspointe House with a report about Benthower's activities.

"He wants to help your wife obtain an annulment on the grounds that she wasn't in her right mind when she married you. He means to pay a bishop and a doctor with funds from your wife's dowry to rush the annulment through the courts, and he wants to split the remainder of the funds with her. He then intends to set her up for the rest of her life on her own property in Durham," said Baker.

William folded his arms in disgust as he paced his study. "Bloody bastard. Why can't he mind his own bloody business?"

After Baker left, William debated asking Cassandra about her brother's annulment scheme, but in the end, he opted to wait to see what happened between them on their trip to Essex. Obviously, she was hesitant about going along with Benthower's machinations, or she would have packed her things already and moved back in with him. Perhaps he could woo her to his side yet, while they were on their trip.

They departed for Essex very early on Friday morning and had about a day's ride ahead of them to reach their first destination, which was Wyndemere Manor, the dowager residence near East Welkin. They made good time and actually arrived at the property an hour ahead of schedule. William explained a little bit of the history of the house, how it had been his grandmother's and now belonged to his mother. They turned into the long drive up to the main house. Apple trees in full bloom lined the drive, obscuring the sight of the house, but eventually the Jacobean building came into view.

Cassandra watched out the window, her excitement palpable, which delighted him. "Oh, William, it's beautiful."

He agreed, but then he had always thought the house beautiful and had fond memories of it from when he would visit his grandmother as a boy. "I'm glad it pleases you."

"May we go in?"

"Of course. There's only a skeletal staff on duty at the moment, so we won't get much of a grand tour, but I think you will like the interior as well. The second and third floors have eight well-appointed chambers each, which could house several women if you put two to a room. And then, of course, a few of the rooms on the first floor could also be converted into bedrooms to house even more."

The coach halted at the front entrance, where he descended first and then helped her down. He knocked on the door to see whether the housekeeper in residence was near the entry, but after a few moments, it became apparent that she was not at hand. He let both Cassandra and himself in through the front door with keys he had gotten from his mother.

"I don't think anyone's around." He closed the door behind him and glanced about the entry. "Follow me this way." He led her first down a corridor to the left of the entry hall and showed her several rooms, including the library and a drawing room, and then he led her down to the opposite end of the corridor where he showed her several more rooms, including the dining room, a salon, and a study. He then took her back down the corridor to the grand staircase and led her upstairs, showing her several of the bedrooms there.

"The third floor is basically the same as the second," he said to her after they had looked into the last room.

"Oh, William, it's all so lovely. I don't know what to say about it."

"Say you'll use it for your shelter."

"But what about your mother? What has she to say about my using her house as a refuge for battered women?"

"She supports your efforts and gives you full permission to use the house as you see fit."

She peered down at her hands, uncertainty clouding her features. "I don't know, William. I don't know how I could ever repay her or you."

"Repayment isn't necessary. Just say you will use it for your refuge."

She seemed to think on the matter a moment, chewing on the corner of her mouth. "I-I guess so."

"Good. It is settled then. How soon do you want to begin moving women into Wyndemere Manor?"

"As soon as we can, I suppose. I will write to Julia tonight and ask her how we should proceed. We have underground contacts in London who help us secret the women out of their situations, but Julia has been the one who has made the arrangements with our contacts."

"I'm certain this house will work out perfectly for your mission."

"Oh, thank you, William. Thank you so much." She surprised him by approaching him and embracing him tightly. He hugged her in return, and as they broke apart, he looked deep into her eyes thinking he might kiss her, but she turned away from him before he could bring his lips to hers.

Frustrated with a lost opportunity, he followed her silently down the hallway and down the stairs into the entry hall once again. They reached the entrance without speaking to one another, and he led her outside, locking the door behind him. He helped her up into the carriage and then took the opportunity to retrieve something from one of the bags he had brought with him, which was tied to the top of the coach. After he had the item, he climbed into the vehicle and sat across from her. He rapped on the ceiling to indicate to the coachman that he should proceed, and they were off to Springwinds Hall, which was about a forty-five minute drive from Wyndemere Manor.

After they had been on the road for about five minutes, he took out the item he had pulled out of his bag and presented it to Cassandra. It was a medium-sized jeweler's box, and she flushed when she saw it.

"I got you a little something to celebrate our first month together, Cassandra. Open it." He handed the box to her and leaned forward with his arms on his knees while she took it.

She removed the top and gasped when she saw the diamond necklace that he had picked up from the jeweler yesterday. She pulled it out of the box, disbelief apparent in her wide eyes. "Oh, William, it's so beautiful. I don't know what to say."

"Say you like it."

"Like it? I love it. Thank you. Thank you ever so much."

"Here," he said as he came over to sit beside her on her bench and took the necklace from her. "Let's put it on you." She turned so that her back was to him, and he undid the clasp and then laid the necklace gently around her neck. He closed the clasp in back and leaned forward to whisper softly in her ear, "It looks divine, even from behind." And he feathered light kisses along the nape of her neck and bare shoulder until gooseflesh appeared on her skin. He took in her heavenly scent of lavender and roses and was hard as stone for her.

"William, I don't—" she whispered to him as he nibbled her ear.

"Turn around a little. I want to see how it looks from the front," he said, not giving her the chance to finish her sentence.

She turned in the seat so that he could see the necklace as it graced her alabaster skin. He raised his eyes to look into hers. "It's lovely." Then he put his arm around her shoulders and gently brought his lips to hers. He kissed them softly and took her lower lip between his teeth and nipped it as he continued to look into her eyes. He saw desire in her gaze, and he let go of her lower lip to run his tongue along the seam of her mouth. She parted her lips for him, allowing his tongue to slide over hers. Though she closed her eyes as he kissed her, he kept his open, watching her reaction to his advances. He broke from the kiss briefly to close the curtains on the carriage so that they had some privacy. Then he returned his mouth to hers.

He kissed her thus for several minutes while he touched a breast, and she moaned as the nipple peaked beneath his fingers through the fabric of her shift and dress. He ran his fingers over her other breast, causing it to peak as well. Then he pulled the short sleeve of her dress down her shoulder a bit and slipped her bodice and undergarments off her breasts, and when he had them bared, he cupped first one full breast and then the other in his hand, running his thumb over one and then the other nipple. She moaned at his touch, and he dipped his head and laved a nipple with his tongue, sliding it around the perimeter until she was groaning with pleasure once again. His cock throbbed when he heard her sounds, and he took the nipple in his mouth and suckled it. He did the same thing for the other breast, which caused her to squirm in her seat—probably to relieve some of the throbbing she felt herself.

He pulled up the skirt of her dress and slipped his hand beneath the hem of her petticoat, sliding it up from the stocking tied just above her knee to her inner thigh. She leaned back against him and spread her legs for him to give him greater access to her, and he found her maidenhair already damp with moisture. He slid his fingers through the mound of curls to her tender inner flesh, where he parted her lips, finding her warm and slick for him. He stroked her swollen clitoris and circled it with his thumb several times as he eased his middle finger into her sheath. He sensed she was about ready to fly apart from how wet she was, as he slid a second finger into her. He moved them in and out of her, still circling her clit with his thumb until she moaned loudly and came apart in his embrace, her flesh quivering all around his two fingers.

He kissed her tenderly until she came down from her high, and then he stared into her beautiful, sated celadon eyes. The love in them was so obvious it was palpable in the air between them. It astounded him, even as it humbled him. And it did something to his own heart until he felt it would burst with some kind of emotion, one he couldn't name. What was this emotion he felt for her? He gazed at her in astonishment and awe. Could it be love?

CHAPTER 13

Two of Swords: Stalemate, blocked emotions, reaching an impasse, denial of feelings . . .

———◆———

WILLIAM WAS ASTONISHED BY THIS nascent feeling he had for Cassandra because it was unlike anything he had ever felt before. It was deeper than anything he'd ever had with any of his other lovers and even more profound than his so-called love for Belinda. In a search of his heart right then, he found that his feelings for Belinda had waned to such a degree that they were non-existent. And whatever it was that he had felt for her in the past paled in comparison to what he felt right now for Cassandra. He longed to tell her how he felt, but the emotions were too new, too raw for him to share with her just yet.

Her breathing returned to its normal state, though the flush of arousal was still evident over her breasts and up to her glowing face. He could have made her come apart again if he'd kept up his stimulation of her tender flesh, but she moved so that he had no choice but to take his hand away from her. She leaned forward and kissed him, and the love in her heart was once again evident in her gaze. She boldly thrust her tongue into his mouth and drew his tongue into her own mouth in a kiss that had him so hard that he feared he might spill his seed in his trousers.

Then she broke from the kiss and looked into his eyes seductively as she untied his cravat. After loosening it, she kissed the angle of his jaw and ran her lips over his bare throat, eliciting a deep groan from him. She opened his shirt and kissed him on his chest, tasting his nipples, driving him insane. Then she took a pillow from the bench and placed it on the floor of the carriage. Kneeling before him, she ran her hands down his chest and abdomen to the placket of his pants and began unbuttoning the flap to release his burgeoning cock. Unsure exactly what she meant to do, he held his breath in heated anticipation as she worked to free him. Once she had him exposed, she held him in one hand as she ran the fingers of her other hand down his length. She looked at his erection intently, as if examining it, studying it. Seeing her in that position was so erotic that, once again, he nearly spilled his seed.

She squeezed and stroked him until he thought he couldn't take it anymore and then—oh, God—she kissed the tip. He was in ecstasy as she opened her mouth and licked the head around its perimeter several times. She took the crown into her lush lips and looked up at him as though she were tasting sweet nectar, and as she began to suck him, his eyes rolled back into their sockets and he lolled his head against the pillows at the back of the seat. After several minutes of reveling in this attention to his penis, he opened his eyes. Through narrow slits, he watched as she licked up his shaft, then down it, and then tongued her way back up to the tip again where she opened for him once more and took as much of his length as she could manage into her mouth and sucked on him.

Where, oh where, had she learned to do this? Vaguely, he made a mental note to ask her where she had gotten her instruction as she repeated her ministrations until he was going to explode if she did not stop. He wanted to feel his cock inside her tight sheath, however, before he finished, so he reached down and pulled her up until she sat astride him on his lap, her skirts up around her waist.

She squealed when he lifted her up until she straddled him, and he thrust his cock into her. She was wet and oh, so tight, and when he was fully sheathed, he held her hips steady as he pulled out of her and then thrust into her once again. He withdrew and then thrust into her several more times, until she took control of the joining and began to ride him up and down his shaft. Again, he wondered where she had learned to do this, and he took her head in both his hands as she rode him. Hair pins flew from her coif releasing her locks in waves of dark tresses as he kissed her hungrily.

He continued kissing her but put one of his hands between them so that he could apply pressure to her clitoris as she rode him. She moaned with pleasure into his mouth and flew apart, her flesh clutching him and bringing him to his own furious release. He pumped and pumped his seed into her until there was nothing left in him.

When his orgasm was over, he panted heavily as he broke from their kiss, and he slouched in utter exhaustion against the squabs trying to catch his breath as he slid out of her. He gazed at her, her hair all disheveled around her shoulders, her celadon eyes sparkling and her face lustrous from her recent physical release, and he realized—not for the first time—how beautiful—

gorgeous really—she was. Once again, her love for him shone in her expression, and his heart swelled with that emotion he'd felt earlier. He nearly told her he loved her right then, but it was still too early, too soon, too new for him to be able to articulate his feelings. He was too afraid of the rush of sentiment he had for her now. It scared him, this love that had been building over the past few weeks for her. He needed time to come to terms with it himself, before he said anything to her about it.

So, instead of telling her how he felt, he ran his hand through her wild locks and said, "My God, you're beautiful."

———————

CASSANDRA WAS panting from their untamed coition, glowing from their love-making, if she wanted to think of it in those terms, until his words stabbed her like a knife to her heart.

"You're so beautiful," he said again.

Beautiful. The word echoing around in her head sliced her to her soul.

Her world came screeching to a halt. How dare he call her beautiful? He would never call *her* beautiful, not when he thought she was homely. That could only mean one thing: he had to have been thinking of Belinda again while they had made love. Pain slammed into her breast once more, and she slapped him across his face as hard as she could.

"What's the matter?" he asked in obvious pain from the slap, his skin turning red with the blow as she got off his lap.

"You were thinking of her again! You were thinking of Belinda." Unwelcome tears formed in her eyes.

"No, I wasn't. I was thinking only of you."

She gritted her teeth and said through them, "No, you were not. You were thinking of her when you said 'you're beautiful.'"

He had once again just made love to Belinda in spirit, while taking her body in reality, and the pain of it was so severe that she gasped for air, trying desperately to avoid sobbing. She righted her clothing until she was no longer exposed to him, and then bent down to the floor searching for her hair pins. She found several at his feet.

"Cassandra, honestly—I was thinking of you and how beautiful you look." His attempt to soothe her with words only made her angrier.

"Stop saying that!" She shook her head in a furious frenzy as she sat across from him on the other bench and began putting her hair up with the few pins that she could find. "I know you are lying." She veritably screamed the words at him.

He righted his own clothing, closing the placket on his trouser and buttoning his shirt and waistcoat. As he tied his cravat, he looked at her in thorough exasperation, as though he couldn't believe she was this upset over something so minor. Minor to him, maybe. But not minor to her.

She closed her eyes, and she was back in the stables almost fifteen years ago overhearing him telling Benthower how ugly he thought she was. Homely, he had called her then. Not at all attractive, he had said of her. And here she was to believe that he thought her beautiful now? Oh, no, he did not think her beautiful now. He had been thinking of his beloved Belinda once again as he made love to Cassandra's body.

They pulled up into the quadrangle of Springwinds

Hall just then. Neither had noticed their surroundings until they felt the coach come to a halt. She straightened out her dress and pinned her hair as best as she could, but before William could get to the door, she opened it and climbed carefully out of the carriage, not allowing him to assist her in any way. She stood on the stone driveway and gazed at the house to take her mind off what had just happened in the coach.

Like Wyndemere Manor, Springwinds Hall was a Jacobean estate. Unlike Wyndemere, it was shaped like an "H," with a huge courtyard in the front of it where they had parked. Vast lawns stretched on either side of the long driveway down to the main road, while the front entrance loomed before her. Under other circumstances, she might have found the front elevation of the house to be lovely. She was not inclined at this moment, however, to regard anything to do with William as lovely.

Servants in red livery filed out of the main entry to greet their new lord and lady, who both appeared, for all intents and purposes, like they'd just been in a row.

"Lord Kingspointe," said the butler as he bowed before William.

The housekeeper curtsied but appeared too tongue-tied to give a verbal greeting.

"Wilkes, Mrs. Shaw, everyone, I'd like to introduce my wife, Lady Kingspointe, to you all." To a person, they all bowed or curtsied before her, their new marchioness, and Cassandra was overwhelmed by the introductions. She heard more names than she could commit to memory. Her forbearance throughout the entire ordeal was tenuous, given the turmoil inside her at the moment.

After the servants had all dispersed, William led her

into the grand entry hall and said in a low voice, "We need to talk."

"No, we do not," she whispered back to him. "I need my room and a bath, if it would be at all possible."

He ordered a bath for her and took her upstairs to a suite of rooms reserved for the master and mistress of the manor. He pointed out several paintings of ancestors as they walked to their rooms, but she didn't have the slightest notion—or care, for that matter—about what he'd said when he was finished. He led her into the marchioness's room and tried to engage her in conversation once again.

"Cassandra," he began, "you're being unreasonable. I don't know why you are so upset. I was not thinking of Belinda while we made love."

"Had coition," she snarled through her teeth. "We did not make love just now—or at any time in the past. We merely had coition. I'll thank you to remember that."

"Fine. I can see there's no sense in trying to talk to you about it when you are in high dudgeon over it. I will see that your things are brought up, and I will leave you alone."

"At last."

"Do you care to join me for dinner?"

"Not in the least."

"Fine, again. I will have a meal sent up for you when you are finished with your bath." He turned to leave, but as he got to the door, he spun around to her and pleaded with her. "Cassandra, can't we *please* talk about what happened? I don't even know what I did."

"Not right now, we can't." She tried for composure as she spoke, but inside, she was shaking with pain.

He left her with obvious reluctance, but when he

was gone, she broke down and started crying—like she had done when she was fifteen years old. She lay on top of the counterpane on the bed and sobbed at her foolish heart, foolish for believing for a moment that William had been making love to her and not Belinda. She should never have let her guard down in the carriage when he had presented her with the diamond necklace. She had been so overwhelmed with the gift, however, that she had not been thinking straight when he began to kiss her and touch her, and she had let him go too far. Then, in the afterglow of her release, she had felt so much love for him—such untamed passion—that she had knelt before him as though he were a king and taken him in her mouth. And then, worse, she had taken him in her body, opening herself up to the possibility of becoming pregnant—if she weren't already pregnant.

She ruminated over the fact that it might be too late for her to worry about avoiding pregnancy because she was over two weeks late for her courses. She wouldn't stress herself about it yet, though, because she had been late for her courses before—sometimes up to a month late, but if she were with child, she would not be able to get the annulment. And she desperately wanted that annulment now. She could not stand to stay with William when he loved Belinda as he apparently did. As she lay on the strange bed in the strange room in the strange house, her heart ached so much that she thought she would die from the agony. This would not do. She would head back to London tomorrow to tell Benthower to go forth with the annulment. If she were pregnant, she would worry about what to do about it later. Benthower most likely needed money so desperately that he would help her conceal a pregnancy and sneak her out of the country to give birth.

With the decision made to proceed with the annulment, Cassandra's spirits improved so that by the time her bath was brought to her, she was most relieved. Findley, who'd arrived earlier in the day with a couple of other servants from Kingspointe House, assisted her in getting out of her clothes—and the necklace—and unpinning her hair and then left her alone to soak in the tub. She sank down into the scented water and tried to forget about everything that had happened today, but when she closed her eyes, all she saw were images of William's face when he told her—or rather, Belinda—how beautiful she looked after they'd had coition. She had seen the love in his eyes, for it had obviously been love—the love he had for Belinda—at that moment, and it had been agonizing to watch.

She tried to put him out of her mind, but she kept coming back to the fact that she loved him as none other, while he loved the duchess. If only she could make him love her, how different things would be. They could be a real couple with a real marriage. She would have his children, and they would grow old together—in love with one another. Tears leaked out of her eyes at how wonderful it could be. The reality was, however, that he would never love her—not the way he loved Belinda—so why think about what might have been? Instead, she distracted herself by plotting out her course of action for tomorrow morning. She would rise before sunup and have the carriage readied for her without telling him about her plans. He would try to prevent her from going, naturally, if he knew, but with any luck, she would be gone by the time he awoke, and there would be nothing he could do to stop her. Vexing man.

———◆———

PROVOKING WOMAN. Thoughts of her—mostly carnal thoughts, thoughts of her hands and mouth all over him—had kept him awake all night, and just as he had finally managed to fall asleep in the early pre-dawn hours, a noise from her room woke him. He put the sound out of his mind and returned to slumber, but there it was again. It sounded like her door creaking slowly shut and light footsteps in the hallway. Was she up at this ungodly hour? If so, what was she doing?

He climbed down from the large bed in the master suite, threw on his banyan, and padded over the thick carpet to his door, which he opened just slightly so that he could peek out of it. Nothing was there in the corridor. Wait. Were those footsteps once again? This time they headed away from him down the hallway toward the stairs, so he quietly left his room and followed the sound of the footfalls. He turned a corner as Cassandra tiptoed slowly to the stairs. Not wanting to startle her, he hid behind a large statue on the landing and waited until she made it all the way down the staircase. When she disappeared around another corner at the bottom of the steps, he quickly but stealthily made his way down the stairs and followed her around the corner.

She tiptoed farther toward the open hall, and he quickly but softly followed her, remaining undetected until she reached the grand entry. She whispered something to her abigail and then headed out the door into the first blush of dawn. A couple of footmen carried her portmanteaux out the doorway behind her, and he quickly strode over to the door as they loaded her luggage onto his waiting carriage. He leaned against the doorway as one of the footmen assisted Cassandra toward the coach. Her slipper was poised to step onto the first rung of the carriage's stairs when William spoke.

"Going somewhere?"

Everyone started at his voice, and she visibly jumped, almost out of her dress. "William! What are you doing there?"

"Why, I could ask the same thing of you, Cassandra."

"I'm just . . . That is, I was just . . ."

"Yes?"

She frowned at him and threw her head back in defiance. "I'm headed back to London, if you must know."

"Are you?"

"Yes. And there's not a thing you can do to stop me."

"Isn't there?" Without waiting for an answer, he walked over to her, grabbed her by the waist, and swung her away from the carriage steps. He set her on the drive and peered down into her large celadon eyes. "You're going nowhere."

"How dare you?" Indignation flashed across her countenance. "You are not my master."

"Indeed I am. I am your husband and your master, and I say you are not going anywhere." Then he turned to the coachman and said, "Sullivan, take this vehicle back to the coach house and do not let my wife borrow it again without my permission. She is not to go anywhere unless I approve it. Is that understood, everyone?"

Sullivan and the footmen all nodded their understanding, as the footmen took her things from the carriage and marched back into the house with them. The coachman then drove the carriage away from the main entry.

Findley, meanwhile, looked to Cassandra for direction. "Go on inside," she said to her maid reluctantly. To William, however, she remained defiant. "You cannot hold me here as though I am some sort of prisoner."

"You're not a prisoner. You have but to ask me for permission before you go anywhere."

"What is that but a prisoner?"

"Be reasonable, Cassandra. It is my carriage. It is only common courtesy to ask me if you may take it. I need to know when someone plans to use it in case I also have need for it so that other arrangements can be made."

"Very well. May I take your carriage to London?"

"What for? We just got here."

"That is none of your business."

"I beg your pardon, but you are my wife. It is absolutely my business."

She crossed her arms and stomped her foot. "Oh, you are insufferable. I don't like this aspect of you, William."

"Just tell me what you need to go to London for, and then I'll decide whether you can use the coach."

"I have business there."

"Can't it wait until I have finished my business here? I'll only be a few days."

"No, it can't wait. It's urgent."

"Perhaps if you told me what this business was, I'd be more inclined to let you go." He approached her and touched her cheek, and she jerked her head away from him.

"It's very personal business and doesn't concern you."

"I've already told you that if it concerns you, it concerns me. Now, if you're not going to tell me what you're going to London for, then you may not use my coach."

"Fine." She glowered at him. "I'll stay, but I won't like it." She turned to go back into the house.

"Cassandra, wait." Exasperation overwhelmed him, and he stepped forward to touch her once again, but she moved hastily away from him. "Would you mind telling me what I have done that has upset you so much that you wish to leave? I mean, what happened between us in the coach that made you so angry with me? What did I do to upset you? I thought we had shared something special after I gave you the necklace."

She turned back toward him and narrowed her eyes, gazing upon him distrustfully. "So did I. But . . ."

After a moment, he encouraged her to continue. "But what?"

She looked down at her hands, which clasped her reticule as if it would fly away from her if she didn't hold onto it tightly enough. Her voice was steady, calm, and quiet. "You were thinking of her again."

"No, I wasn't. I was thinking only of you."

"No, you weren't. You were thinking of her."

"What makes you think so?"

"You called her 'beautiful.'"

"I called *you* beautiful because you *are* beautiful." He stepped forward to take her in his arms, but she backed away from him once again as tears began to fill her eyes.

"No. *You* do not think so, at least."

"I do, too. I think you are gorgeous. The most beautiful woman I've ever beheld, in fact."

"Stop it!" She dropped her reticule, and her hands flew to her ears where she held them so she could not hear him. "Stop saying that. You do not mean it. You cannot mean it."

"Why do you say that?" he implored her, his hands open wide in front of him in frustration.

"Because you said I was ugly."

"When did I *ever* say you were ugly?"

Tears fell from her lashes as she looked down and seemed to recall something very painful. "Nearly fifteen years ago . . . in the stables . . . You told Benthower you thought I was . . .," she paused and continued in a whisper, "*homely*." Her bottom lip trembled but she did not cry.

Vaguely, a memory seeped into his consciousness of a conversation he'd had with Benthower years ago. He saw the two of them in the stables at Benthower Castle, discussing Belinda. He had told Benthower that he thought Miss Hollowsley was the most beautiful creature on the earth and that he loved her, which was the beginning of the end of his friendship with the duke. In that same conversation, Benthower had suggested William and his sister Cassandra would someday make a match, and William had scoffed, calling Cassandra . . . homely. Oh God, had he really said she was homely? What an arse. He covered his face with his hands in shame at the memory. He had said she was big and gawky and homely, and he had also disparaged her nose, her beautiful, classical nose. He'd also complained of her spots, which she'd clearly outgrown because her complexion was now smooth and creamy.

"Cassandra, I-I . . ." He attempted words, but what could he say? Nothing seemed adequate.

"You remember it, don't you?" she whispered.

"You were there?"

"In the hayloft . . . listening to you both. It was wrong of me, I know, but I adored you so much at the time that I followed you nearly everywhere you went with

Benthower. Until you called me homely."

"Cassandra, I was an arse. A stupid, youthful, arrogant, shallow, and most of all, insensitive arse."

"Yes, you were. You were all of those things, but it doesn't change the fact that you don't think I'm attractive."

"That is not so. I think you are beautiful. Please . . . please, forgive me."

"It hurts too much. Like a sword through my heart. I can never forgive you."

"Never? Not even if I—"

"Not even if you let me go back to London," she finished for him.

What he had nearly told her at that moment, however, was that he loved her, that he had been falling in love with her by degrees since they had married. He doubted she would believe him, however, especially if she didn't believe he thought she was beautiful. Not wanting to upset her further, he kept the news that he loved her to himself. "Could we start over and try to build a relationship between us?"

"No. You're not interested in a relationship with me. You just want me for my money. Don't think I haven't figured that much out. Why, all of a sudden, would you give me a diamond necklace and tell me I'm beautiful? You're just trying to soften me up so that I'll consent to letting you use my money to repair your kingdom."

"Is that what you think?"

"It's not only what I think, it's what I know to be true. I know you."

"If that's what you think, then you don't know me at all."

"Well, know this, Lord Kingspointe, I hate you as I've hated no other man." Then she stormed into the house, and at that moment he loved her as he had loved no other woman, including Belinda. He considered racing after her, taking her in his arms, and telling her how he felt, but she would not believe him.

He suspected in his heart that her reason for wanting to leave for London was to tell Benthower to proceed with the annulment, which had been the real reason that he had stopped her from going. He hadn't really cared that she had wanted to borrow his coach without his knowledge or permission. Bloody hell, everything that belonged to him was hers to use. He simply couldn't bear to have her to go back to London to start the annulment. He had wanted to keep her there at the house, more or less as the prisoner she had called herself—and he would have continued to keep her with him against her will but for the fact that she had said that he wanted her only for her money. In that moment, he realized that he loved Cassandra too much to *make* her stay wed to him. He did not want her only for her money. That she thought that of him wounded him deeply. He wanted her for the beautiful, caring human being that she was. He wanted her for the fact that she had adored him as no other person had ever done—and that he, in turn, loved her beyond all measure—but he would have to let her go before she would ever believe that he loved her as he had loved no other woman.

He entered the house with the intent of telling Cassandra that she was free to go back to London and to use his carriage to do so, but she had vanished to her room. It was just as well. He couldn't bear to tell her in person that she was free to go. It would be too heartbreaking. Instead, he would write her a note telling her that she might take his coach and leave, and he would

give her the note just before he set out to visit his tenants' cottages this morning. That way, he would not be
here when she left, and he would not have to endure
the pain of watching her go.

CHAPTER 14

The Tower: Unforeseen catastrophe, sudden upheaval, complete downfall . . .

———◆———

CASSANDRA BROODED IN HER ROOM over her confrontation with William. He had almost appeared sorry that he had called her homely all those years ago. He had also almost looked sincere when he told her she was beautiful now, but she was no fool. He did not think her beautiful now. No, that was a ruse to get her to accede to his request for her money, just as the diamond necklace had been and the seduction in the carriage.

More than ever, she wanted out of this marriage. Her only option for getting the annulment process started now, however, was to write to Benthower and tell him to proceed. To that end, she rang for her maid and instructed her to procure pen, ink, and paper, and when she had those things, she sat down to write the missive.

> *Dear Benthower,*
> *I must be quick, as I hope to get this letter in the post today. Please come and get me. I am stuck in*

*Essex with Kingspointe and have no way to leave,
but I want to proceed with the annulment per the
terms you laid out to me last week, if it is still possible.*
   Yours,
   C.

When she was finished and the ink had dried, she
folded the paper and addressed it to Benthower in
London. She then asked Findley to sneak the letter
downstairs into the outgoing mail. That feat accom-
plished, she relaxed a little and called for some breakfast
to be brought to her room.

While she waited for her food, she got out her tarot
deck to do a reading for herself, recalling the last time
she had looked into the future using the cards. It had
been on the night that she and William had first made
love, the memory of which brought warmth to her
cheeks. Then, of course, there had been yesterday in
the coach with him, which brought even more warmth
to her face. They were so right for one another on a
physical level. She only wished the connection could
reach an emotional level—not just for her, but for him
as well.

She shuffled the cards to clear them of the energy
from the last reading and then shuffled them some
more as she began concentrating on William and her
quest for clarity about their relationship in the past,
present, and future. Cutting the cards into three piles,
she took the top card from each pile. The Lovers was
the first card revealed, representing the past. No real
surprise there. She and William had been lovers, but
that was all past now. She turned over the second card,
which represented the present. The Two of Cups stared

up at her, and that card did surprise her, for it meant a truce or connection was in the offing. Surely that couldn't be right, not after this morning's disastrous interaction with him. How could they ever reach any sort of truce? She shook her head and turned over the final card.

She gasped at the Tower. Shocked and alarmed, she stared at the card as tendrils of dread spread throughout her body at its meaning. Either the future held some calamity and her world was about to crash down around her, or—metaphorically speaking—false beliefs would soon come tumbling down, opening her eyes to some truth. She hoped and prayed that the card held the latter meaning in store for her and not the literal catastrophe it could sometimes portend.

Distressed over the implications of The Tower, she put the cards away as her breakfast tray arrived. As she poured herself some tea, she discovered a letter addressed to her sitting on the platter in between the teapot and a plate of toast. Odd, she thought. Who would have written to her? Then she recognized the handwriting on the paper. William had penned her a note. Her hands shook as she broke the seal and read it.

> *My Dearest Cassandra,*
> *It is with a heavy heart that I write this letter, for it is to tell you that you may go. You may take my—our—carriage and leave. I have instructed the coachman to take you to London whenever you wish to go. I know why you want to return there—so that you can tell Benthower to begin the annulment of our marriage. Never mind how I know this. Just know that it pains me that you would do so. I ask only that you please leave before*

I return this afternoon, so that I don't have to
watch you go.
  Farewell,
  William

She put the letter down on the tray in silent disappointment. Oh, that he was allowing her to leave was surely good news, and yet, that he was allowing her to go so easily was a blow to her heart. Well, what had she expected the letter to say? That he loved her with all his heart and wished she would stay with him to build their marriage? Such a fool was she to have even thought it.

Her appetite suddenly gone, she rose from the table in her room, rang for Findley, and instructed the girl to get her things ready to leave once more. Though nothing had been put away from her earlier attempt to escape, she needed her abigail to coordinate with the footmen to take her things to the entry hall, while she sent word to the coachman to prepare the carriage.

In half an hour's time, everything was set to go. Despite the fact that leaving was what she wanted to do, regret filled her heart and soul at the loss of William and what might have been if only he'd returned the soul-searing love she felt for him. Disappointing man.

———◆———

OVERWHELMING WOMAN. She had no idea how she affected him. He rode his horse down the road, his heart filled with emotion for her. She had become everything to him, yet he had told her she could go. It had to be this way, however. He did not want her to be unhappy with him in a marriage she did not want.

He only hoped she was gone before he returned from his business with his tenants so that he didn't have to witness her leaving.

His first stop was the modest home of his land steward, Jenkins. He hoped the man would accompany him on his tour of the tenants' cottages today. The two of them could then discuss the best course of action with regard to getting the houses repaired. How he would come up with the necessary funds to fix the run-down structures was beyond him, but he would worry about that when the time came.

He pulled up to the hitching post outside the house and tied his horse up to it, while a gaggle of small children—the Jenkins's grandchildren, no doubt— played out front. The lively little group appeared for all the world to be having the time of their lives, their whoops and calls testifying to their fun. Their antics left him melancholy, however. Had Cassandra stayed with him, their children might have played like this one day. As he tried to divert his thoughts from his wife, a plump woman stepped out of the house toward him on the front steps. She was a matronly figure in her white mobcap and pinafore, and he recognized her as Jenkins's wife.

"Lord William! I mean, Lord Kingspointe," she called to him in greeting as she curtsied.

"Mrs. Jenkins, how are you?" He descended from his steed and approached the porch.

"Fine. Just fine, my lord. What can we do for you?"

"I'm looking for your husband. I was hoping he could ride out with me to take a look at the tenants' cottages today."

The woman shook her head. "I'm sorry, my lord, but Jasper has gone into East Welkin on an errand for me."

He shrugged and waved away her concern. "That's no problem really. I shouldn't have dropped by without warning. I should've sent a note around to him yesterday about going out today, but having just arrived at Springwinds, my mind was otherwise engaged."

"How about if I have Jasper catch up to you when he returns? He shouldn't be too much longer."

"That would be fine. I'll be at the Badby cottage first." William mounted his horse and took his leave of Mrs. Jenkins.

He set out once again and in a matter of fifteen minutes, came upon the first terribly run-down cottage on his land, the Badby household. Old and worn, the home badly needed repairs to the shutters, roof, and doors. The thatching on the roof had a good-sized hole in it—visible from the road—and the front door was weathered and hanging off its bottom hinge. How did his tenants even dwell in the place with it in such deplorable condition? The roof should've been re-thatched last summer at the very least, but his brother had probably not had the money to make the repairs.

As William got down from his horse in front of the Badby home, a commotion coming from inside the house captured his attention. He tied his horse to a ramshackle wooden fence surrounding the yard and approached the front door. Noises came from inside, the sounds of a man bellowing and a woman softly weeping. Standing there listening to the domestic dispute was awkward beyond measure, and he didn't know whether to knock or leave. He knocked once just to see if anyone would answer, but the yelling continued unabated, and no one came to the door. Then, smack! It was the distinct sound of flesh hitting flesh.

The woman yelped in obvious pain.

"You s-s-stupid bitch," the man yelled, slurring his words. "Can't you do anything right? I told you I wanted coffee, not tea." The sound of the flesh hitting flesh once again reverberated throughout the cottage.

Without thinking, William opened the door, which was not securely shut due to the broken hinge, and walked into the house. Though he didn't immediately see the man or the woman, he heard them arguing from a room farther back in the house. He followed the sounds to the kitchen, where the man was striking the woman repeatedly across the face.

"Oy, there, Badby!" he called out to distract the man, but Badby paid him no attention.

In an obvious rage against the woman, Badby continued pummeling her in the face and abdomen. Horrorstricken, William stepped into the fray, coming face-to-face with the man. Badby's fist connected then with William's jaw, and he saw stars as he reeled backward.

"Edgar! Stop! It's Lord Will . . . er, Kingspointe," said Mrs. Badby, who had taken cover near the hearth.

Instinctively, William threw a punch back at Badby and landed one on his nose, which started to bleed profusely. Enraged further, Badby socked him in the gut. William doubled over for a moment, and Badby hit him again, this time in his eye. William continued to give as good as he got, and their scuffle lasted several minutes, neither man showing any signs of fatigue. Finally, after he landed another blow to Badby's face, the man grabbed a knife off the kitchen table and swung it at William.

"No, Edgar!" Mrs. Badby screamed.

William backed off, his hands in the air, as Badby

lunged for him, stabbing him in the torso a couple of inches below his sternum. William teetered backwards as he pulled the knife out of his abdomen and dropped it on the floor. Blood flowed from the wound, and shocked at the sight of it, he lost his balance, falling backward toward the hearth. His head hit the brick ledge, while his legs crumpled beneath him and his world went black.

—◆—

CASSANDRA CLIMBED into William's carriage with the aid of a footman and settled back against the squabs in the seat facing forward, while Findley took the seat across from her. As the door closed, she shut her eyes to the reality that she was leaving him for good. It had to be this way, she reminded herself, and despite affirmations that she would not cry, tears dripped from her eyelashes as she rapped on the ceiling of the coach to signal the driver, Mr. Sullivan, to proceed. Without much ado or fanfare, the carriage rolled forward, and they were on their way.

Through bleary eyes, she watched out the window at the scenery they passed. William's land really was very beautiful and pastoral, and under other circumstances, she'd have been happy and proud to call herself his marchioness. The carriage passed a house where several children played out front, and her heart sank with the realization that the baby she likely carried now would have no brothers and sisters to play with, nor a man to call father.

A woman hanging laundry out to dry waved from the front yard, and she waved back. They continued down the lane to the main road where they turned and proceeded through more of William's holdings. A ramshackle cottage lay up ahead and caught her attention with its state of disrepair. He had been right when he said that his tenants' homes were sadly in need of repairs. This one was a mess with a hole in its thatched roof and its shutters and front door hanging off their hinges.

As they neared the cottage, a hysterical wisp of a woman came running out of the doorway. She waved her arms in a frenzied attempt to flag down the coach. Cassandra rapped on the ceiling indicating to Mr. Sullivan to stop, while the distraught woman ran to the carriage door and frantically pounded on it. Cassandra opened the door and was shocked to see the woman's face bruised and swollen. Moreover, her hands and pinafore were drenched in blood.

"Lady Kingspointe, Lady Kingspointe, come quick, come quick!" said the woman who obviously recognized William's carriage from the crest on the door and thus assumed Cassandra was his wife.

Meanwhile, a wild man ran out the front door in a frenzy of his own and took off down the road without stopping to assist the woman. He, too, was covered in blood. What on earth had happened inside that cottage?

"Badby!" Then a different man, one whom Cassandra had never met before, stood in the doorway of the cottage calling out to the man running away down the road.

She climbed out of the carriage. "What's going on?"

"Oh, ma'am, please come quick. It's your husband. He's been stabbed, and he won't wake up."

The world spun out from under Cassandra. She nearly swooned as her knees buckled. They almost gave way there in the road, but she found the strength she needed to stand her ground. Findley, who stood right beside her, offered her an arm, but Cassandra refused it.

She could only ask, "What happened?"

The man who had called out the door after Badby approached them. "Your husband has been stabbed, Lady Kingspointe. I'm going to town for help. I'll bring back the surgeon. Mrs. Badby and you should tend to Lord Kingspointe, meanwhile. He's bleeding something fierce. Get some cloths and see if you can staunch the flow of blood."

Though Cassandra's knees weakened again as she put a hand to her forehead, she managed to remain upright and mustered the fortitude required to handle the situation.

"Thank you, Mr. Jenkins. Be quick about getting the surgeon," said Mrs. Badby.

"I will. And I'll also sound the hue and cry for your husband."

Mr. Jenkins climbed on his horse and rode in the direction of East Welkin. Meanwhile, Mrs. Badby led Cassandra, Findley, Mr. Sullivan, and two of William's footmen back to the kitchen where William lay unconscious face up on the floor in a pool of blood that ran in a dark steady stream from his body. His coat and waistcoat had been removed and his shirt lifted up to reveal a gaping wound in his abdomen.

"William!" Cassandra crouched at his side trying to get him to awaken. "Has he been out long?"

"Yes, my lady. Ever since he fell backwards and hit his head on the hearth," said Mrs. Badby.

"Oh, dear God."

"What should we do?" Mrs. Badby cried as she wrung her hands.

"Abner, Hugh, Mr. Sullivan, help me get his lordship

to a bed." Cassandra took charge and ordered the two footmen and the coachman to assist her.

Mr. Sullivan grabbed William by the feet, while Abner and Hugh grabbed him by the shoulders. All three men hustled him out of the kitchen and onto a bed in a small chamber off the entryway.

Cassandra asked Mrs. Badby, "Ma'am, do you have some clean rags we could use to staunch the bleeding?"

"Of course, of course." She hurried off in a whirlwind to get the rags.

Cassandra bent over the bed and caressed her husband's brow. "There, there, William. It will be all right. I only wish we could move you back to Springwinds somehow." She continued to caress him. Soothing him soothed her as she tried to prevent the threatening tears from falling.

"I'm not sure it's wise to move him so far right now. Let's see what the surgeon says after he tends to him," said Mr. Sullivan who stood beside her.

She nodded as Mrs. Badby returned with the clean rags. Cassandra took several cloths, pulled a chair next to William, and began to soak up the blood that continued to flow from his abdominal wound.

"Oh, William," she whispered to him, her reserve wavering just a little, "please don't die."

Blood quickly drenched the rag that she held to the stab wound, and she would've fainted at the sight and smell of the gore had she not been determined to be courageous for his sake. She stroked his forehead once again with her free hand and kissed him on his brow, noticing for the first time that blood also leaked out of a wound at the back of his head onto the pillow where he lay.

"How did all this happen?" Mr. Sullivan asked.

Mrs. Badby drew a deep breath and said, "My husband—Edgar—and me was fighting when Lord Kingspointe came to the door. He must've heard us and came into the kitchen to see what was going on. He saw Edgar punching me pretty hard and got into the fray. He shoulda just let things be. Edgar's always hitting me. It ain't nothing new. Anyway, Lord Kingspointe got in the way, and the two of them went at it for a good ten minutes. And then Edgar took a knife off the kitchen table and stabbed Lord Kingspointe with it. His lordship fell backward and hit his head on the hearth and got knocked out. Edgar stood there screaming and yelling at me while I tried to get Lord Kingspointe to wake up, but he wouldn't come to for nothing. I was trying to stop the blood with my hands and my apron when Mr. Jenkins showed up. He tried to get Edgar to help him with Lord Kingspointe. That's when you all showed up outside, and Edgar decided to make a run for it. They'll hang him if Lord Kingspointe dies, won't they?" She started crying at that realization and was soon in hysterics.

Mr. Sullivan put a hand on Mrs. Badby's shoulder to calm her. "Don't worry about your husband right now. We need to be strong for Lord Kingspointe. Why don't you go and get some water to wash his wound before the surgeon arrives?"

Cassandra, meanwhile, continued to hold herself together for William's sake. She had to remain brave and not break down when he needed her so. With immense fortitude, she pasted a placid veneer on her face and resolved to be strong for him. The fact that he was in his current circumstances because he had acted to save Mrs. Badby, to defend her from the brutality of her husband, did not fail to strike Cassandra as ironic. He had saved a woman who was being beaten by her husband and, in doing so, was beaten himself. Her very noble William. Always rescuing women in need. Always there to protect those less fortunate. She continued to stroke his brow in an ongoing effort to comfort herself as much as to comfort him. Inside, her emotions swirled between the intense love she felt for this man and the intense rage she felt toward the man who had done this to him.

A little over forty-five minutes later, Mr. Jenkins returned with the surgeon, Mr. Livesey. He and Mr. Jenkins removed William's shirt completely, and Mr. Livesey cleansed both the wound in his torso and the one to his head with the water that Mrs. Badby had provided. The surgeon then stitched the gaping hole in William's abdomen and said that the gash on the back of his head didn't need stitching. He then dressed both wounds with some salve and bandaged them up. When he was finished, he turned to Cassandra. "How long has he been unconscious?"

Cassandra looked to Mrs. Badby for a rough estimate of the time, and the woman wrung her hands together in obvious distress, as she said, "Maybe two hours now?"

"Is that bad?" Cassandra asked warily.

"It's not good," said Mr. Livesey. "But I've seen people with conks to the head go for a couple of days before waking up."

And Cassandra had seen her sister go three days without waking before she died. She tried not to let her mind go to thoughts of Phoebe, but she couldn't help but remember the awful head injury she'd endured that lead to her death. Cassandra must've blanched white, for Mr. Livesey patted her hand to comfort her. "He'll need time to heal is all."

"Is it all right to move him back to Springwinds Hall?"

"I believe so, if you're very careful. If he should wake up, give him this for the pain." He handed her a bottle of laudanum. "In the meantime, I would call for his doctor in London, if at all possible, and have the man take a look at him, especially if infection sets in. Keep the wounds clean and change his dressings once a day."

She shivered at the mention of infection but instructed Mr. Sullivan, Mr. Jenkins, Abner, and Hugh to carry William with great care to the coach. He did not stir as the men laid him across the carriage seat.

The thin veneer of strength that she had tried to project cracked just a little as she climbed up into the coach next to William. She cradled his head gingerly in her lap, and after she was settled, she knocked on the ceiling of the cab to indicate to Mr. Sullivan to roll ahead. William did not move or make a sound during the whole trip, and Cassandra's heart sank at what that meant. When they arrived back at Springwinds, the men moved William from the carriage to his bedroom.

Once they had him safely in his bed, they left her alone with him, and the real torture began. What was she to do now? More than anything, she wanted to crawl into bed with him to comfort him. She broke down then and cried. She couldn't help herself. The enormity of what had just happened finally caught up to her, and seeing William in such peril terrified her. She didn't wish him ill. She loved him. With all her heart, she loved him, and at that, she sobbed.

Then she recalled the last words she had spoken to him. Oh, dear God, they had been words filled with hatred. "Know this, Lord Kingspointe, I hate you as

I've hated no other man." She had spoken the words to him before she had left him in the courtyard this morning.

Overcome with shame, she tried to rouse him by shaking his shoulder. "Oh, William," she said, "can you hear me?" She took his hand in hers and whispered into his ear, "I'm so sorry for what I said. I *love* you as I've *loved* no other person." But he didn't stir. Nor had he stirred or made a sound since being placed in his bed at Springwinds, and she was once again reminded of Phoebe. What if he didn't awaken, like her sister? What if he died in his sleep, as she had done?

That was simply unacceptable, and she would do everything within her power to make sure it didn't happen. To that end, she pulled herself together and sent for his doctor in London.

She stayed by William the rest of the day and night. She got no sleep herself because she was so distraught, but she rejoiced the next morning when he finally began to move a little and to moan and mumble in his sleep, indicating that he was perhaps coming out of his state of unconsciousness. Phoebe had never moved. Never made a sound before she died. Although the little motions in his hands and legs and eyes were definitive signs of improvement, the slight fever he had developed was worrisome and that it continued to rise as the day wore on was terrifying.

She procured some cold water and rags with which she wiped his skin in an attempt to cool the fever, but by afternoon, it was raging hot. She removed his bandage and examined the stab wound. It was red and swollen, but the only thing she could do for it was bandage it again after cleansing it thoroughly. As she continued to tend to him with cold compresses, he mumbled her name.

She grasped his hand in both of hers. "I'm here, William. I'm here."

Then he mumbled the unimaginable. "I love you," he said, and her heart skipped a beat as she dropped his hand in dismay.

Had he just declared that he loved her, or was he, in his delirium, imagining someone else? Belinda perhaps?

"William, what did you say?" Joy wrestled with disbelief as she stood next to the bed.

He mumbled something else, but it was unintelligible. Still, he had said *her* name and then, "I love you," not Belinda's name. Dare she hope that he'd really meant her? For if he loved her, then that changed everything. She would not leave him. She could not leave him. She would stay with him—forever.

She clasped William's hand once more in hers. "I love you, too." As she whispered the words into his ear, she would've sworn he squeezed her hand.

Then she remembered that she had written to Benthower yesterday asking him to move forward with the annulment. She had to write to her brother immediately and tell him to cease and desist. Her second letter to him was as brief as her first.

> *Benthower,*
> *Disregard my previous letter! Do NOT go forth with the annulment. William is injured, and I cannot leave him because I love him, and I believe he loves me. Moreover, I'm fairly certain I am with child, which would therefore make getting an*

annulment impossible.
   Yours,
   Cassandra

She ordered the note delivered to Benthower by special courier and hardly slept during the next two days, staying by William's side the entire time. His fever worsened during that time, and though she continued to apply cold compresses to him, she could not get the fever to break.

At last the doctor, Dr. Lipton, arrived by supper-time the next evening. Weary and haggard, Cassandra explained what had happened as she led the doctor to William's chamber. Dr. Lipton examined him, and she rejoiced when he declared that he would most likely recover fully from the injury to his head.

"When do you suppose he will wake up?" She was hopeful for the first time since the ordeal began that his condition might actually improve.

The portly, middle-aged man took off his spectacles and wiped them clean with his handkerchief. "It's hard to say exactly when, but I would bet within the next couple of days. Don't be surprised if he wakes up a little confused and agitated, though. I've seen patients wake from these spells alarmed and restless. They don't know what's happened to them, and they're a little frightened. Also, he might not remember everything that happened to him before the blow to his head."

"What about the fever?" That bothered her as much as his state of unconsciousness now.

"I'm more worried about that actually. It looks like he has an infection in the stab wound from the way it's draining pus. The surgeon did a fine job of sewing him up, but likely the knife was dirty when it went into him."

"Is there anything we can do to treat the infection?"

The doctor shook his head. "I'm afraid not much. I have some ointment that might help, but it'll mostly be up to his body to fight it. Cover him in plenty of blankets so that he is able to sweat out the infection with his fever."

Dr. Lipton applied the salve to the festering stab wound, while Cassandra rounded up several blankets to cover William. She tucked him in up to his bristly chin, and only when she had him firmly ensconced in his nest of blankets, did she stop a moment to breathe.

The doctor took her hand in his and patted her cheek. "Now, my lady, it is time for you to get some rest. I can tell you haven't slept in a couple of days, and you will need to keep your strength up to be there for Lord Kingspointe."

"I can't leave him, doctor."

As he parted for his own room, Dr. Lipton turned back to her. "Do try to get some rest nonetheless. Doctor's orders."

Perhaps she could lie down next to William and close her eyes for a little bit. In truth, she was so exhausted that she didn't know what day it was. She drew down the covers and climbed into the bed next to him to comfort him. Taking his fevered hand in her own, she was elated when he groaned her name. He did not open his eyes, however, and she whispered into his ear, "I'm here, William. I'm here if you need anything, and I love you." He seemed to smile at her statement, and a tear slipped down her cheek. "William, you must get better. I may be carrying your child, and he or she will need you." She could have sworn that he squeezed her hand for the second time that day. Amazing man.

CHAPTER 15

The Star: A glimmer of hope, promise, healing, inspiration, peace, and serenity . . .

———◆———

ENCHANTING WOMAN. WHAT WAS SHE doing lying next to him fast asleep? He himself had awoken with a start, disoriented and confused about where he was and what had happened to him. He had been about to yell for his valet when he felt Cassandra's arm draped across him in bed.

Then he remembered that just before he had set out for his tenants' cottages, he had written to her, telling her she could go, that she was free to leave him to get an annulment. What was she still doing here? Sleeping by his side, no less? And why did he have a raging headache and a dull pain just below his sternum? Furthermore, why was he all bandaged up? His head was bandaged, as well as his abdomen, and he was practically naked beneath his covers with nothing on but his small clothes. What had happened to him? He tried to sit up without disturbing Cassandra, but when he moved, she instantly awoke and shot upright in the bed.

Her eyes went wide, as if she did not believe what

she saw. "William! Oh, William, you're awake. Oh, thank God, you're awake." She touched his forehead. "And your fever—it's gone."

He looked at her lovely face and smiled. "What happened?"

"Don't you remember?"

He shook his head no.

"It was Edgar Badby. He stabbed you in a fight. You tried to stop him from beating his wife, and he stabbed you with a knife." The details of the confrontation with Badby slowly started coming back to him as she spoke, and the haunting image of Badby repeatedly hitting his wife flashed before his eyes. "Then you fell backwards and hit your head on the hearth. You were unconscious and bleeding when I found you."

"You? You found me?"

She nodded.

"But I don't understand. I told you that you were free to leave. Why are you still here?"

She stroked his face tenderly and smiled at him. "I wouldn't be but for the fact that you were in such peril. I was going to go. In fact, I was on my way home to London in your carriage when Mrs. Badby waved us down to get help for you. And I just couldn't leave after seeing you so badly hurt."

"Then I am glad Edgar Badby stabbed me. I owe him my thanks."

An expression of distress crossed her face. "Never say that. You could have been killed."

Without her, he would have preferred to die. He stared at her in silence, contemplating his next words. Did he tell her he loved her? Or would that set her off, as telling her he thought she was beautiful had done the other day? Perhaps he should let their relationship be what it was right now—companionable. Perhaps he should let her tell him how she felt first, presuming she still loved him. Or did he presume too much? She had, after all, said she hated him the day he was stabbed, and he simply could not take it if she didn't love him as he loved her. Therefore, he was reluctant to tell her how he felt, to leave himself vulnerable to her spurning him, as Belinda had done.

"You could go now—if you wanted to. I'll not keep you against your will," he said.

"No, I couldn't."

His heart raced as to why. Was she implying that she loved him by that statement? "I know you could get an annulment. I had a man check into your brother's affairs after he visited us that one morning, and I know Benthower told you he could get you an annulment, if you had a doctor to declare you feeble or insane. I know you could leave if you wanted to."

"Not so. Benthower said that the bishop wouldn't agree to the annulment if I were pregnant."

This time, he stared at her in stunned silence, not quite sure he understood what she told him. "Do you mean to say . . . ?"

"Yes, William. I believe I am with child."

"Oh, Cassandra." He tried to sit up, but the pain in his abdomen was too much, and he was too weak. He lay back down with a huff. "That is extraordinary news. I am so happy." He stroked his hand through her hair, which was disheveled and hanging loosely about her shoulders. God, she was beautiful. "I want to get up." He started to sit up once again but couldn't manage it.

"Let me get the doctor. To make sure that you are all right before you try to sit up."

"Doctor?"

"Yes. There was no doctor in East Welkin, so I sent for Dr. Lipton in London, and he came all the way here to treat you." She rose from the bed and walked over to the bell pull to call a servant. "Is that not wonderful?"

"Yes. Just wonderful. I wonder what his visit will cost me," he replied not a little sarcastically.

"It is of no concern, William. We have my dowry. Remember?" She pinned her hair up before anyone arrived at his room.

"But I don't want to rely on your money to fix my problems. You will need it for your haven for women whose husbands beat them."

"True, but I shan't need all of it for that purpose. Not if we use Wyndemere Manor to house the women. And we will most certainly use some of the money to pay off the creditors and repair your tenants' cottages. Then we'll decide how best to use the remainder for the women's shelter and for us to live on."

Why this change of heart? What had happened, other than finding him nearly dead, to make her willing to stay with him? He asked her that question.

She peered down at her hands, as though she was wondering what to say and they held the answer. Finally, she looked up at him, her expression difficult to read. "I told you. I believe I am with child. I couldn't leave now, even if I wanted to."

"Is there no other reason?" he asked, hoping she would tell him she loved him.

She looked away from him. "No, no other reason."

Her words were a blow to his heart and the pain so great, he thought he would perish.

"When do you think we could start moving women into Wyndemere?" she asked.

Her obvious attempt to change the subject back to

the shelter annoyed him, but he didn't protest. "As soon as you want. I only need to send word to the servants there to prepare the place for the women so they can move in."

"Then I will go ahead and write to Julia to have her send us some ladies from Lexington House in Hampshire or to send us some victims through the underground in London."

"Good. We shall visit Wyndemere when the ladies arrive and make sure everything is in order."

"Oh, William, it is so good of you and your mother to let us use the house for a shelter."

"It is nothing."

"It is everything." She crossed over to him and hugged him.

"Cassandra, I—"

He was about to tell her he loved her, but the moment was lost when someone knocked at the door, and she went to answer it, finding a maid standing there. She instructed the maid to get Dr. Lipton, and the girl ran at once to do as she was bid.

William, meanwhile, brooded once again over whether or not to tell her how he felt. She might not believe him, and if she didn't believe him, she might get angry with him and decide to leave. Once again, he determined that it was perhaps better if he said nothing—at least, not yet.

Dr. Lipton came to his room and appeared relieved to see that William had awoken. The doctor examined him and declared him fit to try to stand but warned him that he might be weak and dizzy with his first attempts. Dr. Lipton and William's valet, Watts, both assisted him in standing, which he could do only for a little while. He was, indeed, too weak to stay on his feet for very long or to attempt walking very far. While he was up, however, Cassandra had a couple of maids change his bed linens, and when they were done, Dr. Lipton and Watts helped him back to bed.

Before leaving the room, the doctor ordered him to try to eat some broth and bread and to take some laudanum for the pain in his head and abdomen, and William asked Watts to stay and help him shave, while Cassandra excused herself to take a bath.

———◆———

ONCE ALONE in her room, Cassandra knelt beside by her bed and thanked the Lord that William had awoken and seemed all right. She was not a particularly religious woman, but she felt such gratitude for her husband's improvement that she had to express it somehow. She also thanked Heaven that she was probably with child and reflected for a moment about how happy she really was. If, as he had mumbled in his sleep, he loved her, then life was complete and she could ask for nothing more. She had been about to tell him she loved him when he asked her if there were a reason other than the pregnancy that she was staying with him, but she decided against it. Although she longed to tell him how she felt, that she loved him more than she'd ever loved anybody, she would have been crushed if he didn't return the sentiment—or worse, if he said he could never love her.

She put those thoughts away as her bath was brought to her, and when she was alone, she sank down into the warm water. She had not allowed herself any luxuries, like time to herself, since his injury five days ago, so she reveled in the feel of the bath all around her.

After the bath, Findley helped her dress, and Cassandra returned to William's chamber to help him eat some food. Though he appeared a little weary as he sat up in his bed, he had shaved and washed with the help of his valet. How handsome he looked, and her heart clenched with the love she felt for him. She kissed his lips lightly, meaning for it to be just a peck, but when she tried to pull away from him, he held her head in place, and she couldn't break the kiss. She felt his tongue on her lips, trying to part them, and she relented and let him inside her mouth. The world spun away. He tasted of tooth powder and fresh mint, which he must have chewed because he had known he would be kissing her. The kiss heated up, and he groaned deep in his throat.

"I want you," he said against her lips.

"And I, you. But your wound is still too fresh, and you too weak. We'll have to wait until you are up to it."

"Oh, I'm up to it right now." He took her hand and placed it on his hard member. She stroked him through his small clothes, and he groaned again.

"When you are better, William. I don't want you rupturing your stitches—or worse."

"Killjoy," he replied as he kissed her deeply one last time.

She laughed and sat down to feed him his gruel, as he called it. Even though he protested that he could feed himself, she insisted on spoon-feeding him the broth the doctor had prescribed for him. She also broke off little bites of the bread, put them on his tray for him to eat, and made him sip some herbal tea that she had ordered from the kitchen. He ate heartily, and she was thankful for his healthy appetite. She was also thankful that he had shown a physical appetite for her. If only he would tell her that he loved her now that he was awake, then she would be the happiest woman alive. But he said nothing about loving her, and she began to doubt that he had meant it—or had meant it about her—when he had said it in his sleep a few days ago.

Her thoughts must've appeared in her expression, for he said, "Cassandra, what's the matter?"

"Oh . . . nothing. Nothing is the matter." Her words lacked conviction, however—even to her own ears.

"There is something wrong. Please tell me what it is."

She had to think quickly to come up with a reason for her melancholic demeanor. "It's just that I feel sorry for Mrs. Badby."

"Do we know how she is doing?"

"I spoke with her yesterday. She stopped by to see how you were. She is doing as well as can be expected, I suppose. Physically, she is fine and suffers no serious injuries from her husband's abuse. She is quite distraught, however, that her husband is being held by the authorities. She has no other family, and she doesn't know what she will do without him. She wants him back at home with her, of all things. She says she blames herself for his beating her. He is always telling her it's her fault that she enrages him to the point that he beats her, at any rate." She heard the consternation in her own voice. "I don't understand how women whose husbands beat them can want to stay with the abusive brutes."

"Perhaps it's because that's all they know," William said. "Sad as it is, Mrs. Badby's security has been threatened by her husband's incarceration."

Cassandra considered that insight for a moment. "So true. I hadn't thought of it like that. I believe she fears you will turn her out."

"Which I would never do. She can stay on her land for as long as she needs to. We will just hire some hands to help her with the farm."

"Of course, we will help her. It must be very frightening for her to be left without anyone or anything. If she prefers, if she would rather not stay on the farm, she could stay at the shelter for as long as she needs to in order to make a fresh start away from her husband."

"Badby," William said, shaking his head at the man's name. "I knew he was a drunkard, but I had no idea he beat his wife so mercilessly."

"How very noble it was of you to get involved in the fray to protect her, William. I'm just thankful you were not killed."

"And I am thankful I have you with me. Now, tell me," he said. "What is really bothering you? Why do you look so sad? Have I done something to upset you?"

"Absolutely not. I am just fatigued, I think."

"I think perhaps you need a kiss." And so saying, he pulled her from the chair to lie beside him on the bed. "I want you." Reiterating his earlier sentiments, he kissed her mouth. Then he plied kisses along her jaw and down her throat until she was shaking with desire.

"But William, surely you're not fit to make love." She broke from the kiss breathlessly.

"I like that you say 'making love' now instead of 'having coition,'" he chuckled against her neck.

She laughed, too. "Soon enough, we can make love once again."

He strengthened over the next two days, so much so that Dr. Lipton felt he could take his leave. True to his word, William then sent instructions to Wyndemere Manor to have it readied for the women who would soon be coming to stay there. Once they received word that everything was in order at the manor, Cassandra wrote to her sister and told her to start sending women to Essex, and in a couple days' time, she heard back from Julia that she would be accompanying some ladies from London to Wyndemere by the end of the week.

On Saturday, she and William went to look the place over and to greet Julia and the women. They were also going to stop in to see the surgeon in East Welkin to have him remove William's sutures.

As they rode in the carriage to Wyndemere, she asked him playfully, "What shall we call our firstborn if he is a boy?" It had been seven days since he had first awoken from his unconsciousness, and her courses still had not started.

He thought a moment and answered after some consideration. "How about David, after my brother?"

"David," Cassandra said, testing the sound of the name. "Yes. David."

"Of course, he shall never be called 'David' except by us, perhaps. He'll be known as Lord Margate to the world until my demise."

She arched her brow at him. "It's in very poor taste for you to speak of such things, William."

"I apologize, my dear." He blew her a kiss across the coach. "What shall we call a girl?"

"Miranda? After my mother?"

"Lady Miranda." He seemed to think a moment. "That's perfect."

"Oh, William, I'm so excited about the baby that I can hardly contain myself."

"You're not sorry about it then?"

"No. Why would I be sorry?" she asked in genuine confusion.

"Because it means you have to stay with me."

"Yes, that's true, but I am still thrilled about the baby." That didn't come out at all right, and he appeared a little hurt by her answer, so she quickly asked, "Are you not excited about the baby?"

"Yes, of course. You're sure you're with child then?"

"Not exactly positive, no. But sure enough that I believe it's safe for me to start knitting booties." She couldn't help herself from smiling until a memory came to her. "Speaking of booties, do you remember the time Benthower stole my doll's clothes and shoes and hid them from me?"

"I seem to recall some prank or other like that."

"There were many pranks like that with him. I was traumatized carrying around a naked doll in just her blanket. Benthower could be so frightfully mean sometimes, but you rescued the entire wardrobe for me."

"And made an enemy of Benthower in the process, if I remember the incident properly. He wouldn't speak to me for two days."

"It seems you were always rescuing me from some tragedy or other—just like you did several weeks ago at the Wellesley party."

"You know, in eleven days, you will be thirty."

"How kind of you to remind me," she said dryly.

He laughed. "I only mention it because the original deal was that you would take your money and go live on your own then."

"Yes?"

"Well, do you really mean to stay with me?" He paused a moment, and then with his hands on his knees, he leaned forward from his seat in the carriage. He seemed to search her eyes for the answer.

"For now, at least." It was all she could say. Anything

more, and she would've revealed her heart to him. He sat back then and stared out the window. Befuddling man.

———◆———

Discouraging woman. Why did she torment him so with an answer like that? And why wouldn't she just tell him she loved him, like she had the first time they'd made love? He hadn't imagined that, had he? She really had said she loved him, had she not? And the love he saw in her eyes when they'd been intimate in the carriage—this very carriage, in fact—two weeks ago, that had been real, hadn't it? He didn't know any more. Perhaps she was just with him for the baby's sake.

He watched out the window as the carriage trundled toward Wyndemere Manor, and they both remained quiet the rest of the trip. What she was thinking wasn't clearly written on her face, but all he could think about was how much he felt for her.

They arrived at the manor house in silence. He stepped out of the carriage first and then helped her down.

Julia ran out of the front entrance to greet them on the driveway. "Oh, Cassandra, William, how good it is to see both of you."

Cassandra hugged her sister and stepped back from her. "It's good to see you, as well."

"You're positively glowing. You're with child, aren't you?" Julia asked her pointedly.

Cassandra blushed a deep vermillion. "Julia, really. Must you be so blunt?"

"You are with child, though. I can tell. Also, I did a tarot reading the other day, and it predicted the birth of a child coming up. All I could think about was you.

You're going to have a baby, aren't you?"

"Probably," she replied. "But we will discuss all that later. For now, please show us what has been done with the place and introduce us to some of the women you've brought with you."

"First, let me hug you, William," Julia said as she put her arms around his neck.

He winced in discomfort from the wound to his abdomen as she hugged him close.

"Oh dear, you must still be in pain. Cassandra told me all about your ordeal in her letter to me. I'm so sorry for what you had to endure but exceedingly grateful that you are all right."

Then Julia clasped Cassandra's arm in hers, and they both walked into the house. He followed them, smiling to himself at the two sisters, one of whom he loved with all his heart and the other of whom he liked very much.

As they stepped into the entryway, they were greeted by several women, one of whom Julia introduced as Mrs. Wright, the headmistress of the shelter. She was a heavyset woman who looked to be in her mid-to-late thirties. She wore a mobcap and a simple, unadorned gray dress. He took it to be a uniform of sorts.

Mrs. Wright curtsied to them both, and William said, "Welcome to Wyndemere."

"It's my pleasure to be here to help with the cause. Let me introduce you to the women who will be staying here until we can find suitable situations for them away from their husbands," said Mrs. Wright. She introduced each of the women one by one and said where they were from, and one by one, each of the women curtsied to him and Cassandra.

"Thank you very much for opening this place, Lord

and Lady Kingspointe," said a woman who was introduced to him as Mrs. Foley. "I don't know what I'd have done without it and without your assistance."

"We're just happy we could accommodate you," said Cassandra.

In turn, each of the other women offered her thanks to William and Cassandra. Though he was curious about their situations and what had led them to seek shelter from their husbands, he didn't pry.

"May we have a tour of the house to see what you've done with the rooms?" asked Cassandra.

"Of course. Since we arrived two days ago, we've begun to change the setup of some of the rooms on the main floor," said Mrs. Wright, who led them throughout the manor explaining room by room what they wished to do with the place. "The dining room we're leaving the same as it was, of course. It's where the women have been taking their meals. The study and the library we're turning in to sewing rooms where the women can practice their skills in case some of them wish to become seamstresses. Some of the women will work with Cook in the kitchen to better prepare themselves for employment, while others will work with the household staff to prepare themselves for positions as maids, either in homes or at inns. We're even going to use the conservatory and kitchen garden to teach the women the rudiments of horticulture for those who are interested."

Mrs. Wright then led them upstairs to the second floor where the bedrooms were. "We're housing the women in these rooms here on this floor and the next floor. There's a fine space for a nursery on the fourth floor to house the children some of the women have brought with them. We've brought nursemaids from

London to watch over the children while their mothers work."

"You seem to have thought of everything, Mrs. Wright," said Cassandra.

"We've modeled the space after Lady Julia's home in Hampshire. That place has worked well for the women there."

"I daresay it has," said Julia. "It was overcrowded at Lexington House, however, until we moved some of the women to our safe house in London and then here to Essex."

"When do you return to London, Julia?" Cassandra asked.

"Tomorrow, actually. I can't be gone very long due to the fact that I'm sponsoring Violet this Season and chaperoning her to all her engagements."

"I daresay not. Thank you for coming out to Essex with the ladies. I'm sure it was comforting to them to have you here, even for a couple of days."

"Think nothing of it," said Julia. She then asked William and Cassandra to stay to luncheon with her and the women.

After eating, they left Wyndemere Manor for East Welkin where Mr. Livesey resided. How good it would be to get the sutures removed, for they had begun to itch something fierce. When they arrived at Mr. Livesey's home, the surgeon took William into a private room which he had set up as a workspace and instructed him to lie back on a large table.

William removed his coat, waistcoat, and shirt and then hopped up on to the table and lay back as Mr. Livesey had told him to do. The surgeon went to his bag of instruments and drew out a small pair of scissors. He examined the wound to William's abdomen.

"It's healed nicely," said Mr. Livesey, "though I heard from your doctor as he passed through East Welkin on his way home that it had been infected."

"It was, but the pus stopped draining from it, and I've had no fever for over a week now," he replied.

"I'm pleased to hear that."

The surgeon then took the scissors and began to clip the sutures and draw them out of William's skin. The sensation tickled a little, but he knew immediate relief once the stitches were gone. His scar over the wound still itched some but not nearly as much as it had just this morning.

"Tell me, sir," William asked, "Am I able to resume my regular activities?"

"What activities are we talking about?"

"Oh, the normal things. You know, horseback riding, that sort of stuff." Then he added sheepishly, "I guess what I really want to know is can I have conjugal relations with my wife now?"

Mr. Livesey chuckled a little. "I believe so, but perhaps not too vigorously at first."

William was so excited by that news, he sat up perhaps a little too quickly and felt a twinge in the wound.

"Do try to be careful with the scar, Lord Kingspointe. We don't want you developing a hernia at the site of the wound."

"Thank you, Mr. Livesey."

He hopped down off the table, and after dressing, he rejoined Cassandra in the parlor where she sat waiting for him. They took their leave of the surgeon, thanking him for his good work, and stepped into the afternoon sun.

Once outside, he took Cassandra in a feverish embrace and kissed her on the mouth.

"William!" She broke away from their kiss, scolding him. "Couldn't it wait until we got back in the carriage?"

"No, it couldn't. The surgeon said I could resume normal activities."

"So? Why is that worth kissing me in front of the whole town?"

"Because, my dear," he whispered in her ear. "He also said I could make love to my wife."

"Oh." She blushed deeply as he handed her into the carriage. "Goodness. He said that?"

"Yes. Well, no. Not in those words, but he did say yes when I asked him if I could have conjugal relations with my wife." He winked at her and followed her into the coach. "We just perhaps can't do it as vigorously as I'd like to for a while. I have to watch that a hernia doesn't form from my scar. So, I'm not going to ravish you in the carriage on the way home, as was my original plan. We'll have to be good and proper *ton* and wait until we're in our bed tonight, my love." He kissed her once again before taking the bench across from her.

CHAPTER 16

Ten of Cups, reversed: Loss of harmony, anger, feelings of guilt . . .

———◆———

THOUGH SHE REALIZED SHE SHOULDN'T read too much into the endearment, her heart leapt in her chest when he called her "his love." It wasn't an actual declaration of love, but it was something close. And she tried to hold onto it and the hope that he might—in reality—feel for her what she felt for him. Yet, as they rode away from East Welkin, doubt hung over her like a dark cloud, for if he did love her, why would he not just say so?

Distracted with her thoughts, she did not notice him as he reached for her and pulled her across the carriage to sit on his lap. He kissed her hungrily before she could protest, and she responded to his mouth on hers by parting her lips for him. He caressed her body into a fever, and she could not find the will to pull away from him. His hands found her breasts and teased her nipples into peaking, and she groaned into his mouth.

Breathless, she at last broke from the kiss. "I thought you weren't going to ravish me here in the carriage."

"I'm not. I'm merely sampling you. I'm also preparing you for what to expect when we arrive home."

"I think if we continue like this, we won't make it home without having coition."

"Don't forget, now. *Making love* is the preferable term." He pecked her cheek playfully.

"Yes, well, whatever you choose to call it, I think to avoid doing it here in the carriage, I should sit on my side and you on yours." So saying, she slid off his lap and returned to her bench.

"You are very wise to move away from me, my love."

There were those words again—along with the flutter they caused in her belly and in her heart, but they were just a meaningless term of endearment, one he might use with any lady he halfway liked.

"You know what I'd do if I could?" he asked.

"I have a pretty good idea."

"No, no, not that. Well, yes, I would do that, too, of course, but I would also throw you a party for your thirtieth birthday. I'd invite the entire kingdom to attend, and there'd be dinner and dancing and merriment had by all."

"That's very sweet of you, William, but it's impossible, not with you in mourning for your brother. A party is out of the question."

He sighed and nodded. "I'd still like to do something to mark your birthday, though. Perhaps we could have an intimate celebration, just the two of us."

"Oh, I think we could do that. We can even start when we arrive home. It's never too soon to begin the party, after all." She winked at him, and he smiled.

When they arrived home, William helped her out of the carriage and led her into the entryway and straight up the stairs to his bedroom, oblivious to the servants who were scattered here and there cleaning. Once inside his room, he pulled her to him and kissed her with abandon.

His arousal pressed against her belly as she melted in his arms, his hands caressing her body. Her clothing was no obstacle to him, and with little effort, he had her naked before him. He shucked his own attire, and she was delirious with longing as he led her to his bed where he pulled back the covers and laid her down. He stretched out beside her, his arousal now pressing into her hip, her own intimate flesh aching for him.

Before he proceeded, however, he broke from kissing her and put his forehead to hers. Breathing hard, he looked into her eyes. "Cassandra, I want there to be no misunderstanding between us. Make no mistake about it: I want you. I'm making love to *you*. No one else is here with us. Do you understand?"

She peered deep into his green gaze and saw intoxicating desire burning in his eyes. It was the same tangible yearning she had for him reflected back at her, and she nodded. He kissed her once again as he crawled atop her and positioned himself at her entry. She closed her eyes and savored the feel of him sliding into her. He took her in slow, steady strokes, until she thought she would expire from the pleasure, until she flew up and over the edge, writhing beneath him.

He broke from their kiss as his own orgasm overtook him. "Cassandra, look at me."

She opened her eyes, and their gazes locked as he spent himself inside her, his expression hot, intense, and full of raw emotion. She felt it down to her soul. If she had been a more foolish woman, she would have thought that he loved her indeed. Dearest man.

Loveliest woman. That was the most fearsome release he had ever experienced. Who knew that making love could be so earth-shattering when one was actually *in love* with one's partner? He came down from his high and felt himself slide from her warm, tight depths, and he knew a moment of complete, abiding peace, the kind of peace one could reach only after finding his true heart.

Breathing deeply of her scent, a combination now of the roses and lavender he so loved and the musk of lovemaking, he rolled off her to lie beside her. He kissed her forehead as he put an arm underneath her, drawing her body closer to his, her head resting on his chest. They lay like that, entwined in each other's arms and legs, for what seemed like an eternity, content just to hold one another, and he drifted off to sleep, his Cassandra in his arms.

When he awoke, she was still nestled against him, but she was already awake, her fingers making small concentric circles in the hairs on his chest. He was hard once more, and he wanted her again. He watched her as she traced the new scar on his abdomen right beneath his ribs, and he kissed the top of her head. She looked up at him then, her beautiful eyes filled with the look he could only describe as adoration, the same look he had seen in her eyes when they were young. No one ever looked at him like that, with that much—dare he call it?—love. He could only hope she loved him, for she said nothing about how she felt. And he was reluctant to reveal his own heart without an affirmation of that same sentiment from her. He would not do as he'd done with Belinda—confess how he felt only to be painfully rebuffed.

He lay back as she shifted herself onto one arm and

rose up to kiss him, their lips meeting, their tongues entwining with one another's. As the kiss intensified, she climbed atop him, straddling him and taking him deep inside her. It was not just the joining of their physical bodies that overwhelmed him. He also reveled in the joining of their souls. He sensed no boundary between them. They were one.

"Wil-l-l-l." Her voice was full of reverent awe as she reached her climax.

The sound of his name on her lips put him at the edge, and he lost himself in her eyes. "Cassandra," he said her name like a benediction.

Still panting from his exertion, he embraced her and kissed her deeply, a kiss that she returned in kind as she rolled off him to lie next to him. They lay in each other's arms for several moments as they both came down from their respective releases, their breathing returning to normal and their sweat comingling between them. Though their physical union had ended, they were still one in spirit.

CASSANDRA NESTLED next to him and rested her head on his shoulder. She caressed his chest as she basked in the afterglow of their union. She couldn't rate her happiness at the moment, for she had never before felt the euphoria that she did now. Emotion overcame her, and she choked up as though she would cry, while a tear crept out of her eye.

"What's the matter?"

She looked up at him as apprehension flashed in his expression.

"Nothing's the matter, except that maybe everything is too perfect. I don't want this moment to end."

"Neither do I, but don't cry. Please don't cry. I couldn't take it if you started crying."

"I'll try not to. It's just that I'm so emotional lately."

"Don't be. We have our entire lives to live and make love like this." He kissed her lips and playfully circled her nipple with his finger. Then he chuckled to himself as though he were laughing at some private joke.

She sniffled and then asked, "What's so funny?"

"You know, Lady Kingspointe, I'm curious. There's something I've been meaning to ask you about."

"And what is that, Lord Kingspointe?"

"Well . . .," he said as he continued to play with her nipples with one hand while resting his head on his other hand. "I don't quite know how to express it. I've just never made love to anyone as passionate as you. You seem to relish lovemaking, in fact. You also seem to know things about pleasing a man that I wouldn't think you could possibly know. How is that?"

She laughed softly at his observation. "I suppose it's because I've read the *Kama Sutra*."

"And what is the *Kama Sutra*?"

"It's an ancient illustrated manual from India about the art of lovemaking and how to be a good husband and citizen."

"A good husband?"

"And citizen. I'll certainly give it to you to read."

He threw his head back and laughed out loud. "How did a proper English lady like you end up with an ancient picture book from India about the art of lovemaking and how to be a good citizen?"

"And husband, don't forget. I got it from my sister Julia. She and her husband Niles lived in Calcutta for a while, a few years ago. She had it translated and a copy made for each of us—Phoebe, Bess, Violet, and me. It's a fascinating read."

"No doubt, it is. Do you have it with you by any chance?"

"No, I'm afraid not. My copy is in London, but I'll show it to you once we get back to Town." She brushed her lips over his and then lay her head on his chest, listening to his heartbeat and imagining it beat for her.

They rarely left his bedchamber over the next ten days, feasting mostly on each other and taking the occasional sustenance that they ordered to his room. During that time, her love for him only intensified, if that were possible, but how he felt about her remained a mystery. He had not reiterated the sentiments he had spoken aloud while he was unconscious three weeks ago. Therefore, in a rare moment apart, while he was downstairs tending to some pressing correspondence the day before her birthday, Cassandra took out her tarot cards and did a reading once again to seek clarity about her relationship with William.

She sat at the table in his room, and laid down the first card. It was the Two of Cups. Love, affinity, a spiritual union. Those were just some of its meanings. Her belly dipped at the possibility that it meant that William loved her. Of course, it could also mean the obvious—that she loved him. The second card was the Ten of Cups, reversed. Her heart clenched at its meaning, for it indicated loss of harmony, anger, and feelings of guilt. Hope began to fade with this card. Then she drew the third card, and all hope went out the window. The Three of Swords—three swords piercing a heart. There was no mistaking its meaning: heartbreak and separation. Would it be her own poor heart that would soon be breaking?

William startled her when came up behind her and

touched her on the shoulder as she regarded the cards. "Well, my love, what do they portend today?" He blithely used the empty term of endearment she had come to resent over the past ten days.

"Oh, nothing of import." She tried not to sound too dejected, but his words left her sullen and irritable. She begrudged him calling her "his love" when he wouldn't say out loud that he loved her.

"What's that one mean? The one with the swords through the heart? That can't be good."

"It has many meanings."

"What does it mainly signify?"

"As you might imagine, it can mean heartbreak," she said soberly.

"Well, not for us, my love. I know I would never hurt you, and I don't think you would ever hurt me. The cards must be wrong."

"In general, the cards do not lie."

He ignored her statement and removed his banyan as he took her hand and led her from the chair to the bed where he proceeded to ravish her. He had kissed her senseless and had his member poised to enter her when a knock sounded at the door.

"What the . . . ?" he said, annoyance heavy in his voice.

Cassandra chuckled to herself at his frustration and giggled aloud as she watched him get up off her and the bed with his raging erection, throw on his banyan, and stomp to the door.

"Who is it?" he growled, his member deflating.

"Wilkes, sir." The voice was barely audible through the door.

William opened the door just a crack. "Well? What do you want? And it had better be good."

"You have visitors, my lord." Wilkes's voice was unruffled by William's tone.

"Well, tell them I'm indisposed!"

"I tried to tell him that, sir, but he insisted I get you at once. Or rather, he insisted I get the marchioness."

"He? Who is he?"

"The Duke of Benthower, my lord. He would not be put off."

"Put off? I'll put him off. Tell him to wait."

"He said if I don't produce you or the marchioness at once, he will begin searching the house for you until he finds you, beginning with your bedchamber."

"Bloody hell," William cursed.

Cassandra, meanwhile, had risen from the bed and begun dressing and pinning her hair up so that she was almost ready when he turned back to her. She had a sinking feeling as to what this was all about.

"You're not leaving, are you?"

"One of us has to go down there right away. Or he *will* come up here after us."

He cursed again, this time using a much stronger expletive.

"Why don't you let me talk to him first? I think I may know what is going on." She continued to fix her hair in the mirror above his dresser.

"What is that? And why can't he just take a seat in the rose salon until we are decent?"

"Because he is Benthower and must be obnoxious, and if I'm not mistaken, he's here because of a simple misunderstanding. Hopefully, I should be able to handle it and straighten everything out."

"Very well. You go on ahead. I'll be down in a second." He turned toward his clothes, which hung over a chair, and began dressing.

Cassandra surveyed her appearance in the mirror and only hoped that Benthower would not be able to tell she had been freshly tumbled by her husband. How embarrassing that would be. She left William in his room, and went out to the hallway. From the stairs, she could hear her brother blustering about something in the entryway. Tea. Evidently, yes, of course, he would have some tea. What a silly question. She hurried down the stairs and came face-to-face with the duke . . . and his wife. Oh grand. The duchess was here, too.

"Your Graces. What an unexpected surprise." Her unenthusiastic reception did not seem to bother either her brother or her sister-in-law. "Let us go to the rose salon."

Without much ceremony, she led them to a room done mostly in dusky pinks, with hints of blues and golds here and there. The duchess seated herself on a brocade sofa covered in roses with swatches of blue and gold interwoven to offset the flowers, while Benthower took the matching chair across from her. Cassandra remained standing.

"What do you want?" Her question was short and to the point and not a little rude.

"I should think you'd be happier to see me, Cass. I came as soon as I could."

"What are you talking about?"

"Your letter. The one in which you requested an annulment. I came as quickly as I could when I got your letter."

"My letter?" She paused, recalling the note she had sent to her brother. "I sent that letter over three weeks ago. I'd hardly say you came quickly."

"Well, it took me this long to get the annulment proceedings going for you. Luckily, I'd had the officials begin the process in the consistory court in Raventon after I first talked to you about the annulment a few weeks ago—just in case you wanted to move forward with it. I had to convince the chancellor there that you had been remanded into my care, and as your caretaker, I had to provide the libel to begin the annulment. I also had the doctor provide his deposition that he examined you and found you were not of sound mind at the time of your vows and that you are still quite insane. I provided a deposition with the other details of your case as well. It's moving ahead posthaste."

"What?" The room began to spin as her brother kept talking.

"It's almost done, Cass. You'll be a free woman in a few short weeks. You don't have to thank me. Just your payment will be enough."

"Michael, what have you done? This is outrageous!" She began pacing the room. What would this mean for William and her?

"Didn't you send me a letter telling me to go forward with the annulment of your marriage?"

"Well, yes, but I sent you another letter telling you to call it off. I told you I wanted to stay with William. I love him."

Benthower scoffed at her declaration, while Belinda chafed in her seat. Cassandra glanced at the duchess, intrigued by the expression of alarm that crossed her face. She half expected her to say something, but the woman remained silent.

"I never got that letter," said Benthower.

"Never got it? I sent it by special courier the following day."

"I never got it," her brother insisted.

"I believe you lie, Michael." She hissed the words at

him.

"You wound me with your harsh words, Cass. I would never lie to you."

"Ha!" She could say nothing more in retort. Benthower was lying through his teeth, but she couldn't prove it. Worse, she was disturbed that the annulment was moving forward and that she and William would soon be effectively never married.

"Well, anyway, it is done."

"What is done?" William asked as he strolled into the salon at that moment. He was as handsome as she'd ever seen him, and Belinda sat up straighter when he walked into the room.

"Ah, Kingspointe. You deign to join us at last. Indecent, were you?" Benthower laughed at his own remark, his sarcasm amusing only himself.

William ignored the duke's attempt to goad him. "What is done?"

"Your annulment, old chap. I have managed to have it started in the consistory court in the Diocese of Raventon and to move it along as quickly as possible—no easy feat, let me tell you. Nor cheap. But it is done. Soon, you and Cassandra will never have been married."

"What?" William shouted. "Who told you to go forth with the annulment?"

Cassandra stopped pacing and turned to him, distraught. "I did." They were two of the hardest words she'd ever had to utter.

"When?"

"The day you were injured—before I saw how badly you were hurt. I sent a letter to Benthower telling him to go forward with the annulment when you wouldn't let me leave Springwinds Hall."

He was wounded. She could tell by his anguished expression. "How could you?"

"I'm so sorry, William. I–I desperately wanted out of this marriage at the time, but you wouldn't let me go to London. So, I wrote to Benthower instead. I asked him to come get me. I swear to you, though, that I sent him a letter by special courier the very next day telling him to cease and desist. He claims he never got my second letter."

William said nothing, but the injured look on his face told her everything she needed to know. Because of her, he was suffering. Pitiable man.

———◆———

TORMENTING WOMAN. She had begun the annulment after all. That realization hurt more than he would have thought—was a knife to his heart, in fact—even though he had told her she could go forward with the annulment. It was illogical for him to be this upset and angry with her for doing something he had told her she could do, yet the thought that she would ever want to be away from him for whatever reason deeply troubled him, and he wanted to throw something. He looked around the room for an innocuous missile to hurl at the fireplace and noticed Belinda for the first time sitting on the sofa and looking at him coquettishly from beneath her lowered lashes. He was unmoved by her blatant flirtation with him and, in fact, it made him want to toss a vase at the hearth even more. Benthower, meanwhile, ignored his wife and gloated over his victory. Bile rose in William's throat, and he felt it wise to leave the room.

"I have to go." Without further explanation, he stormed out of the salon. He would go for a ride on his horse to clear his head.

"William!" Cassandra called after him, but he did not turn around.

He flew down the hallway, unmoved by the sound of Cassandra's hurried footsteps behind him. He raced to the kitchen where he startled a couple of scullery maids putting dishes away and exited out the back of the house for the stables. He assumed Cassandra had tried to follow him, but she didn't know the lay of the house as well as him, and he must have lost her somewhere between the salon and the kitchen, for she was not behind him when he stepped out into the open air.

He ran outside through the kitchen garden for the stables, which sat among the outer buildings of the estate. He swiftly saddled his horse by himself, fearing any moment that she would catch up to him. He did not want to speak to her while in his present mood, and despite his shaking hands, he had the horse ready to go in record time. He hopped on his steed and trotted out of the stables just as she rushed up to him.

"William, please stop. Let me talk to you." Her voice was plaintive, and the desperation on her face clenched at his heart.

He said nothing to her, however, and galloped away instead.

"William!" He heard her call his name, but whatever else she said was lost in the wind.

He kept riding, turning into an open meadow away from the house, not really knowing where he was headed. He just wanted to get away from Springwinds. He couldn't stomach Benthower and the duchess, and he couldn't talk with any sort of rationality to Cassandra. He was hurting too much. He was too afraid of how much she meant to him. The thought of losing her, the thought that she would leave him for whatever reason, petrified him. He was frightened that she meant so much to him and that his world could come crashing down around him without her.

He rode hard until he came to a wooded area just beyond the glade and took refuge among the trees. The woods, however, reminded him of his horse ride at Wellesley Manor nearly nine weeks ago when he had come upon Cassandra walking in the rain and insisted that she ride his horse back to the house with him. Had that been a mistake? If he had never offered her a ride, they would never have started speaking civilly to one another, and he may not have offered to help her with her predicament then with Sir Lionel. And he would not be in the pain he was in now.

Oh, Cassandra, Cassandra. How much he loved her. Belinda had been nothing to him by comparison. In fact, no other love compared to the love he had for Cassandra. She was warm and kind and so passionate with him that he grew hard thinking of her—as usual. Their lovemaking these past few days had been earth-shattering for him. He wanted nothing more than to hold her in his arms for all eternity, and he was afraid that it was not the same for her. He feared that she did not feel for him what he felt for her. If she had felt for him *half* of what he felt for her, she would never have been able to ask Benthower to go forward with the annulment. With this realization, he turned his horse around and headed out of the woods. He was not ready to return home yet, so he headed the opposite way, toward East Welkin. Although it was early, he would go into town and get drunk and forget about her for a while.

CHAPTER 17

Three of Swords: Heartbreak, betrayal, separation, rupture, emotional pain . . .

———◦————

CASSANDRA RETURNED TO THE HOUSE with a heavy heart. She wanted nothing more than to find William and tell him how much she loved him. She had, in fact, called out the words to him as he rode away, but she doubted he'd heard her above the clopping of the horse's hooves. And even though he hadn't declared his love for her, she would tell him how she felt now because he was everything to her. She could tell by the expression on his face as he left the salon that he had been deeply hurt that she had written to Benthower asking him to go forth with the annulment—even though she had recanted her request in a second letter.

She returned to the salon and found Benthower still sitting there unmoved by the drama between her and William. Belinda, on the other hand, positively glowed as she sat drinking the tea that Wilkes had provided her. She took a sip and smiled broadly when she noticed Cassandra had returned. Why was she so happy about her and William's misery?

"Cassandra," Benthower said as she entered the room, "I'm glad you're back. Let him go. You're better off without him. We will return to London tomorrow."

"I'm not going anywhere without William. He will be back."

"Perhaps. But do you really think he's right for you? You're so independent that you would be better off on your own. If you're worried about the baby, we'll secret you off to the Continent where no one will ever know about it. You can have your baby there and then return to Durham where we'll have a cottage built for you and the child. You'll say you adopted the babe."

She stared at him for a moment through narrowed eyes. "That's strange, Benthower. How did you know about the baby? I haven't said anything about it to you yet."

He looked like he was well and truly had at that point but tried to cover his perfidy by saying, "Will told me."

"Impossible. You haven't spoken to William alone since you've arrived. And I know he didn't write you about the news."

Benthower just peered at her haughtily through lowered eyelids but didn't reply.

"You did receive my second letter, didn't you, you snake?"

"Cassandra, I—"

"No, don't try to explain. I know that's what happened."

"And what if it is? You're better off without Kingspointe. You're in my care now. Accept the annulment when it's finalized, dear sister. It's a gift really—and just in time for your birthday. I'll take you north to Durham where you can live in peace."

"Get out of my sight, Benthower. I don't want to see you."

The duke stood. "What about my money?" His question was beyond audacious, but his expression told her he was utterly serious in asking it. "And the money for the bishop, the chancellor, the doctor, and the witnesses?"

She huffed. "The doctor didn't even examine me!"

"He took my word on faith."

"What a fool he was then. And just where did you find witnesses to testify that I was insane at the time I married William, for the love of God?"

"That's not important. What is important is the fact that you now owe all these people considerable sums of money."

"Neither they—nor you—will get money from me, Michael."

"Fine. Maybe your husband will honor your debt."

"Ha! How soon you forget. He will no longer be obligated to pay my so-called debts when the annulment is finalized," she snarled at him and then left the room. She wanted nothing more than to have William with her at the moment. Where was he? Distressing man.

———◆———

TORTUOUS WOMAN. Why couldn't he drink her away?

"Chilton, my good man, set me up with another three fingers of whiskey, won't you?" William tapped his glass as he slurred his words.

"Pardon me for saying so, milord, but I think you've had enough to drink."

"Not nearly enough. Not while I can still remember her name. I just can't seem to drink her out of my mind."

"That bad, is it?"

William nodded.

"What happened?" Chilton seemed genuinely interested in William's story as he passed a wet rag over the surface of the bar.

"She had our marriage annulled. Oh, I told her she could do it, but the fact remains that I didn't want her to. She went and did it anyway, and soon we will no longer be husband and wife."

"That's brutal, milord, but I don't think drinking yourself senseless will help the situation. Why don't I have my wife make you some coffee so you can sober up for your ride home? Gladys," he called toward the small kitchen adjoining the pub.

A woman with rosy cheeks and a mobcap poked her head around the doorjamb.

"Please make his lordship some coffee."

Gladys nodded and retreated back into the kitchen.

"Bah. Another drink here, barkeep. There'll be enough time to sober up later, when she's gone."

Chilton regarded him a moment. "You love her, don't you?"

William squirmed under the barkeep's scrutiny. "More than words could ever say."

Chilton rubbed his bristled chin as though he were deciding what to do. William, meanwhile, tapped his glass for more whiskey. The bartender relented and poured him just enough liquid to cover the bottom of the glass. William gulped it down and then rose to leave.

"Perhaps you should sit a while, milord, rather than heading out just yet. Gladys is making you some coffee."

"I will be fine." He slurred the words as he tumbled off his barstool and landed on the floor.

Chilton dashed around to the other side of the bar and helped him to stand. William teetered as he got to his feet and then sat with a huff when the bartender led him back to the stool.

"You'll stay for coffee?"

William nodded.

A little while later, Gladys brought out a steaming mug of the brew and set it down before him. William mumbled his thanks, watching as Chilton kissed his wife and thanked her for her services.

"'Tis no problem whatsoever. You know I would do anything for you, my sweet," she said to her husband.

"That's why I love you and keep you around," said the barkeep. He patted his wife's bottom affectionately as she turned back toward the kitchen.

William watched with some resentment the interplay between Chilton and his wife. Obviously, they seemed to have a warm, loving relationship, the kind of relationship he had wanted with Cassandra. He envied the way the barkeep had had no difficulty telling his lady he loved her. Why couldn't William do the same with Cassandra? Why had he kept his feelings for her bottled up all this time? Why had he not been able to tell her he loved her yet?

He could only attribute it to pride. Pride and fear. Pride over the fact that she hadn't told him she loved him yet, but after the way Belinda had rebuffed his sentiments, he had not wanted to reveal himself to Cassandra before she confessed how she felt about him. He had not wanted to suffer the same kind of pain and anguish he had over Belinda's rejection. And then there was the fear, fear over the fact that he didn't think Cassandra would believe him even if he did tell her how he felt. He'd thought if he told her he loved her that she would become angry with him once again, like she had on the day when they'd made love in the carriage and he'd told her she was beautiful. He thought she would believe he was lying to her.

Yet, he had to overcome his pride and suppress his fear. He needed to tell her how he felt about her, regardless of how she felt about him. Life was too short, too capricious to guarantee a person happiness. He had nearly died not long ago, for God's sake. One had to seize the opportunity for joy when he could because one might never again get the chance. He should have told her he loved her the moment he realized it. Perhaps she would never have gone through with the annulment had he told her how he felt about her. He couldn't be sure of that, but what he could be sure of was that he had been foolish to bolt away from the situation like he'd done. It had solved nothing. He suddenly needed to talk to her. He needed to tell her he loved her. Now. He set his coffee mug down and turned to the bartender. "Thank you, Chilton. I must be going."

"You feel up to the ride home?"

"Yes."

"Good luck, milord. And Godspeed."

He took his leave of the bartender and got on his horse and rode back to Springwinds Hall. It was very late when he arrived, past ten o'clock, and he wanted nothing more than to go to Cassandra and talk to her, to tell her he loved her, to make love to her. As he walked into the main entryway, a light spilled from a room down the hall—his study. With relief, he paced toward the room. She must surely be waiting for him there. He stopped at the door and stared at the chair behind his desk.

"Belinda. What are you doing here?"

She answered him in her sultriest voice, "I've been waiting for you, William."

"What for?"

"I wanted to talk to you." She stood and walked seductively toward him.

"Again, I ask, what for?"

"I think it should be obvious."

"And what if it isn't? What if I have no idea what you're talking about?"

"No doubt you must have wondered why I came out to Essex with Benthower."

"Not really."

"I'm here for you, William. I've missed you these last few weeks. I never see you anymore." She closed the distance between them and stood right before him.

"That's because I've been in Essex," he said as though it should have been obvious.

"Still, you're not the same. You never seek me out any more, like you used to do."

"Things have changed, Belinda. I'm not the same man I was a few weeks ago."

"Don't say that." Her lips formed an insincere pout as she brushed a lock of hair from his forehead. She leaned in and whispered, "Come to me tonight."

"I'm married now."

"You won't be soon," she whispered again. "You'll be a free man. Come to me like you've always wanted to do. I love you, William. Don't you see? I was a fool all those years ago for putting you off and marrying Benthower. He doesn't love me. Not really. All he ever wanted was my money, but I long for you, William. I want you more than anything. I *love* you."

Years—*years*—he had waited to hear those words from her lips, and yet now, they left him flat. Not a beat of his heart did they affect. He was unmoved by them or by her. "And I love Cassandra."

"No, you don't. You may think you do, but you don't really love her. What has she got to offer you? She's a fishwife and a harridan, and she's not at all handsome."

"Don't ever say that about her again. She's the most beautiful woman I've ever seen."

She pouted her lips once again. "You used to say that about me. What happened?" Her words grated on his nerves, petty and whiny as they were.

"I told you. I fell in love with Cassandra." And in the shadows of the room, the lines around and beneath Belinda's eyes became visible to him for the first time, and she looked so old. Her scent surrounded him, also. It was a cloying, musky smell that made him long for fresh air and the sweet scent that was Cassandra.

As he was thinking about his lovely wife, he paid Belinda no attention, and before he realized it, she was right in front of him, closing in on him, kissing him on the lips. The kiss was cold, unaffectionate, without passion—like kissing a snake, and he felt nothing for her except revulsion. He had no time to react, however, as she stuck her tongue in his mouth and tried to parry it with his own. She tasted of stale wine and the dinner she'd had, not at all like his Cassandra. Repulsed by her, he tried to push her away, but she wrapped her arms firmly around his neck as she continued kissing him, and it was like being embraced by a serpent. Then she slithered closer to him and rubbed her body against his, further repelling him. He lifted his arms to hers to break the hold she had on him, but she would not let go and, in fact, drew him closer to her body, if that were possible. They were clenched in an embrace from which he could not extricate himself.

———————◆———————

CASSANDRA GAPED in anguish from her vantage point at the study door. Why, oh why, had she come downstairs looking for him? William's and Belinda's lips were locked together in a kiss so fierce, it almost shook the room. It shook her, anyway. The pain. Oh, the pain— it was a punch to the gut, unlike anything she'd ever experienced before, and she nearly doubled over from the agony of it.

She held on to her pride, however, and neither of them noticed her as she backed quietly away from the doorway. How she managed to walk away with as much composure as she did, she would never know, but she headed for the staircase trying to hold in the tears. By the time she rounded the corner, however, they were streaming down her face. She hurried upstairs to her room and broke into a sob as she closed the door behind her and ran to her bed.

So, that was how it was going to be, was it? Without so much as an attempt at reconciliation, he was going to turn to Belinda for solace, was he? At his first opportunity, he was going to be with that bitch, forgetting about Cassandra. Well, she should have known that anything they had together would always be overshadowed by the love he had felt for the duchess all these years, would pale in comparison to what he felt for Belinda. Her heart sank to the very lowest depths it had ever been with the realization that compared to Belinda, she was nothing, especially to him. No one could ever be what Belinda was to him.

She cried for what seemed like forever—until she heard him return to his room next to hers. She went silent, then, as the sounds of his door closing filtered through their adjoining door. He knocked about his room for a few moments, and then the handle of their connecting door turned. She didn't want to speak to him, wasn't prepared for a confrontation with him, so she pretended to be asleep. She lay on her side away from the door and pulled the covers on her bed up to her chin and closed her eyes.

She listened intently as William opened the door and walked into her bedroom. He padded over to her bed and touched her lightly on her shoulder. Still, she pretended to sleep, hoping he would go away. She sensed him waiting a moment to see if she would awaken, but when she didn't move, he kissed her on her cheek. He smelled of liquor and a vaguely familiar musky scent that reminded her of her sister-in-law, and she wanted to sit up and scream when his lips touched her skin. She remained still, however. He then padded away back toward the door, which opened and closed softly, and he was gone. She opened one eyelid slightly to make sure he was not there and then opened them both. When she was certain he had left her room, she wiped the kiss he had given her from her cheek, disgusted at the thought that he had just kissed Belinda before he had kissed her.

The sudden need to get away from him and Springwinds Hall was overwhelming, but where could she go at this time of night, and how could she get there? She wanted a friendly shoulder to cry on, someone she could talk to about what she had witnessed with him and the duchess. She desperately wanted Julia or Violet or both at that moment. However, they were both in London at Julia's townhouse. She contemplated how she could possibly get to London by herself. Her options were to take William's carriage, to go by stage-coach from East Welkin, or to ride back to London with Benthower and the duchess tomorrow.

Of the three options, taking William's carriage seemed the most difficult. For one thing, she would have to wake the coachman and a groom to get the carriage ready, and she was afraid one of them would get a message to his lordship that she was attempting to leave. Would he even try to stop her? Or would he willingly let her go now that he had Belinda? In either case, she didn't want to see him or speak to him, so she decided against taking his coach.

That left either riding back to London with their graces or taking the stagecoach from East Welkin. There was absolutely no way she was going to endure the close confines of a carriage with Benthower and Belinda, especially on her birthday, so that left the stagecoach as her only option. If she started walking to East Welkin in a couple of hours, she would be there by early morning to catch the first stage out of town. Riding a stagecoach would be most uncomfortable, but she would tough it out for the chance to get away from Springwinds. And of course, she would have to bring a maid with her. She would leave Findley here at Springwinds to deal with William in the morning, and take a chambermaid or scullery maid with her instead.

While she waited for him to go to sleep, she jotted him a quick note. It was short and to the point.

Lord Kingspointe,
I saw you with the duchess tonight. I am leaving

you to each other.
    Lady Cassandra

She placed the note and the ring he had given to her in Nether Wrigsby on her pillow, and when she heard no more noise from his chamber, she gathered her pelisse, bonnet, and reticule and silently left her room. She sneaked past his door without a sound and made it to the staircase undetected. From there, she went upstairs to wake Findley, whom she had sent to bed after learning that William was back.

"Findley, I need you to wake up," she said, shaking the maid to rouse her.

"What is it, my lady?" The maid rubbed her eyes.

"I'm leaving for London."

Findley's eyes shot open. "Now?"

"Yes, now. And I don't want Lord Kingspointe to know about it, so I'm walking to East Welkin tonight and taking a stagecoach in the morning."

"But, my lady, that is so dangerous."

"Nevertheless, that's what I'm going to do. I need you to get a maid to accompany me. And be discreet."

"Shan't I go with you?"

"No. I need you here to put Lord Kingspointe off in the morning. I've locked my door to him so that he can't get in there too early. You are to tell him I don't want to be awoken until after eleven."

"He'll be angry and concerned that you are gone," Findley warned.

"Don't worry. I have left him a note explaining everything."

Findley did as she was told and went to wake a scullery maid to accompany Cassandra into town. Cassandra also procured a lantern for each of them to carry to light their way. After she had assured the frightened and bewildered girl that everything would be all right, she and the maid set out for East Welkin. She would go to London and forget all about William. Bloody man.

———◆———

ENDEARING WOMAN. Today was her birthday, and he had dreamt of her all night long. He jolted awake, however, with an excruciating headache. Apparently, he had drunk more than he thought he had last night. He looked at the clock on his dresser and realized it was still early, however—only seven o'clock. He sat up and threw off his covers. He wanted to talk to Cassandra about yesterday, about why he had left when he found out about the annulment, and about their future together. More than anything, he wanted to tell her he loved her. They would either have to stop the annulment or get remarried to one another, this time in the Church. If they got a start soon, they could head to London yet today so that they could apply for a special license as soon as possible.

He got out of bed, threw on his banyan, and rang for his valet. If Cassandra weren't already awake, he would wake her himself so that they could get going. Perhaps they could even make love quickly in celebration of her birthday before they set out. He crossed to the door leading to her room, but when he turned the knob, it was locked. Odd, he thought. When would she have locked the door? She had been asleep when he had left her room last night, but perhaps she was already awake this morning. Perhaps she was dressing or bathing and didn't want him barging in on her privacy. He knocked but received no response.

He heard a knock on his own door, and on answering it, found Watts there with some fresh water for his morning ablutions.

"Where's Findley?" he asked.

"I believe she's still upstairs."

"Please have her come down. I'd like her to get Lady Kingspointe for me at once."

Watts left to get Cassandra's abigail, and William, meanwhile, took the water and emptied the pitcher into the basin on his dressing table. He washed himself, and rather than waiting for Watts to return, shaved himself to save time. He dressed and then bided his time in frustration waiting for Watts to return with Findley. He knocked on Cassandra's door once again. And once again, nothing. He went out into the hallway and tried to open the main door to her room, but it was locked as well. He had keys to the room somewhere, just not on him. Findley, at least, had keys.

An appallingly long while later, Watts returned with Findley.

"There you are." William couldn't hide his abject irritation. "I've been waiting for half an hour."

"I'm sorry, my lord," said Watts. "Findley was indisposed."

William ignored his valet and turned to the abigail. "Findley, I'd like to get into Lady Kingspointe's room to speak to her. She doesn't answer my knock."

Findley didn't speak for a moment as she fidgeted with her apron. Finally, she said, "Lady Kingspointe left instructions that she wasn't to be woken until eleven."

"Well, it's seven-thirty. That's close enough. Besides, she and I need to get ready to leave for London as soon as possible. Go ahead and unlock her door so that I can wake her."

The maid drew a deep breath, exhaled, and did as she was told. Her hands shook as she unlocked the door, and then William entered Cassandra's room. Her bed was empty, and the ring he had bought her in Nether Wrigsby sat on her pillow next to a note addressed to him. His heart lurched as he snatched up the note and quickly read it.

"Bloody hell!" Rage washed over him, not at Cassandra and the fact that she was gone, but rather at Belinda and the fact that she had kissed him last night and that Cassandra had seen them together.

"Find—ley!" he shouted, as though the maid had stepped out of hearing distance.

"Yes, my lord?"

"Where is Lady Kingspointe?" His voice and manner were gruff, but he made no apologies for his mood.

The maid hesitated, obviously afraid to speak.

"Do you know where she is?"

Findley nodded timorously.

"You can tell me. You must tell me," William said a little more gently.

"She's gone to London, sir."

"Bloody hell! How? Did she take my carriage?"

"No, sir," Findley replied and then remained quiet.

"Would you mind telling me how she did go to London then?" Though his patience was running thin, he forced himself to be gentle with the question.

"She was going to take the stagecoach from East Welkin."

Exasperated, he scrubbed his hands over his face. "And how did she get to East Welkin if she didn't take my carriage?"

"She walked, sir."

"Walked?! Bloody hell." For the third time, he cursed

as he stomped about the room irritably. "When did she leave?"

"Very late last night."

He threw his arms up in frustration. "Oh, for the love of . . . Didn't she realize how dangerous it was for her to walk out alone in the middle of the night?"

"She had a maid with her."

"That's hardly reassuring, Findley," he replied irritably.

He instructed Watts to pack a bag for him and then ordered for his curricle and a groom to accompany him. He wanted the curricle because it was lighter and swifter than his large carriage, though he doubted he could catch up to the stagecoach given it had probably left East Welkin around six this morning, but if he left now, he could make it to London by sometime this afternoon or this evening.

He was on his way out the front door to board the curricle waiting for him in the drive when he heard his name. He turned to see Belinda hurrying down the stairs toward him.

"William, I need to speak to you. You left so abruptly last night that we didn't get a chance to talk."

"Now is not the time, Belinda. Besides, we said all there is to say."

She appeared wounded, genuinely wounded, and her voice wavered as she said, "But what am I to do? I love you."

If that were true, then he felt pity for her. He truly did, for he had been in her predicament—loving someone for years whom he could not have and who did not love him in return. "Well, don't do the same thing I did for the past fifteen years. Don't pine and suffer for someone you can't have, Belinda. You're married to

Benthower. You chose him over me. Love him."

Tears shimmered in her eyes. "But he doesn't love me. Not like you. Besides, he has his mistress now."

"I'm sorry. I truly am, but there is nothing for us, Belinda. I love Cassandra, and I have to go find her."

"Why? Where is she?" she asked petulantly.

"She saw us kissing last night, and she has gone to London. I must leave now to find her." And without a look backward, he ran out the door to his curricle and headed for London.

———◆———

Exhausted and sick, Cassandra watched out the window as the stagecoach pulled up to the coaching inn just outside of Chelmsford a little before seven. What a way to spend her birthday. She had been on the road for only an hour, and she didn't know how much more of this infernal ride she could take. The coach was not sprung well, so that every little rut it hit caused the vehicle to shake and rock violently. The constant lurching made her sicker than she already felt from the baby, and the sweaty, stinky bodies packed snugly together inside the tight space of the coach made her so nauseated that she had to get out and rest at the next stop, if only so she could cast up her accounts. She used the privy and then rented a small sitting room where she and the maid Nettie could rest from the road until she felt well enough to continue traveling. The next stagecoach was scheduled to leave at nine, and she was certain she would feel more herself by then.

She ordered some tea for Nettie and herself, and revived somewhat after drinking the hot beverage. She even chanced eating a bit of crumpet, as she was feeling a little better since having thrown up. After eating and drinking, the fatigue from not having slept all night overwhelmed her, and she lay down on the settee that was in the sitting room to rest a bit before the next stage arrived. She fell asleep quickly, oblivious to the rest of the world.

She opened her eyes a while later and then bolted upright when the clock in the hallway struck nine. Damn it! She glanced over at Nettie, who was sleeping soundly in the chair across from her. She must have dozed off, too, after Cassandra had gone to sleep. Now, the both of them had overslept and possibly—probably—missed the nine o'clock stage. She rose from the settee and nudged Nettie.

"Nettie, wake up."

The maid wiped the sleep from her eyes and looked around in bewilderment. "What is it, my lady?"

"Make haste. We overslept."

"Goodness, what time is it?"

"It's already nine. Now, go. Run out to the desk and see if we've missed the next stagecoach."

"Yes, ma'am." Nettie yawned loudly, stretched her arms and legs out before her, and then stood to do as she was told.

A short time later, the maid dashed back into the room and slammed the door behind her, appearing spooked by something.

"What's the matter?" Cassandra asked with concern.

"I saw Lord Kingspointe out there."

"Oh, no! Please say it isn't so. Where? Did he see you?"

"At the front desk. I was asking if the nine o'clock stage had gone yet, and I think he mighta saw me from the side." Nettie wrung her hands in obvious anxiety.

"Do you think he recognized you?"

"Maybe. He saw me yesterday putting dishes away in the kitchen. He looked at me kinda funny today, like he mighta known me from somewheres."

"Did he follow you or see where you went just now?"

"I don't know, my lady. I'm so sorry!"

The maid appeared so agitated, Cassandra feared she might faint. "Oh, don't worry yourself too much about it, Nettie. Has the nine o'clock left yet?"

"No. It's still outside. Apparently, a horse needs to be reshod before they can leave."

Cassandra peeked out the window overlooking the coaching yard. The stage was sitting in the yard down one horse, and there was William talking with the driver, while his groom skulked about the yard accosting patrons as they left the inn. He was most probably searching for clues about her. Oh, dear. This was not good. She'd never be able to sneak out the door and onto the coach with the both of them lurking about asking questions.

She continued to watch William out the window as he spoke with the coachman. He did not appear pleased at all. He put his hands on his hips, as if he were unhappy with the news from the driver, and then turned to head back inside the inn.

She hustled over to the door to her room and opened it a fraction, peeking out the crack. From her vantage point, it was difficult to see anything, but she heard William down the hall asking the clerk behind the desk whether he had seen a woman fitting her description. Her heart pounded in her throat as the clerk, whose voice she did not recognize, said no. She thanked Heaven that he was not the same person who had rented out the room to her and Nettie and, therefore, had never seen her.

She heard William ask the clerk if he might check the inn for any signs of her, and the clerk agreed to let him search the dining room and down the hallway for her.

She quickly and quietly shut the door and bolted it. There was no back door, so she was well and truly stuck in the room with no way out. He knocked on doors here and there in the corridor, asking for her but having no success, of course. He got to her door and knocked on it, calling out her name. She and Nettie, however, remained as still as statues, making no sounds whatsoever. Finally, she heard William's footfalls move on to the next door down the hall. Eventually, after he seemed to have tried all the doors along the hallway, the floorboards in the hallway creaked as he walked back toward the front desk. She held her breath and moved once again to the window overlooking the coaching yard. He exited the building and headed for his curricle. He climbed up next to his groom, and the carriage rolled away. Within moments, he was out of sight. Troublesome man.

CHAPTER 18

King of Swords: A just, ethical, intellectual man with dark hair and light eyes, who is brilliant, caring, and wise . . .

———◆———

WORRISOME WOMAN. WHERE THE HELL was she? He had not passed her on the road to East Welkin this morning, nor had he seen her at the coaching inn in the village. He had to assume she had made it onto the stagecoach this morning with no troubles because the alternative was too horrible to consider. But if she had been on the stagecoach from East Welkin, then she had to have passed through the coaching inn in Chelmsford on her way to London, for it was on the stage route. Yet, the clerk at the Chelmsford inn had not seen anyone resembling her. Nor had the driver of the coach been able to give him any clues as to her whereabouts. Of course, the driver had just pulled into Chelmsford from the north, so he would not have had her as a passenger.

In his gut, though, he had the feeling that Cassandra had been hiding from him in the inn the entire time that he'd been searching for her. He thought that he had seen one of the maids from his own kitchen standing there at the front desk among the crowd of people,

but he wouldn't have sworn to it as he had only seen
her in profile. He wished he'd had the foresight to get
to know all the names and faces of the new servants
at Springwinds so that he could've said for sure that
she was one of his employees. He would have asked
the girl whether or not she was with Cassandra anyway had he been able to find her again, but just as
quickly as he had spied her, he turned, and she was
gone. Nevertheless, he had to press on to London, for
even if they were back at that inn, they would eventually make it to her sister's house in Town. He figured
that had to be her destination. Where else would she
go? To his house? Not bloody likely. To Benthower's
house? Even less likely.

As he drove down the road in his curricle, he contemplated how he would tell Cassandra he loved her.
He wanted nothing more than to take her in his arms
and show her how he felt, but he feared that she would
balk at his touch. Should he, then, just blurt out his
feelings the moment he saw her? Or should he say
he loved her with a little more finesse than that? Of
course, the latter would be better, but how did he even
get to that point when he had to explain about Belinda
first? Would she accept as truth the fact that Belinda
had kissed him and not the other way around?

Such a whirlwind was his mind that it took him a
while to notice that his lead horse, one of a matched
pair of bays, trotted along as though it was lame. Its
strange gait and the fact that its head nodded up and
down with each movement of his hind leg were sure
signs that something was amiss. He pulled the horses to
a stop, and he and the groom hopped down from the
curricle to check the animal. A careful examination
revealed that the gelding's hind left foot had a large

abscess that must have been causing the animal considerable pain. The horse would no longer be able to haul the curricle.

He instructed his groom to wait with the horses and the carriage while he walked to the nearest farm, which they had passed about a half a mile back, for help. He'd have ridden the healthy horse over to the house, but the animal was not broke for riding.

He walked briskly and arrived at the farmhouse about twenty minutes later, hot and sweaty. He wiped his brow with his handkerchief and knocked on the front door of the house, where a tall young woman, who appeared to be a maid by how she was dressed, greeted him from behind the doorway. She had dark hair and green eyes and so reminded him of his Cassandra that his heart clenched in longing for his wife.

"Good morning," he said. "Allow me to introduce myself. I am Lord Kingspointe from near East Welkin."

"Good morning," she replied in a voice barely above a whisper. She curtsied to him but didn't provide him with her own name, nor did she show him into the house.

"One of my horses has taken lame up the road a bit, and I was wondering if I might speak to the gentleman or lady of the house about borrowing an animal from them for a short time."

"Wait one second, please," she said, again barely audibly. She closed the door on him and disappeared into the house.

Several minutes later, the maid returned with a middle-aged woman in a mobcap and white muslin day dress and then introduced William as Lord Kingspointe. The older woman clucked her tongue at her servant and said, "Molly, really. When are you going to learn? You should have invited his lordship into the parlor and offered him some tea." She turned to him and curtsied. "My apologies, my lord. I'm Mrs. Pierce. Won't you come in? I'll have Molly put on some water for tea."

"I thank you, ma'am, but what I'd really like is to find out whether or not I might borrow a horse. One of my own horses has gone lame with an abscess in its hind hoof, and I need another to carry my curricle just to the next town. I'd pay you for your trouble, of course."

"Oh, it'd be no trouble. I think we could work something out, at any rate. Let me take you around back to the stables where you can meet my husband and make arrangements with him."

So saying, the woman invited William into the house and led him through the rooms to the kitchen in the back, and from there, out to the garden. They wended their way through rows of newly planted vegetables and various herbs, and he followed her to the back buildings, among which was a modest stable.

"Mr. Pierce? Mr. Pierce, are you in here?" Mrs. Pierce called into the stables.

"I'm over here." A muffled, masculine voice came from a stall at the other end of the building.

Mrs. Pierce led William to the end of the stalls where a tall man sweating with the exertion of his labors pitched some hay to a skinny mare. After his wife made the introductions, Mr. Pierce bowed at William, while he returned a nod.

"Lord Kingspointe here would like to borrow our horse to draw his curricle just to Creston Ridge."

"I'd be prepared to pay you a guinea to let me borrow the animal."

Mr. Pierce leaned on his pitchfork and laughed out loud. "For a guinea, I'd let you keep the animal."

"That won't be necessary. I just need to get to Creston Ridge to hire another animal."

"Very well. All's I've got to loan you is this old nag here named Daisy. She's trained to haul a carriage but ain't broke to riding. You're welcome to her for as long as you need her."

"It won't be too long. I'll just need her to get me to Creston Ridge, and then we'll figure out how to get her back to you."

The arrangements agreed upon, William set off once again at a brisk pace leading Daisy to his curricle. All the while as he walked, he couldn't help but wonder where Cassandra was now. He sent up a little prayer that wherever she was, she was safe.

———◆———

CASSANDRA SAT on the front facing bench in the coach next to an open window, holding a fragrant handkerchief to her nose to mask the smell of the sweaty bodies stuffed inside the stagecoach. She was thoroughly nauseated once again and slightly jealous of Nettie, who had the good fortune, at least, to be riding up top in the open air. The stagecoach hadn't left Chelmsford until ten due to the necessity of reshodding one of its horses, but Cassandra was grateful they were on the road now and wouldn't be bothered again by William and his groom.

Not more than twenty minutes later, the coach seemed to be slowing to a stop, and she looked out the window to see what the commotion was about. Oh, lord. William's curricle was parked by the side of the road. Her heart thumped in her chest as she recognized his carriage. Dear God, he wasn't hurt, was he? She prayed nothing was wrong with him. Both of his horses were unharnessed and eating grass in the meadow next to the road. And while the groom appeared weary and apprehensive, there was no sign of William. She shot straight up in her seat when she realized he was not by the curricle.

The stagecoach came to a complete halt beside the other vehicle, and the driver called down to the groom, "Is something wrong here, sir?"

"Just one of our horses has come up lame. My lord went to the nearest farmhouse for help. He should be back any moment, if you could wait for him."

Cassandra's heart began to pound. Was William all right? Oh dear, what if he was hurt? She longed to know he was doing fine, and yet, she didn't wish to see him, for fear he would make her return to Spring-winds Hall with him. What if she'd come all this way only to be thwarted by running into William out here on the road to London?

"I hate to say this, but we really should be moving along. That is if you have everything under control and no one is hurt. We're running late as it is, and we really can't wait for him," said the driver.

"No, no one is hurt," the groom replied. "Thank you, though, for stopping to check on our situation."

Vastly relieved that William was not hurt and that the stagecoach would be moving on, Cassandra kept her head low and her face hidden beneath the large brim of her bonnet so that William's groom wouldn't notice her or recognize her. She only hoped Nettie did the same up top.

The rest of the ride to London was uneventful, and at long last, the stagecoach pulled up to the Oxford Arms in Warwick Lane. It was still early—only four o'clock. Cassandra wanted nothing more than to see her two sisters. She rented a hack to take her and Nettie from the coaching inn to Julia's leased townhouse where both Julia and Violet were staying for the Season. The hack ride was nearly as abominable as the stagecoach ride had been, and by the time she arrived at her sister's place, she was ready to throw up once again. She managed, however, to hold on until she made it to the front door. She asked for a chamber pot before she asked for her sister, and after casting up one more time, she felt relieved enough to ask for Julia and to send Nettie below stairs for a respite and some food.

"Cassandra!" Julia appeared at the door just in time to see her throw up. "I'd wish you a happy birthday, but you don't look so well. Goodness. Tell me what is happening."

"Julia, may I have some water?"

"Yes, of course." She turned to a footman and said, "Please get Lady Kingspointe some water." Then she led Cassandra into the drawing room and sat her down on the settee.

"It won't be 'Lady Kingspointe' for long. Soon, it'll be 'Lady Cassandra' once again."

Julia cocked her head to one side like a confused terrier. "I don't understand."

"The annulment is underway. And just in time."

"But how?" Confusion flashed across Julia's features. "I thought an annulment was out of the question."

Cassandra explained how Benthower had begun the process for the annulment by manipulating the bishop, chancellor, doctor, and witnesses to testify on her behalf. She also explained that she had been upset at first by the fact that he had moved forward with the arrangements without her permission. "But now I'm glad about it. Joyful even. I couldn't be happier. Soon I will be rid of William forever." But even as she spoke the words, the tears that threatened to fall from her lashes belied her true feelings and the pain she was in.

Julia took her hand and squeezed it. "Why, what's the matter then?"

"Oh, Julia, I saw him kissing Belinda." Cassandra swiped her eyes with her handkerchief.

"Who? William? How could he? I had no idea he was such a bounder."

"He's always been in love with her. Evidently, that'll never change. And I won't stay with him, Julia. Not while he has her. I can't do it. I just can't do it." She inhaled sharply as she tried to gain control of her emotions.

"Nor should you have to. You will stay with me."

"I will have to go away soon, however, because of the baby. I can't have the child here in England when I am unwed. I'll have to go abroad."

"Of course, dear, of course." Julia took Cassandra in her arms and caressed her back to soothe her. "Well, we will certainly go somewhere far away while you have your baby, but I don't want you to worry about that now. Is there anything I can do for you at this moment?"

"I believe I'd just like to rest for a couple of hours."

"As well you should. And then when you awaken, you should accompany Violet and me to Almack's for an evening of diversion to celebrate your birthday."

"I don't know if I am up to a night out. I'm not at all well, and I haven't anything to wear. Plus, I'm still supposed to be in mourning for William's brother David and shouldn't go out."

"Nonsense. You are no longer obliged to mourn William's brother if you'll soon be unwed to William. And as far as a dress, you can wear one of Violet's or mine."

"But I've put on so much flesh because of the baby that nothing will fit me, especially in the bosom."

"If we work quickly, we can have my maid Burton let out the bust on one of our dresses a little. Violet has a beautiful white one with pearls woven into the bodice and silk florets ringing the hem. It will be perfect, and you will look stunning in it."

"I don't know, Julia." She sighed at the thought of going anywhere without William, even though she was still infuriated with him.

"Oh, say yes, Cassandra. We'll have such fun. You need to forget about that man and have a nice time, especially on your birthday."

Cassandra shrugged her indifference.

"Well, just think about it at least. We don't have to leave until eight-thirty, which gives you several hours to rest. Maybe you'll feel up to it after a nap."

"Fine, fine. I'll consider it."

"Wonderful. Now let's have Burton measure your bosom and get to work on that dress in case you wish to go later on."

Cassandra nodded, thankful for her sister. "I don't know what I'd do without you, Julia. If Kingspointe should come here looking for me, please don't let him know I'm here. I don't want to speak to him."

"As you wish."

Julia then took her upstairs to a bedroom, made her comfortable, and ordered some tea and biscuits for her, even though Cassandra wasn't sure she could eat them. Before her tray arrived, Julia's maid Burton came into her room to measure her bust. When she was done, another maid delivered her food and drink, and Cassandra nibbled at a biscuit and drank some tea. Though she felt physically better, she was still emotionally overwrought. How would she ever mend her broken heart after the crushing blow it had taken when she had seen William kissing Belinda? She tried to tell herself that it should have come as no surprise that he and the duchess would end up with one another somehow. She had always suspected they had been together in some fashion, anyway.

Fatigued from the tribulations of the day, she readied herself for her nap and wearily went to her reticule to search for the few articles she had brought with her on this trip, among them her hairbrush, and was frustrated when she couldn't find the thing. She dumped the contents of her bag onto her bed, and her tarot deck fell out onto the counterpane. She had forgotten that she had carried it with her from Springwinds, and she was struck by the fact that all the cards remained face down except for one. Staring up at her from the pile of cards was the King of Swords. She immediately thought of William. Under other circumstances, she would have taken the card to portend that he was coming back into her life. But that was impossible now.

Then she was reminded of the reading her grandmother had done for her on the eve of her debut. Cassandra had drawn the King of Swords that night, and against the advice of Grandmamma, she had turned William down for the first dance that evening. Perhaps if she had accepted him, then things would have turned out much differently than they had. Perhaps they would have formed a bond that night, and perhaps they might even have married eventually, as her grandmother had predicted. She was sick at the thought of what might have been and quickly put the cards away. Oh, how she still loved William. Regrettable man.

———◆———

UNSETTLING WOMAN. She was probably asleep now after having such a long, arduous day of travel. It had taken him four hours to arrange for his horse to be replaced and to get the borrowed mare back to the Pierces, so he hadn't arrived in London until nine o'clock that night. He decided to skip going to his house and went to Julia's townhouse first instead. The place was mostly dark when he arrived around nine-thirty. Though he realized it was too late for a visit and that he should turn around and go home rather than disturb anyone, he was too anxious about Cassandra to do anything but descend from his curricle and approach the front door. He knocked, and a beleaguered footman answered. William asked to be admitted, but the footman told him that everyone had gone out for the evening.

William didn't believe him. "Is Lady Kingspointe here?" He used her married name rather than "Lady Cassandra."

"I'm not at liberty to say," said the servant.

William took that as a "yes" and stated adamantly, "I'm not going anywhere until I've seen Lady Kingspointe. It's urgent that I talk to her."

"I told you, sir, they went out for the evening." The footman refused him admittance until William, taking a page from Benthower's book, threatened to barge in and search the house himself for his wife, at which point the servant asked him to wait in the entryway while he offered to get Julia's maid. The footman then disappeared upstairs, and not long thereafter, William heard the vague murmur of voices coming from the landing. A good length of time later, Julia's maid came downstairs and greeted him in the entryway, not offering to show him in.

"What can I do for you at this late hour, Lord Kingspointe?" she asked him.

"I've come looking for Lady Kingspointe. She left Essex early this morning headed for London, and I have reason to believe she has come here."

"She's not here."

He didn't believe her, but rather than arguing about it, he began yelling loudly in the entryway. "Cassandra? Are you here?"

"Really, Lord Kingspointe," said the maid. She waved the footman over to help him to the door.

William would not be put off. "Cassandra! I'm not leaving until I talk to you!"

"Shush! It's late. I think it best that you leave, sir. *Now.*"

"Cassandra!" he raised his voice even louder than before. "Cassandra! I know you are here."

"Please be quiet, Lord Kingspointe. You'll wake the neighborhood. Lady Cassandra and her sisters went out for the evening," said the maid a little desperately.

"Oh? And where did they go?" he grumbled.

"I'm not at liberty to say."

"Please, madam, I must know where she is. It's imperative that I see her. Won't you please tell me where she is?"

The maid seemed to think on his request.

"I'll bluster even louder than I'm doing now if you don't tell me where she is."

Finally, the frustrated maid lifted her arms in defeat. "Almack's. They've all gone to Almack's."

It was Wednesday. Of course they would go to Almack's—probably to celebrate Cassandra's birthday with some dance and bad refreshments.

"Thank you, ma'am. Thank you so much." He took her hand and kissed it and then turned to leave. He'd have hugged the girl had it been at all appropriate. He left the house and bounded down the front steps to his curricle. Of course, this meant that he had to run home to change from his trousers into his damned knee breeches so he would not be turned away from the door at Almack's by the haughty patronesses. It was just after ten, but if he hurried to Kingspointe House and dressed quickly, he might just make it to Almack's before the doors closed at eleven.

His house was dark and quiet when he arrived, and he startled a sleeping footman when he burst through the front door. Watts was not with him, of course, so he had the footman wake Moreland, the butler, and he commandeered the man to assist him with his wardrobe. Oh, he could pick out his own clothes and even manage to dress himself, but if his breeches required pressing at all, then he would need Moreland to do the honors.

He selected his breeches, which indeed needed some ironing and set the butler to work on that task. Meanwhile, he sent the footman for some water so that he could wash off the dirt of the road before heading to Almack's. When his water finally arrived, he washed and even shaved so that he didn't look like a complete barbarian. Once he was dressed and ready to go, he made certain he also had his voucher for admittance to the infernal club. Then he bounded down the stairs and out of his house to the street where his curricle remained parked. He and his groom were finally on their way at about ten to eleven. He would be cutting it close with respect to the arrival time, but surely he could make it. He had to make it. He had to see her as soon as possible.

Traffic was snarled around St. James's and in King Street due to the crush at Almack's, and he couldn't find a place to park his curricle near the entrance. The Season was in high celebration these days, it being nearly June. And though William detested the marriage mart, he had purchased a voucher for Almack's—and been granted one by the snobbish patronesses—for this Season so that he could, ironically, search for a wife. Now, by some bizarre fluke of fate, he had himself a wife whom he loved with all his being. Or rather, he didn't have her, thanks to her meddling brother. Why was Benthower always disrupting his happiness?

He put the duke out of his thoughts as he searched for a place to park. Nothing was available near the entrance because of all the vehicles parked everywhere, and in fact, he couldn't even drive down the street to have his groom drop him off. The closest he could get to King Street was Pall Mall, which would have to do, for his pocket watch indicated it was one minute to eleven. He had practically no time before they closed admittance to the club. He, therefore, handed the reins over to his groom while he jumped out of the curricle and ran from Pall Mall to Almack's.

He arrived sweaty and breathless at two minutes past the hour, but it didn't matter. He was going to see Cassandra, whether the patronesses liked it or not. He sensed there was going to be trouble because already an attendant was giving him problems about the time, telling him it was too late to enter.

———◆———

Cassandra was enchanted by the beeswax candles illuminating the ballroom and reflecting off the mirrors. The whole effect made the room appear even larger than it already was. She was glancing up to the pavilion at the orchestra, which was warming up for the next dance, when she felt a tug on her elbow.

She turned and was completely surprised to see Lord Wakefield by her side.

He bowed, as she curtsied. "If you aren't already taken for the next dance, Lady Kingspointe, would you do me the honor of accompanying me?"

The next dance was a waltz, and though she didn't really want to dance with Wakefield due to the unsavory propositions he'd made to her during their dances at Julia's ball several weeks ago, she couldn't turn him down, not without being rude beyond all measure.

"No, I'm not already taken, and of course, I would be happy to dance with you," she lied. She took his proffered arm, however, and followed him to the dance floor.

With reluctance, she stood next to him waiting for the music to begin. In truth, she wanted only William beside her, and not for the first time since she'd departed from Springwinds Hall this morning, she began to feel remorse for having left him. She was such a hothead sometimes. Had leaving been the right course of action? Or should she have waited to talk to him about what she witnessed between Belinda and him? Perhaps there was a logical explanation as to why they had been kissing, and yet, as she heard the words in her head, she knew that was ludicrous.

Logical explanation. Ha! One kissed a woman because one wanted the woman. The only logical explanation was that he was still in love with Belinda, and she must have returned the sentiment to some degree, given the way she returned the kiss.

The waltz started, and once again, her thoughts returned to the moment.

"Where is Kingspointe this evening?" Wakefield asked, a smirk on his face.

"Oh, he is otherwise engaged and unable to join me and my sisters here at Almack's."

He leaned in a little closer to her. "You know, if you were my lady, I would never leave you alone for a moment." His low, unnerving voice was calculated to seduce.

Her cheeks flamed, and she was momentarily rendered speechless.

"You blush, Cassandra." An indelicate gleam shown in his eye.

"Lord Wakefield, I haven't given you leave to use my Christian name. You must desist."

"Ah, but there is something between us, my dear. We have an understanding, you and I."

"I'm not sure I know what you're talking about, sir."

"Only that you and I could be together, sweet, if you'd just consent to letting me come to you one night this week." Once again, his low voice unsettled her. "I'll be discreet, of course."

Warmth rushed to her cheeks with his words, and she shuddered at the thought of being with the man. Though momentarily rendered speechless by his offer, she gathered herself together and looked him squarely in the eye. "As I've told you before, Lord Wakefield, I'm a married woman." Which was rubbish, and she knew it. Soon she would no longer be married to William, so why she persisted in pretending she was still wed to him eluded her. Still, she added, "I could never betray my husband like that."

"That's funny, my lady." His lips formed a cunning smile. "Because I heard that the two of you were no longer together and that your marriage is being dissolved. No easy feat, I understand, but it is being done nonetheless."

My, how quickly news traveled throughout the *ton*—thanks to Benthower, no doubt.

She hesitated a moment as she considered her answer. "While it is true that I will soon no longer be married to Kingspointe, I still can't entertain the notion of an assignation with you, Lord Wakefield. I mean you no offense. It's just that I'm not inclined to an involvement at this time."

"You wound me, my lady. I have wanted you since we danced at your sister's party. You are the most beautiful creature I've ever beheld, and I could ravish you here on the dance floor."

How she wished she could hear those words from William's lips instead of Wakefield's, but he was not here to say them. Even so, she shook off thoughts of her erstwhile husband. "You shouldn't say such things, Lord Wakefield."

Wakefield merely grinned wolfishly at her.

"No, you shouldn't," growled a familiar voice. She turned as best she could in Wakefield's grasp and saw William standing behind them. His mouth snarled, while his eyes held a feral gaze trained on Wakefield, and her heart nearly leapt out of her breast with joy at seeing him. "Unhand my wife." That he'd called her his wife further undid her.

They'd stopped dancing, but Wakefield's arm remained around her possessively. And as she looked about her, she noticed a commotion on the ballroom floor. All dancing had effectively ceased, while the dancers angled their heads for a better look at William, Wakefield, and her. Meanwhile, two attendants and Lady Jersey stalked over to William.

"Very soon, Kingspointe, she will not be your wife anymore," said Wakefield.

"That is only due to an unfortunate misunderstanding and a technicality that I hope to remedy as soon as possible."

Cassandra's heart raced. What could he mean?

Meanwhile, Lady Jersey and the attendants accosted William on the dance floor, one attendant grabbing his left arm and the other his right. "Really, Lord Kingspointe, how dare you barge in here past the attendants!" she said with severe indignation. "It's unheard of. You arrived after eleven, so they could not admit you. You must leave, sir. You must. This simply isn't done."

"I'll not leave without my . . . er, without Cassandra." He tried to wrest free of the men holding him.

"She's with me tonight," said Wakefield as he drew her closer to him. She tried to break free of his grasp, but he held her too tightly.

"Unhand her, I said," William growled.

When Wakefield only smirked again, William broke away from the men holding him and swung his fist at the earl, landing a punch right across Wakefield's nose. The earl stumbled backwards as blood gushed from his face and ran down onto his cravat.

"Lord Kingspointe! Really, sir, this is beyond the pale, and it must end. Now!" said Lady Jersey, who appeared to have had an apoplexy, so shocked was the expression on her face.

"I'm not leaving without my wife." He grasped Cassandra by the upper arms and kissed her in front of Lady Jersey and the entire *ton*. It was not a chaste kiss either. He pulled her to him, and she felt every inch of his arousal for her against her abdomen, as his tongue stole past her lips. He tasted of mint and tea, and she wanted to lose herself thoroughly in the kiss. He broke from it, however, and panted as he gasped for air. "I *love* you. I should have said it long ago, but I was afraid you didn't feel the same for me. Now I don't care. I love you, and I'm going to shout it to the world, regardless of how you feel about me. I love you, Cassandra Poniard, as I've never loved another woman. I don't know how to make you understand that you are my heart and my soul and that I want you back."

Momentarily flummoxed by the emotions fluttering through her heart and the sensations flowing throughout her body, she could only stare at him in wonder. She recovered herself a few seconds later. "But what about Belinda? I saw you kissing her."

"I was not kissing Belinda."

"Really? It certainly looked to me as though your lips were locked with hers."

"What I mean to say is that she kissed me. I did not kiss her. There's a difference. Can't you understand that? I love you. I would never kiss her when I love you so much. I had come home from drinking at the pub in East Welkin last night hoping to talk to you about the annulment." He paused only long enough to catch his breath. "I thought you were waiting for me in the study when I got home, but instead it was Belinda. She approached me and kissed me. I had no idea that you saw us, but when I went to your room to talk to you about it afterward and about the annulment, you were asleep."

Lady Jersey appeared spellbound by their conversation, and the attendants stood back and regarded them with a mixture of awe and disbelief on their faces. Indeed, the whole crowd seemed transfixed by the scene that was unfolding before them on Almack's dance floor.

"That's your story?" Cassandra asked.

"Yes, damn it, and it's the truth." He raised his hands in exasperation and then wrapped his arms around her and hugged her tightly to him. "I do not love Belinda. I love you. I have never loved any woman the way I love you. You're my life, Cassandra. I can't live without you." He took her hand and kissed it. Then he pulled something out of his pocket and got down on his knees—both knees—in front of her and the entire *ton* and held up the ring he had bought her in Nether Wrigsby. "Please. Please take this and wear it. We'll have the annulment proceedings halted as soon as we can. And if the petition can't be withdrawn, then I'll apply for a special license for us to wed as soon as possible. Only, please marry me, Cassandra. I love you. With all my heart, I love you."

Tears formed in her eyes, and she swallowed past the lump that had formed in her throat. She wanted nothing more than to believe this man, to fall into his sensual emerald eyes and get lost in them forever. She wanted to believe he was her King of Swords, but she was scared, scared to love him with the depth of feeling she had for him. Scared that she could be hurt so easily because she loved him so much.

"I love you," he whispered. His plaintive stare undid her, however, and she could no longer resist his entreaty, could no longer resist his pleas.

Tears—tears of joy—spilled from her eyes, and she nodded her assent. "I love you, too, William. From the depths of my being, I love you and always have. Ever since I was a little girl, I have loved you. You are now and forever will be my heart and my soul." She stroked his cheek, and he turned to kiss the palm of her hand.

"Will you marry me? For real, this time?"

"Yes, of course."

He rose from his knees and took her in his arms once more and kissed her. "I want to make love to you," he whispered in her ear.

"Here?" she said as a joyous giggle bubbled out of her.

"No, we might lose our vouchers if we did it here," he replied with a wink and a smile.

She laughed at his remark.

"Let's go home." He caressed her cheek with the backs of his fingers.

"As you wish."

"Never leave me again, Cassandra."

"Oh, William, I won't." Then she kissed him, her King of Swords.

EPILOGUE

Ace of Swords: Triumph of great force, such as love; resolution of obstacles; a birth of special significance . . .

Essex
October 1817

CASSANDRA SHUFFLED HER OVERSIZED DECK of cards, the ones given to her by her grandmother, while Lady Miranda lay in her cradle beside her on the floor. At just nine months old, she looked thoroughly angelic as she sucked her left thumb, slumbering sweetly, oblivious to either of her parents.

"Are you concentrating?" William whispered as he nibbled Cassandra's earlobe. He had come to stand behind her at the table where she sat.

"Well, I was," said Cassandra, exasperated.

"I am sorry, but I find you much too enticing to resist."

"Do try to control yourself, sir," she said with a laugh. "Or don't you really want to know what our next babe will be?"

"You're certain you're with child again?"

She turned over three cards: the Knight of Swords,

the Page of Cups, and the Ace of Wands. "If I weren't sure from my symptoms, I would be certain from the cards in this reading. The last two undoubtedly signify fertility and an upcoming birth."

"And the first?"

"That the baby shall definitely be a boy this time. Miranda will have a brother."

"Ah. Lord Margate is on his way, is he?"

"I would say so, yes."

"Well, my love, now that you have satisfied your curiosity, blow out your candle and let us go back to bed."

She touched his cheek with her finger and smiled. "You have a mind with a singular purpose, I have noticed, Lord Kingspointe."

"What man married to you would not have one thought on his mind, Lady Kingspointe? Come. While she sleeps soundly."

She blew out the candle and followed William to bed. He kissed her properly and said, "I love you, my beauty."

Cassandra smiled. "And I love you."

In her heart, in her soul, she was happier than the cards could ever have predicted she would be.

Acknowledgements

MANY THANKS TO MY DEVELOPMENTAL editor, Bev Katz; my proofreader, Hardy Garrison; my critique partner, Rachel Frye; and everyone at the Killion Group. I'd also like to thank my beta readers, Julie Button, Amy Kenny, Jennifer Stoiber, and Angie Thibault for their invaluable insight and constructive critiques. And of course, this book would not have been possible without the love, encouragement, and support of others not mentioned above, including my husband, Jim; my son and daughter-in-law, Kevin and Ashley; my parents, Tom and Judi; my mother-in-law, Marty; my brother and sister-in-law, Tom and Holly; my dear friends Deborah, Mark, and John; and my mentor, Lisa.

ABOUT THE AUTHOR

ANNA DURBIN IS THE AUTHOR of charming tales of the Beau Monde. Having grown up reading sagas of chivalry and romance, she began crafting her own elaborate stories in her imagination at a young age. It was only natural that she would one day write them down. Her first novel, King of Swords, was a 2012 Golden Heart® finalist.

Despite years of study in the biological and physical sciences, her true love has always been the literary arts. Inspired by her favorite author, Jane Austen, Anna adores the Regency Era and writes period pieces set during that time that show love conquering adversity. Oddly, for all her love of science and history, she is a faithful devotee of the New Age. She discovered tarot cards in a New Age shop in Minneapolis during a high school class trip one year and has been enchanted with them ever since. She enjoys weaving the symbolism of the tarot deck into her storylines.

Anna has lived in ten different states throughout her lifetime, from California to New Jersey. A Midwesterner at heart, she was born in Kansas and raised in Iowa. Currently, she lives in Wisconsin with her husband and works as a technician for local government.

OTHER TITLES BY ANNA DURBIN

Kings of the Tarot Series
King of Swords—Book 1
King of Wands—Book 2
King of Cups—Book 3
King of Coins—Book 4

For more information about these titles,
please visit Anna at
www.annadurbinauthor.com